RACING ON THE EDGE 1

A NOVEL BY SHEY STAHL

D1522066

**Warning: This book contains adult content,
explicit language, and sexual situations.**

Cover Art: Allusion Graphics, LLC and Elaine York
www.allusiongraphics.com

Interior Design and Formatting/Proofing:
Elaine York, Allusion Graphics, LLC

Author
ACKOWLEDGEMENTS

Some authors place their acknowledgments at the end of the book, others at the beginning. After writing this story, I believe the correct placement, for me, is at the beginning. The words spilled across these pages wouldn't be possible without the following influences.

The boy—I can honestly say that you are the only person who really knows me in ways I've never had to explain. Time stands still when I'm with you, the memories we've created influence me in ways that can't be described with words but alive with gestures. You support me no matter what I put you through and allow me to share my time with you and my characters floating in my head. Your willingness to eat out so I can write all the time, and the ability to look past the laptop to see the television is appreciated. Thank you.

Mom—you told me when I was younger to follow my dreams. This is me trying, for you. Thank you for always supporting me in anything I do and pushing me when I needed a push.

Sister—thank you for laughing until you cry when I'm trying to explain something to you. Not many of us have the ability to do that in life, and you do. Thank you for always being there when I need someone to listen, even if you do laugh when it's not funny. Also, even though I don't feel that way at the time, love that you laugh at me when I make a fool of myself. At least one of us thinks it's funny.

Dad—I've learned over the years, through my own strange tendencies, my dry sense of humor comes from you. Lucky me. I wanted to write a book that would draw around the way I grew up and my favorite memories you provided with racing. Thanks to you, I honestly feel the racing comes to life in this book. I hope I've captured that in these books because they are some of the best memories I have from growing up at the local dirt tracks; including the one where you rolled me down a hill in a sprint car tire when I was five.

Honey Girl—though you're still very young, and I hope you never read this, and maybe just skip to this page only, I love you. I never truly understood the bond between mother and child until I looked at you. You throw plenty of fits right now and treat me as if I'm your personal jungle gym and punching bag, but I can look past that and see the love … I think.

Finally, thank you to those who pre-read my stories, offered input, all the local racers who allowed me to interview them, gave me inside information, and pushed me along the way to do this.

For The Boy who has taught me more about the way an internal combustion engine works than I ever thought possible. Thank you for not only being my best friend all these years but also helping form this story with your knowledge of engines and mechanics.

Where there is love there is life.
Gandhi

Table of CONTENTS

Hooked Up – When someone uses this term they are referring to a car that's performing at its best.

"This is beautiful," I told him, climbing into the back of the truck.

Jameson had already laid the blankets in the bed of the pick-up truck.

"I came out here last year when I was racing in the Busch series," he said conversationally, pulling me onto his lap where he sat on the edge of the tailgate.

The faint sounds of "Wicked Game" playing over the stereo hummed around us.

"Really," I gave a sidelong gaze at Jameson. "Who was the lucky girl?"

"I told you," he let out a soft chuckle against my shoulder. "I haven't been with anyone in over a year. I came out here by myself. In fact, I actually spent the night texting you from this *exact* location."

I couldn't say anything to that.

What would I say?

He didn't give me a chance to think about it before he turned me around so that I was straddling his hips.

His lips skimmed along my collarbone and then back again before removing my tank top as the song continued.

I was stumbling through this, deeper in love with this man, yet he remained clueless.

He honestly had no idea how madly in love I was, or did he?

"You're so beautiful, honey," he whispered leaning in for the most passionate kiss I think I'd ever had.

When he pulled back to look at me his expression changed and took on a soft edge.

His mouth opened as though he wanted to say something, but no words came out and he stared back at me with his hand resting against my cheek.

I wanted to say so much in that moment. It seemed fitting.

I wanted to tell him how much I loved him and how much I've always loved him, but like him, I didn't say anything. I gazed back at him wondering why the words wouldn't form.

Feeling myself nearing tears, I leaned in kissing him again and then removed his shirt.

Jameson rested against the bed of the truck and closed his eyes. I skimmed my fingers across the muscles in his chest, down the ripples of his stomach to the sharp lines of his hips.

Rocking my hips against him once, the friction of our clothing caused him to moan and grab my hips securely with his hands, moving me the way he wanted.

I took everything he gave me that night, knowing I was falling deeper and deeper into whatever this was between us, but I also couldn't make myself care.

This was fun, this was exciting, and this was us.

Everything with Jameson and I was always so simple and easy that I couldn't think of a reason why this couldn't be, too.

I also knew it wasn't enough. I would want more.

1

Aero Push

Aero Push – If another car follows another too close, the air from the lead car doesn't flow across the following vehicle the way it should. It will go over the top with a downward force on the front and then narrows. When that happens, the car can't turn easily in corners resulting in the front of the car pushing up the banking toward the outside wall resulting hints the term aero push.

"Would you like two tickets?"

"No. Just *one* ticket for Charlotte, North Carolina," I paused trying to relax myself. "The ticket is already purchased by Jameson Riley. I just need to confirm with you apparently."

Peering down at the chips in my toenail polish, I touched them up with a black Sharpie I found beside the bed.

"What city?" the woman with Southwest Airlines barked back at me.

I gathered she was just as annoyed. After being on the line with her for the last twenty minutes, I hated to tell her she wasn't exactly my favorite person either.

Glancing out the window as I paced, a slow but constant mist of rain fell. A steady flow of cars came and went through the parking lot of the dorms at Western. Most of the students were heading home for the summer, as was I.

"Like I said the first five times, *Charlotte*, North Carolina," I wanted to add some choice words at the end, but I refrained.

I couldn't be sure what I'd do five minutes from now if I was still on the damn line though. A girl can only take so much this early in the morning without coffee. And personally, I believe in our constitutional right to speak our minds. In fact, I think more people should exercise this right, in my opinion.

"Did he make the flight for today?"

My God.

Before answering, I sighed dramatically attempting to let her know how frustrated I was.

"Yes," I gritted out, my leg continued to bounce as I sat there waiting. "He said he did."

Once I finished coloring my toes, I tossed the Sharpie aside.

"Is it first class or coach?"

"He said it's first class."

Personally, I blamed Jameson for all of this bullshit I was going through right now. The jerk called me at two in the morning to tell me he clenched the pole for the NASCAR Winston Cup Coca-Cola 600 race tonight and needed his good luck charm there. I hadn't seen a race in person since Daytona—I figured I owed him that much.

I was also inclined to think I was not fully awake when I agreed to fly across the United States for the weekend.

Who does that kind of thing?

Me. I did that shit.

Why? Because I was an idiot, that's why.

Jameson Riley is my best friend who also happened to be a NASCAR Winston Cup race car driver. After taking his precocious racing talent from the bullring dirt tracks of the Pacific Northwest to the elite levels of auto racing, he did it.

From the time I met Jameson when we were eleven, we've been inseparable, up until a few years ago when I decided it was time to finish my bachelor's degree and actually attend classes as opposed to traveling with him and his family. The first year I tried doing both, traveling with them and online classes. That never worked in my favor so I had to physically attend school if I was going to graduate.

For myself, I needed to go to school. Most of my life I had never really had much direction and at some point, I realized where that was leading for me. Pit lizard for life.

Personally, there was nothing wrong with that if you asked me but I decided that I just needed to do it.

That left me in Bellingham while my friends were traveling all over catching any race Jameson could on the east coast and mid-west.

Finally though, after three years at Western Washington University, I finally graduated last week. I was now a free woman. No more late night study sessions cramming for mid-terms. I could finally have a life of my own.

Even if that meant being a pit lizard again.

That's when I knew that life of my own would eventually lead back to Jameson. It always would.

When I first enrolled in college, it took me some time to decide what I wanted to do with my life. I was that girl constantly putting it off while taking classes like pottery or art to avoid having to *actually* make a decision. But when my dad, Charlie, said he didn't raise a pit lizard for a daughter, I made the decision to go into Business Management. That sounded sophisticated enough for me.

For me, college ended my "Pit Lizard Phase" of following Jameson around. You know, I wouldn't even say I followed him around either because I was there for a reason. It may not have always been the right reason but it was a reason.

When I decided to go to school, I felt left behind. In a sad way I thought they would forget about me but no, they didn't. Especially Jameson and his sister. I still heard from Jameson every few days and weekly calls from Emma checking in on me.

They certainly hadn't forgotten.

The year I stopped traveling with them and went to college, I honestly think it had more to do with me wanting to get over Jameson.

Unfortunately that didn't happen. If anything it made my feelings stronger.

Four years after Jameson left Elma, Washington, for his chance at a career in racing, all that dedication to a sport that gave very little in return, had worked out for him. This past winter he signed with his father's new NASCAR Winston Cup series team Riley Simplex Racing and got a full sponsorship from Simplex Shocks and Springs, a manufacturer of, well, shocks and springs for race cars.

And now here I was flying out to see Jameson's first Coca-Cola 600 race and wondering where this would leave the relationship we had. The thing was, if he asked me to fly to the North Pole to see Santa Claus with him, I would. Which leads me to today. Flying across the states to see him.

It's crazy to think how quickly Jameson went from being an average Saturday night sprint car racer to racing in NASCAR.

Running roughshod through the Busch Series last year, he won fourteen races so Jimi, his dad and car owner, decided it was time to move up to the cup series.

For his first season, he was doing remarkably well. On his second start in Rockingham, he won his first career cup series win. Alas, I wasn't there for it.

He did thank his best friend on national television and that was comforting to a certain degree. I still had to watch it on TV instead of being there and experiencing the excitement first-hand. I must have cried for an entire week, but I made my decision to finish college, and I did just that.

For me, the worst part about not being there for the win was him calling me from victory lane because he wanted to hear my voice. Talk about making me feel like an asshole. Those were the times I regretted trying to make something of myself.

When I finally finished getting my ticket, I headed out the door in a mad rush to SeaTac Airport. As I waited for my truck to warm up, I sent Jameson a text to let him know I would be there tonight.

Got my ticket, be there at two. Someone had better pick me up!

He responded instantly, which surprised me. Lately it took him hours.

Headed to interviews. Can't wait to see you! Alley will

pick you up. :)

Naturally, I smiled like a fool over his texting excitement to see me.

I managed to make my flight on time, despite the Seattle traffic and many instances where I flipped people off. Once inside the airport, I also found the need to stop by Starbucks and pick up an iced white chocolate mocha.

This was probably the best decision of the morning. Who knew what type of shenanigans I could get into at an airport, surround by other people, *without* caffeine.

For most of the flight, I thought about how I really couldn't believe that I was doing this, among other things. What kind of idiot dropped everything for a guy that she knew didn't feel the same way about her?

Me. I do that shit.

To us, the story behind Jameson and me was pretty simple but also complicated. And though it started back when we were kids, the relationship itself, for me, changed the summer we left home in the hunt for the USAC Triple Crown title. The summer of 1998.

When Jameson graduated high school, he finally convinced his sprint car World of Outlaw champion father that he was old enough to pursue his racing dreams. Jameson had been racing since he was four years old, but Jimi made the stipulation that he graduate from high school before he could move to the East Coast.

Graduation day came for Jameson and he headed east with his older brother, Spencer, Spencer's girlfriend, Alley, and Emma, Jameson and Spencer's younger sister, who graduated a year early just so she could come along.

Naturally, when he asked me to come along, I did without a second thought. Now, up until that point, Jameson had always been my best friend, never anything more. Sure, we'd done the teenage experimenting with each other, but it had never led to anything. We had remained just friends.

That summer shit changed drastically. Not only did it test our relationship as friends, but it changed it. Surrounded by the lingering sweet sting of methanol, a mystifying greatness emerged from a single dream of one boy. The only boy in my world. Between those dirt tracks, sleeping in the truck along the side of the road and eating a shitload of fast food, I became captivated by Jameson Anthony Riley as he fought to be his own man.

I fell in love with him. There was no way around it.

Looking back on those times, during high school I could feel my feelings for him shifting, but *that* summer they really took on a life of their own and became something I just couldn't ignore. Believe me when I say I tried.

Most would wonder by now, what was Jameson like? Who is this guy who holds my heart?

Jameson Riley was an asshole. He was temperamental, childish at times, and could easily put a toddler to shame with the fits he threw. He overreacted, had textbook aggression issues, and was flat out arrogant.

And I loved him regardless because underneath all that was a magic about him that literally captivated you.

Just like any single-minded athlete, he had a burning desire to race, and that's all he did. That overreacting side and that single-minded athlete mentality was who he was and how he got to where he was now. I loved that about him too.

No matter what, I was there for Jameson through it all. Through engine problems or the set-up deficiencies, the runaround he got from track owners, other drivers and sponsors, I was his safety shield in his crazy life as he would say. If he needed anyone, I was there. If he needed to talk in the middle of the night, I put aside everything to be there for him.

Despite being that so called safety shield, I was *never* his girl. Jameson had one girlfriend in high school, Chelsea Adams, and more nameless one-night-stands than I cared to know about. Believe me, I witnessed it first-hand those summers and it wasn't pretty.

And then there was me. His friend sitting in the wooden bleachers with rusty nails, wishing he would see me for who I was—absolutely perfect for him—but to this day he remained oblivious to how I really felt for him.

No one knew how I felt about Jameson aside from Emma, Alley, and probably his mother. Being women it wasn't hard to catch on with my pathetic attempts at flirting those summers we traveled. And believe me when I say there were many times that I wanted to slap myself.

Finally, the captain came over the intercom to announce our final descent into the Charlotte area.

Scrambling around, I hurried up and put my iPod and laptop away. I was finishing last quarter's books for my dad.

Once graduation day came for me, Charlie, my dad, wasted no time throwing me into the family business of managing the track. I knew his intention was to have me take over when he retired. I think the jerk has been grooming me for this since I was a kid, but if you'd asked him, he would just smile.

It has been just Charlie and me since I was six. My mother, Rachel, died of breast cancer when she was twenty-five. After her death, we moved from Aberdeen to Elma, Washington, and that's when racing caught my attention.

Soon after the move, Charlie purchased Grays Harbor Raceway, a 3/8 oval clay racetrack off Highway 8. I was literally around racing every weekend, and it was eventually how I met the Riley family.

The first time that I saw Jameson Riley, it was Memorial Day weekend, the summer of '92. I was eleven years old.

Now that I think about it, it was eleven years ago this weekend.

The night we met, I was at the track one Saturday evening for the weekly races. I remember that day distinctly because it was one of the hottest days in Washington's history. It was something like a hundred and two degrees that day. When your average summer temperature reached maybe eighty ... that was hot.

Jameson liked to joke that this had something to do with him and his good looks.

There I sat with a red rope licorice in hand, when a black sprint car caught my attention. With their thunderous rumbling and slide jobs, sprint cars were always my favorite cars to watch. Sprint cars are small open-wheel, high power-to-weight ratio beasts that can reach one hundred forty miles per hour on some tracks.

I chose a seat close to the fence to feel the dirt and wind of the cars hit me when they would broad-slide into turn one. Some call me crazy, but I loved to get right in the middle of the action, despite the lack of visibility. I also enjoyed the burn in my eyes from the methanol and that growling pop they made when they lifted in the turns.

The black speed demon went from sixth to first in two laps straight. I'd never seen the car race here before, let alone seen someone race the way he did. His agile movements on the track were so smooth and so precise balancing right on the edge of control. Once he chose a line, he was set and determined—he'd easily slide past two or three cars in each corner.

I continued to watch him the remainder of the night. He not only won the heat race I watched first, but the trophy dash, the B-Feature, *and* the A-Feature—he was the talk of the night.

Listening closely, I tried to pay attention to the announcer to catch his name, but you couldn't hear anything over the roar of the cars and cheering fans.

When it came time for the trophies at the end, I made my way to the pits to find my dad. It was usually the only time I saw him throughout the night.

I glanced at the flag stand when I got past the entry gate. From the distance, I could see a *boy* emerge from the car appearing to be the same age as me.

I thought for sure he would be a full-grown adult with those racing chops. Not to mention the legal age to be in a sprint car was sixteen. Charlie frequently bent the rules back then on age limits, though, so that was no surprise.

There the boy stood with the biggest grin on his face having smoked men three times his own age in an 800-horsepower sprint car weighing 1,400 pounds.

The fact that he could even drive that machine in a straight line was impressive enough for me. I doubt I could even push-start the damn thing, let alone make it through turn one.

I managed to make it down to the pits to find my dad. Not exactly the easiest task when you're a little over four feet tall. I spotted Charlie standing outside the CST Engines car hauler talking to Jimi Riley, so I walked over to them.

Jimi was racing in The World of Outlaw Series—it was rare to see him here on a Saturday night unless the series was in town. The Riley family lived here in Elma, but we rarely saw them around since they traveled so often. With an eight-five race schedule each year, it was grueling and allowed little time to be spent on the West Coast.

"Hey, kiddo how you been?" Jimi asked me as I stood beside my dad.

"Good sir, how are you?"

"It's Jimi, honey, not sir. I'm good." He smiled and his stance shifted gesturing to the hauler behind him. "Have you met my kids before?"

"No si—Jimi." Even though I supposedly went to school with them, I never recalled *actually* meeting them.

"Let's introduce you then." He glanced around for a moment. "If I can find the little shits."

There were so many people standing around waiting to get a glimpse of Jimi you couldn't decipher who was who, let alone find anyone shorter than five feet tall.

"Jameson ... Spencer ... get over here!" Jimi hollered over his shoulder reaching out to sign a few autographs for a couple kids who made their way past the adults.

"Coming," the boys yelled barreling out of the back of the car hauler.

Jimi smiled reaching for the younger one by his race suit.

It was the speed demon.

"Sway, this is my son, Jameson. I think you two are the same age." Jimi shook Jameson's shoulders. "And this is my other son, Spencer." He ruffled Spencer's hair. "I've got a daughter, Emma, but who knows where she disappeared to."

"She's selling T-shirts," Spencer said.

With his black wavy hair, Spencer Riley looked very different from Jameson. They both had the same intensity in their eyes, but

Spencer's were bright blue and Jameson's were green. I saw the similarities in the crooked grin, too, the one that had me blushing.

"It's nice to meet you both." I shook both their hands.

They both smirked when I did that, which made me want to punch them in the face, especially when Jameson winked at me.

He was the most beautiful boy I had ever seen with bright, grass green eyes that complemented the rust color of his wavy hair, which curled out into loops at the ends.

I wasn't really into boys at eleven years old, but he was one pretty boy. I'd met Nancy, Jimi's wife, once before so I recognized that Jameson resembled his mother rather than the Riley side with black hair and blue eyes.

"You did great out there tonight," I said to the pretty boy knowing my face was a pretty cherry red color, much like my red rope.

"Looks like you follow in Jimi's footsteps," my dad added putting his arm around my shoulder. I looked down, embarrassed, but quickly looked up when I heard Jameson chuckle.

He smiled widely at us. "Yes, but I'm better." He nodded his head arrogantly while my dad and Jimi both start laughing at the suave confidence of the cocky little eleven year old.

By the end of the night, I was running around Grays Harbor Raceway with the Riley family.

I think the bigger picture here was what happened that night where the clay met the rubber, as Jimi would say. A racer was born in the sense that his dream came alive that night while racing on the edge.

Making my way from the plane, I was able to make it through baggage claim without bitch-slapping anyone. Balancing my purse on top of my suitcase, I made my way down the escalator into the Charlotte Airport.

I heard Alley and Spencer before I saw them, bickering as usual. Those two fought all the time. It was actually rare that they got along.

Only a few seconds before I made my way off the escalator Spencer, Jameson's older brother, had his arms locked around me in a steel trap as he hugged me.

"Whew," his arms wrapped tighter. "I've missed you, Sway!"

"Hands off, shit head," I muttered trying to pull away from him. "I can't breathe with you crowding me."

I liked a certain amount of personal space that Spencer never could provide. He knew nothing about personal boundaries.

Spencer was the type of guy you always had to keep your guard up around. With his unpredictable offensive behavior—you never knew when he'd strike, and you'd be the brunt of one of his stupid pranks. For a reason unbeknownst to me, I was one of his favorite targets and always had been. After spending more than a few minutes around Spencer, you'd understand why zookeepers give most animals toys.

If you kept them distracted, they're less likely to attack. I honestly believed this theory worked on children, as well.

Why do you think their toys are shiny? Distractions, it's all about distractions.

Always keeping Spencer occupied was my number one rule. If he was allowed time to think of any predatory attack, you would undoubtingly regret it. I loved Spencer like a brother, but the fact that he had to repeat the third grade *twice* should give you an inclination as to the type of behavior he exhibited.

Honestly though, if you didn't know any better, you'd think he was raised by a pack of wild animals.

I stopped trusting Spencer years ago—around the time when he allowed me, while camping in the woods, to wipe my ass with poison ivy knowing damn well it was poison ivy.

To this day I still haven't forgiven him.

"Spencer, for Christ's sake you're going to squish her," Alley grumbled beside us. "Put her down."

"Jameson is so excited to see you." Spencer finally let go to set me securely on the ground. "He actually cracked a smile this morning."

I stumbled for a second, finding my footing while tugging my underwear out of my ass. "How is he?" I was trying to hide my excitement that he implied Jameson was excited, but my voice had a certain beseechingly dismay to it.

Why wouldn't it?

Before Spencer could answer my question, Alley grabbed my suitcase and began lugging it with her. "We have to be back at the track in an hour. Get your ass moving." She turned to wink at me once. "We've got a busy night and no time for bullshit."

Alley, Spencer's wife now, was the team manager for Riley Simplex Racing and Jameson's publicist for good reason. She didn't put up with bullshit from anyone, including Jimi. She loved her job, even though it meant keeping Jameson and his team out of trouble and constantly defending Jameson's actions to NASCAR. She had a way with words, that one did.

I finally caught up with Alley and her long ass legs when we made our way into the parking garage. "Do you have to walk so fast?"

"It's good to see you again," Alley teased throwing one long scrawny arm around me. "You ready for this?"

"Uh, what does that mean?" My eyes shifted anywhere they could to avoid her questioning steel blue eyes. "Is there something I should know? Last time you asked me if I was ready for something I ended the night with six stitches in my ass."

Alley laughed it off but suddenly I was worried.

What if he had a girlfriend he didn't tell me about?

I then began thinking of all the ways I could kill her off if that were the case. I couldn't have another woman in the way, I just couldn't. High school and Chelsea were enough for my sanity. If he had a girlfriend now, I'd probably be sent over the edge and commit murder.

Alley sighed throwing my bag into a black SUV, her eyes holding concern. "Okay, I'm gonna say it. You need to hear it, *clearly*. I want to be sure you don't get hurt." She took a deep breath. "There, I said it."

"Is he with someone now?" My voice betrayed me and cracked a little. My heart was trying to qualify for a race at the way it was beating rapidly, waiting for her to answer.

Alley shook her head. "No, not that I'm aware of. But I also don't ask." She smiled. "I just want *you* to be careful. You know him."

I knew Jameson had one-night-stands—it was obvious. But since

Chelsea, I hadn't seen him in a "relationship" with anyone. And I wasn't sure you could even call his time with Chelsea a relationship. It was more of a convenience for him.

Alley, and even Emma, his younger sister, felt like Jameson used me to his own advantage. Which I guess maybe he did from time to time, but I didn't care. I should have ... but didn't.

Alley seemed to be waiting for an answer so I said, "I will."

Spencer got in the back of the SUV, his attention on his cell phone mostly but smiled when I said that I would be careful. He knew too.

Clearly I was lying. I was never careful and hardly ever rational when it came to Jameson. Now wouldn't be any different.

"Where's Lane?" I looked around to see if he was hiding from me inside the SUV. Right about then I realized they wouldn't have left a child in the car while inside the airport, or at least I would hope they wouldn't be that careless.

"He's with Jameson at the track." Alley frowned, her lips pursed. "The kid loves his uncle more than his own mother."

I laughed because it was probably true. Alley and Spencer's three year old son, Lane, thought Jameson was the world.

Me and this kid—we had a lot in common.

"It's been an interesting morning so far," Alley said conversationally merging with traffic.

"Why?"

"Well ... the team was fined fifty thousand for a fuel additive of methanol and ethanol." I gasped mainly at the fine, not the reasoning. "Gordon thinks the crew added it after qualifying."

"They wouldn't do that, would they?" My eyes darted to Spencer.

"Hey ... have some faith," Spencer defended. "I just found out. We'd never cheat *like* that. You know as well as I do NASCAR is very specific on rules—especially fuel and tires."

I knew that. As with any racing division, they monitored both carefully as that's where most teams cheated. But not Jameson; he never needed to. Every team pushed boundaries as a child did. They tested the authorities to see how much they gave and took, but there were still some things you just didn't mess with.

"So in other words, Jameson's in a shitty mood?"

"Not since he heard you were coming," Spencer said relaxing into the seat, his weight shifted so he could see out the windshield. "Stupid fuck has been antsy all morning."

Well then. He's is excited to see me. Hot damn.

The traffic on I-85 toward Concord was light as we made our way to Lowes Motor Speedway. I really wanted to see Jameson before the drivers' meeting knowing once the meeting was finished he had interviews, driver's introductions, and then the race. I remembered in Daytona it was hard to get a moment alone with him on race day with all the hospitality visits he had. After hearing about the fines, I wanted to be sure he was all right. For someone who put so much of himself into his racing, he always took this sort of thing hard.

Entering the pit entrance was much like my experience at Daytona earlier in the year. I've been around racing almost my entire life and have watched more races than I could ever remember, but to attend my first NASCAR Coca-Cola 600 race where my best friend was starting on the pole, was a feeling I couldn't describe. There was so much excitement swirling around me between the fans sporting his number proudly, to the news reporters, other drivers, and the officials.

To truly understand the exhilaration surrounding a race like this, you had to actually attend it. I can't explain it any other way. That's the only way to *truly* experience it. The lights, the sounds, the smells, can't be captured any other way than feeling it first-hand.

This wasn't some small town bullring dirt track where the pits consisted of an open field, and the grandstands were wooden bleachers with missing rusty nails. This was Lowes Motor Speedway where the best racers in NASCAR battled it out.

As soon as Alley stopped the car next to Jameson's motor coach, my door flew open, but before I could escape, she grabbed my shirt tossing me back in the leather seat.

"Sway, you can't go running around looking for him. You need a hot pass." She handed me a pass. "Besides, you're small enough someone might mistake you for a lost child."

"I thought I got a pass in the garage?"

"You already have one—Jameson got it for you."

I knew enough from my experience with the pit lizards at Daytona to know the difference between plastic and paper. I also knew that a "plastic pass" ran around twenty five hundred dollars and was *not* transferable. The fact that Jameson purchased a "plastic pass" for me had me thinking, but should I put any weight to the significance?

Glancing down at the hard pass they had made, I noticed one addition I was sure NASCAR did not add.

Under Sway Reins was *"Jameson's Pit Lizard"* written in black sharpie. I turned sharply to glare at Alley when she shifted her eyes to the back seat at Spencer and then back to me.

Without letting on, I placed the pass around my neck and grabbed the first thing that I could think of to throw at Spencer's head, which happened to be a front spring we had picked up for Jameson's car from the shop on the way here.

"What the fuck was that?" Spencer wailed clutching his face. "I think ... I'm ... *bleeding*. I am bleeding!"

Sure enough, he was bleeding, profusely, from right above his left eyebrow.

"Suck it up, asshole. You deserved that, and you know it." Stomping toward the garage, my pit lizard pass flailed behind me in the breeze.

"Babe, I think I need stitches." Alley examined his face closely before reaching in her purse to stick a Spiderman bandage on his forehead.

"There." She kissed his forehead right above his eye.

"You're fine!" I yelled over my shoulder as they trucked along behind me.

For only being five foot two and barely a hundred and five pounds, I could throw a mean front spring when needed. I grew up at a racetrack ... I could protect myself. Sure, there were times I may need to make use of car parts to assist me in protecting myself, but I *could* do it.

Since I'd been around racing most of my life, I could also smell my way to the garage off the fumes alone. I didn't need a damn escort. I had pit lizard instincts. I was sure I could smell a race car idling a mile away.

As I rounded the corner to the garage area, cars were scattered along the bays, revving engines and preparing for race day activities.

Just like my pit lizard instincts for racing, I had an instinct for Jameson and could pick his raspy velvet voice out like a needle in a haystack.

He was yelling over the revving, gesturing at the rear of the car. There he stood next to his race car talking with his crew chief, Kyle Wade.

I let out a truly pitiable sigh and trailed Alley and Spencer toward Jameson's bay.

There were drivers, media, crew members, and cars scattered throughout as they prepared for the night race.

I looked around, but like the pathetic pit lizard I was, my eyes immediately found Jameson, and it was as if everything else disappeared as though the world stopped.

So corny.

With his hand resting on the hood, his eyes were closed listening to the car as he made an adjustment under the hood.

I heard him holler over the rumble of the engine. "I was tight coming out of turn three yesterday during ..." was all I could make out before another engine in the distance revved drowning him out.

Sighing again, I looked around at the paddock. Only problem, I *couldn't* focus, not with the dirty thoughts in my mind listening to Jameson talk car.

No standard dirty talking for me; I like a man who talks car. The first time I heard Jameson say camshaft, I wanted to rip my clothes off and ride his camshaft reverse cowgirl style.

My eyes shifted back to him, wanting another look. Just one.

Squinting into the sun, I took in the rest of his appearance. Dressed in a black T-shirt and jeans that were met with his usual worn black Pumas. His rusty hair that seemed darker than usual was all over the place, nothing new, but it had always suited him the way it looped out at the ends. I sighed and shook my head when I noticed the shadow along his sharp jaw, loving the scruff he was sporting. He was hot, like greasy mechanic hot. I had a thing for a man who knew his way around an engine.

I focused for a moment thinking about Jameson getting to know his way around my internal combustion engine and, more important-ly, my crankcase. And if you don't know what a crankcase is, it's a metal casing in the engine that houses the camshaft, crankshaft, and a few other parts in reciprocating engine. This is why I called my va-gina a crankcase. It made perfect sense to me.

After all, I wouldn't mind housing Jameson's camshaft. And the camshaft, well, it's a long shaft inserted into the crankcase that ro-tates. Naturally, I would refer to this as a penis.

"Sway?" Someone yelled for me in the distance but it wasn't Jame-son. "Is that you?"

He had stopped his adjustment under the hood but hadn't looked up yet. His head remained bent forward peering down at the car, one hand rested on the hood over his head.

Fuck he looks so good. Sexy and delicious.

My eyes searched for who called my name. It was his spotter, also Emma's eye candy, Aiden Gomez, who had called my name and was jogging toward us.

Trying to hide behind Spencer didn't do any good. I was heaved into a hug from Aiden as he swung me around.

Aiden Gomez was a tall, lanky guy with blonde curly hair that stuck out from under his hat. He was a cowboy straight up from the deep south of Pickard, Alabama. I'll spare you my stereotypical thoughts of folks who come from Alabama because let's face it, in NASCAR, I was surrounded by the mullet madness from the southern states.

Aiden was cool, though, for a spotter. I had my own feelings on spotters. They were good people—but crazy if you ask me. Anyone who could stand hundreds of feet up in the air and hang over a railing was certifiably insane in my book.

Jameson met Aiden last year while he was racing in the Busch Series, and when Jameson got the opportunity to race in the Winston Cup Series, he asked Aiden to come with him as his spotter. Emma was the most excited because it meant that she got to be around him more. They had a secret love for each other that hadn't been revealed to the big brothers, if you know what I mean.

"Don't tease her, Aiden. She's feisty today," Spencer advised rub-bing his forehead. "Nearly took my head off."

"It grazed your eye." Aiden finally set me down. "Where's Emma?"

"Uh ..." Aiden gave me a tentative smile, his eyebrows scrunched. "She said something about getting you something to wear for tonight and left for the mall. She took Lane with her." I was just about to protest when he held up his hands. "Don't hate me."

Emma ... *oh Emma* ... she took every opportunity she could to make me her dress up Sway-doll. The last time I let her dress me in Daytona, I looked like the Fourth of July exploded on me.

I loved Emma like a sister, but sometimes I wanted to kill her.

Actually, most of the time I wanted to kill her. She had this ridiculous obsessive-compulsive disorder, much like her brothers; that seemed to be heightened by her need to control other people and lather herself with lotion.

I wished she'd leave me alone and go back to counting, applying ungodly amounts of lotion, and sanitizing everything she saw, but no, what would be the fun in that for a deeply troubled sadistic shopaholic like her?

The answer: nothing. Just like her brothers, they lived to annoy me in ways I found loving. They were my family.

"Well ... she's wasting her time." I huffed. "I'm not wearing anything she picks for me." I crossed my arms like a spoiled child.

I wasn't lying either—I refused to play dress up tonight.

I had *other* plans. My exact plan was convincing Jameson that he loved me, too, and letting his camshaft meet my crankcase and test out my bearing alignment (a process to make sure all bearings are aligned so when the camshaft is run through, no binding occurs). Or, maybe we could do some thrust bearing (a type of bearing that's designed to support high axial load while rotating). Or if things really go my way, I could do some micro polishing (a procedure that cleans the camshaft with high speed polishing belts) ... I could go on for days like this. I had a name for anything sexual, and it wasn't what it was commonly referred to.

To me, the inner workings of an engine bore little resemblance to the actual function and instead bore a strong resemblance to something of a sexual nature.

When you think about it, *really* think about the way an engine operates, you'd be absolutely amazed at how closely it resembles sex. I'm not very mature as I'm sure you've guessed by now.

Spencer and Aiden were grumbling about the fine issued by NAS-CAR when they stopped and smiled over my shoulder.

I turned sharply to see what they were smiling at only to see Jameson making his way over to us with a huge grin.

God I love that grin!

I ran at full speed toward him jumping in his arms, and yes, I wrapped my legs around his waist. It was everything I had hoped for, and then some.

"I've missed you Sway, *so much!*" he breathed into my neck.

If I wasn't already in love with him, I fell in love, and so did my crankcase with my legs still tightly wrapped around his waist. I wanted him to confess right then that he loved me too but maybe that was wishing too much of him.

Right about then, I realized my crankcase was making all kinds of justifications that my mind would have no patience for, if it were still in charge. Warmth spread over me when I could feel his strong arms flex as he held me against his body. His breath blew over my neck, shivers ignited down my body firing nerve endings into race mode. I hoped like hell he didn't feel me trembling in his arms.

"I've missed you, too," I said softly breathing in the smell of his sun-kissed skin. He smelled of racing and summer, two things my senses had memory for.

At my words, Jameson turned his head kissing my cheek, his lips lingering. Pathetically, I found myself leaning into his touch.

"Oh Jesus," It must have looked inappropriate because Alley cleared her throat beside us. "Do you two need a room?"

I looked over at her pursed lips in a hard line while she glared at me.

Jameson laughed setting me on my feet beside him, his arm wrapped around my waist pressing me securely to him.

"I can't believe all this. It gets crazier every time I see you!" I mocked punching at his shoulder. "Will you sign my arm? Or my ass?"

Or my chest.

His eyes narrowed at the willing appendage, my arm, and before I could retract it in time, his tongue darted out licking me. Seductively I might add.

"There's your autograph. Want me to sign your ass too?" He rolled his eyes, looking to Alley. "What's the plan for tonight and after the race?"

I looked down at my arm, coated with Jameson drool. "I'll never wash my arm again."

He laughed beside me, leaning into my shoulder.

Do I wipe it off? No, not me, I left it there. I wasn't lying. I might not ever wash it again.

"You have the drivers' meeting in an hour," Alley reminded him, but kept tending to Spencer's eye. I felt bad, but only for a second, a brief second.

Jameson chuckled, eyeing Spencer. "What the hell happened to you?"

"Your best friend there decided to try and take my head off with a spring." You could literally hear the resentment in Spencer's voice.

"That's my girl." Jameson nodded in approval. A shy grin appeared as though he was hiding a secret. Knowing him, he probably was and that made me fall a little deeper.

"Listen." Alley smacked his shoulder grabbing his attention. "You have the drivers' meeting and then introductions start at four. After the race you have to make an appearance at Howl at the Moon in downtown Charlotte."

Jameson turned to me, a sly smile tugged at the corners of his mouth.

"So what … did you get a hotel room, or do you want to stay in my motor coach?"

"Alley got me my own room," I told him, hoping he didn't catch the fact that I was giving him ogle eyes, also instinct for a pit lizard.

"Damn," he smirked. "Well, I guess that means I have to return you to your room tonight. Or you could stay in my motor coach."

When I came for Daytona I had stayed in his motor coach so I had an idea of where that could go. Let me tell you, I was willing to let it go there.

Alley smacked at his shoulder. "You're staying at a hotel tonight dipshit. You leave town tomorrow morning after an interview. Which you better not be late to."

Jameson nodded and then looked at me again and then back to Alley. "Am I staying at the same hotel as her?"

"Yeah."

For a moment, a brief moment, I thought I saw disappointment in his eyes.

With the way he looked down into my eyes, the rest of my internal components lined up on the same side as my heart and crankcase. We were all ready and *willing* to do whatever Jameson Riley wanted.

Suddenly I had an idea of what he wanted. He liked to party. And by party I mean get drunk and make bad decisions. We both did.

"I'm not getting drunk tonight, Jameson," I warned as he lugged me toward the garage.

The last time I got drunk with Jameson on my twenty-first birthday, I ended up with a tattoo on my ass of God knows what, but it strangely resembled his lips. He had a matching tattoo that *also* strangely resembled my lips.

Actually, that wasn't the last time we got drunk together. There was the time after the tattoos that we ended up doing body shots with Jameson puking in the parking lot for an hour afterward.

Moral of this outcome, we shouldn't get drunk together.

It *never* ended well.

"So you say," Jameson pulled me by the hand. "I bet I can convince you otherwise." He paused, the smirk still present. "Besides, I have another ass cheek that needs branding and so do you, honey," he teased with a slap to my ass.

If there was one quality about Jameson that most failed to recognize, it was that he had the negotiation and debating skills of a seasoned politician. No lie. If he wanted me to do something, he could convince me in a matter of seconds.

I knew one thing—this pit lizard was going to have a *good* time tonight.

Groove – This is a racer's slang term for the fastest way around the track. A high groove takes the car closer to the outside wall and the low groove takes the car closer to the apron.

Jameson took me around before driver introductions started and introduced me to everyone with Simplex Riley Racing. The team had grown since the last time, and even though I'd met most of them in Daytona, there were a few additions to the team.

Some of the pit crew was new, like Ethan and Gentry, both affable guys who fit in well to the combination.

His crew chief, Kyle Wade, was still the same. I stayed with him while Jameson did pre-race interviews and talked with his teammate, Bobby Cole.

If you were to spend time around a racing team, at the track or even away, it wasn't hard to figure out who the driver was. Maybe it was the type of personality racing interested. Just the same, you could tell who the crew chief was as he was the one carrying as much of a burden but with less pay.

"How's he doing?" I asked Kyle knowing he'd give me an honest answer if I asked. He cared about Jameson and worried about how this life was effecting him.

Kyle was a burly guy, not as large as Spencer was, but similar to a teddy bear with his olive skin, brown hair and puppy dog brown eyes. He was adorable, if that was an appropriate word to use for a twenty-nine year old man. I thought it was. Every time I saw him, I wanted to cuddle him and spoon-feed him applesauce, because that was not weird at all.

Kyle joined Riley Simplex Racing around the same time as Jameson so it took a few races for them to get into a groove together. The turning point came when Kyle made the right call in Rockingham—that led to the victory.

Jameson respected him, and you needed that in a crew chief. And let's face it, Jameson rarely respected anyone besides his parents.

"Oh, you know. Still the same moody asshole he's always been." Kyle placed his arm around my shoulder leaning into me. "Although, once he found out you were coming, the boy was in a surprisingly *good* mood," he hinted with a grin and a waggle to his brow.

Everyone on his team, and other teams for that matter, thought something was going on with Jameson and me since Daytona. Even though I wanted that, I denied the accusations, as did Jameson.

Annoyed at the invasion into his personal life, he would usually bark something along the lines of, "Fuck off, mind your own business."

Our relationship did appear relatively strange. We hugged and held hands from time to time. Hell, we'd even made out on some occasions, but it was always held to friend standards, for the most part. Don't get me wrong, there were times when Jameson and I experimented with each other growing up, but clothing always remained intact ... most of the time. I say most of the time because there were times when my memory was a little faded due to alcohol consumption.

So from the outside, we *could* look like *more* than friends. Either that, or they saw right through my tough exterior and saw that I was madly in love with this man.

After the drivers' meeting, I watched as a news reporter from ESPN approached Jameson after he finished up with FOX Sports. "Hey Jameson, you got the pole. Do you think you have a chance at winning?"

"I think we have a chance." His eyes dropped tipping his sunglasses down. "This Number Nine Simplex Ford is running great. Both practices we were up front. I would expect to see us stay up front," he said leaning against the side of his hauler.

His weight shifted to one side appearing relaxed, his eyes told another story, which was why he slid the sunglasses down. There seemed to be emptiness about him I couldn't place. Or maybe it was a defining edge of who he was, and who he wasn't, in a sport that constantly tried to mold a triangle to fit within a circle. Since his first race, I witnessed this side emerging through interviews. Now there was no ignoring it.

Some thought Jameson was just another arrogant rookie trying to prove himself. The way he regarded other drivers and reporters, basically anyone outside of his circle, wasn't from arrogance but vulnerability this life had created for him. It was a something you rarely found in a racer with his impulsive reputation.

"Now let's talk about this hefty fine handed down this morning by NASCAR ..."

Jameson hung his head, a slow shake revealed his aggravation. Just as the shifting of the wind, the tension crept over him. His left hand reached across his body running the backside of his hand down his jaw. In a gesture that seemed straightforward as maybe satisfying an itch, I knew the weight behind it.

"I don't really have much to say about it," he told them, his voice taking on a throaty rasp from all the interviews today.

The reporter continued to ask questions. Jameson snuck a drink of water before running his hand through his hair. With a contemplative tug, his gaze focused past the reporter to the track.

He hated doing interviews, absolutely hated it. So it was easy to see the frustration as one reporter after another hounded him for interviews. I guess you had to keep in mind how quickly he went to a household name to understand his frustration with the constant media attention.

Growing up racing on dirt, he'd been measured one of the local boys even though his dad held royalty status among the racers. Even when Jameson raced USAC (United States Auto Club), it was nothing compared to the attention he received once he was thrown into the Winston Cup series. When he won his second race at Rockingham, his lifestyle became as fast as his driving. It was unbelievable the following he now had.

With the way NASCAR had evolved over the years, these guys were hounded like rock stars.

Watching him also brought out the pit lizard in me, as I was slobbering over every move he made, every wink he gave me—every tug of his hair, every crooked grin.

Let's just say my rev limiter was working on overdrive trying to control my engine from exceeding its maximum rotational speed and exploding. I had it bad. But all things considered, I was okay with that—for tonight anyways.

The rest of the afternoon, we hung around in Jameson's motor coach waiting for driver introductions to begin and catching up with everyone who I hadn't seen since Daytona in February. Though getting to the motor coach was a task.

To give you an idea of the following Jameson had now—it took about fifteen minutes to make it to his motor coach with all the garage groupies wanting his autograph.

Let me take a moment here and explain the difference between a garage groupie and a pit lizard. A garage groupie is a teenage fan who knows nothing about NASCAR or even who's leading the points battle, and usually only cares about the younger drivers. Now, a pit lizard is a woman who hangs around the pit area, has a certain driver in mind, and will do anything in her power to sleep with them.

Since I was twenty-two, knew everything there was to know about racing, and only had one driver in mind—I fit the pit lizard category, sadly. The difference here was I wasn't interested in a one-time bearing assessment. I was looking for forever. *We* deserved forever.

When the garage groupies attacked Jameson on the way to the motor coach, he laughed nervously trying to sign everything they shoved at him and posed for a few pictures. When some fourteen year old asked him to sign her stomach, I snickered beside him. He politely declined telling her she was a little young for that sort of thing.

Once we made it back to the motor coach, things quieted down *until* Emma returned.

"Oh my God," Emma wailed as she flew at me. Once inside, she tackled me to the floor. "I thought Jameson was lying when he said you were coming!" She puckered her lips to kiss me.

"You kiss me, and I *will* punch you." I clenched my fist in anticipation that she would try this—she had before. Instead, she giggled and got off me, straightening her tailored clothes I was sure cost more than my rent.

Emma was smaller than I was, but the little hooker could knock the wind out of me in a heartbeat. Jameson helped me up, since Emma was obviously too distracted by her purchases to realize she'd just laid me flat.

I sat down on the couch and waited for her to attack me again, but I knew next time she'd be trying to take my clothes off—which she had also done in the past.

"Where'd Lane go?" Jameson asked taking a seat on the couch next to me with a plate of grilled chicken and steamed vegetables in his hands.

"With Alley at the playground." Emma didn't bother looking up as she prodded through the bags. "Found it," she chirped holding up a skirt that looked like something a woman wore in the stone ages because that's all the fabric they could spare for clothing.

This indigo denim skirt wouldn't even cover my ass cheeks.

Then she proceeded to pull out a shirt that, for "Emma standards," was actually something I might wear. It was gray sheer fabric with a black swirled design. The sleeves were short and tied up on the shoulders by pieces of the shirt that seemed to be missing on the sides.

It wasn't bad, for a pit lizard to wear.

If the shoe fits, I might as well wear it. Again, I admitted how pathetic I was.

But it wasn't the clothing that clenched the deal for me.

When she dug out the black heels, I started to object but was quieted by a low whistle Jameson let out beside me.

"Are you wearing *that* tonight?" he asked shaking his head slowly.

After setting his empty plate aside, his other hand that wasn't on my shoulder ran through his hair once.

"I uh—"

"Yes, she is," Emma announced proudly.

Jameson smiled but remained cryptic. "You won't be introduced to any more people tonight." He winked at me. "Just so you know."

What the hell does that mean?

Did that mean he didn't want people to see me? Did it mean he liked the outfit? By the way he was eyeing the skirt, I decided that was it.

Emma never stopped talking the entire time I was getting dressed in the tiny bathroom of Jameson's motor coach which, by the way, wasn't all that small. It was certainly bigger than my dorm bathroom, and you had to turn sideways to squat on the toilet in that bathroom.

"You wouldn't believe it, Sway," she sighed on the other side of the door. "He told me he loves me."

Tugging on the skirt trying like hell to make it longer, I asked, "Do Spencer and Jameson know?"

"Fuck no, and don't you tell them." She smacked the door with her tiny fist. "I mean it, Jameson needs to concentrate on racing, and Spencer would go apeshit if he knew I was fucking Aiden."

I flung the door open; slapping her in the face forgetting the doors opened the wrong way.

"What?" I yelled. "You're fucking him ... when did this happen? How come you didn't call me?"

Emma was too busy rubbing her forehead where the door smacked her to answer me right away. Turning to look in the mirror, she examined her red mark and then spilled the news. "It happened in Richmond." She grinned, that same mischievous grin both Spencer and Jameson possessed. The same grin that had you guessing what they were thinking and knowing damn well it was dirty. "I didn't say anything because you and Jameson talk every day. You would let it slip ... I know you."

True, I couldn't keep anything from Jameson. Anytime I heard that smooth voice, my willpower crumbled and I talked.

On top of that, I couldn't keep a secret to save me life. It was as if

I had the cure to cancer and couldn't wait to tell everyone. I'm utterly amazed I haven't told him how I felt yet.

Emma continued to go on-and-on about Aiden and his magic fingers.

I stopped listening around the time she started talking about his ability to make her see stars within thirty seconds because, frankly, I was jealous as hell.

Not only did I wish Jameson and I were humping like them, but my crankcase hadn't seen any reciprocating motion in over a year. I was getting desperate, obviously by what I was wearing.

Inhaling a deep breath, I stepped from the bathroom and looked over my appearance.

Hot damn.

Starting with my hair, long reddish-brown messy waves draped a heavy curtain over my shoulders. The shirt came down low enough so you could see the faint start of cleavage *but* left enough to be desired. The skirt, well the skirt was illegal, that's all there was to it. It covered enough that I wouldn't be arrested for indecent exposure, but if I bent over, that was another story. My legs looked surprisingly long with the heels on, though, and muscular.

They looked damn good I must say.

"You look hot," Emma told me applying some makeup to my face.

Rolling my eyes, I gave in. "Why do you do this to me?" I tried to turn my head toward her, but she yanked it back the other way.

"Because you're trying to convince my big brother he loves you, too."

"Is that so ...?"

"I see right through you, Sway." Her eyes narrowed suspiciously. "I know what you're up to."

And here I thought I was being sneaky—guess not. I was an idiot savant after all and made a mental note to work on being sneaky later.

"Do you think he feels the same way?" I whispered.

I could feel my cheeks getting hot as soon as I spoke the words. Once they were out, my ears started to glow like one of those glow-worm dolls I had when I was younger.

"Sway," she sighed placing her makeup bag on the counter, pausing for a moment as though she was deciding exactly how to let me down easy. "Jameson ... he loves you. It's easy to see that, but with Jameson, he doesn't know what *that* love means yet. I don't know if he ever will. Right now, he's focused on his career, and it's hard for him to see anything past that right now."

Well damn, that wasn't what I wanted to hear.

I wanted to hear that, yes, he loved me and wanted to go steady. Okay, well it's not 1950 so I didn't want to hear "let's go steady," but I did want to hear that he loved me.

Emma concluded her Sway-whore makeover and let me go. I grabbed my bag from the couch, threw some black flip-flops inside and a black zip up hoodie to cover myself.

I felt exposed.

Emma was still going on-and-on about Aiden when we walked out of the motor coach, but quickly silenced when she saw Spencer standing outside with Alley.

Just one foot out the door and Spencer started howling like an idiot. "Jesus Christ, Sway." He then proceeded to fan himself.

Jameson, now dressed in his racing suit, had his back turned to us doing an interview with SPEED but looked over his shoulder once he heard Spencer.

Never failed, any time I saw him in his racing suit my heart skipped. He looked hot. And by hot I mean I wanted to fuck him silly.

Jameson tried to turn around when the reporter asked him a question but his head kept turning back to me. Stepping down, I stood against the motor coach. I convinced Emma to let me wear the flip-flops for now until later when we had to go to the bar. Even then, I had some concerns about the heels.

The reporter was trying desperately to keep Jameson's attention, but he kept his eyes on me.

"Does the penalty from earlier deter you at all from concentrating tonight?"

"No, I don't agree with the fine, but there's nothing I can do about it right now." Jameson peeked at me again. "They watched us add two drums prior to the race so we'll have to prove it to them tonight."

"So what do you think your chances are for a win tonight?" The reporter shoved the microphone in his face. "You're strong on these one-and-a-half-mile tracks, do you think you can pull it off?"

Still not looking, Jameson answered, "Uh..." He finally turned around but not before his eyes raked down my body once. "I ... I think we have a good chance. The car is really strong. It's hard to say what will happen in the race; it's a *long* race. A lot can happen in six hundred miles," he told him while he rubbed the back of his neck with one hand and looked over his shoulder once more.

This time his brow furrowed and his eyes squinted a little—like he was trying to figure something out. I thought he was looking at me, but his eyes focused behind me on a crowd gathering at the motor coach beside his.

Jameson looked over at Spencer who was putting on his gear for the pits and motioned with his head for Spencer to come over toward him.

Once he was close enough, Jameson whispered in his ear words I couldn't hear.

Spencer then nodded and walked back over to us with a smirk.

"What did he want?" Alley asked looking down at her Blackberry. "He needs to get to driver introductions. Why can't this asshole ever learn anything about time management?"

"He wants a moment alone with Sway before driver introductions." Spencer smiled, his head tipped to the motor coach. "He said to meet him in the motor coach."

By that point, I was breathing heavy, and my heart started pounding.

What did he want? Did he not like what I was wearing?

"Okay," I said hesitantly and made my way back inside to wait.

My nerves were getting the best of me, and I thought I was going to vomit any second when the door opened causing me to jump.

"Didn't mean to scare you," Jameson said closing the door behind him. He didn't look up and sat down beside me, staring at my bare legs and shook his head. "You're fucking hot in that outfit," he said lasciviously leaning into my shoulder.

"Uh ... thanks."

I really wanted to say hot enough for you to...*Ah, shit stop this.*

Jameson started to say something and I missed the first part. I was distracted that he said I was hot.

"I just wanted you to know that," he finished, eyeing me cautiously.

"Wait, what?" I asked confused.

"Were you not paying attention to anything I said?"

"No ... I was distracted."

"Pay attention." He placed his hand under my chin, his eyes gauging. "Chelsea's here."

"What?" I started to panic. What would Chelsea be doing here, in Charlotte, at a NASCAR race of all places? This was unacceptable to me for a number of reasons I'm sure you could understand. "You mean Chelsea Adams, as in your ex-girlfriend?"

He nodded, flinching at the word "girlfriend."

"She's here because she's dating Tate Harris ... or so I've heard." Jameson let his hand fall from my face leaning back into the couch and groaning. "I think she's trying to make me jealous or something, but *fuck*, I haven't seen her in five years."

"Are you?"

"Am I what?"

"Jealous ...?"

"No!" he gasped, his features revolted. "She can fuck every racer out there for all I care. She's a bitch."

"So ...?"

"Listen." He slowly turned his head to look at me. "I wanted you to know she was here so you weren't surprised if you saw her. She's always been jealous of you, and I would hate for her to start something tonight."

"Eh, no worries, buddy," I said dismissively. "You saw what I did to Spencer earlier."

Jameson laughed loudly. "I'd pay you a million dollars if you threw a spring at her."

I grabbed his hand with mine shaking it. "Deal."

"Hurry up asshole." Alley beat against the door. "You have one minute."

"All right." Jameson rolled his eyes. "Be there in a second." He looked back over at me, and then my legs. "Not what I need to be thinking about," he murmured with a pensive frown.

The door slammed behind him leaving me wondering what that meant. I sat there for a minute before Emma came back in. "You coming?"

"Yeah." I followed Emma to the grid where the cars were starting to line up along pit road in the order they qualified. The setting sun provided a shine over the cars that reminded me of a Saturday night at the local tracks.

About three hours before the race, with crews setting up shop, everything on pit road kicked into high gear. Most of the time pit road doesn't cool down for about two hours after the race. It's the most stressful part of the track and swarming with various crew members, visitors, officials, and drivers.

One word of advice: don't touch anything, and don't get in their way. They all had a job to do, and one simple mistake can cost them the win. I repeat, don't touch anything. And, yes, I said this from experience in all my times spent in the pits at the local dirt tracks. This was no different. Believe me, these guys have *everything* where they want and need it. Just simply moving a hammer can set everyone off.

I wanted to stay down there until the race started and watch Jameson get in the car, something I really enjoyed about Daytona, but I decided against it when I saw Chelsea hovering around.

An encounter with her wasn't ideal for me since I hadn't seen her since high school.

She looked the same, honey blonde hair and beautiful blue eyes. Her jeans appeared to be painted on, and her shirt was so low that I thought I saw a nipple.

I hated her. Maybe despised was a better word. To put it simply, she was perfect and I was plain. She looked like she belonged on the cover of a magazine, and I looked like I belonged at the strip club with the way I was dressed.

Casually, Chelsea looked my direction toward Jameson's car but didn't make eye contact with me. She probably didn't recognize me with so little clothing.

Emma caught on by the look on my face. "Rub your tits on the car."

I choked on my own spit, which was easy to do when you think about it. A quick inhale with the right amount of saliva and you've accomplished this. "What?"

"You know, mark your territory." She pushed me toward the car, and I stumbled against the front fender. "Rub your tits on the car."

I spun around and slapped her across the face, not hard, but enough that I felt I got my point across to her. "There's something wrong with you."

Emma did have a point.

I *should* mark my territory, but I wasn't about to give that little bitch the satisfaction of realizing I was jealous. Not gonna lie, I did think about turning around but decided to keep walking to the grandstands. There were cameras everywhere and surely I'd be caught and Charlie would blow a head gasket if he saw the fun bags on display on national television.

Before driver introductions began, Emma, Alley, and I made our way to the private suite in the upper Terrace Ford grandstands. Jameson's sponsor, Simplex Shocks and Springs, had the entire room rented out—most of which was occupied by corporate representatives, but his family was also up there.

I had yet to see Jimi and Nancy so when I walked into the suite, I wasn't surprised to see them already sitting there with Lane, who was bouncing up and down with his little Simplex hat and shirt on. He looked adorable sporting his uncle's gear.

"Where's Aiden?" Jimi asked Emma with his cell phone to his ear.

"Uh ... how should I know?" she mumbled, and I could tell she was starting to get nervous.

"Cut the shit, Emma." Jimi glared her direction. "Kyle needs to talk to him."

Emma sighed in relief, visibly relaxing. "He is in the spotter stands."

Jimi turned back to his phone and began talking to Kyle again while I made my way over to Nancy.

"I'm so glad you could make it, sweetie." Nancy swept me into a hug. "We've missed you."

Over the years, Nancy Riley had become a mother to me. Since my mom died when I was only six, I needed womanly advice from time to time—Nancy never let me down.

Even the time I started my period in class in the eighth grade, she was there to take me to the store for tampons, and even showed me how to use the damn things since the kid behind the counter at the mini-mart couldn't show me.

This was also not something I would've allowed Charlie to do.

Could you blame me?

It looked as though a homicide took place in my underwear. I hardly wanted to share that with anyone, let alone my dad. I had a hard enough time convincing myself I wasn't dying. I honestly thought I was bleeding internally and spent a good amount of time trying to convince myself that I wasn't.

"I'm glad I did, too." I sniffled against her shoulder letting an emotional tear or two slip. "I hate being away from everyone."

Before I had a chance to really have an emotional breakdown, Emma nudged my shoulder.

With a good amount of enthusiasm, I stood and looked down toward the center of the track in time to see Jameson approach the line of drivers waiting to be introduced and Lane running at me.

"Auntie Sway!" he screamed.

I reached down and picked him up. "Hey buddy, how are you?" I tickled his sides and he squirmed in my arms, letting out a small giggle. "Look, who's that?" I pointed to Jameson who walked onto the stage as the track announcer said his name.

"Jameson Riley, driver of the number nine Simplex Ford!"

Oh sweet Jesus.

The entire place erupted with screams that were almost deafening as they caught a glimpse of Jameson approaching the stage.

"Where my daddy at?" Lane asked Alley as I handed him over to her.

"He's in the pits, buddy," she ruffled his honey-dusted hair. "If you watch closely right there you can see him when Uncle Jameson pits." She pointed to Jameson's pit stall. "He will be the one carrying the jack."

Spencer was on Jameson's over the wall pit crew who took the jack around both sides of the car during the pit stops.

Smiling, I took a deep breath when Lane started rambling on about Jameson and how he was going to be a race car driver like him someday.

My focus wasn't with this adorable boy, but with greatness below making his was on stage. Jameson stopped, waved to the crowd and then made his way from the stage, the vulnerability rippling from his quick humble exit from the intensity of the crowd.

This was all so new to him that he hadn't had a chance to adapt to it. He stumbled through his freshman season so far, though he was doing well, he wasn't concerned in the politics of it all and the overwhelming curiosity into his personal life. Racing, for Jameson, was an outlet, a place where he could be himself.

Taking in the sights before me, though I mentioned this before, I hadn't realized how popular of a driver he had become. Just his demeanor today indicated the change.

Everywhere I looked people wore hats, shirts, jackets, and foamy fingers all with his name and number.

My best friend *was* a super star.

Once driver introductions were finished, the National Anthem was sung, jets flew overhead, and the drivers were in their cars. I put on the headset Jimi handed me.

When I was in Daytona, I didn't get to listen to his in-car audio, and I was a little disappointed so Jimi let me listen this time. Emma and Alley followed suit in putting on their headsets.

Lane wanted to listen, but Alley made it clear Jameson had a potty mouth so he couldn't listen.

The kid pouted for a good ten minutes like his father. Lane and Spencer's personalities were spitting images of each other, but Lane resembled Alley with his honey blonde hair and blue eyes.

Eventually my favorite saying was announced over the speakers: "Gentlemen, start your engines!"

And the deafening roar that followed vibrated my entire body, even in the suite. There's something to be said about forty-three cars starting their engines at the same time. The smell, the rumbling in your chest when the engines revved, I was in race car heaven.

"All right boys, let's have a good race here. Keep focused," Kyle said over the radio talking to Jameson and the crew. "It's a long race, let's keep our heads."

All the over the wall crew—the spotter, crew chief, car chief, and driver—could speak to each other throughout the race. The only people who spoke directly to Jameson during the race though were Kyle, Aiden, since he was the spotter, and his teammate, Bobby Cole.

Kyle was able to talk to Jimi, if needed, Mason Bryant, the car chief who delivered orders to the crew, and other drivers' crew chiefs. Kyle also had direct lines to the engine specialist, Harry, and the tire specialist Tony. From time-to-time, engine or tire issues were brought up throughout the race and Kyle could get advice from them when needed.

The cars were making their way onto the track when Terry Barnes, one of the announcers with ESPN, tapped into Jameson's radio. "Hey Jameson, it's Terry, you copy?"

"Yep," Jameson said, the radio cracked echoing static.

"So kid, you got the pole, think you got a chance?"

"I think we do. It's a long race and a lot can happen, but we've got a fast race car."

God, his radio voice was even sexy.

"Well—good luck kid," Terry said. "It's a long race, take your time."

"Thanks."

Jameson was quiet on the radio for a lap as he warmed the tires and talked with Bobby about who was starting third behind him. I watched closely as he scrubbed the tires in a back-and-forth controlled swerving motion they used that warmed and softened the rubber on the tires. They did this for better traction and speed.

"All right, Jameson—two laps to green, bud," Kyle said over the radio. "Your pit road speed is gonna be at 5400."

"Copy that, 5400," Jameson acknowledged. "So when I come out of four, that yellow line, is that the line for pit road?"

"Yeah," Aiden replied. "Start breaking after the wall when pitting. You're pitting right after the number sixteen pit."

"10-4."

I felt like my heart was in my throat by now, it was all so hard to grasp. Daytona was my first NASCAR race, but this was the Coca-Cola 600, a night race.

Not only did it bring back the summer we shared, but it also reminded me of what it took him to get here. That alone was enough for me to get all riled up.

Ask anyone in the racing community and they'll tell you that there's something about a night race that leaves everyone with a high and with Jameson on the pole, it made it even more exciting.

I also think it had something to do with the fact that I've always loved a Saturday night at the races. It reminded me of the good ol' days at Elma with Jameson racing.

Humming with anticipation, my legs were starting to shake.

Thankfully, I took the heels off and opted for the flip-flops for now, or I'd be on the ground with these jelly legs.

"Are you okay?" Emma whispered in my ear.

I was annoyed with myself as the butterflies in my stomach threatened to fly their way out. I couldn't even look at Emma. My eyes fixed in submission on Jameson as he swerved back and forth at the front of the line.

The second pace car separating the cars pulled off allowing the field of forty-three cars to bunch together tightly and double up for the start.

It was different seeing them in a double file on start, when growing up I was used to the 4-wide salute the sprint cars put on. It's definitely something to see and a sight you'll remember.

The lead pace car in front of Jameson and Tate Harris kept position leading the cars down the backstretch, it's lights out indicating the last pace lap.

"Here we go Jameson, coming to the green flag here," Kyle told him. "Watch your shift. Don't spin the tires."

"Jameson, it's Aiden." Emma smiled so wide I thought her face would stay that way. "Kyle's right, coming to the green this time."

We all held our breath as they came out of turn four to the green, the pace car darted onto pit road.

The entire crowd was on their feet screaming, as were we, in contest to the noise on the track.

The cars remained side-by-side as they crossed the start/finish line with a roar.

"Green flag, green flag," Aiden chanted with hurried edge. "Outside one ... Harris is high ... outside middle ... outside rear ... clear."

Cars darted for position; some shifted high, some low, all with the same controlled but aggressive movements. Tate and Jameson remained in line until turn two.

By turn four, Jameson had a two-car lengths gap between him and the rest of the field.

"Nice Jameson, good start," Kyle praised. His main purpose throughout the race besides making the calls on the pit box was to keep his driver calm and collected throughout the race. "Stay focused, hit your marks."

Letting out the breath I'd been holding, I relaxed slightly as the race fell into a rhythm of green flag laps.

Jameson was quiet on the radio, said little unless he was asking where someone was at on the track and the occasional remark of, "What the hell is that guy's problem."

Growing up racing sprint cars and midgets where in-car radios were never allowed, he usually didn't say much over the radio. That was until he was upset about something. With a race that spanned six hundred miles, it was bound to happen at some point.

It was long race. They didn't call it NASCAR's longest night for nothing. It broke up the time to be able to hear what was happening over the radio and the pit stops were always entertaining. Jameson was such a hothead with them.

On lap two-ten, the caution came out for a wreck right in front of us that collected the four and the ten of Tate Harris.

"Caution's out ... car spinning in turn one ... go high."

"Who's spinning?" Jameson asked.

"Four car, hit the wall hard," Aiden told him. "Collected Harris with 'em,"

"So what do think, bud," Kyle came over the radio, "Any changes?"

"Don't touch a goddamn thing!" Jameson snapped. "The car's

fucking perfect. This bitch is cornering like it's on rails."

And *that* is why Lane can't listen.

"All right so … four tires boys … no adjustments and fuel," Kyle ordered, the crew who stood ready on the wall waiting for Jameson to get to the stall.

"I need a bottle of water," Jameson told the crew.

He had the first pit at the end of pit road so it seemed to take forever for him to get there. Once they made it to the stall, we couldn't see much from the suite but relied on radio chatter.

"Three … two … one … wheels straight, foot on the brake." The crew went to work but got stuck on the left rear when a lug nut wasn't tight, causing Jameson to fall behind five spots on the exit.

"One lane … one lane … hard, hard, there you go." Aiden guided him through pit road traffic. "Cross over on entry … there you go."

"You guys act as though you've never performed a pit stop before. My god!" Jameson yelled. "How'd I lose five spots?"

"Sorry bud," Kyle said. "There were loose lug nuts on the left rear."

The remainder of the race was spent with Jameson and Kyle arguing strategy, and Jameson telling him to shut the hell up a few times.

Jameson came over the radio at lap three-forty. "How many more laps?" You could tell by his tone, he was exhausted.

"About sixty," Kyle answered.

"If I ask again—ignore me."

Jameson had fallen back to seventh and wasn't all that pleased by this. Every time he pitted, he lost at least four spots.

Jimi was pissed and yelling at Mason, the car chief, over the radio to tell the crew to get their shit together.

Jameson, well he was quiet, which was a good indication that he was livid.

The stream of profanities that flowed when he fell back to third, after making his way to first again before this last caution, actually hurt our ears.

"Oh Jesus, you guys … what the fuck!" Jameson shouted. "How can we win if every time we have a pit stop you fuck it up and we're down three more spots? I don't know how many times I've passed this fucker in front of me!"

"They're working on it," Mason clipped.

"They're working on it?" Jameson mocked sarcastically. "We all have a job to do out here. Get it together!"

I could tell Mason was just as disappointed with the pit stops as Jameson and Kyle were. From our position in the tower, you could see the crew hanging their heads in shame. They didn't need to be told they weren't holding their own, they knew.

Both Emma and I had to pull the head phones away for a moment as Jameson continued his ranting.

When he drove past the front stretch, you could see him throw his water bottle and pound the steering wheel with his fists. After a few laps, he was quiet again.

At five laps to go he was running second when the caution came out. "Cautions out, turn three low."

"Stay out or no?" Jameson asked.

"Uh …" Kyle paused for a moment.

"*Kyle* … we can't be hesitating like this."

"I know that, Jameson!" Kyle snapped back. "How's the car? Do you need any adjustments?"

"With a few laps to go, nothing's gonna change. I'm tight, but we're better on the short runs anyhow."

"Stay out then," Kyle told him. "Just keep calm."

When the green flag dropped, Jameson was in third. When the white flag waved, he was one second behind the fourteen of Darrin Torres and gaining quickly. His last lap times were enough to break the track record.

"Your last lap time was—"

"Don't tell me lap times," Jameson snapped getting a nose under Darrin. "If I want 'em—I'll ask for 'em."

Jameson went high, and Nancy and I gripped each other tightly as he came out of turn three. We all held our breath when he entered turn four neck and neck with the Darrin.

I literally stopped breathing when they came across the finish line together. You couldn't tell who won.

Everyone turned toward the screen waiting for them to announce the winner. The instant replay played repeatedly as they tried to decipher the winner. Within a minute, it was decided.

"Who won?" Jameson asked impatiently. "Come on! Who won?"

Jameson had won by three tenths of an inch.

"You did, bud," Kyle answered. "Nice racing!"

"Seriously?"

"Yes," Kyle laughed, "seriously."

All we heard was Jameson screaming over the radio causing everyone in the suite to break out in laughter.

"Whew!" He seemed to have let out the breath he'd been holding. "Not bad for a dirt track racer from Washington!" Jameson yelled, his voice shaking with excitement. "*Fuck yeah!*"

The crowd erupted into another booming screaming fit, and I couldn't help but get excited with them. It was in the air tonight.

I smiled when Alley and Emma started jumping with me.

We all turned to Nancy who started jumping along with us. Soon, Jameson's Nana, at seventy-two, started jumping.

Jameson swung his car along the front stretch and revved his engine, the rear tires creating a curling cloud of smoke.

I wanted to run down there and throw myself across his hood when he revved his engine. It was as if he was a lion and I was a female lioness in heat.

He yanked the window net down, pumping his fist in the air as he did a burn out in the infield holding the checkered flag, grass and dirt soaring in the wake.

Since the Chili Bowl Midget Nationals, I hadn't seen Jameson win a race in person. And as I sat there watching him, I couldn't help but cry knowing what it took him to get here.

Witnessing it first-hand, I lived it with him over the years and it was just as much of a reward to see him like this now as it was for him.

He did it—he won the Coca-Cola 600. The preeminent rookie driver, my best friend, captured NASCAR's longest night.

I think what stood out most to me in that moment, here was Jameson, doing what he loved, doing what he was born to do, and I loved that I was here sharing it with him. I felt as though I was a part of that.

The rest of his family and I made our way down to victory lane to wait for Jameson.

When he pulled the car in, you could barely hear anything besides screaming fans.

I studied his every move as he stripped away his gloves, neck brace, removed the air tube from his helmet and then unbuckled his helmet.

Collecting himself, he leaned his head back against his seat for a second before removing his helmet.

When he finally removed it, he ran his fingers through his mop of sweaty hair. That's when I got a good look in his eyes for a moment. That arresting fire, that intense self-assured stare, was glistening with tears.

Immediately I was crying again. In all the years I'd known Jameson, I'd never seen him cry, ever, nothing even close to a tear. Even the time Spencer accidently-on-purpose had hit him in the junk with a tire iron when he was fourteen. He had never cried. But *now*, his composure was wavering. And that had me wavering.

He shook his head and swallowed, his hands trembling as he tried to compose himself. Not only was he completely worn out, this was an important race to him. He always wanted to win in Charlotte having never won here before in all the USAC events they ran and with his entire family being here this weekend—it was emotional for him.

To him, a win in the heartland of NASCAR, in a series that no one thought he'd make it in, meant far more than a win at any other track on the circuit.

Why?

Because to him, winning in the heartland showed he could be that mystifying greatness he was pegged to be. And he was.

After a moment, he pulled out his ear buds, took the steering wheel off and placed his sponsor's hat over his matted hair.

Kyle made his way over to the car, placed his head inside and then ruffled Jameson's hair. Jameson grinned shaking his hand. Kyle then grabbed a beer and handed it to Jameson who opened it taking a slow drink.

When he glanced in our direction, my eyes caught his.

He winked and reached up to hoist himself to the edge of the window, beating on the roof, enlivening the team wedded to him.

Collective shouts erupted, victory lane roared to life, with an astounding adulation for a boy, who I grew up watching, command respect with his ability.

Whistles and clapping mixed with beer, champagne and Coke spraying.

Let me tell you something about celebrating in Victory Lane. Shit gets in your eyes when it's sprayed, and you can't avoid it. Beer and champagne don't sting nearly as bad as Coke does when it gets in your eyes. I don't know what's in the stuff, but that shit burns.

Swinging his legs over the side, Jameson stood on the edge of the window frame, let out a laugh and launched himself into his crew where Spencer caught him.

His team swarmed with friendly ribbing and hard pats to his back. Their solidarity was hard to find with every team on the series, as it was hard to attain. This team had casualness to each other and a trust—despite the problems with the pit stops—that formed over time. It was easy to see this team, reveling in the victory, and knowing that they could be a champion team as they all saw the bigger picture.

You feel it and maybe understand it, in part, but the unity between a racing team is what drives it forward leading them to victory. Without it, a win could hardly be appreciated.

Soon the announcer was in Jameson's face asking questions, but he motioned for me to come over before he started talking.

I wasn't sure he wanted me to come over until he yelled, "Get over here, Sway!"

I trotted my happy little pit lizard ass right over.

Smiling down at me, he wrapped his sweaty arms around me for a burly hug I deemed *completely* appropriate.

"I'm so proud of you," I whispered in his ear—his damp hair falling against my forehead.

"Thank you for being here. It means everything to me," he whispered back before placing a quick kiss on my lips.

This alarmed me.

For one, the sensation left me weak in the knees, and two, there were reporters everywhere.

I could hardly attack the boy like I wanted to, or could I?

The announcer stuck the microphone in his face, and I backed away toward Nancy and Emma who made their way over letting Jameson talk to the media.

"Jameson Riley, you heard go from Kyle and you did." Spencer screamed in the background causing another bellowed uproar from the team behind us. "Tell us what you did there at the end to catch Darrin Torres."

"You know, we had an unbelievable car throughout the entire race. The car wasn't as good on the long runs so we lucked out with the green white checker," Jameson told them, still smiling. "We had some problems with pit stops, but we had a fast car to make up for it. It's pretty awesome to win here on Memorial Day weekend. Despite everything that happened in the Winston and with the fine earlier today, all I can say is it feels good to win." He looked over at his family. "My family is all here ... even my Nana was able to make it. I need to thank my sponsor Simplex Shocks and Springs ... all the people that support us, CST Engines, my dad for giving me a chance."

"Let's get him over here." The reporter motioned for Jimi to come over. Jameson wiped sweat from his neck with a towel that Alley threw at him.

"Jimi, what do you think of your son here?" He shoved the microphone in his face.

"I knew he had it in him." Jimi smiled. "We're very proud of Jameson." He reached for Jameson, heaving him into an embrace, and whispered something to him.

For a moment, Jimi's hard demeanor shifted showing him remembering what it took for his son to get here, in Victory Lane. This, the sounds, vibrations, smells of racing and the rouse of the night around us was what completed Jameson and, in turn, was highlighted in Jimi's eyes having made this dream possible.

When Jameson pulled back, he was all smiles.

He had conscientiously tried for so long to gain approval from Jimi as well as separation to become himself even though he still looked to his father for praise.

What Jameson never realized, but then, maybe he did after winning the USAC Triple Crown during our summer together, was that he never needed to separate himself.

Kyle remained near the car, his humble demeanor breaking into a smile of both honor and gratification. The announcer turned to him. "Kyle, you seemed to make the right call there to stay out."

Kyle shook his head and patted Jameson on the back. "Nah," he drew out with coyness. "That was Jameson's call."

"Well, it seemed to be the right one. Congratulations."

I watched him in awe as he finished the last of his interviews.

This man made talking to the media sexy.

Once interviews were finished it was time for the "hat dance" as they called it. The "hat dance" was where drivers and their teams wore the hats of their various sponsors, snapped a picture and then moved onto the next one, usually around twenty or so.

It was actually somewhat comical to watch. There were a few times where half the team had the wrong hat on where others didn't.

It had to have been confusing, but did provide us some entertainment.

Alley, Emma, and I excused ourselves to wait back at the hauler for him to finish. Standing near the doors, Alley talked to Simplex on the phone when Jameson returned with Aiden and Spencer.

"Congratulations," Alley screamed over the noise of the engines from the car returning to their haulers.

Jameson hugged her and wiped his sweaty face over her shoulders. "You're an asshole," she snapped and punched him in the stomach.

Emma threw a towel at him, and he wiped off his face.

"Hi." He smiled once he was close enough and took a drink of the Gatorade Aiden tossed him.

I laughed. "Hi."

"I have a press conference to do," he said nonchalantly with a shrug. "You're coming to the bar, right?"

I wanted to hit him and hump his leg at the same time when he smirked like that.

"I'm not sure," I said with a shrug. "I might go check out this Bobby Cole driver. See if he'll take me home." I shook my hips at him.

Jameson's eyes narrowed. "You better be here when I'm done,

Sway." He pulled on the strings of my sweatshirt, his eyes darting to my lips and then back again.

"Whatever." I countered slapping his hand away with a giggle.

Alley was telling him it was time to go, but he leaned closer. The thick scent of racing engulfed me.

"I'm not kidding. You better be here," he warned and hip checked me.

Emma, who was standing behind me, placed her head on my shoulder. "Pit lizard."

I turned glaring at her.

"Whore who's fucking her brother's friend," I quipped back reaching for the black heels she dangled in my face.

I had something to prove tonight, and I was going to need those damn shoes.

Victory Lane – The spot on each racetrack's in-field where the race winner parks and celebrates victory. It's sometimes referred to as "winners circle."

It was nearly midnight when Jameson finally finished with the contender conference (a press conference with the top five finishers from the race and their crew chiefs) and post-race interviews. Now we were finally on the way to downtown Charlotte where Jameson was required to make an appearance at the Howl at the Moon bar.

The thirty-five minute drive from the track was filled with Jameson, Aiden, and Spencer recapping the race and pit stops. Spencer had been just as disappointed with the pit stops as Jameson.

Emma, Alley and I elected to crack open the mini-bar half way through the drive. Since Jimi and Nancy decided to make it a night and gladly took Lane with them, Alley and Spencer were making use of the grown up time. Lane, who wouldn't get out of Jameson's car after the race, ended up falling asleep in there and had to be carried, lifelessly, to Nancy and Jimi's hotel room.

"What was wrong with Bobby's car?" Spencer asked Jameson.

"Fuck if I know. He was really loose coming out of four. Hell ... I think he pegged the wall a couple times." Jameson leaned further back in the seat and took a drink of his beer. "A couple of times I thought he'd give me a push on the restart, but he hung me out to dry."

Alley smiled at Jameson. "Gordon called." She held her phone up. "The car passed post-race inspection ... they're dropping the fine, too."

"Seriously?" Jameson perked up.

"It was a bullshit fine anyway," Spencer added.

Alley slipped her phone inside her bag. "Regardless, we're a new team. We don't need publicity like that. It's good they dropped it."

Jameson nodded, his gaze fixated on his beer.

The poor guy was beat. He'd spent four hours manhandling a race car—he had a right to be tired.

If it were me, I'd be curled up in bed right now.

Eventually the talk turned to what we were all going to drink once we got to the bar. Howl at the Moon had some of the best drinks around, like the Purple Rain.

As luck would have it, the Omni Hotel where we were staying was up the street. I had a feeling we might want the short drive after this escapade.

I sat there silently listening and drinking my beer beside Jameson.

When we first got inside the limo there was about a foot between us. Every so often, Jameson scooted over to whisper something to me and never moved back.

So now, here we were shoulder-to-shoulder, hip-to-hip, left leg-to-right leg, and I was in pit lizard heaven.

My left hand was holding my beer, and I kept my right hand busy with the outside paper label. God knows what my hands would do if they didn't have something to occupy them. They probably would have checked out his gearshift and then moved on to figure out what size gears he was running.

You sound totally stupid.

Jameson showered before we left and changed into a pair of jeans that matched my skirt and a black button down shirt that he had rolled the sleeves up to his elbows. Emma dressed him, in case you were wondering how we ended up matching. He was insanely hot and smelled even better with the faint smells of racing fuel and burnt rubber lingering on his skin.

If only they made racing fuel cologne. I laughed at myself thinking back to the commercials they used to do with racing fuel as cologne.

Jameson turned his head toward me, grinning when he heard my chuckle. "Get drunk with me tonight."

"I don't think that's a good idea, sport," I objected shaking my head. I crossed my legs, and Jameson's eyes that were once focused on my face slowly moved to my bare thighs.

His eyes met mine again, and his intense stare had me blushing in seconds. He didn't say anything for a long moment—just looked at me until Spencer's laugh interrupted us.

Jameson licked his lips in a deliberately casual way. His head angled to one side before he brought his hand up to his face and rubbed down the sharp line of his jaw, his eyes holding mine. "I won the Coca-Cola 600." His nose scrunched in the cutest way and motioned with two fingers for me to lean closer, so I did. Then he whispered in my ear. "That's a big deal." I felt his lips graze my earlobe. "*We* need to celebrate."

"Fine," I huffed, pulling away from him slightly and pretending to pout while he smiled triumphantly next to me.

I think I let out a noise that was near a squeak but closer to a snort. It sounded stupid ... not at all sexy.

I wasn't mad he wanted to celebrate by drinking. I needed the liquid courage tonight more than ever. I didn't want to appear too *eager*.

"Can I make one suggestion?" I asked when I could speak again.

"Is it a lewd suggestion?" Jameson raised a questioning eyebrow at me, a raffish smile plastered across his lips.

"Surprisingly, no." I smiled holding up a finger in front of him. "No tattoos."

His bottom lip protruded out, the smile threatened again tugging at the corners of his mouth. "Where's the fun in that, Sway?"

Something seemed different about us. I couldn't place it, but it was there. Instead of taunting, he was teasing in a flirting way.

Regardless, it was messing with my head though, and more alcohol was definitely in the cards tonight.

Once we made it to the bar, Spencer got shit-faced drunk, Alley was pissed because she ended up wearing an entire bottle of Jack Daniels down her dress, Emma was trying her hardest to stay away from Aiden and his cowboy hat, and Jameson ... well, poor Jameson looked uncomfortable as ever.

It might have had something to do with the fact that I bent over in front of him to grab the bottle of Jack Daniels that Spencer had spilled on Alley. Let's just say that I forgot I was wearing a skirt.

Okay, okay ... I didn't forget. I knew *exactly* what I was doing.

This was what I liked to refer to as Pit Lizard 101.

When the limo pulled up to the bar I wasn't prepared for the swarm of fans that inundated Jameson when we stepped out.

Everyone was yelling his name, screaming for his autograph, and I'll be honest with you, it was a little overwhelming.

Jameson smiled politely at the insanity declining to sign anything until he was inside.

After hearing them, I intended on staying in the car until Jameson grabbed my hand. "Come on, Sway."

I shook my head. "I lied. I don't think I want to go inside anymore. What's wrong with the mini-bar in here?" I asked.

"Spencer drank it all."

When our eyes met, I knew he saw my fear.

"Don't leave me hangin' ... you promised," Jameson intoned, leaving me weak and vulnerable. I hated being either one. Especially around someone like Jameson Riley.

"I hate you," I seethed stepping out, careful to keep my goods covered.

Jameson watched my every move as I stepped out, shamelessly letting his eyes rake down my body.

With a devious smirk, he slowly winked at me. "You don't hate me, honey, and you know it." Pressed against his body, his lips dipped to my ear. "I have a surprise for you tonight anyway."

If it involved his camshaft, I was all for it.

Eventually we maneuvered our way inside the bar. Spencer and Alley were arguing, Emma and Aiden were inches away from each other and looking like they are about to kiss any second, and I was so close to Jameson's side you'd think we were glued together.

And believe me, I wasn't complaining.

Once inside, it wasn't hard to spot Tommy, our friend from high school and the mechanic for Jameson's sprint car team. Not only was his orange hair loud and stood out, but he was also chanting Jameson's name as he stood on the bar.

My eyes scanned the bar looking for familiarity and the low lights set a comfortable ambiance.

Most of the crew was waiting at a large table that the bar had reserved for us and the alcohol flowed in abundance. When we reached the table, Kyle pulled Jameson into a hug, which meant Jameson had let go of my hand. I wasn't okay with that.

What surprised me was once Jameson let go of Kyle, he quickly reached for my hand again.

Maybe he does have feelings for me. Maybe he's loved me just as long.

Unlikely, but a pit lizard could dream.

The bar was uncontrolled. Media, fans, various team members, sponsor reps, and even other drivers hugged the very edges of the room.

Everyone, including me, wanted a piece of Jameson. Everyone wanted to talk to him about the race and the win. Everyone wanted to get a picture with him ... wants, wants, wants.

I'll tell you about wants ... My *want* was working overdrive as I observed him working the room, shaking hands with everyone and mingling.

I had a feeling he didn't know who most of these people were but he pretended. I, on the other hand, had no idea who anyone was until Alley and Jameson took me around and introduced me.

"This is Melissa Childers," Jameson said motioning with a tight nod to the short brown haired woman standing before me. "She's a public relations rep for Simplex."

"Hey dude," Tommy threw an arm around Jameson. "Justin and Tyler flew to Terra Haute for tomorrow's race. They said to tell you congratulations and this girl hello," Tommy tugged on my hair.

"Thanks," Jameson replied with a wide smile.

Melissa, who remained beside me, shook my hand and chatted as Jameson moved through the crowd to greet fans and a few other drivers who made an appearance.

Seated securely in the corner, wanting to control myself for once tonight, I kept an eye on Jameson from a distance. That alluring mysteriousness circling him captivated me as it always did.

He stood in the shadows of the bar; wanting a distance from those around him he wouldn't get any time soon. Not tonight. Watching the crowd, he seemed agitated. As if he was struggling with something he couldn't say.

Shrugging to an unheard question from the man seated next to him in a dark suit, Jameson tossed a smirk my direction. A reassurance I definitely needed right then. The man walked away after that leaving Jameson to himself for a moment until the next person requested his attention. It seemed to be an endless cycle, and I knew then *why* he stayed in the shadows.

Beneath the many layers of Jameson was that vulnerability about him that you didn't see too often in racers, as I've said. Personally, I think most racers owned this trait, but you didn't know, or cared enough, to be aware of it.

Jameson seemed uninterested in the fans surrounding him, yet he didn't move from his place at the bar as he knew he *had* to be here. I think he knew if he moved Alley would kick his ass.

It was times like this where I could feel the change in him. He was still the same Jameson, but I was afraid of what he had to be on the outside and if he would be able to protect him and his dream.

Despite the lack of attention he seemed to have to those around him, I could still see the restlessness and the loneliness that this lifestyle had created for him over the past few years. That was the side you could see in most drivers these days. It was as if the lifestyle was destroying who they were inside just to live a dream.

Jameson's eyes appeared distant and unseeing for a moment as he searched the crowd appearing to be looking for someone. Me, I hoped.

Looking at him now, you wouldn't know that this was a man who'd won a race. He appeared annoyed.

Tommy walked by ruffling his hair. His distance gave way to the gesture, and he cracked a smile at his longtime buddy.

That's when Jameson stole a sideways glance my direction and a familiar heat spread over me. He was still that boy I grew to love. He was still Jameson.

I smiled, seeing the authenticity I've always known and loved about him.

Another fan approached him for an autograph, his body shifted toward them to offer them a little piece of him. Dragging his hand through his hair, a careful smile formed, but I could see he was uneasy with the close proximity of the fans. He was nervous and apprehensive.

A reporter with FOX Sports made it known she had an attraction for Jameson by basically hovering over him.

This only made me want to push him against the bar he was leaning against and fuck the boy senseless right in front of her.

You sound like a jealous high school girl with insecure emotional issues, I told myself. Well I wasn't in high school and didn't really have any insecure emotional issues but jealous ... party for one, please.

"I've seen that look before, Sway," Alley whispered in my ear taking a seat next to me at the large dark wooden table.

So much for my private stalking.

I didn't look up quickly finding interest in tracing the cracks in the wood with my fingertips.

Turning, I glared past her, my eyes focused on Jameson. "Who is that hanging on him?"

"Ashley Conner, she's a reporter with FOX Sports." Alley looked over the drink menu, never looking up. "She does this *every* weekend."

Throwing my arms against the table, I groaned letting my head fall against my forearms. "He's slept with her—hasn't he? Jesus. Why am I so stupid?"

I don't know why I asked if he slept with her. I knew the answer by the way they looked at each other. She was trying her hardest to flaunt her tits in his face, and he was looking everywhere else he could to avoid her. Over the years, I'd seen this exact dance between him and nameless pit lizards.

Alley sighed. "I don't know," her tone was dismissive as it always was when speaking of Jameson's encounters with women. "My contract doesn't include monitoring Jameson's sex life. They don't pay me enough for *that*."

I was on the verge of tears when she turned in her seat and forced me to look at her.

"I'm warning you," Alley pointed at me. "Don't do what you're thinking."

"I didn't ..." I began and was quickly silenced by her murderous glare.

"I know you, and I know what you're thinking. You think if you sleep with him you can convince him he loves you."

Am I really that transparent?

In an attempt to hold on to any remaining dignity her glare didn't destroy, I didn't say anything.

"Don't do it," she warned once more and then called the waiter over. "Here, pick something." She tossed me a menu. "We're getting drunk."

Spencer, sporting a new Spiderman bandage above his eyebrow, sat down next to me and swung his arm around my chair.

"I suggest you remove your arm," I warned grimly, my mood turning for the worst.

Screaming or crying, either one was a good option as I watched woman after woman throw themselves into Jameson's arms. Trying to analyze his every move, I knew Jameson, and I knew exactly what he did when his interest was piqued. So far, he showed none of those signs; he actually appeared uncomfortable with it all.

"Spencer," Alley's voice brought me back around to reality.

Spencer, who'd been staring at the menu, flinched looking over at her but quickly looked the direction of the door when Alley mouthed something to him.

"What are you guys whispering about?" I asked scanning the room to see if I missed something. My eyes focused on the bar to see Jameson and a guy standing inches from his face.

He was around the same height as Jameson, dirty blonde hair, but I couldn't see anything beside that with his back to me.

I did notice the tall blonde attached to his hip and thought that she resembled Chelsea.

We watched for a moment but when Spencer rose knocking his chair to the ground, I realized that the conversation between Jameson and this guy was getting heated.

Disdainfully, Jameson set his beer down and stepped forward. His eyes took on that dark glower I also knew well.

The woman at the guy's side seemed uninterested and disappeared into the bathroom while the guy continued to talk to Jameson, waving his arms around as if he was explaining something.

Alley and I got up following Spencer over to the bar where we picked up on what was being said. By now, the entire bar was listening.

"Just because your dad provided the ride doesn't mean you're hot shit, Jameson," the guy said.

Once closer, I recognized him as Darrin Torres, driver of the number fourteen car that Jameson beat for the win tonight.

Darrin and Jameson had history dating back to their days racing USAC and had frequent run-ins so far this year—including a very public brawl after the Winston a week ago.

Jameson leaned back against the bar again creating distance, trying to appear as if he didn't give a shit. He probably didn't.

"Darrin," Jameson spoke slowly shaking his head, his voice surprisingly calm—it sounded all the more threatening that way. "Just because my dad owns the team I race for, doesn't mean I can't drive. Who won tonight?"

"By three-tenths of an inch," Darrin snorted with a glib smile. "Hardly a win."

Jameson laughed darkly, the impassiveness remaining imperturbable. "Any way you want to look at it Darrin, I won." He looked away from Darrin. With a nod, he motioned for the bartender to get him another beer. "How does second place feel?"

"How does that $50,000 fine feel?"

Jameson laughed.

"Oh, I don't know ... didn't you hear?" His hand casually dragged along the stubble of his jaw. "They dropped the fine." His eyes then scanned Darrin. "Said the test came back inconclusive and nothing was found in the post-race inspection. Try harder next time."

I didn't know Darrin had anything to do with the fuel additive in his car, but I wouldn't put it past him.

Darrin stepped closer and grabbed Jameson by the collar of his shirt causing Jameson's beer to spill. "Listen you little shit," Spencer appeared threateningly beside Jameson. "Stay out of my way on the track, or you *will* regret it," Darrin warned.

Jameson came on like a charging bull shoving Darrin backward. Before Spencer could react, Jameson delivered a hard left hook to Darrin's jaw, jerked him forward by the shirt and held a broken beer bottle pressed to his neck.

Spencer, who stood close to me in a protective stance, shook his head muttering something along the lines of "southpaw," but I couldn't make out much else.

I'd seen enough of Jameson's frequent pit brawls over the years to know his left-handed pop could get you unexpectedly. Spencer used to say that Jameson had this advantage over others, even him, because lefties came at you backward. I'd say that from the blood pouring for Darrin's lip that he could attest to this theory.

"Don't *ever* threaten me again." Jameson growled in his ear making no attempt to back away. His voice was sharp enough to cut glass sending waning chills down my spine.

Before Darrin could counter to the anger pulsating from Jameson, Spencer and Kyle were breaking things up, and the owner was escorting Darrin from the bar.

Jameson was yelling at Aiden and Spencer as they pinned him forcefully against the wall struggling to control him.

I tried to get over to him, I knew I could calm him down, but Emma and Alley were tugging me toward the bathrooms in the other direction.

"I don't have to pee, let me go," I groaned as they pushed me through the door.

As if the night couldn't get any worse, I ran into the person I thought I would never have to see again.

Chelsea Adams.

"Well," Chelsea said looking directly at me. "It's been a long time, Sway."

"I wish I could say it's nice to see you, but it's *not*," I replied glaring at the perfect bitch.

She rolled her eyes.

"Is that Jameson you're salivating over out there? He's looking good these days."

I pounced on her like a jungle cat, slamming us both to the ground in the middle of the bathroom. I'm not sure what got into me, but I was livid. I hated her in high school and now she thought she could walk into his life again and pick up where they left off ... not if I had anything to say about it. Drawing my fist back, I punched her square in the mouth.

Moments passed and I stayed perched on top of her throwing punches, pulling her hair and scratching.

"Get off me you whore!" Chelsea screamed from underneath.

"Who are you calling a whore?" Emma lunged for Chelsea as well.

Word got out quickly to the rest of the bar about the gladiator style fight going down in the women's bathroom. Doors were broken, mirrors were smashed, hair was ripped out, blood and tears were shed.

It looked like they filmed part of the movie *Fight Club* in there.

Alley, Emma, and I were unscathed though.

"What the fuck happened in here?" Spencer asked stepping over the broken door. His eyes focused on Chelsea wiping her mouth. "Holy hell ..."

Jameson and Aiden stood in the doorway their questioning eyes scanning.

"Hey boys," I said as casually as possible. "Just freshening up."

Jameson was looking at me with an amused expression patiently waiting for an explanation. Tommy stepped inside the bathroom and burst into laughter tossing me a glorified smile.

I grabbed Jameson by the arm and fluffed my hair with the other hand. "Let's get drunk now."

I never saw Chelsea again that night, and I think the key factor there might have been my intoxication.

A Hurricane Bucket, a Purple Rain, a Lucille's Sweet Tea, and one Loose Goose. I was done for.

I couldn't even form a coherent word … even when I tried.

Jameson wasn't doing any better with Tommy holding him up as he explained how he thought today's youth, present company excluded, had no work ethic.

Alley and Spencer had left to go get Lane since Spencer had to drive the motor coach to Pocono tomorrow.

Emma complained she was tired so Aiden *conveniently* became tired at the same time. They left together. Thankfully, Jameson was too drunk to notice.

This left Jameson, Kyle, and Tommy with me at the bar when Jameson decided to duel some guy on the piano. No one knew he had the piano chops, too, and left the entire bar, still bursting with people, in a complete frenzy, me included.

Eventually I was alone with Jameson and he was pulling me toward the dance floor to dance to "Purple Rain" since we were, in fact, drinking a Purple Rain drink.

This was his reasoning at least.

Drawing me against his chest tightly, he whispered the lyrics of "Purple Rain" to me with a low gravelly voice that left me trembling in his arms. What sent me over the edge was when he threw his head back and belted out an utterly raw verse.

It seemed the more I drank, the more my plan was set in stone.

I was going to fuck this boy tonight. I was sure of it.

My biggest problem when drinking was that I had all the bad ideas floating around in my head. When alcohol got involved, they turned into bad decisions. Over the years I'd become accustomed to this, but don't think I didn't want to sue the makers of tequila a time or two for their persuasive influence.

These bad ideas convinced me that I would make him see me for me and that I was perfect for him. The drunker I got, the easier it was to forget that he was a superstar now and not just my best friend. He was the boy I grew to love. After a while, I went with it.

All night it seemed that he was giving peculiar looks, his eyes cutting and smiling. It warmed me and he looked as though he was seeing me as the girl who was always there for him and not some pit lizard. He looked at me like I was the only woman in the room who mattered to him.

I must have been staring at him because when he snuck a glance at me, he smirked. "What?"

I bit down on my bottom lip then slowly pulled my straw in my mouth and took a drink before saying, "Nothing," then winked at him.

Slowly, and I do mean slowly, he sucked his bottom lip in, bit down and then gradually let it drag against his teeth.

"You are the most *beautiful* woman I've ever met," he crooned pressing a tender kiss right below my ear.

I was drunk, plain and simple.

Tanked, toasted, spent, hammered, smashed, intoxicated, plastered, and sloshed ... whatever you want to call it. Jameson and I could barely put one foot in front of the other when the limo driver dropped us at the hotel around four in the morning.

Somewhere between the dancing and serenading, I decided I was going to do whatever my engine and crankcase wanted—as noted, alcohol played a strong role in this. Since my crankcase and engine were in charge, *they* decided I'd stood by watching far too long now.

I watched as he won the Coca-Cola 600 tonight. I watched as he whispered an entire song in my ear and, let's face it, he could have been whispering how to change a tire and I would have melted.

And then to top it off, he told me I was the most beautiful woman he'd ever met. Okay, well yes, he was drunk when he said it but still, he said it, *to me.*

My attention turned back to Jameson fumbling with his room key. He seemed resolutely focused on getting the door open.

Leaning against the wall, I searched for mine in my bag. Reaching down, I slipped my heels off. My feet now resembled hamburger from all the blisters.

Jameson, with some determination and focus, managed to get the key in the door but fell through the door when it opened, landing on his ass in the entryway.

We both started laughing as he lay down on the floor. "I think I broke my ass."

"I'll let you get some sleep, Jameson. See you in the morning." I started to walk away, but stopped when I felt his hand grasp my ankle.

"Where you going, honey?" I looked down and I was met with the most intense burning stare. Where his eyes were once restless at the bar earlier, they were now focused and alive.

The green, though bloodshot, seemed brighter but in the same sense, they seemed darker with a carnal desire. I knew the look well as I had it plastered upon my face throughout the entire evening.

That burning stare traveled up my body focusing on me as he waited for my answer.

"To my room," I choked out, though I'm not sure he heard me or maybe it was that I couldn't hear myself over the loud thudding of my heart in my ears.

I should have been concerned with how fast my heart was beating, but all I could focus on was the green in his eyes contrasting against the black in his shirt and the way he was looking at me.

His head skewed to the side slightly as though he was waiting for me to do something, anything.

Nervously, I stood in the doorway hovering over him. He bent at the waist to sit up wrapping his hands around my legs and leaned in to my right leg.

"Stay," he whispered against my calf.

His lips brushed against my skin in a tender way, but the predatory gaze he unleashed told another story.

Kneeling down beside him, I dropped my shoes and bag to the ground, providing quite the sight with my illegal skirt. "You're drunk."

"So are you," he pointed out. His hand reached to touch the side of my face. "I don't care that we're drunk."

I intended on helping him up, but it didn't end up that way when I leaned forward. Arms crossed, legs gave way, bodies tangled together and hands went wild. Before I knew what happened, I was lying on top of Jameson with my legs on either side of his hips.

Propped up by one arm, I looked down thinking he was going to tell me to get up, but nope, he stared at me. His right hand moved from my leg and touched my cheek again.

What did I do next?

I did what any aptly minded pit lizard would do. I leaned down and pressed my lips to his once. I planned on one kiss—just to remember the feeling. But he surprised me when his mouth opened and his tongue swept over my lower lip.

So while I intended on this one kiss, my crankcase had other plans, as did Jameson.

His mouth pressed to mine urgently, rough with a hard desperate edge. When his tongue entered my mouth, I gasped, forgetting how nice that felt. Over the years, we had kissed often, to which I had *always* enjoyed, but I had failed to remember the giddy high that it had gave me.

I moved my hips, shifting my weight when my hands found his hair. It didn't feel strange; it felt right—natural and familiar.

He groaned into my mouth, the want emanating in his voice. "Sway ..."

His hands flew to my hips and guided me down on top of him—flush against his pelvis and *oh ... oh ...* hold up ... caution flags out ladies and gentlemen. We not only had an oil slick down on the track, but we had a camshaft searching for a crankcase.

I froze, wondering if he was going to push me away at any moment, but he didn't. We had been here before, but he always stopped quickly before anything escalated, collecting himself. Only now he wasn't stopping.

Instead, he pushed his hips up to meet mine. "Jesus Christ, Sway ..."

Still kissing me desperately, his impatient hands began working my shirt over my head. The pit lizard in me was thrilled, and I ripped the motherfucker off letting it fall beside Jameson's face.

He grinned, a lopsided grin against my lips, chuckling at my sudden onset of rage against the poor fabric that used to be a shirt. Like an engine exceeding its maximum rev limiter, my willpower and need for him couldn't prevent any unforeseen damage.

I realized right about then that the door was still wide open so I tried to maneuver my legs to kick the door shut but didn't succeed.

"Just a second," I whispered and with one last kiss—I got off Jameson and pushed the door closed.

Once I was away from his warm embrace, I began to comprehend what was really happening.

Did I want this? Did he? Would we regret it in the morning?

Before I had time to regret anything we'd already done, I felt him approach me from behind. A strange electric pulse sang between us causing my breathing to become ragged.

Placing both hands against the door to stabilize myself—my body anticipated the contact. I could smell him—feel him getting closer.

With nervous energy pulsing throughout my body, my nerves felt primed for it—waiting. The silence between us was heavy and tense. My body felt like it was being pulled toward him by the energy between us.

Jameson leaned in—his chest pressed against my back covering my hands against the door with his own, his fingers interlocked with mine.

I could feel the rise and fall of each strained breath in his body. His lips pressed to my bare shoulder and then he kissed me slowly leaving wet kisses over my skin until his lips found my neck.

The fire in me was burning. He stopped there, and then grazed his tongue back down the path he'd made, sending a shudder through me.

"I *want* you so bad," he whispered, echoing my exact thoughts, his voice and body trembling.

I couldn't respond. I wasn't aware that a voice could sound so pleading while with so much urgency. Over the course of our friendship, I'd never seen him like *this* before.

I maneuvered myself turning around in his arms.

We stood there facing each other—me without a shirt, his jeans intact with his shirt open in the front.

The muscles in his stomach flexed and contracted with each labored breath he took. I could tell his resolve was crumbling when he swept his shaking hand across the back of his neck.

It felt as though each of us was daring the other to make the next move.

My eyes met his, and I thought I would see love or something resembling the emotions I felt for him, but all I saw was the hooded lust burning deep with hunger.

His breathing remained heavy, shit, he was nearly panting as he watched me like I was his prey. And it was impossible to miss the way his hands trembled as they reached for me again.

Letting go of any hesitation I may have had, I lunged for him. Jumping in his arms, his hands immediately flew to my ass as he attacked me, my kiss silencing his guttural moan. We stumbled back against the wall with an animalistic grunt, the drywall cracked against my back, but that didn't stop us.

Driven with want, we seemed to be eagerly searching for the unknown. We weren't necessarily searching for the same want, but we were searching for it with each other.

I kept asking myself what I was doing, but I was doing what felt natural to me. It was instinct and adrenaline coming together, but there was the familiarity there, assuring me; I was safe with him and *he* wanted this.

We wanted this.

Throughout our entire friendship, it was easy to see there was a sexual attraction between us. I always wondered if it was me. Judging by the camshaft rubbing against me, it wasn't my imagination.

Happy hour had begun and our clothes were all over the place and in pieces, with the exception of his jeans.

It didn't take long and I was on my back on the king size bed in the middle of the gigantic bedroom. His kisses were frantic, hands were as determined as they were when he was steering a race car. Only now, he was steering me. Pushing, pulling, and dragging my body against his in all the ways he wanted.

"Tell me to stop," he whispered, and I could feel the hesitation in each move he made.

It was evident he wanted this, but he held a certain amount of ambiguity. Pulling back, his eyes hooded with that same hesitation and lust.

"*Please*," his voice broke when his breath caught. "Honey ... tell me to stop."

Though he was saying this, he didn't stop. His fingertips ran over my lips searching my eyes for an answer, an answer he didn't want.

As I said, we'd been like this before but stopped. Stopping now didn't seem like an option for either of us. But I also had a feeling this was his way of making *this* my decision.

I didn't want him to stop. I wanted this just as badly. I always had and now, for the first time, my insecurities surrounding this didn't matter and I threw myself into it.

"Don't," I mumbled pulling him closer, my legs wrapped tightly around his waist. "Please, don't stop."

There, I told him.

He pulled back again, his eyes searching mine, and I could see the struggle within as he stilled himself above me. With each breath, our chests moved slowly but with a rapid pace that gave away our feelings. We both wanted it.

But I could also sense his hesitation. He was afraid to move knowing there was no going back. We couldn't take this back once it happened. When he entered me he was, in more ways than either of us understood, claiming me.

What would that mean?

Sometimes you think you want a taste, but is a taste ever enough?

I honestly believe no one could have just *a* taste. This went beyond physical attraction. For me, this was bone deep and would never change. With the way I was drawn to Jameson, both frightening and exciting, this couldn't be just a taste.

"Sway, I ..." his voice faded, his eyes opening and flashing with an emotion other than the lust we were both feeling.

"I know," I said softly. I had no fucking idea what I was agreeing to.

I just said "I know," but really, what did I know?

Then, to add some fuel to the fire, I said, "I want you."

"I want you, too."

That pretty much sealed the deal for me and soon all thoughts were lost when he leaned forward and kissed me.

"Oh God ... it's been a *long* time," he moaned.

You and me both, buddy.

Jameson broke away for a moment, the clanking of his belt buckle registered, bringing me back to what this was as he pulled his jeans and underwear down before returning to the bed, pressing his warm naked body against mine.

It was then that I realized that I was completely naked, too. Took me long enough to realize that. I'd only been that way for the last ten minutes.

I couldn't see very well, the only light was coming from the bathroom down the hall, but I could see *enough* to know I was in trouble.

Growing up, I always knew the Riley boys were well endowed but *this* ... I may require medical attention after this. I may have even gasped at this thought, but I couldn't be sure with all the noises he was making. We were both being very vocal.

Settling between my legs, his lips grazed over my bare nipples. Slowly, he drew my left nipple into his mouth and sucked gently and then let his teeth graze it before pulling back, repeating the process with my other nipple.

I was dying ... a slow agonizing death, wrapped in his warm steel embrace.

Suddenly he jerked back looking at me, his brow scrunched together. "Are you okay? I mean ... are you sure, Sway? We've never ..." A shaky hand rose to run through his mess of hair.

Is he nervous? Why is he shaking so badly?

I nodded, my cheeks blazing like the fiery sun. If I didn't know any better, I'd think he was nervous at the way he was shaking. But I knew Jameson well enough that he was never nervous, why would right now be any different?

When his eyes met mine again, he looked worried. "I ... uh ... are you sure? We've never ..."

We've never ...

He kept going back to that. Of course we've never. One of us always stopped.

Could I do this? If it meant other women were nowhere near him, then yes, I could do this. If it meant that by some slim chance he would realize he had feelings for me too, then yes, I could do this.

I nodded again.

Jameson flashed a soft smile leaning over the side of the bed for a condom in his wallet. I wanted to look when he put it on, but I didn't. I think I was too nervous.

The hesitation returned for a brief moment before his eyes found mine again and I saw a glimpse of that boy I grew to love. With his body pressed tightly to mine, you couldn't hide much of anything. I could feel him against my thigh and knew he could feel my chest against his chest. Why I was thinking of our body parts pressed together I'm not sure, but that's what I was thinking.

Knowing this was about to happen, I swallowed slowly feeling the rapid beating of our hearts and trying not to focus on pressing body parts and more on the actual boring about to take place.

Then, with a slow lazy kiss, our bodies joined. He pushed forward gradually with a growl that sent shivers and goose bumps all over me, his body trembling with each movement.

I can't believe we're actually doing this! We're actually having sex! He's not pushing me away, he's pulling me against him and his camshaft is inside me!

The feeling I got when Jameson entered me was amazing, sappy even. I felt complete.

Pathetic. You're pathetic.

He gasped and I let out a shaking sigh against his lips as I adjusted to him.

"Are you all right?" his voice hindered by his harsh breathing. "Should I ... stop?"

I couldn't form the words so I simply shook my head against his shoulder placing a kiss into his neck and pushed my hips up letting him know I didn't want him to stop. My hands moved over the breadth of his hard shoulders urging him on.

"Are you sure you don't want me to stop? I can stop." He sort of laughed a breathless chuckle and shook his head against my fore-head. "That's a fuckin' lie. I can't stop."

I laughed and then stared at him wondering if I was dreaming.

Is this really happening?

Now I've had sex before with a few different people, but Jameson quickly put them to shame when he had me screaming like a porn star within two minutes.

His hips moved slowly for a while, his hands curled under me pulling me into his movements, holding me tightly to his body. So tightly, it felt as if his life depended on it, and I desperately wanted his life to depend on it.

Intensity and impatience marked everything from his movements to his kisses and I wasn't about to complain.

Holding my hands above my head against the pillow, his head dipped down to whisper in my ear, "You don't know how long I've wanted this."

Say what?

All I could do was moan loudly and then he reached down hitch-ing my leg farther up his hip.

"You like that?" he grunted against my shoulder, most of his weight shifted to rest against his arm that was bent near my head supporting him.

"Yes, harder."

Jesus, you sound ridiculous.

Jameson chuckled breathlessly. "That I can do," he growled in my ear fisting his hands through my hair, tugging gently before he flipped us over so I was on top of him. "You like dirty talking ... don't you?"

I became undone completely with everything, all around me. It was his voice, so low and vibrating that I could feel it pulsing through-out my entire body, every nerve ending reaching out to him. It was his touch, one that I knew so well—firm, yet soft, and focused.

It really was everything and *so* much more than I ever thought possible. So many times, I wondered what this would be like and now it was happening.

"Yeah," I moaned eventually to his dirty question because I really did enjoy the dirty talking. You could tell me how to change spark plugs and I was a quivering mess.

Right about that point, I began to sound as if I was auditioning for a Ron Jeremy movie. I was ashamed at how vocal I'd become.

"I can tell you like car talk, too ...," he whispered in that low gravelly voice he had from time to time. I moaned again when his lips found the sensitive skin on my neck rough with need. His teeth drug over the path he'd made. "Proper amount of lubrication makes inserting the camshaft easier, you know?"

My response was to moan. I seemed to be doing a lot of that.

He had my body bending in directions I never thought were possible without needing an MRI the next day.

He also, to his utter amusement, had me screaming at the top of my lungs at times, and a few instances where I was sure I saw twinkling stars.

Wanting to see how worked up I could get him, I did everything I could to drive him just as insane.

My theory that he, too, was losing control was confirmed when his head fell back against the pillow, his eyes squeezed shut as he shook his head resisting. "Ah honey, slow down ... *please,* slow down," he moaned taking a firm hold on my hips.

I was grinning like a fool.

He was also very thorough, too; I'll give him that. I swear he covered every inch of my five-two frame with kisses or nips and the occasional pinch or lick.

What wasn't that comforting was his attention while my ass was in the air with him between my legs behind me.

For one, I'm not sure about the rest of society, but for me personally—my ass in the air wasn't really a comforting position, unless you're a dog. Let's face it: your asshole is public knowledge when you walk around on all fours like an animal.

And for me, I'm not that comfortable with my ass in the air or my asshole. I'm just not. Especially when the person behind me was Jameson Riley.

Thoughts of my asshole in the air didn't last long and soon I drifted completely with the kissing, the sucking, the pinching, it was all almost too much.

Where'd this boy learn all this and why had I waited so long to indulge? That's what I wanted to know.

We were molded together. You couldn't tell where I ended and he began. But when he sucked down on my nipple once more, I couldn't hold off.

Thrashing around beneath him with total futility, his hands held me in place tightly against him and the mattress. With a tingling that started in my toes and settled in my tummy, I literally screamed Jameson's name loud enough for the entire hotel to hear.

Forget the porno audition.

Apparently, I was now trying out for the opera.

Jameson chuckled against me, my breathing turned to something resembling a woman in child labor or an animal in heat. It had been way too long since I last had sex, that's for sure.

I soon realized Jameson was past the point of stopping or being able to go slow as his breathing was turning from heavy to panting gasps—grunting with each movement. My head hit the headboard with each thrust while his hands moved from my hips to the pillow behind my head, grasping it tightly as he prepared himself.

I wanted to stop time, slow this down and make it last forever, but I knew I couldn't. After waiting for so long for this, it seemed to be fleeting quickly. I kept thinking I was dreaming until he would move or say something, his voice bringing me back, and I realized it *was* happening.

"Oh God, Sway," he grunted, his body trembling for control, I knew the feeling. "Shit ... I'm sorry ... can't hold on any longer ..." His head fell against my shoulder, his teeth sinking into my skin as he threw himself into his movements. "*Fuck*," he cried out.

My legs wrapped around his waist, and I held onto him anywhere I could, desperate to make this last longer.

He gasped, his body jerking, his eyes squeezed shut tightly as his forehead rested against mine.

A few thoughts ran through my mind. The first was that, at least he didn't squeal like a pig. Mike Tanner, a past fuck did, and I was very alarmed. And secondly, *hot damn* we just had sex.

Collapsing on top of me, his head turned to the side, his ear pressed against my racing heart. We laid there, breathing as if we ran a marathon, which we kind of did, when Jameson rolled moving the sheets over us.

Once he pulled out, I felt as though a cold breeze blew over me at the lack of contact between us. He surprised me, though. He didn't go far. Sliding to the side, he tugged my body against his trailing kisses across my shoulder.

He cuddles after sex?

If possible, I think I fell deeper in love.

After a couple minutes, I felt his smile pressing a kiss into my hair.

"Why were we not doing that from the beginning?"

"You're so weird." Tossing my arms over my face attempting to mask my embarrassment and any chance at crying, I shook my head. "Because, we were eleven you pervert."

He chuckled, but said nothing more.

Moments passed and the surge of adrenaline mixed with anxiety and fear overwhelmed me. Suddenly I felt sick as tears threatened again. I wouldn't cry. I wouldn't let myself. If anything, I'd blame it on allergies or something just as ridiculous.

All my brain focused on was, *would he regret this in the morning?*

More moments passed where we remained, the fear embedded further with no relief.

From the morning light coming in through the cracks in the curtains, I could vaguely make out his expression.

Lying on his back, arms contently resting on his stomach, I steadied his sedated breathing. His left hand rose to run through his hair.

What really caught my attention was the intensity marking his gaze. His eyes were open staring at the ceiling, the restlessness returned, as did that vulnerability. I couldn't stop my mind from convincing me he'd regret it. Maybe that's why he wanted me to tell him to stop.

Once Jameson was asleep, I couldn't take lying there as the gnawing anxiety got the best of me. Turning over, I took in his softened features. With his unkempt rusty hair, the freckles on his nose, he reminded me so much of the boy I fell in love with amongst the methanol and clay of the Northwest.

Who was I kidding? He was still *that* boy. Jameson hadn't changed and I knew that. And knowing that, I shouldn't have been so worried he'd regret this because the boy I fell in love with wouldn't. He was still my best friend above all else and sleeping together wouldn't change that.

Or would it?

Here I go again.

The haze of intoxication was starting to lift and reality was setting in.

Feeling sick again, I decided to get some water or run away, one of the two was a good idea.

You'd think his room would have water since it had everything else but nope, just alcohol. No surprise there though.

I threw on Jameson's shirt from last night and stepped out the door, tentatively. I glanced outside but no one seemed to be around.

Half-naked, hair all over the place, I made my way down the long hallway of the Omni Hotel and Resort in search of water.

When I rounded the corner, I ran right into Emma.

No, scratch that—I fell over Emma because for God knows what reason, she was on her knees in front of the vending machine.

"What the hell, Emma?" I grunted peeling myself from the tile floor, slipping on ice cubes that were scattered everywhere.

Emma started picking up the ice chips frantically and dropping them in a bucket. "What does it look like? I was getting ice and water."

She looked over me once, scrutinizing my appearance and then shook her head. "Where are your clothes?"

"Where are yours?" I challenged. Emma wasn't wearing much more than me with Aiden's t-shirt and cowboy hat. "Nice hat," I added.

She smiled again and looked more closely at my collarbone that was sporting a purple bite mark from Jameson. "Did you ... *oh God*, Sway, you didn't?"

"Shut up!" I snapped shoving her against the vending machine. "You have *no* room to talk. Whose saddle were you just in?"

"Saddle?" Emma glared but appeared nervous. "Don't tell Jameson about me and Aiden."

"Don't tell Alley about me and Jameson then," I countered letting go of her.

"Deal." We shook hands.

"Well, was it what you hoped for?" Emma asked as we made our way back down the hall to our rooms. "I heard you. You sounded like a damn hyena in there," she added laughing hysterically.

I pushed her again, knocking her and her ice chips against some innocent guests' door. "I hate you. I really do."

When I made it back inside the room, Jameson cuddled against my back. I thought he was sleeping but his breathing hitched when I kissed his arm that he'd placed around my shoulders, pulling me closer.

"Have you ever thought about this before?" he asked. His voice was out of breath and low but smooth, as it always was.

"Thought about ...?" I tried to be vague as though I didn't know what he was asking, even if I did.

"This ..." his answer was just as vague. His arms flexed around me and he kissed my shoulder once, his lips warm.

"Yes and no," I told him honestly, because right now, I couldn't tell him how I really felt.

For someone who never ran from anything and spoke her mind frequently, I couldn't tell him that this was all I've thought about for the past four years. The words wouldn't form.

In his arms that morning, I knew then that nothing would ever be the same between us. This wasn't something where two people casually slept together.

It couldn't be.

Not with the thirst I had.

Happy Hour – Slang term for last official practice session held before an event. Most of the time it will take place after qualifying and all other practices.

I think I'm dead. One eye opened assured me.

I was dead.

That's all there was to it. Surely, there's no way someone could feel this *badly*, and still be alive. My throat felt like the Mojave Desert. My head felt like someone hit it with a baseball bat, and my body felt like jelly.

I laid there for a good ten minutes, wondering if I truly was dead. Stretching, I intended to get up, when my arm bumped something causing me to jump.

What the hell?

I felt movement on the bed and someone groan beside me. Once I turned my head, I groaned myself.

Not only did I *know* that particular groan, but even so much as turning my head, hurt like hell. Bringing my arm up, I covered my face to block out the blinding light coming in from the morning or afternoon sun.

I continued to lay there for a moment trying to remember anything that happened last night when reality hit me—slapped me across the face, actually.

It came back to me in flashes, the race, the bar, Chelsea, the dancing, the kissing, and Purple Rain.

And then in a rush, without warning, the sex came back to me based on the soreness between my legs.

Then *who* came back to me ... Jameson ... *oh God.*

What if he regretted it? What if he doesn't even remember what we did?

I turned over onto my back, covering my head with a pillow now, wondering what I was thinking last night. Friends with benefits, *jeez*, you have truly lost your mind this time.

Just as I decided that I would be perfectly content never removing my head from under that pillow, Jameson groaned loudly beside me and flung an arm around my waist.

It was at that point I realized I was still completely naked, in bed with my best friend, Jameson Riley.

While I was starting to regret not putting some clothes on before we went to sleep, he grunted, moved closer and pressed his body against mine and *oh my* ... he was hard.

Hot damn that's nice.

What did I do next? I started giggling.

Why?

When I was nervous, I giggled, and right then, I couldn't speak and I could barely even think so, I giggled.

"*Ugh* ... Sway," Jameson groaned once again covering his head with a pillow. "Stop laughing ... head hurts ..."

Well, at least he knows it's me beside him.

This had me giggling even more because I, Sway Reins, slept with my best friend Jameson Riley.

"Oh ... God ... stop your fucking laughing," Jameson groaned again, tossing a pillow at me.

His legs tangled with mine under the sheets, and his erection pressed against my thigh.

I had the sudden urge to stick my head under the sheets and get a good look at him since I didn't see it last night. I refrained though.

I giggled once more, my head throbbing at the noise and causing Jameson to cringe and tighten his grip around my waist. "I swear to God ... if you don't stop, I will push you out of this goddamn bed," he warned in a serious rough voice.

Eventually I stopped giggling and Jameson made no attempt to push me away or off the bed. Instead, he kept his arm firmly around my waist and his hips pushed against my thigh.

Before I could decide what was going to happen next, his cell phone started ringing on the nightstand beside me.

"*Fuck* ... that's worse than you laughing," Jameson grumbled reaching over me pressing his chest against my own.

Completely on top of me, he answered the phone, "What?"

I was hyperventilating.

Let me take a moment here to really explain what kind of position we were in. I was lying on my back, legs spread, completely naked—kind of like last night. Jameson was completely naked as well, on top of me and between my legs.

We were in quite the predicament here.

"What time do I *have* to be there?" Jameson sighed. I could tell by the voice coming through the receiver that he was talking to Alley. "Wait ... what time is it now?" Jameson looked around the room searching for a clock.

Glancing over my shoulder, I looked at the alarm clock to see that it was already four in the afternoon.

Great, my flight leaves at eight tonight.

I tried to push Jameson away so I could get up and get dressed but he grabbed my hand with his and pushed it above my head.

Apparently, I wasn't going anywhere.

His eyes narrowed at me, shaking his head no. "Yeah, Alley, I'll be there at six. I need a few ... hours though," Jameson added with a wink.

Say what?

Alley apparently wasn't happy about this judging by the screaming. "Bye, Alley," he simply said tossing his phone on the floor.

My head turned, looking anywhere but in his eyes that I could feel penetrating me. Speaking of penetrating, I could feel something else awfully close to penetration.

Jameson let go of my hands and placed his right hand against my cheek forcing me to look at him.

"Look at me, honey," he said, softly kissing along my jaw.

I couldn't help the tears that were forming. I tried—believe me I tried. When I finally looked at him, my emerald green meeting his smoldering green, I couldn't place the emotion his held.

Why am I doing this to myself? You know this isn't going to change anything. This is stupid and one of the worst ideas you've ever had.

"You okay?" he asked leaning in to kiss me. His lips pressed to mine once, twice, three times and then his tongue grazed my lips. His other hand came up holding my face securely to his while he attacked my mouth with passionate hungry kisses that left me weak and incredibly vulnerable again.

Hard and ready, all he would have to do is push once. Just as his hips flexed forward, a loud knocking interrupted us.

"Jameson, open the goddamn door!" Alley yelled outside smacking the door. "Don't you ever hang up on me again asshole!"

Jameson put his fingers to my lips and pushed forward causing me to let out a loud moan. His hand covered my mouth, chuckling above me with that damn smirk.

I'm not all that surprised this amused him, as he loved pissing Alley off. It was like a game for him. He wasn't happy until she'd called him an asshole at least once throughout the day.

"Shhh ... if we're quiet ... she'll leave," he whispered in my ear and pushed forward once more.

I openly cried out when he bit down on my shoulder again, cut off by his mouth that clamped down on my own, causing both of us to groan.

We moved together languorously but the door opening quickly interrupted us again.

Jameson stopped suddenly and pulled back to look at me, his eyes wide with panic.

Fuck, fuck, fuck!

"Jameson ... she can't see me in bed with you," I whispered, but was silenced by a pillow covering my face.

Was this supposed to be hot?

For some morbid reason, it was. I really needed help if him holding a pillow over my face turned me on.

I couldn't see any more, but I heard Alley's heels clicking against the wood floor when she came into the bedroom.

"Get out of bed you shithead!"

"How the hell did you get a key?" Jameson growled back at her. And yes, in case you're wondering he was still inside me, his body trembling to stay motionless.

"I reserved the room for you. I have a key," Alley replied with a sour edge. "For Christ's sake Jameson, you have a woman in bed with you?"

Oh Alley ... It's even worse than you think.

"Get out!" Jameson yelled in a no nonsense tone.

"No," she objected. "Get up!"

"Well, I'm not getting up with you in the room!" He snorted. "I'm naked."

Yes, you are, with me underneath you.

"What the hell is taking so long in here?" Spencer's bellowing tone echoed throughout. "Whoa ... dude, who's under there?"

You couldn't miss the inquisitiveness in his voice, and I'm sure by that point he was trying to see who was underneath Jameson.

I'm so glad my face was covered because it was the color of the devil's ass right then, and I was moments away from breaking out into a giggle fit. I giggle when I'm nervous. I can't help it.

It's amazing the thoughts that go through your head when you're naked and in this predicament. I won't go into details but some were even alarming to me and I was used to my daily rambling thoughts.

Jameson sighed loudly, throwing his head forward against my shoulder. "Get the fuck out!" he yelled loudly against the pillow vibrating my entire body with his menacing voice.

This was so mortifying.

And who joined the party next?

Jimi.

"Jameson," he began as he entered the room, I assumed.

I couldn't see to know this for sure, but his voice suddenly tapered off when he took in the sight before him. I can only imagine what this must look like.

"What the hell, why …" I heard him sigh dramatically. "I *don't* even want to know." Now they were all in the bedroom of the hotel room. Spencer was laughing hysterically; Alley was yelling at Jameson, and Jimi was yelling at Alley and Spencer to leave the room.

Jameson, probably mortified, was shaking his head in disbelief against the pillow covering my head.

I was now giggling.

It was so unbelievable … really, it was. Here I was lying underneath my best friend, his camshaft inserted in my crankcase with three other people in the room.

Good times.

"All of you shut up!" Jimi barked over them. "Get out now! Jameson, get this girl out of your goddamn room and get dressed. You have an interview with SPEED in less than two hours."

Jimi ushered Alley and Spencer out of the bedroom, but I could still hear them arguing in the other room about why I wasn't in my hotel room, which had me panicking again.

Jameson removed the pillow from my face and smirked.

"We need to get up …" he whispered in a low throaty voice but never attempted to move.

Instead, he pulled back and then pushed into me again. His eyes fell closed with the motion. Mine did not. They were fixated on the door that was still wide fucking open. And though their backs were to the room, what if they turned around?

"Jameson." My eyes were very wide by this point. "We *have* to stop …" I pushed against his chest, but he didn't budge, just continued with tenacity. "Jameson …" I tried again but my voice faded when one of his hands fisted in my hair and the other reached down to my … ignition switch.

"I can't, Sway … I *want* you …" he moaned. "I can't stop … I can't. Not after last night."

"Your family is right outside the door," I whispered incredulously trying to point out the obvious reason *why* he had to stop.

"Fuck 'em."

"Jameson, get up!" Jimi bellowed from outside the bedroom.

"Oh, goddamn it," Jameson growled against my shoulder.

I've talked about this before, but this dirty heathen ... has a quick fuse. All of a sudden, his arm raised, his left fist slammed into the headboard, the wood splintered and cracked loudly.

"GET THE FUCK OUT OF HERE!" he roared at them causing me to jump. It's been a while since I've heard him so angry.

Have you ever seen a two-year-old throw a fit?

It usually happens suddenly and in the midst of this fit, their tiny arms flail around and they reach for anything they can to get their two-year-old point across.

That was Jameson.

So because punching the headboard did nothing, he then reached for anything he could reach without pulling out of me, which happened to be an empty beer bottle.

The glass shattered against the wall causing me to jump again and Alley to yelp.

Jameson didn't stop at that. He then reached for the lamp on the nightstand and chucked it across the room as well, it too shattering.

"I mean it!" He warned them in a blistering snarl. "Get the fuck out of this goddamn room right now!"

No one said anything, including me.

They knew he'd keep throwing shit until they left. He'd destroy the entire hotel to get his point across.

Believe me, he'd done it before.

Finally, we heard the door close as they left. I sighed in relief, thankful that Nancy and Emma hadn't joined the party, or worse, Tommy; wherever the hell he had disappeared to last night.

Jameson was panting against me from the sudden onset of rage but his movements didn't halter. His hands returned and fisted tightly against the pillow my head was resting on. His lips were at my neck now, trying to control his breathing but it was coming in irregular gasps. He managed to rasp out, "Fuck, you feel good," against my neck that left me shivering.

With the intoxicating haze lifted, the closeness I felt to him now was unlike anything I'd ever felt before.

I knew this wasn't going to last very long by the way he was moving against me, but the idea of a quick, naughty, illicit, qualifying lap had me panting just as hard as he was and giving way to the pleasure.

My hands flew to his back as my fingernails sunk in, my orgasm overtook me in waves, causing him to push into me harder and harder, pushing me farther up the bed into the splintered headboard.

We're old friends, this headboard and me.

After a few quick thrusts, Jameson threw his head back exposing his neck for me, groaning my name.

The sound vibrated my lips as I attacked his neck with wet kisses. He shuddered above me and then collapsed against my chest.

I welcomed the weight of his exhausted body. I've waited years to feel this man heavy, spent, and relaxed above me.

As I laid there trying to catch my own breath, I thought again about what had just happened and started giggling.

Jameson growled while he nuzzled his face in the crook of my neck, his two-day scruff tickling my skin. "You're going to give me a complex if you keep laughing at me like that."

I giggled again.

Eventually Jameson made it to the bathroom to get ready. Once dressed, he sat down on the bed next to me.

I was still wrapped in the sheet because I didn't have any clothes. Jameson ripped my underwear and bra off with his teeth, destroying them last night. I ripped my shirt off like a whore, so that left my skirt and heels.

"You should probably get dressed," he suggested running his fingers through his hair. "Even though I prefer you naked." He winked.

"I would ... but I don't have any clothes," I reminded him. "They're in my room."

He raised an eyebrow at me and then smirked. "Sorry, I guess I lost control last night." His fingers lightly traced the mark.

I shrugged pulling the sheet up feeling exposed. "It happens." I looked away from his gaze.

I was really starting to freak out and felt like bursting into tears at any moment having agreed to any of this.

There seemed to be a suffocating silence lingering when Jameson moved closer to me on the bed but didn't look up. Gently, he took my hand in his own, rubbing it softly. "Don't leave tonight," he pleaded, although he spoke more to his hands than me.

I didn't look up; my eyes remained fixated on the bed as a pensive silence lingered once again.

"Jameson, I can't stay here." My voice sounded strange, probably because I was saying one thing but meaning another. "Charlie needs me at the track."

He nodded taking a deep breath. "Please ..." he mumbled softly, almost so softly that I couldn't hear him.

"Why?"

Jameson still hadn't looked up even though I was staring at him now. I had never seen him act like this before, so I asked again. "Why do you want me to stay, Jameson?"

Tell me you want me to stay because you love me.

He tilted his head to one side before answering, "Because, I need you here." His eyes slowly met mine, and I saw an emotion I couldn't quite place again. It was as if he was begging me not to pry, to give up trying to figure him out. "I ... you ... keep me grounded." He offered me a bolstered smile and the restlessness from last night returned. "Come with me to Pocono and Michigan. Then we're in Sonoma again ... you can go back after that. It's closer to Washington."

I groaned, leaning my head against the headboard, looking up at the white ceiling. "What are we doing, Jameson?"

"What do you mean?" He actually sounded confused.

How can one person be so clueless to this!

"This." I motioned to the bed. "What is *this*?"

I have to know what he thinks. Does he want more? Will he ever want more?

I leaned my head forward again, looking into his eyes. That's when I saw that this isn't going to be what I had hoped, but I also saw that same emotion that I couldn't place. He was hiding something behind those beautiful eyes.

"We're friends ..." he paused, swallowing. "But I'd like to keep doing what we did ... I liked it." He took a drink of water from the bottle he'd been holding, concealing his smirk.

"What if someone else comes along that's not a friend and you want *that* with her?"

You sound like a jealous high school girl.

"That won't happen." His voice sounded almost disgusted that I asked that.

"You're Jameson Riley—you have women throwing themselves at you, why me?"

"Because Sway, you're my best friend." Jameson sighed again, leaning back against the bed on his elbows.

It distracted me when his shirt came up revealing the sharp lines of the hips leading down to the promised-land.

Before I could get *too* distracted, Jameson's voice interrupted me, "I trust you, and I can't trust anyone right now." He leaned closer to me pulling my legs against his chest. "This can be fun, Sway; let's just … have a good time together. Keep it simple."

Have a good time? Keep it simple?

Maybe—can you do that?

Doubtful—can you do this without getting your heart broken?

Absolutely—do you want to have fun?

Without a doubt—do you want to stay with him?

I'm so screwed.

I knew my reasoning was completely off and incredibly stupid. I knew I was going to get hurt, but I decided, once again, to put Jameson's needs above my own and reached for my cell phone to call Charlie.

The conversation with Charlie didn't go as planned. And it wasn't even his anger that upset me the most. It was his disappointment that I would be with Jameson again for a few weeks. I think his exact quote was, "Sway, he's using you. It's a shame that a girl as smart as you can't see that."

Way to make me feel like a complete asshole.

Despite all this, it didn't change my feelings or way of thinking as this (indulging in too much alcohol once again) ended in me sleeping with my best friend. Wasn't that what I wanted all along? Yeah, it was, but just the thought of "friends with benefits" to Jameson Riley was freaking me out a little … *okay*, a lot. But then I thought about how much I wanted this. I didn't want to be another pit lizard to him; I would be more if it killed me trying. Stupid logic I know, but fucking sue me. I was a woman on a mission.

Jimi had bought a Citation Bravo Jet last year, which made traveling for their entire family easier. Half the time Jimi was on the opposite side of the United States from Jameson and that made the jet nice.

The Riley's still kept a home in Elma, but they also had homes in Mooresville and Jacksonville Beach.

Jameson had recently started building a home near his parents in Mooresville, or Dirty Mo as we referred to it.

Unfortunately, the house he was having built on Lake Norman wouldn't be finished until December. This left him staying at his parent's home.

He hated it.

When we walked outside the hotel to get the car Alley had rented for Jameson to get back to Mooresville, I burst into laughter.

Jameson, well he was *not* laughing. "You have to be kidding me." He threw his bag down next to the Dodge mini-van and kicked the left rear tire.

Growling, he pulled out his cell phone to call Alley.

"You're such a fucking bitch!" he shouted and snapped the phone shut. Turning to me, he glared. "Get in."

I couldn't stop my laughter, but eventually I did get in when he threatened to leave me there if I didn't stop laughing.

Much of the drive to downtown Charlotte was spent with Jameson complaining about the speed the mini-van refused to do, how he hated living with his parents, how he was going to get Alley back, and if I thought anything was going on with Emma and Aiden.

Remembering my pact with Emma, I denied the accusations and conveniently changed the subject to something sexual.

He was easily distracted when the subject involved sex. What man wasn't?

"What did you mean when you said it's been a long time?" I suddenly blurted out.

Jameson choked on his water. "Huh?"

My cheeks flushed in embarrassment and I whispered, "Nothing," pretending to look out the window, avoiding eye contact.

"Don't do that," he snapped back at me.

"Do what?"

"Ask a question like *that* and pretend that you didn't," he said as he avoided looking at me and we pulled into the parking lot of the SPEED studio.

"Answer it then," I said boldly.

"It has been a long time," he shrugged indifferently.

Looking anywhere but at him, I asked, "How long?"

Jameson groaned loudly parking next to a red SUV. "Over a year."

I laughed ... scratch that, I giggled hysterically almost to the point of tears.

"You're such a shit!" Jameson barked at me. "And how long has it been for you?"

I stopped laughing instantly. Oh, how quickly the red flag can be thrown.

"A while." My cheeks burned.

He brought his right hand up to my heated cheek. "Don't get shy on me now, honey."

Damn him.

"A year, maybe longer," I mumbled suddenly finding my hands very interesting.

I snuck a glance over at him and his face was scrunched as if he was trying to remember something and then he reached for his Simplex hat on the dashboard. "With who?" he asked quietly putting the hat on. Almost methodically, he adjusted the fit to the way he preferred it.

It was my turn to choke; not on water, but on my own breath, at his question. "Huh?"

"You heard me." Though the hat concealed his expression slightly, his eyes narrowed at me.

"You don't know him." I knew this answer wasn't going to work, but I tried anyway. I could hardly admit to myself that I had slept with Mike, the guy who squealed like a pig when he came, let alone tell Jameson.

Jameson shook his head slowly, his eyes penetrating. "That's *not* what I asked."

It was useless. He'd get it out of me, anyway.

"Mike Tanner," I finally said after a moment of silence.

"Where'd ya meet him?" He reached over the front seat for the posters in the back.

"Skagit, he was racing outlaw late models there one night when I was there with Tommy."

Jameson was quiet, eerie quiet, sitting next to me. The only sound was the squeaking from the sharpie marker as it drug across the posters. His jaw was clenched, body tensed. I could see the muscles in his jaw flexing.

"Who was your last?" I tried breaking the silence.

"Couldn't tell you." He signed one more poster and then shoved them inside a white plastic Simplex bag. Still not looking at me, he shrugged his shoulders carelessly. "I never got her name."

I've known Jameson for over eleven years; I could tell he was irate by the way he slammed the door of the mini-van when he got out. Why he was so upset over this was beyond me.

I'm sure it had something to do with Mike being a race car driver. I should have lied and said he was a construction worker or something, but Jameson and I don't lie to each other. We never have.

I felt badly for this poor Kim woman who was stuck doing the interview with Jameson. She started on the wrong foot by flirting with him.

What did Jameson do?

He said and I quote, "That's unprofessional," in a sharp demeaning tone and followed it up with, "Besides, you're not my type."

And to think she still has to perform an interview after that.

Jameson could be a real jerk when he wanted to be, and his demeanor could turn on a dime. Having experienced this first-hand on many occasions, I sort of felt the need to apologize to everyone he encountered and tell them it was my fault and not to take it personally. But I didn't. I simply sat back and watched the hot, possessive, angry side of Jameson emerge for nothing more than pure entertainment value.

Waiting for the interview to begin, I observed his behavior much like I did last night. These interviews, the press and media, weren't part of the lifestyle he wanted.

His passion and vast talent for racing had suddenly created a life for him that he had a hard time adjusting to at times.

"Jameson," Kim began, crossing her leg over the other, sitting in the large director's chair. "Can you tell us how you got started in racing? You're only twenty-two, when did you start racing?"

I can imagine how many times he has told this story over the years.

Jameson shifted in his chair and sighed before he began to tell his story—a story I knew first-hand as I was a huge part of it.

"Well, let's see, I started racing quarter midgets just before I turned five. My dad was racing in The World of Outlaw series so I learned a lot by watching him and the other drivers."

"I heard you raced sprint cars, too." Kim smiled. "When did you start racing those?"

"I was eleven. My dad moved me up to sprint cars but not full-time because you had to be sixteen at most tracks. So I continued racing midgets and sprints when I could. When I turned sixteen, I began racing on the Northern Sprint Tour and the USAC Silver Crown Series as well as the USAC Midgets.

"The day I graduated, my older brother, Spencer, his girlfriend at the time, Alley, my younger sister Emma, and my ..." Jameson's eyes met mine. "... best friend, Sway, traveled east with me. I raced in the USAC Divisions and The World of Outlaw series collecting trophies and winner's checks just big enough to make it to the next track. I raced anything I could whether it was my car or for Bucky Miers and Monty Evans, both long-time friends of my dad." Jameson leaned back further in the chair. "I drove, and Spencer worked on the cars along with a few of our buddies who were able to help out. Emma, Alley, and Sway all helped in any way they could. That summer we ended up capturing the USAC Triple Crown title, which is a national title in all three of the USAC divisions."

"And those are?"

Jameson chuckled. "Well USAC runs three national divisions of midgets, sprints and silver crown cars, all open-wheel. If you win the championship in all three divisions, you get the Triple Crown. To date, Bobby Cole, my teammate, and me, are the only drivers who've ever won it."

"Wow," she seemed shocked. "That's impressive."

Jameson nodded taking the compliment about as well as he took her flirting.

"So the Triple Crown paved the way?"

"Yeah, I guess you could say that." He gave a contemplative nod. "From there, I was able to land some sponsors that smoothed the way to bigger races with better payouts. In January of 2001, I met Tate Harris at the Chili Bowl Midget Nationals in Tulsa through my dad and Bucky. He introduced me to a representative with Simplex Shocks and Springs, about the time my dad was thinking of starting a NASCAR team, and the rest is history."

"Is your family still a big part of the operation?"

"Yeah, my dad is the team owner. My mom and sister run my fan club. My brother is on my pit crew." Jameson's eyes shifted back over to mine. "It means a lot to me to have my family nearby. It reminds me of what's real."

"I hear you started your own sprint car team this year, too? How's that going?"

"I did. Right now, I have two cars racing in The World of Outlaws. I have my buddies Tyler Sprague and Justin West in the cars. They used to race USAC with me growing up. They're doing an amazing job." Jameson leaned forward and took another drink of water.

"Do you still race sprint cars when you can?"

He laughed. "I try, but Simplex doesn't like it all that much. It's a liability issue on my part if I was to get injured while doing it but ... dirt track racing is where I came from. It's a part of me and I refuse to let that go."

"Once you go dirt you never go back sort of thing?" she teased.

Jameson laughed softly staring at his feet as he pulled his hat down further shadowing his eyes. "Yeah, I guess that's the saying."

"So let's talk about this season. You won your second start in

Rockingham; you won the Winston and *another* on Saturday night at the Coca-Cola 600! Do you think you have a chance at the cup title this year?" Kim asked.

"I think we do. The win last night put us only sixty-three points behind Darrin Torres. I wasn't sure how competitive we'd be in our first full season with it being a new team, but I think we have a shot at it," Jameson said nodding his head and rubbing the back of his neck.

"Now we heard NASCAR dropped that hefty fine they handed out on Saturday night. Can you tell us about that?"

"There's not much to tell." He shrugged. "As far as I know, the fine was dropped because the test turned out to be inconclusive."

I think she knew he wasn't going to give her the inside scoop so she finally let up.

"Well, Jameson, thank you for coming and good luck with the rest of the season."

Jameson stood, shook her hand politely, and then headed for the door without another word.

Once we were back in the car, I realized his mood was still the same.

He didn't look at me and instead headed to Mooresville. The drive wasn't long, but *eventually* we started talking again.

Half way there, Jameson plugged his iPod into the stereo and put it on shuffle. He had a vast music collection of Van Morrison, Eagles, Linkin Park, and *every* song by Lynyrd Skynyrd.

One particular song, "Simple Man," came on and Jameson began to sing along.

He had an amazingly smooth, but raspy voice that could leave any woman a puddle of oil in his drain pan. And let me tell you, he could do one hell of an Eddie Vedder baritone.

This particular song was one of Jameson's all-time favorite songs. It was relaxing and held a special meaning for him. He always said he listened to it when he needed to remember where he came from and as I sat there and listened to him singing along, the truth behind the lyrics was easy to see.

A few verses caught my attention, similar to "Purple Rain," and I knew there was nothing behind him singing that particular verse louder than the rest of the song but again … a pit lizard could dream.

My hand was resting lightly on my knee when Jameson shifted in his seat reaching for my hand, pulling it to his lips to place a tender kiss on it. "Does it hurt?"

"Huh?"

Does what hurt? Yes, my crankcase!

"Your hand," he clarified.

"Oh that … *uh* … no, not really." I smiled briefly. "You owe me a million dollars though."

"Pfft." Jameson shook his head. "I said a *spring*, not your hand." He kissed my knuckles once more. "Though I am proud you punched her. I would have, but it's frowned upon to hit a woman."

"Frowned upon, really?"

This seemed to have broken the ice between us again, and the rest of the drive was filled with laughter and witty remarks, our usual selves.

We arrived back in Mooresville around ten that night, and Jameson's mercurial mood had returned.

Now he was planning his attack on Alley for the mini-van and walking in on us.

If there's one thing I could say about Jameson and his practical jokes on people, it was that he never did them half-assed.

We eventually agreed upon a plan of action and called Kyle to have him order it, insisting on the part being sent overnight.

On the way to his parents' house, we stopped by Burger King because we were both starving. I was so exhausted by the time we got there. Thankfully, Jameson's parents weren't home so we didn't have to explain why I was there … well, for tonight anyway. I was sure that there would be questions when I arrived with him in Pocono.

His parent's house was huge. It literally reminded me of something you would see on *MTV Cribs*, only built for a racing family.

The house was situated on fifteen acres, complete with a quarter-mile oval track in the backyard, a pool that could accommodate the Olympics, and enough bedrooms to shelter a small village.

Once we got upstairs, I headed toward the guest bedroom at the end of the hall when Jameson grabbed me by the arm and slammed me against the wall. It wasn't rough, just enough that he took my breath away for a second.

"Where do you think you're going?" Jameson asked with his lips at my ear. His tongue darted out and then he nipped my lobe with his teeth.

"To the guest room?" I mumbled breathlessly watching his intense eyes find mine.

"Wrong." He picked me up bridal style and carried me up to his room on the third floor.

Once in his room, I couldn't tell you what happened when the door closed. I couldn't tell you what happened when we broke his bedroom door. I couldn't tell you what happened when we fell through the closet door onto the floor. I couldn't tell you *any* of this because I was in such a state of overdrive by this man that I was actually delirious and incoherent.

When I woke up the next morning, I wondered why I was on the floor in Jameson's closet surrounded by broken furniture and clothes that had been ripped off hangers.

It was a disaster.

At least I had my bra on, well half on with one of my funbags falling free.

Somehow, I feel like less of a slut with a bra on ... stupid, so stupid.

Tucking myself in, I surveyed the rest of me. I was wearing one of Jameson's ties around my neck, which was not all that concerning as I could imagine how it had been used. I was also sporting a pair of his boxer briefs.

How and why I was wearing these random items was a mystery to me.

I glanced around the large walk-in closet and was rewarded with an absolutely magnificent sight; it was Jameson Riley, lying on his back, naked.

Nothing, and I mean *nothing,* was more beautiful than the sight before me. I stared at his face. His messy hair looked like he had just done some press forging (a process where you forge hot metal between dies in a press to make the metal stronger) in a closet the entire night.

His beautiful face looked content; his lips pushed out into an adorable pout. His defined chest, amazing ripped stomach, and the sculpted cut lines of his hips that led down to the biggest motherloving camshaft ever engineered.

Christ Almighty, he was a sight.

I've seen a few ... okay, only three ... but this one topped them all including the few that I'd seen in pornos Alley and Emma had forced me to watch in high school.

How did that fit in me? That was a very concerning thought for me.

I brought my knees up to my chest and curled into myself, comforting my crankcase and wondering how she hadn't exploded yet.

I realized once I did that particular curling move that I was paying the consequences of our press forging. I commonly referred to press forging as aggressive sex. If you have ever seen metal press forged, it's *very* aggressive.

My legs burned and they felt like I had tried out to be a Navy Seal or something similar.

And judging by the shaft my eyes were currently fixated on, I'd say that happened, more than once last night. I couldn't tear my eyes away from him.

Until Jameson's light laughter startled me.

Embarrassed, my eyes quickly darted to his meeting his amused expression in embarrassment.

He stretched slowly and put his arms behind his head.

"Like what you see?" he asked with a smug smile.

"Eh ... I've seen bigger," I quipped quickly running into his bathroom hoping to get away from him.

That was one race I was not going to win.

Our debate about him being small officially ended when he had me pinned against his shower wall.

We spent a good part of the day inside Jameson's room ... *and* the closet.

Kyle called around three that afternoon to let Jameson know the part he ordered was in and that he needed to drop off Justin's helmet at the race shop. Jameson had a friend of his paint some new graphics on the side for Justin.

On the way over to Spencer and Alley's house Jameson turned to me, his eyes focused. "You down for this?"

"Sure."

He gave me a skeptical glance as though he thought I was lying. "It could mean jail time."

"My arrest record was shot long before this," I reminded him.

When Jameson and I were sixteen, we were arrested for branding the ass of old man Roger's cow with an iron that said "Grade A Piece of Ass." That wasn't the first time I'd been arrested, and I was sure it wouldn't be the last.

"Good point." He smiled and plugged his iPod into the stereo of his truck—he ditched the mini-van once we got back to Mooresville. "Here's a song to get us prepared."

And with that, House of Pain's "Jump Around" flooded the truck, and we jumped around like complete idiots that we were.

Once we were parked outside of their house and eyeing the said target, Alley's precious cherry red Mustang, Jameson pulled me into the bushes on the side of their house.

"Here's the plan," he whispered in my ear.

Keeping focused was hard; it was distracting as hell when he whispered like that.

"You go inside and distract her. Pinch the boy or something."

"The boy has a name, you know," I pointed out.

Jameson glared slapping me on the ass. "Pay attention." He put on the hood of his black sweatshirt. "It'll take me ten minutes tops to change the horn."

I started laughing at how focused he was on this entire prank. It was as if it was a mission directed by the Secret Service or something.

"What does the horn say?"

Jameson flashed me a wicked smile nodding his head arrogantly.

"Move, I'm a ruthless bitch."

"She's going to kill you." I pulled my hood over my head as well.

"She deserves it." He nodded to the house. "Now go, we don't have all night. I have to swing by the race shop."

Going in there alone, concerned me for a number of reasons, some more than others.

"If it will only take a few minutes why do I have to go in there?" I asked. "Jameson, she will pry it out of me," I pleaded.

Not only that, I was afraid she would find out what I was doing with him. I'm sure I've covered this before, but I was not known for being sneaky. I lack that particular set of desired skills.

Jameson was silent for a brief moment and then frowned. "Another good point," he mused looking at the house and then the car. "Fine, stay right here. Keep watch."

Then he jumped over the bushes and snuck toward Alley's car all stealth-like. It was very entertaining to watch.

My time waiting wasn't long. He returned in five minutes with a huge grin that quickly disappeared when we heard voices from behind.

Darting back into the bushes with me, we crouched down between the branches. One particular branch kept tickling my ear, and I snapped and broke the fucker off.

Jameson looked at me as if I was crazy so I punched him in the stomach.

The voices got closer, and I saw that it was Aiden and Emma. Unfortunately, they stopped a few feet from us on the side of the garage, right in our line of sight and started making out.

I knew what was going to happen next so my hand flew to Jameson's mouth before he could say anything and give our covert operation away.

"Shhh ... Calm down," I whispered.

His jaw clenched; his entire body tensed.

"Don't tell me to calm down!" he barked in a whisper pulling my hand away. "Did you know about this?" He motioned to Emma and Aiden *still* making out.

I didn't answer, just played with my broken branch, avoiding eye contact.

"You knew?" he asked incredulously attempting to get up. "How could you *not* tell me?"

"Jesus Christ, Jameson!" I yanked hard on his arm and he collapsed on my lap. "She's twenty-one and *in love* for the first time. You get it?"

"*Apparently*, I don't."

I really couldn't understand *what* the big deal with all this was but he was adorable when he was mad. "You're cute when you're mad."

"Whatever," he glared. "You should have told me."

"Calm down."

"No." His arms crossed over his chest. "I'm mad."

Emma and Aiden were still kissing so I needed to distract him.

I couldn't believe I was resorting to this but I was. It was either this or poor Aiden wouldn't be walking tomorrow.

"Would it help if I showed you my boobs?"

He was quiet for a moment before replying with, "Maybe." He motioned with a quick flip of his hand. "Show me and let's see."

Ashamed with myself, I flipped my shirt up, and his eyes immediately lit up like a kid in a candy store.

He was like a damn child.

Emma and Aiden finished their make out session and ventured inside so that I could pull my shirt back down. It took some persuasive convincing on my part but we eventually made it to the shop to return the helmet and did *not* go inside Alley's house to kill Aiden.

No one was at the shop when we arrived, which surprised me. I figured there would be guys there working on the car since they are leaving for Pocono tonight.

When we entered the large warehouse-looking building, Jameson turned on lights as he went.

Once the fluorescents lit up the main floor, I was in pit lizard heaven. That heaven was glorified when I saw his cup car parked by the bay door, ready to be loaded on the hauler.

I skimmed my fingers along the sharp line of the body, gliding over the black glossy paint. My fingers skated along the rear quarter panels, along the door, down the front quarter panel and against the hood with ease.

It was beautiful. I had a thing for race cars that either made me squeal with delight or horny.

I thought Jameson was in the office, but he surprised me when his hands touched my hips, his fingers pressing lightly into my heated skin.

"See something you like?"

How many times was I going to hear these exact words today?

"Maybe I do," I began turning in his arms. My eyes scanned the shop when they settled on an engine perched on a hoist. "Isn't that supposed to be in the car?"

Jameson looked over his right shoulder and then at me again. "Yeah, but the bearings are misaligned—they have some work to do on that one. I think it's going back to Grandpa's shop tomorrow."

I smiled knowing where this was going when he smirked. "What's bearing alignment?"

Knowing damn well I knew what bearing alignment was he was only playing along. "Well," he began, slowly pushing me against the side of the car. "When you have bearing misalignment, and an engine turning 9,000 RPMs, that's not *good*. You see ..." His fingers that were gripping my hips trailed delicately up the curve of my body before cupping my cheek and his thumb brushed my lips. "All bearings have some internal clearance which can accommodate a certain amount of *thermal expansion* and misalignment." He pushed forward again, this time his hips showed *his* thermal expansion. "But when that clearance is fully consumed, then metal-to-metal impacting occurs with high dynamic stress ... and bearings fail." His eyes searched mine, hungry and glowing with desire.

Playing my part well, I asked, "So why so much focus on bearing alignment? I mean ... I understand it's not ideal, but what do the bearings do?"

Jameson's smirk widened; he knew what I was doing. His head tilted to one side, his eyes penetrating my very being with one look.

"It keeps the camshaft moving with ... ease."

"And your camshaft, is it moving with ... ease?"

"I think I need to check the bearing alignment." His lips found mine. "I seem to be experiencing some ... thermal expansion."

He didn't give me time to respond before picking me up and carrying me over to the front of his race car.

In the process of doing this, he knocked over a drip pan, and we slipped in the spilled oil, landing against the hood.

Jameson looked down at my jeans that now had oil covering them, giving me a lopsided grin. "Look at that, those are ruined," he mused. "You'll have to take them off."

Moments later there I was, pit lizard-style, spread out on the hood of his race car, naked, my bare ass sitting directly on his Simplex logo and damn happy about it.

He removed his black sweatshirt and t-shirt, oil smudges smeared across his jaw.

Just when I figured he was going to drop his pants, he surprised me, flashing a wicked smile. Pulling my hips to the nose of the car, he dropped to his knees.

Sweet Jesus.

"In order to properly check the bearings ... I *need* to do some deburring of the crankcase."

He's going to kill me with all this car talk!

Leaning forward so his lips were on the inside of my thigh, he took in a deep breath and then placed slow deliberate kisses along each thigh, groaning a loud luscious groan. "I can't wait to taste you." His voice alone was enough to put me into overdrive.

In my head, for some reason, I was singing Nine Inch Nails, "Closer."

Me, and others at times, found this somewhat concerning but in addition to inappropriate giggling, I heard music in my head at the most *inappropriate* times.

Panting uncontrollably, I threw my head back against the hood and stretched my arms up against the Lexan windshield, already so close with just fingers.

As soon as his mouth replaced his fingers, I was no longer in control of my body movements.

Jameson roughly grabbed both legs near the tops of my thighs and pulled me closer to him with a low growl.

As good as that felt, I *really* wanted him, now, after that reaction. "Jameson, *please* ..." I moaned.

He chuckled against me.

"Please what?" he grunted.

I whimpered. "Inside ... need you ... inside."

I was amazed I could even string the words together to form that sentence, given it wasn't complete, but I shouldn't expect so much from myself.

"Not yet, honey," he murmured in that signature raspy velvet voice. He continued his ministrations until I was literally screaming his name once again today.

I was trembling, panting, quivering, shivering, and shaking; whatever verb you want to use ... I was in complete disarray on the hood of Jameson Riley's race car as he tended to my crankcase as if it was the holy fucking grail.

Just when I thought I had died and gone to heaven, he pulled away, stood, slowly drew his bottom lip between his teeth and dropped his jeans to the ground.

I got a glimpse of the lust driven desire from his eyes that were mean enough to scare a wild animal as he crawled on the hood and inched up my body as if he was hunting his prey.

Hot damn.

What did I say in that moment?

"Roarrrr!" complete with a hand gesture.

Yep, in that moment *that's* what I chose to say.

I was amazed I didn't belt out the lyrics to him.

Jameson fell against me in a fit of laughter at my reaction, but he didn't get distracted for long.

Nudging my legs apart with his knees, he placed one hand behind my left knee and hitched it up his bare hip.

Bending forward at the waist he leaned his face against mine and whispered in my ear, "This is something I've *always* wanted to do with you."

Did he just say what I think he said?

"Huh?"

Jameson didn't waste any time at all before pushing himself forward into me.

"I've … uh … nothing," he mumbled hooking his hands on the top of the hood for leverage.

He went in for the kill, assaulting my neck with wet kisses and soft nips while his hips rocked against mine. The steel hood was not designed to support the weight of two grown adults and began to flex beneath us but that also did nothing to deter Jameson.

We didn't last long before I was once again moaning like a whore as he started in with the dirty heathen car talk pushing me over the edge.

"You like that, honey?" Jameson grunted reaching for a fist full of my hair, wrapping it tightly around his fingers and tugging gently.

"You have the most amazing camshaft!" I blurted out.

"Fuck!" Jameson cried out slamming his right fist against the hood beside my head, the steel vibrated causing me to once again jump. His other hand was still holding my thigh securely to his hip. "I love the way you say camshaft," he growled right before his head fell forward against the hood above my shoulder.

I turned my head to get a good look at him, his eyes remained closed, his brow furrowed in concentration and determination, biting down on his bottom lip.

I wanted to take a picture of that face right there, blow it up and hang it on the ceiling in my bedroom.

By that point, we were both panting, my ass was stuck to the hood, and I was sure I had sticker burn.

My hair was caught in an air vent, my toe was stuck in a hood pin loop, and Jameson was still trembling above me. His hands were gripping my shoulders tightly, holding me against his chest.

I was afraid to move or even breathe.

Drawing in a shaky breath, he whispered, "We should … get off the hood." Still panting, he placed a row of soft tender kisses along my collarbone.

He can be so sweet.

"Yeah, we should," I agreed, but we still made no attempt to get up.

I didn't know if we actually could. We'd worn ourselves out today.

What is this, like round six ... maybe even seven.

Eventually, we did peel ourselves from the hood that was, indeed, dented.

Jameson laughed when he looked down. "This is the one we're taking to Pocono, too."

Laughing at him, I put on my oil-saturated jeans about the time Kyle came walking into the shop with Gentry, his younger brother, trailed close behind.

Kill me now.

At this point, Jameson still hadn't put his shirt back on. Not that I minded, but now they were going to know what we were doing, *in* a race shop, *on* the hood of a race car.

Jameson had oil smudges on his face and neck with his hair looking like it could easily have its own zip code.

Who am I kidding, I'm sure I didn't look any better, my hair was all over the place, I had oil literally everywhere *and* I was missing a shoe.

Kyle approached us while Jameson slipped his shirt over his broad shoulders.

"What happened in here?" Kyle glanced at the oil on the ground *and* on the hood of Jameson's car.

"I spilled some oil and we ... slipped in it," Jameson replied throwing some shop towels on the ground to soak up the mess.

I was still searching for my other shoe when I found it on the spare pit box. I climbed up there and retrieved my shoe while Gentry and Kyle started loading the hauler.

Usually this would have already been done but Jameson insisted on taking this particular car to Pocono so they had to reload the car and the back-up car.

Kyle ran his fingers across the dent, his head quirked to one side. "Jameson, why does the hood of your car look like someone sat on it?"

I sunk as far down in that damn pit box as I could without falling. What did Jameson do?

He smiled, his head tilting slightly, but didn't look up from his spot on the floor where he was cleaning the oil.

"That's because someone *did* have their ass on the hood of my race car, Kyle." And then he looked up and proceeded to nod his head arrogantly with that stupid dirty smirk plastered across his face.

I wanted to kill him.

Kyle shook his head in disbelief. "I don't even want to know."

I didn't think I could be any more embarrassed than this morning in the hotel room, *but* this surpassed it.

Gentry, standing beside the pit box, nodded his head as he let out a low drawn out whistle. "Damn."

Once again, embarrassment did not do this justice.

"See you later, bud." Kyle grinned at me. "And careful with that engine over there—it's going to be sent out for bearing alignment and sonic testing, wouldn't want to disturb it."

I said nothing because there wasn't any point adding any fuel to that particular fire. In a matter of minutes, we'd dented a hood and coated the floor with oil. Just imagine what we could do to that engine.

"What's a sonic test?" I asked pretending to be shy when the guys left and we remained cleaning up our mess.

Jameson's warm eyes darted to mine from the floor. He grinned with an adorable nod. "Hmm ... You don't need much recovery time, do you?"

"You should know by now that I can go all night," I told him with very little wavering on my part. I may have shifted my stance but other than that, I was strong and confident. I was winning this battle to make up for all the embarrassment.

He inhaled a breath before letting it whoosh out and smiled. His hand came up as he leaned against the side of a toolbox running it across the back of his neck. "Sonic testing uses high frequency sound energy to measure material ..." He looked up at me, the warm green in his eyes darkened. "It measures the material *thickness*."

I nearly fucking fainted because when he said *thickness*, his entire body shifted toward me, his breath blowing across my face. It couldn't have been much more erotic than that right there.

"And how does that work?" I provoked him, stepping closer as well.

Once again, our bodies were nearly touching; just one slight movement and we'd be welded together. The lack of touching was providing all the heat in this. Jameson may have been the driver, but he knew engines, my engine to be exact. He knew my particular engine didn't need to be heated prior to the race but goddamn did he know how.

In case you're wondering, this is a real term, too. In sprint car racing, it's common for the guys to "put heat in the engine" prior to the race. They do this by hooking the car up to a machine and bringing the engine and cooling systems up to race temperature. The main purpose of this was to get the most horsepower during the race.

I had no problems in that particular area, that's for sure. My engine was up to race temperature in a matter of seconds.

Jameson's eyes searched mine as he spoke, watching me intently. "The machine sends out a signal and measures the time it takes to echo back. The longer it takes, the *thicker* the material. It measures the cylinder wall thickness as well as the cylinder heads."

"Is it an effective test ... this sonic testing?" I did this snicker-snort of thing because it was the only other noise I could make at that moment so I didn't moan and ruin the dirty engine talking.

Slowly, he drew in his bottom lip, his tongue dragging across it just as slowly as his eyes squinted slightly. "It's a very effective test, *if* done correctly." His breathing increased when I reached forward and grabbed him by his shirt.

"Let's see how long we really can go."

"I think we have enough heat in the engine." He leaned closer breathing a throaty string of words in my ear that sealed whatever deal I wanted. "And I can also ... go *all night long.*"

Rev Limiter – A rev limiter is used to keep the engine from exceeding its maximum rotational speed and exploding into pieces of very expensive shrapnel and to stay within the speed limit rules on pit lane.

"So how was getting caught the morning after?"

"How the fuck did you know about that?" I growled at Emma with a mouth full of food.

"Spencer, who else?" Emma took a bite of her eggs, chewing slowly. "Look at it this way; they don't know it was you."

I let out the breath I'd been holding since she started talking. "I can't say the same for Jameson," I warned. "He knows about you and Aiden."

"What do you *mean* he knows?"

"That's exactly what I *mean*, Emma." I answered taking another bite of my blueberry pancakes. "We *saw* you." I raised my eyebrows at her as we sat there in the corner booth of the Cracker Barrel restaurant in Downingtown, Pennsylvania.

We had arrived in Pennsylvania early this morning and decided to get some breakfast before Jameson had to be at the track.

Alley and Spencer were already at the track so Jameson invited Emma and Aiden to come along with us and I knew the reason why.

Emma slouched in the booth throwing her tiny arms over her

head. Aiden was in the bathroom and Jameson suddenly had to make a phone call when Aiden got up.

I'm pretty sure he was having a conversation with him about what we witnessed. I actually feared for Aiden's safety, which was why I kept looking over my shoulder to see where the hell Jameson had disappeared to.

Emma perked up with a sense of alarm. "Wait?" She glanced around suspiciously. "Where did Jameson go?"

I tried to play it off, I really did, but my facial expression must have betrayed me.

Emma threw her napkin on the table. "That *stupid* protective asshole!" she spat and tried to get up. "Why can't he mind his own business?"

I jumped up and pummeled her, knocking us both against the back of the U-shaped booth.

"Calm down." I grabbed her head and pushed it into my chest, and began petting her spiky black hair as if she was a damn cat. "Just calm down, he probably wanted to have a few *words* with him."

Emma was pissed so I knew my usual tactic of showing my boobs to Jameson to calm him down, wouldn't calm Emma down.

I tried a different approach, petting her.

"Get off me!" she snapped pushing me away. "He is *not* having a few words with him and you know it. Look what happened to Ryder?" Her eyes scanned the restaurant. "Since when has Jameson ever used his damn words? He only knows violence." She sighed shaking her head dejectedly. "Poor Aiden, he doesn't stand a chance against Jameson when he's angry."

She was right, poor lanky Aiden didn't stand a chance.

We both looked up when we heard shuffling of feet to see Jameson sit down across from me and begin nonchalantly eating his pancakes again. He never said a word, just continued looking down at his plate and eating as though nothing had happened.

I'm inclined to think that later especially when Aiden returned.

With a bloody lip, bloody nose, and the beginning of a black eye, Aiden sat down just as calmly as Jameson had.

One look at him and Emma went into a fit of pure hysteria.

She was yelling at the top of her lungs at Jameson while Aiden remained silent beside her, looking down at his hands.

Just like any other situation I was faced with, I started laughing because Emma was acting like an Umpa Lumpa on crack and Jameson...well, Jameson was being Jameson. Refusing to look up at any of us, his face set like stone in a grim expression eating his pancakes.

"I can't believe you, Jameson!" Emma screamed and then burst into tears causing Jameson to *finally* look up.

I don't think he ever intended to hurt Emma but it went that way.

"Just because you're incapable of having a *normal* relationship with anyone, doesn't mean I can't." Emma told him. "I love Aiden."

Slowly, Jameson shook his head but didn't say anything. His gaze dropped to his plate once again as he continued eating.

"You're such a hypocrite, Jameson." At this point, Emma was pissed that Jameson was not paying attention to what she had to say, so she added fuel to the fire. "You think I don't know what you two are doing?"

I dropped my fork about the time Jameson's jaw clenched.

He slowly looked up at Emma and I would not want to be on the receiving end of that glare he was now giving her.

"This has *nothing* to do with me or Sway," his voice venomously warning.

Those who knew Jameson well knew that right now was the point that you quit while you're ahead or you can officially say you've reached the point of no return.

Sitting there as quietly as I possibly could, I watched Jameson and Emma stare at each other.

Aiden's eyes shifted toward me so I mouthed, *"I'm sorry"* to him. He winked.

I think Aiden knew this was coming and knew damn well once Spencer found out, he'd probably have another black eye and possibly a broken nose.

With a dramatic sigh, Emma reached beside her purse and threw a box of posters into Jameson's lap.

"Sign these." She stood reaching for Aiden by the arm. "You're an asshole Jameson and don't *ever* involve yourself in my love life again."

We officially reached that point of no return.

And this is when the temper of the two-year-old emerged.

Jameson slammed his fist against the table knocking glasses and plates around. "You don't know *anything* about love, Emma." He clipped. "You're twenty-one years old."

"And you do, Jameson? You're exactly fourteen months older than me." Emma placed her hand on her hip, tears still spilling down her reddened cheeks.

Jameson didn't say anything just continued to stare at her. Even though I remained sitting across from him, I could distinctly see that warning look he was giving Emma to shut up.

But she didn't and I couldn't blame her. She was mad and she should be. Having two older brothers, Emma has always been on the receiving end of the brotherly witness protection program.

"Do you really think this is going to end well for either of you?" Emma gestured between us. "You're incapable of loving anyone for the *right* reasons, Jameson. You're going to break her heart." She turned to me. "And *you* need to wake up and see that."

Turning on her heel sharply, she stormed out of the restaurant with Aiden, leaving me with an absolutely *livid* Jameson.

He was quiet for a long moment with his eyes fixated on the place where Emma was once standing. I knew exactly what was coming.

My mind began counting down to the eruption as if it were a missile launch for detonation.

"Fucking bullshit," he mumbled under his breath.

With that two-year-old temper, suddenly he grabbed the edge of the table flipping it over into the middle of the restaurant sending food, glass, silverware, and drinks everywhere across the floor.

Everyone starred at Jameson, *including* me.

And to think this was a family restaurant.

"C'mon." He ordered sharply grasping my wrist as we made our way to the cashier, stepping over the mess.

I didn't say a word and followed behind him, carefully avoiding the questioning glances surrounding us. I assumed they were all wondering if I was with a lunatic. I wanted to say, "Don't mind him, he's unstable."

Jameson threw two hundred dollars at the timid cashier. "This should cover our meal and the mess."

Shaken, she nodded slowly taking the money as Jameson stormed out, slamming the door behind him.

Once we were in the parking lot, he got in the car without saying anything.

And though it would have been completely inappropriate at that moment, I nearly giggled just to lighten the mood.

We sat there quietly, I holding in my laughter, and Jameson gazing out the windshield as though he was trying to burn a hole through it.

After a few moments, he started the car and drove silently toward the track at Long Pond.

I felt bad for Emma, seeing her so upset as, over the years, she had become like a sister to me. The last thing I wanted was to see her upset, but I was also irritated she brought me into the argument. She was right though.

I knew I was heading for heartbreak but I also knew that if I didn't stay and see where this went between us, I would *always* regret it and if I thought I would regret not doing something, I did it. So a hint as to how I got into this particular situation with the raging bull next to me.

To understand me, you'd have to understand my childhood.

My mom died when I was very young and though I have vague memories of her, I will never forget what she said to me the last time I saw her alive. My mother kept her sickness from both Charlie and me. She didn't tell Charlie until she only had a couple months to live. Rachel *always* lived her life to the fullest; each day doing exactly what she wanted to do and when she wanted to do it. She never let anyone else dictate when or how she did something. Looking back, she did this because she knew she was sick and had very little time left. She wanted to experience everything life had to offer her at twenty-five and she did.

The day she died, I was sitting in her room with her. I'd made her a Valentine's Day card and was reading it to her. Once I finished, she smiled and gave me a hug. I curled up in the hospital bed that she had called home for the last two months.

And then she gave me her farewell speech.

"Sway, mommy needs to tell you a few things, okay?" I nodded with tears in my eyes. "Mommy is very sick, you know." I nodded again.

Charlie had told me on numerous occasions that mommy was sick and wouldn't be around much longer. I didn't understand what that meant at the time, but being six, I went along with it. Thankfully, my child innocence provided me with not understanding the magnitude of this.

"Baby," she began softly, "you know how much mommy loves you right?"

I nodded again and continued to listen to her low strained breathing with my head rested on her chest.

"I want you to remember that. I want you to live each day like it's your last. If you have something to say to someone, say it to them, don't wait. When you're older and you find someone that you love, don't waste time. Tell them you love them. If there is something you want in life, make it happen. Don't settle for anything because you think you can't have what you really want."

I was crying because I knew this was her farewell speech to me. Even with the innocence I had in the situation, I knew enough that this was the end.

"I was very young when your father and I had you. I don't regret having you at all. You've brought so much to my life and showed me love that I thought people only dreamed of having. When you were first placed in my arms, I was scared that I'd made a mistake. That I would mess you up somehow but in my moment of fear, you looked up at me. Right then, when I was met with the most beautiful emerald eyes I've ever seen. You gave me this look and in that instant I knew I could do it. I knew I could do it because you'd be there to show me how and you have. You showed me there's so much more to life than personal possessions. There's love and the love between a mother and her child is beyond anything I could have ever imagined. Just remember that sweetheart."

I never completely understood what she intended by the speech, but as I got older, the speech began to make sense and I never forgot it. Rachel lived her life to the fullest and she wanted me to do the same.

From that point on, I did things because *I* wanted to, not because someone else wanted me to, except when that someone else was Jameson. I couldn't explain why I held myself to different standards with Jameson, but I did. I loved him and nothing changed that for me.

My logic was off and I've come to the conclusion that I'm completely insane but for now, for this time I was with him, I was going to have fun and live this life to the fullest. I spent entirely too long waiting to see what would happen. I was the doer now!

I told Charlie I'd be home in time for the Modified Nationals and then after that was the Big E Weekend where the Northern Sprint Tour and the Outlaws would be in town. That meant I would get to see Jameson that weekend as well. He had two cars racing in The World of Outlaws so naturally Jameson said he'd make an appearance for it.

After that, his schedule would be hectic until the end of the season.

We could make this work, even if I were only a friend with benefits, at least I'd be seeing a lot of benefits.

That was my logic.

Completely irrational, foolish break your heart logic, but it was mine. So for now, I was going to enjoy my three weeks of friends with benefits and put my emotions aside.

That was my plan. Not that it would turn out well but it was my plan.

Once we pulled into the pit-entrance, the race weekend was in full swing and Jameson was now in race mode.

It might not have been the best timing, but I decided to try to make him see Emma's side. I didn't want him going into practice upset, as he tends to get a little hasty out there if his mood is off.

"Jameson, you should apologize to Emma and Aiden," I suggested, looking at the ten text messages I had from Emma apologizing for bringing me into the argument.

"I will *not* apologize to Aiden. I *will* apologize to Emma, when she calms down, but Aiden ..." He shook his head. "He had it coming. I asked him repeatedly if anything was going on and he said no." He turned his head to look at me. "That's what he gets for not being honest with me in the beginning."

"Have you ever thought that maybe he was afraid to tell you?" I pointed out in the form of a question.

"Oh, please, spare me the bullshit. He's an adult not a five-year-old! If he has something to say, he should say it."

"You can be scary when you want to be and Spencer ... well, there are no words for Spencer. I don't blame them for not wanting to tell you guys."

He looked at me with a shocked expression, his brow raised. "You're taking their side in this?"

"I'm just saying you should be nicer to them about this."

"I will not. If Aiden has a problem with me then fine, he can come and talk to me about it." Jameson showed his credentials to the NASCAR officials and then pulled through the gate when she waved him by. "I'm not apologizing."

Pulling up to the motor coach in the driver's compound, sure enough poor Aiden was sporting another new black eye, but he looked relieved to have everything out in the open. At least they wouldn't have to sneak around. Jameson and I, however, still had to sneak around.

Last night, after the race car incident, I told Jameson my crankcase needed a day's break. It was not only sore, but I had a serious case of sticker burn that was making it a little difficult to sit today *or* walk for that matter. If you've ever had rug burn before, the result is similar.

I had a feeling this "day break" was also part of Jameson's anger issues today, especially when his hand was sliding up the back of my shirt once we are in the motor coach, alone, in the bedroom.

He was supposed to be getting his race suit on for practice, but he seemed to have other ideas about that.

I slapped his hand away. "Jameson ... no."

He sighed bringing his lips to my collarbone, kissing along it. "Please, honey ... I *need* you." His voice was low and strained and was not helping my resolve one tiny bit.

"I'm sore," I whined with a pouty lip.

"Too much align boring?" He raised an eyebrow while backing me up toward the queen-sized bed.

In case you're wondering what the fuck align boring is—it's a process that some do to an engine that involves taking a metal rod and pushing it through the crankcase repeatedly to make sure everything inside the crankcase was properly aligned.

"Yeah!"

"You know, align boring assures proper bearing alignment as well. With all that misalignment we took care of last night, maintenance is just as important. I'm only looking out for you."

"I know, but you're camshaft has too much lift." This was my next attempt.

"Are you suffering from valve binding?"

"What in the hell is valve binding?"

"That's when a camshaft has too much lift ..." His hips pushed forward showing me just how much lift he had. "It opens the valve spring too far creating *valve binding*."

I pushed against him trying to get away. "There's something wrong with you." I laughed once, but then gained control over my expression and crankcase, which was back to making justifications the rest of me couldn't play along with today.

"I just need a day. My ass hurts and my crankcase feels like I let the entire goddamn state of North Carolina align bore me."

Jameson growled pushing me down on the bed, my legs automatically spread.

"I will be the *only* one doing any align boring when it comes to your crankcase ... *only* me." His arms wrapped under and over my shoulders, pulling me snug against his hips.

Of course, he was ready, and my willpower was crumbling for his lift and those damn justifications.

"Hello, Mr. Possessive." I chuckled trying to squirm away.

"I'm not apologizing for that either." His grip tightened. "You will only be my *friend with benefits*, no one else's."

"Does that rule apply to you, too?"

Oh God, shut up!

Despite this, he laughed against my neck. "Of course it does."

Jameson pushed his hips against mine revealing his excitement. "Now let's see about this valve binding problem you have."

"Jameson." I tried again to push against his chest. "I'm serious I need a break."

Pressing his hips against mine one last time, he let out a deep sigh before rolling away. "Damn it!"

Once he was dressed, we made our way to the garage where Jameson forgot about me turning him down. Instead, he was focused on the race car now and the job he had to do.

Well, until Nancy approached us. Chipper as always, she bounced into the garage area, her rusty hair pulled back under her Simplex hat.

"Oh Sway," she breathed reaching for me. "You're here again?"

"Yeah, I'm going home after Sonoma." I pulled away and handed her the posters Jameson signed earlier this morning. "Just taking a summer break after college."

Jameson walked over to sign a few die-cast cars for the Children's Hospital that Nancy brought with her.

"Jameson," Nancy said sternly, her green eyes glaring. "Now, I don't ask a lot from you at home because you're rarely there, but I *expect* you to respect our home while you're living in it." She poked his chest with a black sharpie. "I expect you to clean up your bedroom and fix the closet. What the hell happened in there? It looks like a gang bang took place." Nancy stood there waiting for an answer.

Rubbing the spot his mother poked, Jameson let out a loud laugh as my cheeks began to heat rapidly. "Well a '*gang bang*' implies a group of people. There were only two," he replied still signing the various items Nancy was handing him.

I giggled when he said "gang bang" because he resorted to air quotes to get his point across.

"Well," Nancy actually looked somewhat relieved that her son didn't have a gang bang in her house, "just clean it up."

Once she walked away, Jameson started laughing walking back over to his car to get ready for his first practice session.

This weekend they were racing at Pocono Raceway in Long Pond, Pennsylvania. It was a two-and-a-half favorite. He preferred the mile-

and-a-half and the short tracks—said it reminded him of his dirt track days growing up.

I sat on the pit box with Kyle—listening to the in-car audio—when Jameson went out for practice.

"You copy, bud?" Kyle asked when Jameson made it onto the track.

"Yep," Jameson confirmed while the radio crackled.

"All right Aiden, he's all yours," Kyle said. "Let me know how the car feels bud."

The first few laps were quiet while Aiden and Jameson talked back and forth guiding him through any traffic that was out there. They seemed better.

Jameson and Aiden had been friends for the past few years now; I'd hoped that something like this didn't get in the way of their friendship and so far, it didn't seem like it was going to. That's the cool thing about men, other than the fact they get to stand to pee, which I envied. Once they express their anger for someone and get what they needed to off their chests, they seem to forget all about what went down. Women should take some pointers from them.

I watched as Jameson got loose in turn three, the car jerked sideways and brushed the wall, Kyle cringed beside me. "Damn it."

"Brushed the wall, turn three," Aiden announced. "No damage."

"Looks like you got your hands full there." Kyle looked over the lap times on the computer. "What's the car doing?"

Jameson was quiet for a moment and then came on. "I'm all over the fucking place. I can't keep the damn thing straight. I can't drive in as hard in three, but I can go anywhere I want in the other turns."

"Bring it in," Kyle told him. "We're gonna put it on the scales and change the springs."

After another two laps, Jameson brought the car in the garage and the crew went to work on the adjustments.

Lounging around in the garage area, he talked with Tony, the tire specialist, for a few moments. He thought something felt off about the tires they were using, but Tony assured him they were the same.

Jameson was involved in all aspects of the car. That stemmed from Jimi. Growing up, Jimi had made it clear to Jameson that he couldn't just drive the car. He had to understand the cars, be able to build them and fix them when needed. In a way, that's what made Jameson the type of driver he was today.

Most drivers drove these days, but Jameson could do about anything to a race car and there wasn't anything he couldn't drive the wheels off. His understanding of how everything worked together along with his driving ability made for a lethal combination on the track.

While I waited for him to finish explaining the handling of the car to Kyle and Mason, Alley walked into the garage, her heels clicking against the concrete.

"Is he done yet?" she asked annoyed. She looked pissed.

"I think he will be in a minute, why?" I leaned back against the wall trying to appear calm.

She glared toward Jameson. "I just have a bone to pick with that asshole." She turned to me. "When did you get here?"

Shit, don't panic and be sneaky.

"Oh ... I never left." I tried to act all nonchalant about it so she wouldn't catch on, but I still hadn't improved on being sneaky. "I traveled with Jameson from Charlotte."

By the grace of God, Jameson walked over right about the time she was starting to figure it out.

"You're an asshole!" Alley yelled pushing him into the wall beside me.

Jameson smirked steadying himself by reaching for me. "I have *no* idea what you're talking about." He put his arms around my shoulders wrapping around my chest and then used me as some sort of defense shield against the "Alley wrath" as he frequently called it.

"Oh, I think you *do*, Jameson." Alley got right in his face. "My son called a one year old little girl a ruthless bitch because of you."

Both Jameson and I started laughing.

I know it shouldn't be funny that Lane called a little girl this but it was funny. I only wish I could have seen it. Lane had the cutest little chipmunk voice. It was probably adorable like those Subway commercials with the kids talking.

"Stop laughing, both of you," she snapped changing her focus into work mode. "Jameson, you have an autograph session in an hour. I suggest you get to it. After that, you have a meeting with Simplex and an interview with Track Pass at six."

Jameson nodded to everything she told him pulling his racing suit down around his waist.

Alley started to walk away but turned when she reached the bay doors at the edge of his car. "Oh, and Jameson," she glared directly at him when he glanced up at her, "paybacks are a *ruthless* bitch."

Jameson rolled his eyes imperviously sitting on some tires before pulling me onto his lap.

"Uh ... should I be sitting on your lap here in public?" I asked glancing around the garage. The crews were all distracted by their duties; I still thought this was rather public of him.

"Fuck what they think."

"Hmmm." Part of me wished Chelsea would walk by right about now. Punching her didn't seem like enough. I wanted her to see this, Jameson and me together, in public.

Now you really do sound like you're in high school.

"Have dinner with me tonight," Jameson whispered pushing my hair off my shoulder to reveal my bare skin that wasn't covered by my tank top.

"Friends with benefits go to dinner together?" I raised an eyebrow.

He nodded his head once. "Well," he leaned forward and put his lips at my ear. "We are *exclusive* friends with benefits. And I say we make our own rules to this." He kissed my neck softly before pulling away. "So if I want to take you to dinner, I think I have every right to, as your *exclusive* friend with *his* determined benefits."

"*His* determined benefits," I repeated.

"Yep," he said popping the "p" at the end.

"So what are *his* determined benefits anyway?"

"I can't give my secrets away just yet." His eyes sparkled. "What would be the fun in that?"

"Does it involve more race cars?" He piqued my curiosity when he said his determined benefits.

Jameson winked. "I would say race cars could be arranged." He smiled wickedly leaning into me again. "Do you wanna go for a ride in my race car?"

"*Actually*, I'm dying to go for a ride. I'm being serious. I *really* want to take a ride in your race car."

"Really, you want like a *real* ride in my car, as in *that* race car?" He gestured toward his car parked beside us.

I nodded my head like a five-year-old wanting candy or a pit lizard in heaven—either way, I was ecstatic at the possibility.

"Let me talk to the officials and see what they say."

He acted as if this wouldn't be a problem, but I wasn't getting my hopes up. I knew the NASCAR track officials had rules against this kind of thing. It could potentially be a *huge* liability if something were to happen on the track.

Jameson went out for another practice session after the crew finished the changes, so I went with Emma and Nancy to set up his autograph session.

Emma and I talked and, of course, I forgave her.

How could I not? She was the closest thing I had to a sister.

"I want you to be careful with him." Emma looked close to tears again. "I know that he cares for you, that's evident, I just ... he's focused on his career right now, and Jameson doesn't know *how* to do both. He doesn't want to get hurt either."

I nodded because I knew.

I knew he was incapable of offering me anymore than his exclusive friend with *his* determined benefits, but I didn't care.

My logic was so messed up it was becoming hard for me to even realize how far we were really getting into this. It had only been going for a few days now but with every touch, every kiss, every tender word spoken between us, my heart was falling deeper and deeper in love with him. Before long, there'd be no going back. Therapy would be my only answer, and *lots* of ice cream.

"I can handle it, Emma."

Walking toward a box of t-shirts, I began taking them out of the box, one-by-one, to avoid anything more detailed into my stupid logic.

I was screwed.

Once I had all the shirts lined up, I stepped back to examine the way they looked. Again, it was entertaining to me to see a boy I grew up with plastered all over the place, as though he was a huge star. The difference, he *was* a huge star now.

"So you must be Sway Reins?" a man asked from behind as I day-dreamed.

I turned to see Darrin Torres standing there with a grin.

"I ... uh ... yeah, I'm Sway."

He reached for my hand. "It's nice to meet you, Sway. I'm Darrin Torres."

"I know who you are."

"So I see you're with Jameson's team?" he hinted, looking at the t-shirts I had arranged.

"Well, no. I'm helping out. I'm ..." my voice trailed off because I couldn't really say "fuck buddy" in public, or could I?

"His girlfriend?" Darrin finished.

"No ... We're ... I'm not his girlfriend, *just friends*."

"Oh." Darrin smiled, his eyes dropped from mine to my lips and then back. "Does that mean I can take you to dinner tonight?"

Christ he's bold.

"No, it doesn't mean you can take her to dinner tonight," I heard Jameson's furious voice from behind.

Darrin laughed darkly, his eyes focused on Jameson standing behind me. "I wouldn't advise starting anything here with all your fans around, Jameson," Darrin suggested motioning toward the crowds gathering around, all waiting to catch a glimpse of Jameson. "I wanted Sway to know there are ... other options for her beside *friends*."

You couldn't miss the way he articulated the word friends, implying he knew exactly what we were doing.

Turning around, I focused on Jameson instead, pushing his chest. "*Jameson*, he's right. Don't do anything stupid," I warned attempting to catch his gaze.

Jameson bypassed me and stood face-to-face with Darrin. "Stay away from Sway," he snarled, his body instinctively preparing for a fight.

His voice lowered, and they exchanged a few words we couldn't hear until Darrin shook his head slowly and started to walk away. "Good luck with the ... *friends* thing."

I turned back to a fuming Jameson and hit him in the shoulder. "Stop it. You have an autograph session."

With the help of Emma, we finally got Jameson calmed down enough to have a seat and show his fans a normal human side and not the crazed lunatic he could be.

Once around his fans, he began to enjoy himself and gave them the attention they deserved after waiting in line all morning just to see him.

As with any scheduled autograph session, he was attentive to each fan. He smiled, posed for pictures with them if they asked, and actually stopped to have conversations with them. Still, a piece was missing. I knew him well enough to know this wasn't him; this was the guarded version he had around his fans.

The garage groupies annoyed me and disturbed my daydreams.

They were clingy, way too chipper, and downright slutty for being underage. I didn't think a twelve-year-old could be slutty, but today, one who was wearing a mini skirt shorter than mine and a bikini top revealing her non-existent chest to Jameson proved me wrong.

He looked up and took a double take when she leaned forward but what I thought was a double take of *"Hey, look at her"* was quickly squashed when Jameson shook his head, signed her poster and then threw a shirt at her and told her to put it on.

Emma and I laughed for a good ten minutes when she stomped away over to Paul's hauler to get his autograph.

Paul Leighty was another rookie in the cup series this year and yes, I will admit, Paul was attractive with his dark skin, brown eyes and one hell of a body, but I was a sucker for my tall beautiful rusty-haired hot head.

Finally, the autograph session was over, practices were finished up, Jameson finished his interview with Track Pass and we were now on our way to dinner at the Tokyo Tea House in Pocono Summit.

It was strange going out to dinner with him now. Over the years, we'd gone out on many occasions, but it felt different now. I wasn't sure how to act around him so I stayed quiet in fear I would say something incredibly asinine because of the lack of oxygen to my brain.

It was all going to my lungs trying not to hyperventilate.

Jameson noticed my lack of conversation and heavy breathing during dinner and threw an arm around my chair as we were sitting at the sushi bar.

"Why are you so quiet?" he asked leaning into my shoulder.

I shrugged and gave him a small tentative smile. "No reason," I lied.

My heart was pounding in my chest trying to pump more blood to my brain.

"Is it because you're horny?" Holding my gaze, he seductively licked sauce from his thumb.

"You're such a pervert." I took another bite of my spicy tuna roll keeping my stare ahead of me. "Is that all you think about?"

He wrinkled his nose but nodded. "Sadly, yes."

"You never used to be this perverted, what happened?"

"Mmm … My friend with benefits." He leaned closer, his lips at my ear when he started with the whispering. "She seems to have brought out some hormone enraged fifteen-year-old boy in me that can only think about sex …" his voice lowered with a husky edge. The hand that wasn't wrapped around my chair started at my knee and began to trace lightly up my thigh.

His feather light touch alone was enough to make me want to rip his clothes off right there in that damn restaurant and make him scream my name in front of this poor man serving our sushi rolls.

Jameson continued with that damn whispering, and I soon realized this was part of his plan that he wouldn't reveal earlier, *his determined benefits.*

"All I think about now is her amazing body wrapped around mine and broken furniture." His hand traveled closer to the Promised Land, inching along with both determination, but also enough hesitation; it was enough to drive me mad. "And race car hoods …" he breathed heavily, his hand reaching my crankcase and then dancing circles around my ignition switch, "and bearing alignment." His lips pressed to my neck once and his tongue darted out, licking me. "Assembly lubes and align boring. God, honey, the affect you have on me is ... unbelievable."

Hot damn!

My hand flew up in the air as though I had the golden ticket.

"Check, please!" I suddenly yelled.

In actuality, I did have the golden ticket; only it was a little more in the shape of a camshaft and calling my name.

Jameson chuckled against my neck and leaned forward to pull out his wallet.

"Someone's *eager*."

On the way back to the track, his hand never left my leg and neither did the feather light touching or the dirty car talk whispering he did so goddamn well.

"I don't get it," I said reaching for my bag on the floorboard. "How did you go a year with that sex drive?"

Jameson shifted in his seat. "Is that really a question you want an answer to?" He looked at me with a strange expression.

"Well yeah, I asked, didn't I?"

He let out a nervous chuckle. Jameson was a lot of things but nervous or shy was never one of them.

"Were you lying when you said it'd been a year?"

"No, I wasn't lying," he assured me. "It's actually been longer than a year. The last time was in Vegas last March, well over a year ago."

"So you ..."

"You're not actually going to make me say it, are you?"

I looked at him confused, completely lost as to what he was referring to. I don't think I'd been this confused since I saw my first penis. Imagine my surprise when I found out it had balls attached to it and was covered in hair.

Jameson sighed loudly rolling his eyes dramatically, annoyed by my confusion. He glanced over at my puzzled expression closing his eyes as though he didn't want to say it.

"Jesus Christ, there's uh ... *other* ... you know ... ways to satisfy the urge," he hinted, and I *finally* understood what he was insinuating.

Self-lovin'.

Not only because it was funny to me that Jameson Riley would have to resort to "self-lovin'," but also because I found the idea of Jameson and his "self-lovin'" incredibly hot and all I could do was giggle.

"You're such a shithead!" Jameson barked pushing against my shaking shoulders.

"Do you remember," I paused drawing a much-needed breath, "when Jimi used to refer to it as bleeding your pressure valve?" More giggling escaped me.

"I'm not really amused by this," he shot back, watching my break-down in disbelief.

Once I stopped laughing, the car hummed in silence for a few moments before I broke it. "Why do you ... I mean, you ... *uh* ... have women all over you."

Surely, he's had opportunities. Look at him, who wouldn't want him?

"I ...don't know." He shifted in his seat again. His shoulders seemed tense, that vulnerability rolling from him in waves. "I guess I got to a point where I got tired of it. They only wanted one thing from me or they were in it for the pit lizard fame. They didn't want me; they wanted the lifestyle. And anyone who did want something more than a one-time thing, I couldn't offer it to them." His eyes shifted from the road toward me briefly. "This isn't the *ideal* lifestyle for a relationship, Sway. I'm on the road at least forty weeks out of the year, sometimes longer. How can I ask someone to make that type of commitment?"

I got the feeling he was implying a lot more in this conversation than he was letting on. Like the fact that he couldn't offer me what I want. He was telling me he couldn't offer me more than what was going on right now.

"Did you apologize to Emma?" I asked wanting to change the subject away from this. I reached for my gum in the bottom of my bag.

"Yeah, we talked."

"Do you understand *why* she didn't want to tell you?"

Jameson sighed. "I get it. Spencer and I can be scary."

"Spencer can be scary," I clarified shoving the stick of gum in my mouth and then offering him a piece. "*You* on the other hand, you're like ... the Incredible Hulk."

"Am not," he replied defensively taking the gum.

I gave him an unconvincing look. "Really, what did you do to her first boyfriend when you caught them making out?"

"Pfft," he snorted. "That fucking brat deserved it."

"Or what about the time you found out she lost her virginity to Ryder?"

"Hey," he barked back at me. "I'm still friends with Ryder."

"Probably because he's afraid you'll kill him. He's keeping his enemies close."

Jameson was in complete denial of his anger problem. The boy could snap in a matter of seconds and be a *completely* different person. He had multiple personalities as I called them and they didn't always get along.

"So what's the deal with you and Darrin?" I handed him his water bottle.

Just by the constant media attention surrounding them, I knew the gist of the rivalry but still, there seemed to be more to it than the standard "rubbing is racing" term.

"He's had it out for me since Daytona," Jameson answered. "Before the race, his girlfriend, Mariah ... well, let's just say she made it known she was *interested*. I didn't respond to her advances or anything, but she told Darrin that I hit on her."

I'd never seen Mariah before, but now, I felt the need to know what this woman looked like. She was probably beautiful like all the other pit lizards wandering around the track on race weekends.

"Seriously, she did that?" I asked incredulously, my eyes wandered to the passing cars headlights. Briefly, I was reminded of our time spent traveling together that summer, how different it seemed now.

"Yep." Jameson shifted in his seat again and switched hands on the steering wheel, turning at me with his shoulders. "She's a bitch, and he's a real fucker on *and* off the track, well, you saw." He threw his right hand up in the air before letting it dangle loosely over the wheel. "Not only did he wreck me back in USAC, but once I got to cup he spun me around on pit road in Phoenix and then ran into me after the fucking race in Dover. Each week it's something else. You saw the Winston ..." he sighed in frustration. "It's hard to believe in a sport with guys who are supposed to be professionals—he can't get away with the things that he's pulled. I still think he was behind the fuel additive in Charlotte."

"Has Mariah talked to you since then?"

"No."

I knew Jameson well enough to know he hated the drama of all this. He only wanted to race—not to be embroiled in the trivial high school bullshit that came along with some of the other drivers in the series.

Our conversation continued like this for a while until we arrived back at the track and I was surprised to see that we didn't pull in toward the paddock. *Instead*, he turned and drove to the garages.

"Where are we going?"

"You said you wanted a *ride*." He waggled his eyebrows.

"Did you clear it with NASCAR?" You couldn't miss the excitement in my voice.

"Yeah," he chuckled at my enthusiasm. "Gordon said it would be fine."

I'd always wanted to ride in a cup car and could hardly mask my excitement.

I was giddy as hell when he strapped the helmet on me *and* nervous as hell when he pulled on the track. He stopped the car on pit lane and shut the engine off to explain some rules he apparently had.

I was scrunched on the passenger side, which if you've ever seen the passenger side of a cup car, there was not one.

Crammed in between roll bars, the discharge nozzle for the fire extinguisher and me were getting *real* acquainted.

Jameson pulled his helmet off so he could talk to me, nervously running his fingers through his distraught mess of hair. (delete nervously from here).

"Now, this isn't safe at all, so I *won't* be going full speed."

"No, no, no ... I want the full experience." I shifted my ass slightly to get the nozzle out. "Fuck safety."

He chuckled giving me a lopsided grin. "We'll see about that ... now, if for some reason we ... *uh* ... crash ..." He shook his head at the thought. "Just ... hold on to anything you can." He gave me a tortured expression. "This is a bad idea, Sway, maybe we shouldn't do this."

"Tsk, tsk, tsk, Jameson. When have we ever done *anything* that was a good idea?" I was trying to emphasize our situation.

"Good point." He loosened his belts. "I'm not wearing these if you don't have any. So, let's see ..." He gave me a wicked smile and stared at me for a moment. "Just hold on tight, honey." He leaned over and placed a kiss on my helmet, flipped my visor down, and put his back on.

Taking note of his every move, I watched as he flipped switches and then shifted the car into low gear keeping his foot on the clutch revving the engine a couple of times.

Craning his neck to look over at me, he winked once.

I couldn't focus on anything with the revving, the roar alone vibrating my girly bits in a *very* nice way.

It wasn't lost on me, though, that we were doing something incredibly stupid. Here Jameson was paid millions each year to race, and he's taking his car out for a joy ride with no belts. It wasn't exactly the smartest decision either of us had ever made.

All thoughts were lost when he revved the engine once more.

There's something to be said about the sound of a stock car revving to life that I can't explain, it's a sound ... but it's *the* sound, if that makes any sense at all.

I bit down on my lower lip when the car began to move at a slow speed down pit lane, then on the apron of the track.

Jameson took his hand off the gearshift and gave me thumbs up. I gripped the roll bars tightly and gave him thumbs up as well, letting him know I was ready for *my ride*.

Even over the engine and the wind, there was no doubt he could hear my screams when he slammed the car into high gear as we hit the straightaway.

I had no idea how fast we were going, but I could have sworn on a stack of bibles, I saw Jesus when my face was inches from the wall on the third straightaway. It was exhilarating, terrifying, and hot as hell all at the same time as I watched him push this 800 horsepower race car around the track. The adrenaline coursed through my veins, pumping throughout, shaking my very core with excitement.

Never in my life had I ever been so scared of dying, in awe of how addictive this could be, and pushing yourself to the limits. After all these years, I finally understood the rush he got out there.

Jameson remained focused, occasionally glancing in my direction. I could tell he was nervous, having me in here with no seat belts on, wrapped around roll bars with a discharge nozzle in places he only wished to be right now.

Watching him was probably the best assembly prep I'd ever had and the boy wasn't even touching me. Dressed in jeans and a t-shirt, I could see his forearms contracting with each shift and the way his long fingers gripped the black wheel, the quick movements his feet made while working the clutch, brake, and gas simultaneously—it was addicting to watch.

Suddenly he shifted down to the low gear, pulled down on the apron in turn two, and jerked the wheel left. The car whipped around throwing us into a burn out. And if the driving didn't turn me on, the revving of the engine and the smell of the burnt rubber pouring into the cockpit of the car sealed the deal.

After a few more laps, Jameson slowed the car down, pulled onto pit lane again and then drove into the garage. The tires still smoking—the thick burning smell swirled through the bays, hovering in the air like fog.

Jameson was breathing heavy when he reached over, killed the engine and pulled off his helmet. I pulled mine off as well and tried to fix my helmet hair, completely useless.

"That was *amazing*," I said breathlessly shaking from the adrenaline.

Jameson nodded and then grinned but said nothing.

"So what are all these switches?" I knew most of them, but I wanted some dirty car talk, and I knew damn well he could provide it.

He chuckled, giving me the smirk again. "Well, let's start on your side." He raised an eyebrow. "I know you know what all this is, so I'm just humoring you with this shit."

I let out a little giggle knowing he saw right through me.

"All right, so what is …" He looked at the way I was sitting. "Up your ass right now is the discharge nozzle for the fire extinguisher. And this," he pointed to the switch to the left of it, "is the fire extinguisher switch for suppressing the chemicals?"

I nodded as he pointed behind the seat. "And that's the fire extinguisher." He then pointed toward the dash in front of me explaining the switches from right to left. "This one here is the master switch. It shuts down the electrical system in an emergency. These," as he pointed to a cluster of switches, "are the auxiliary switches. They turn on the back up ignition system, ventilation fans, and my helmet cooling system." He paused placing his hand over the gearshift. "And this … is the …" Jameson licked his lip slowly and winked once. "Gearshift."

Now it was my turn to shift uncomfortably.

He then pointed to the dash in front of him. "This is the starter, ignition and cooling fans. This one is the engine gauge cluster that tells me the oil pressure, voltage, and fuel pressure." He moved on to the tachometer. "This one monitors my RPM, and then this switch shuts off the engine in an emergency situation."

I swallowed; this was *almost* too much to handle.

"And here, on the wheel, we have my radio button." His eyes scanned the cockpit for anything he hadn't explained yet, "Any questions?"

By now, I was panting and so was Jameson. I didn't realize anything besides my own excitement during his allocution, but this was turning him on just as much.

His head tipped back against the seat. "Come over here, honey." He rasped in a thick gravelly voice.

Eagerly, I tried to shimmy my way over there all sexy-like, but it didn't go down that way; in fact, it looked rather ridiculous from the outside.

There were switches, roll bars, a gearshift, a fire extinguisher, and random shit everywhere.

Eventually, I was able to get close to him after he removed the steering wheel and tossed it on the dash.

Just as hot and bothered as me, he was grabbing me in any way he could. And though it was also frustrating that we couldn't really maneuver very well, it was incredibly erotic, providing an alluring temptation that was within reach but couldn't be achieved.

"Goddamn it," Jameson grumbled against my lips when he couldn't get me close enough. The poor boy was grunting, pushing, pulling, tugging, anything he could do to get me closer.

My fingers inched to him following a path along his leg. I had other plans when I slowly unzipped his jeans. "I have something in mind."

His eyes shot up to mine. "What are you ...?" his voice trailed off as his eyes widened in surprise. "Oh ..."

"This is going to be difficult, but I need this," I gestured south with a nod. "In my mouth ... right now."

"*Fuck* ..." Jameson cried out slowly pulling his jeans and boxers down, revealing himself to me.

I've only handed out a few camshaft micro polishings in my time (which is a thorough cleaning of the camshaft to keep from thrust failure—which would be horrible by the way), and I'd never finished one or given one to such a monstrous shaft before. Though I was terrified, I decided to go with it and try.

After sneaking a quick glance at Jameson's lust stricken eyes, I lowered my head in his lap and darted my tongue out to taste him. Jameson took a sharp intake of breath, arching his back slightly and raising his hips when I did that.

Just do it, Sway, don't be scared of the colossal shaft staring at you. Just do it.

After my Nike pep talk with the perverse pit lizard within me, I lowered my mouth, slowly wrapping my lips around him. There was no way I'd be able to get all of him in my mouth, so my hand had to assist.

His camshaft was perfect.

Seriously, though, if he weren't so good at racing, I'd think he could have a job modeling this flawless member. I felt drunk on his scent alone, the taste and the feel of him inside me.

"Jesus Christ, honey, you're amazing ... *God* ... don't stop," he groaned. His eyes focused on my ministrations as he moved my hair aside for a better look—the other hand was on a roll bar gripping it tightly.

I don't think he would have let me stop at that point. And I didn't as I drew him back in, grazing my teeth gently along his sensitive skin. I bobbed, I swirled, I stroked, and I licked.

I could tell by the way he was moaning my name over and over again, that he was close. There was no more dirty heathen talking, there was no more teasing. It was breathless moans of pleasure, pleasure I was causing.

Hot damn!

I was on a mission, and I'd finally found something that made Jameson Riley speechless. Well, aside from him moaning my name, but that seemed to be the only word he could form, so he threw his head back and held on, his hips squirming and lifting to meet my stroking and sucking.

I don't know what our newfound fascination with race cars was, but I wasn't about to complain. I will say that trying to give someone a good micro polishing in a race car that only had one seat and a shit-load of obstacles in the way was extremely difficult; in fact damn near impossible.

What was even more impossible ... getting some alone time on a race weekend.

"Jameson, are you in here?" Alley called into the garage when she opened the door that was not more than ten feet from the car we were currently in.

During the race weekend, the cars were held inside the garage area under lock down. Being in here wasn't even legal and neither was the public display we were putting on.

Just another embarrassing situation to add to my dossier.

It wasn't lost on me that it was damn near three in the morning so why she was looking for him wasn't really a concern, but it did cross my mind. I stopped my bobbing but, of course, kept him in my mouth. What kind of pit lizard would I be if I let go?

"What are you ...?" Alley looked closer I'm sure.

Naturally, I couldn't tell, because once again, my head was buried. Only this time, I was in Jameson's lap, and my mouth was *still* wrapped around his camshaft assuring his thrust bearing wouldn't fail.

"Jesus, Jameson," Alley balked. "You're such a whore."

He laughed. "Let's face it, Alley, you've caught me in *worse* positions."

I was half-tempted to bite him because now I wanted to know what's *worse* than getting caught micro polishing in a race car.

Instead of biting, I decided to make this more awkward for him by continuing my efforts.

His hand flew back to my hair, trying to stop me, but I was determined you see.

"Whore!" Alley yelled and I assumed began to walk away by the shuffling. "Gordon wants to see you in the morning. Something about doing a burnout on the track …" she sighed loudly about the time Jameson threw his head back against the seat. "I don't even want to know how much you're going to get fined for that little stunt out there."

I don't think Alley was looking at him because when I snuck a peek at him, his head was leaned back and his eyes were closed.

"Are you even … Jameson … oh, *how disgusting*!" she wailed and stomped toward the door leaving both of us laughing, but the laughing didn't last long, especially with the vibration it created around him.

"My God," His hands flew to my face trying to pull me up. "Honey … you … I'm … *you* …" he moaned trying to pull me up again.

Shaking his hands away, I doubled my efforts causing him to give up and finally let go. His hips moved once, then again with a shudder and a scrumptious groan as Jameson let go completely. He tightened his grip on the roll bar and his hips jerked as I once again showed him just how skillful I was in the art of engine maintenance. All this, him, the noises he made, the feelings I was having were a pit lizard's dream come true—my dream come true.

Moments later, he pulled me up and I returned to getting to know the discharge nozzle.

Jameson sighed with a whoosh of breath shaking his head. "*Good Lord*, that was amazing."

I giggled at the admission and kissed his hand that was now on my cheek. "I couldn't help myself after that *ride*."

"I'll say."

"Do you think we will ever be able to have sex without being caught?"

Jameson gave me a lopsided grin, his cheeks flushed from the micro polishing.

"Where's the fun in that? Besides, now I have to get Alley back again." He waggled his eyebrows.

"So, are you in trouble with NASCAR now?"

"Uh, well not really, but the burn out ... that wasn't part of the deal I made with Gordon." He lifted his hips pulling his jeans up. "I probably shouldn't have done that," he said shrugging his shoulders once and then lifted himself up on the window to step out.

After he was out, I succeeded in getting untangled from the roll bars. I gave the discharge nozzle a little pat after our time spent together and hopped out of the car to lean against it as Jameson buttoned his jeans and fixed his t-shirt.

Once he was finished, he leaned into me, effectively trapping me against the side of the car once again. "So ... let's head back to my motor coach. I need to repay you," he whispered softly and then leaned in for a kiss.

"That's ... okay, you don't need to. Like I said, I'm sore."

"Silly Sway, no align boring needs to take place for me to repay the favor." He dropped to his knees in front of me, his eyes rose to meet mine through his long thick lashes. "I'm fairly certain this crankcase needs some proper deburring."

Good Lord, that has to be the sexiest thing he does.

Lifting my shirt, he kissed along the band of my jeans, his fingertips dipping inside.

Now as nice as the hood of the race car was the other night, I still remember the sticker burn my ass currently had and if we dented that hood again, Kyle would kill us.

As it was, they already had to steal the hood from the back-up and put it on the primary car. And let's not forget the incredibly awkward conversation with Jimi about *how* the hood was dented in the first place *or* the questioning glances from the rest of his team.

"Jameson," I moaned when he unbuttoned my jeans and swept his tongue along my hipbone. "Not here. Let's go back to your motor coach." I managed to get him back on his feet. "Wait, where are Alley and Spencer staying?"

I didn't want to get caught again, or for Alley to figure out I was who Jameson was being a whore with.

He laughed a loud, adorable laugh against my neck he was currently kissing, oh the kissing, he never stopped. When we were alone, his lips were never far from my skin.

"They're staying in Pocono. Alley probably just came back because I'm sure Lisa called. Gordon probably didn't tell her he told me I could take you for a ride," he assured me.

His hand reached out to tap my ass leading me outside.

Hopping on his back, we made our way back to his private motor coach in the drivers' compound.

Leaning my head down to kiss his neck, I whispered against his cool skin, "Since we'll be alone ... *you* might want to prepare yourself for a long night."

Jameson nodded his head in approval, his eyes dancing with excitement. "Sleep's overrated," and without missing a beat he spun me around so I was in front of him, legs still wrapped securely around his waist, "And honey," he leaned in to give me an ardent kiss, "You *should* prepare yourself."

Heat Cycle – When tires are heated, and then cooled down, it's gone through a heat cycle. When it goes through a heat cycle, the tire compound will harden, which can make the tire perform at a higher level for a longer period of time.

The next morning, I woke up to the sound of Spencer's laughter. Not necessarily a *bad* sound to wake up to, but I didn't want to wake up in the first place. Jameson was draped around me like his last victory flag, which wasn't a surprise. Since we started this *friends with benefits*, we'd barely gotten any sleep and were seeing a lot of benefits as friends.

Tangled in skin, there I was lying underneath Jameson, naked, listening to Spencer tell Aiden about how he once snorted powdered sugar for a quarter when he was five.

With wide justifiable eyes, I examined my surroundings.

Jameson's motor coach was a complete disaster. We went back there after the ride and made sure we made use of the alone time on the couch, in the tiny bathroom, in the bedroom, on the floor and up against the walls.

With only a few feet separating each motor coach in the drivers' compound, I'm amazed no one called security on us.

Furniture was broken, sheets were ripped from the bed, and the mattress was half on the bed and half off, leaving us on the only section that remained stable.

Beside me, there was a pillow that somehow was torn, leaving feathers all over the place, and our clothes were scattered throughout the forty-five foot motor coach. I could *actually* see my bra spinning around on the ceiling fan—talk about a wild night.

The alone time seemed to be over with by the sounds of all the commotion going on outside. Either that or security was waiting for us.

I tried to move thinking I was actually going to suffocate any minute if I didn't free some part of my body. The only problem, I couldn't move. Body parts were tangled in every direction sealed together by sweat. His body was like fire and he was heavy—really heavy.

Jameson began to stir a few moments later, groggy but stirring.

His head lifted to look up at me. "Jesus," he glanced around and then frowned at our bodies. "Can you even move now without pulling a muscle?"

Freeing one arm from underneath him, I giggled. "Probably not."

"Fuck, I have to get to practice ... but," he started kissing the other arm that he was still lying on, "I don't wanna get up."

And he didn't get up. Instead, he moved his hips against my leg and then positioned himself between my legs, reaping in *his* determined benefits.

"Again?" I asked with a slight giggle and then a sneeze when a lone feather tickled my nose. "Is the door locked?" I rolled him onto his back straddling his hips, a position I'd become accustomed to lately.

Jameson gave me a lopsided grin, his eyes sparkling with desire. "Yeah, I locked it last night." His voice had a certain drawl that made it sound gravelly and *incredibly* sexy.

Another hour later, I was getting dressed in the bathroom when I heard the door to Jameson's motor coach open.

"Jameson, have you seen Sway?" Alley asked Jameson who was out in the living room portion of the motor coach. "I can't find her?"

I was hoping Jameson had gotten his own clothes back on. That wasn't the case when she said, "Jesus, Jameson," I could literally hear her roll her eyes. "Put your fucking pants on. The last thing I want to see is *you* naked again."

That would be a no on the clothes, and now I knew what he was referring to the other night about catching him in *a worse position*.

"I thought I locked that," Jameson grumbled. I could hear him scrambling around putting his clothes on.

"Well, you—" her voice cut off when she heard a loud bang coming from the bathroom ... me.

Apparently, and though I knew this already, I was not being sneaky, *still*.

In my attempt to get dressed faster, I stumbled and knocked over the shampoo bottle that was on the sink, sending it flying into the granite shower stall, not at all sneaky.

Fuck, Fuck, Fuck!

"Who's in there?" Alley asked.

"None of your fucking business is *who's* in there!" Jameson barked back at her. "Get out."

I could tell by the pitch of his voice he was starting to get annoyed that everyone kept walking in on us. "Who are you calling?"

"Sway," Alley snapped at him. "Why do you care?"

Where is my cell phone?

Shit on a shingle ... I was screwed. My cell phone was in Jameson's motor coach, on Jameson's nightstand, next to Jameson's bed, where Jameson's sheets, pillows, *and* mattress looked like an F5 tornado touched down, *and* it was ringing.

Damn it, I knew I should have put it on vibrate.

I was cut off rather abruptly from my internal worrying by Alley. "Tell *Sway*, I was looking for her when she comes out of the bathroom."

The door slammed behind her followed by a loud thud of what I assumed was Jameson throwing something at the door.

Slowly, I peeked my head out the door spotting Jameson sitting on the couch putting his racing shoes on.

"So ... Alley knows, huh?" I asked standing against the counter in the kitchen a few moments later.

Again, he didn't say anything as he tied his shoes.

He looked pissed. Watching his quick brisk movements as he yanked on the strings tightly, my pissed theory was confirmed.

"Are you mad?"

He didn't say anything for a moment, his eyes focused on the floor but eventually he did speak. "I'm tired of everyone walking in on us." His tone was off, and I knew then there was something more to this than people walking in on us.

"Is that all?"

Taking in a slow, controlled deep breath, he leaned back against the couch, running his fingers through his hair once. His hair stood on end in the wake as his hands flopped down in frustration. "I just … why is it such a big deal that Alley *not* know about us?" He sounded offended that I would want to keep this from them. "Are you ashamed?" Sighing, he reached for his cell phone beside him as though he'd said something he didn't intend to say.

Momentarily, I stood there until my brain caught up.

"Uh … I … she …" I sat down beside him trying not to look at him in fear he'd see through my paper thin skin when it came to him. "She warned me to stay away from you because they think I'm going to get my heart broken."

Jameson nodded tightly. "Do you think that?" he asked softly, not looking at me and if I didn't know any better, I'd think he wasn't even paying attention by the way he focused all his attention on the phone in his hand, but I also knew better.

Be tough, Sway! Don't get emotional now; be tough.

I smiled ruefully at him hoping he didn't see the sadness. "Why would I think that … we're just friends with benefits?"

That didn't sound very convincing.

His eyes shifted to me and then dropped quickly to his phone. "Right," he mumbled with another cold nod.

Nervous I gave myself away completely, I started to fidget.

After a moment, Jameson tossed his phone on the couch, stood, and pulled his racing suit over his shoulders zipping it. "Well, it's none of their fucking business if we're humping anyway," he said giving me a wink. His expression didn't match the gesture, though. It seemed almost, forced.

"Humping, really? Are you like twelve years old?" I teased attempting to lighten the situation with humor. After all, he was doing the same.

"Whatever," he pulled me up from the couch against his chest. "Wish me luck."

"For what?" I wrapped my arms around his waist, savoring the content feeling I got when I was wrapped around him.

"Practice," he said kissing me. "My car is shit."

"Eh, you'll do fine. Besides, what we did last night gave it good luck."

"If I win, you may need to repeat that *every* weekend. You sure you can handle that?" He gave me a wicked grin, his eyes watching mine intently.

"That would *suck* for me," I replied with lewdness.

Jameson leaned forward; his lips finding my neck, then my jaw and then back to my lips. "*Suck,* indeed," he mumbled drawing my bottom lip inside his mouth, sucking gently.

After a few more kisses and inappropriate groping, Jameson left for practice so I sent Emma a text to find out where she was.

Emma sent me back a text saying she was at Jameson's merchandise hauler near the grandstands unloading shirts so I decided to make my way over there.

Just as I stood to leave, Spencer came crashing through the door.

"Oh, hey, I didn't think anyone was in here." He grinned looking around. "What are *you* doing in here?" he asked suspiciously, his blue eyes full of amusement.

"None of your business," I snapped pulling a sweatshirt from my bag on the floor.

"What are you two doing?" Spencer stepped closer to nudge my shoulder playfully. "I know something is going on. He smiles now."

"Nothing is going on—we're friends."

"Naked friends."

"Shut up," I told him annoyed that I was even talking to him about this.

He shook his head, smirking. "Denial ..." His eyes focused on the bedroom. "What in the hell happened in here? It looks like a pack of wild animals were let loose in here."

Wild animals ... it didn't look that bad here.

Spencer reached for my bra that was still on the ceiling fan. "Do you need this?" He spun it around on his finger.

Jesus Christ, how many mortifying experiences can one person have in the span of a week?

I snatched it away from him; he smirked like Jameson.

"Fuck off!" I shouted and locked myself in the bathroom again.

"You're not fooling anyone!" Spencer yelled after me.

Thankfully, the shithead left so I finally came out of the bathroom.

Before I even made it twenty feet outside the motor coach, I saw Chelsea with a tall red-headed woman approaching me.

Don't look at them, don't look, pretend you don't see them.

"Sway," Chelsea chided in that nasally obnoxious voice that I despised so deeply. "You're still around ... I thought for sure Jameson would have sent you home by now."

They both stopped directly in front of me, looking taller than ever in their heels. I looked like a midget next to them in my worn out gray flip-flops.

Who wears heels to a racetrack anyway?

To me, personally, with the way everything is spread-out, heels are the worst choice possible. And after Charlotte, the blisters on my feet could attest to that.

"Chelsea," I greeted and turned toward the red-haired woman. "I don't think we've met." I reached for the red-head's hand. She raised a perfectly manicured eyebrow at me. "I'm Sway."

"Sway?" her brow furrowed. "That's a ... strange name."

"Yeah, well, my parents had a thing for the Rolling Stones back in the day. Too much reefer maybe."

"Rolling Stones? How does that have anything to do with your name?"

"It's a song," I told her still holding my hand at bay. "And you are?"

Reluctantly she reached my hand. "Mariah," she answered through pursed plump lips.

Oh great, another beautiful woman, wait a second ... Mariah?

"Oh," I said loudly, my eyes widening. "You're Chelsea's lover. *Wow*, you two make such a cute couple." I stood there amused with myself. "I've heard so much about you, Mariah. It's nice that you two could find each other."

"Jesus!" Chelsea sighed dramatically. "We're not a couple, Sway."

"No, no, no." I waved my hand around dismissively. "It's okay; you don't have to hide it." I smiled because by both their livid expressions that I implied they were lesbians had them so pissed and me happy.

Job well done, Sway.

"Well, I need to be going, Jameson needs me." I smiled again clapping my hands together in front of my face. "You two look *so* happy together." I all but skipped away to the merchandise trailers.

That was so worth it.

Once at Jameson's merchandise trailer, I was conveniently greeted by Alley of all people.

Regrettably, for me, I couldn't help the way I was walking and it didn't go unnoticed. My ass hurt so bad from the sticker burn and my crankcase … well that was another story all together. Her and her goddamn justifications got us into this to begin with.

"Good morning, sunshine," I chimed as cheerfully as possible.

Alley glanced over her shoulder at the way I was walking toward them, her eyes probing as she examined me. "I'm surprised you can even walk after the way that motor coach looked." Her tone was sour.

"Actually," I tugged on the back of my shorts. "It wasn't the motor coach that was the worst. It's the sticker burn I got from the hood of his race car."

"Wow!" Alley rolled her eyes. "I warned you once, and I won't say it again. If you get hurt, don't come crying to me." She handed Emma a box, though her eyes remained focused on me.

Emma stood there looking in between us both wondering what the hell was going on.

"Why is it such a big deal to everyone what we do with each other?" I asked, getting annoyed that everyone cared so much if we were, using Jameson's term, *humping.*

Alley threw her arms up in the air. "Because, Sway," her expression changed, softened, "You're *our* friend, too. I've known you as long as I've known him. If this doesn't work, and I doubt that it will, not only does Jameson lose his best friend, but we do, too."

I felt my face crumble at her words. "I wouldn't do that to you guys."

"I warned you because Jameson has no clue what's going on, he can't see it. And, at this point, I'm not sure that you can either."

Why does everyone keep saying that?

Before I could ask her, Alley's phone rang.

She glared down at the screen. "*Great*, Gordon's calling." After a moment of silence and more listening, she hung up without so much as a goodbye.

"See," she held out her phone. "That little stunt you guys pulled last night has Jameson being called to the principal's office."

I just rolled my eyes.

Jameson wouldn't care, and neither did I. That was one hell of a ride and worth it to me. After his reaction to the micro polishing, I'm sure he felt the same way.

Jameson was still on the track when I made it down to pit lane and stepped on the pit box next to Kyle. Mason sat on the other side of him focused on the laptop in front of him as he entered data.

Kyle looked furious obsessively clicking a pen in his hand, his knuckles white.

"What's up?" I asked, almost scared to know.

Kyle pulled his headset aside handing me the spare set next to him. "Darrin is all over him out there," he hollered over the rumble of the cars and then positioned the headset back against his ears. "I know. There's not much I can do. Hang in there."

Once I adjusted my own headset, immediately I heard a fuming Jameson coming through the scanner.

"What the fuck? I mean ... *Christ Almighty,* this is practice, not the goddamn race. Why is he crowding me?"

"Middle two, middle one, clear low ... four car high, fourteen low on the inside ... at your door ... at your rear ... clear," Aiden announced as Jameson passed Darrin again coming out of turn one.

We couldn't see but we could follow him watching ESPN on the laptop that Kyle had opened.

They were all over this with the media. The series point leader and the second place car battling in practice was a headliner for sure, probably just as good as the headlines after the Winston.

Just the few laps I'd been watching of this, they seemed to be playing this cat and mouse game with each other.

One would lead, then the other before Darrin would slide up the track on him and purposely take his line forcing him to run another. Which would have been fine, it's practice after all, but as soon as Jameson found another line and gave Darrin room, Darrin would hang back and find him again.

"Kyle," Jameson's voice was less than thrilled. "Go talk to Frank. I wanna see what his goddamn problem is. If he bumps me one more time, I'm slamming his ass in the wall," Jameson warned. "I'm not gonna take this shit much longer."

"Calm down," Kyle told him trying to ease his frustrations, but really, there was no use now.

Once Jameson got riled up, it was pretty much impossible to calm him down. You just had to wait for the storm to pass.

"Don't tell me to calm down, Kyle!" Jameson snapped back. "It's bad enough I'm fishtailing all over the fucking place, but now I got him all over me. I can't keep the car straight. We're lucky I haven't wadded it up already."

"Mason went to talk to Frank," Kyle replied and then threw the clipboard across the pit box. It smashed against a pile of tires on the ground beside us.

I asked Kyle, "That bad eh?" as he busied himself looking over the lap times and the last adjustments they made to the car, tugging at his hair in frustration.

Everything was kept electronically in the team's laptop so that they could immediately decipher lap times, fuel mileage and adjustments they had made to the car. That way, if they made an adjustment that didn't work; they could document it and know the result the adjustment had.

Kyle sighed shaking his head. His eyes rose to meet mine as he pointed to the screen in front of him. "Jameson's right." I watched the screen closely with him. "The car is all over the place. We made a spring adjustment but it's still off." Kyle motioned with his hand gesturing how the car would move up the track on Jameson. "When he drives into the corner, it wants to come around on him. That's *exactly* when Darrin gets on him." He flicked his hand in disgust toward the screen. "He's trying to make him crash."

"Cole, you copy?" Jameson asked.

"10-4, what's up?" Bobby replied. "I see you got your hands full up there."

"Where the fuck are you? Help me out up here."

"I'm about two seconds behind you." I could see Bobby coming out of turn four. "I'm pulling off though. I got a flat right front."

"Well fuck," Jameson scoffed. "That's just *great*."

Kyle got back on the radio again after entering some data in the computer and talking to Mason. "Bring it in. We need to make some adjustments to the springs," he told him. "I want to try putting a wedge in the rear springs and make a track bar adjustment. Tony wants to change the air pressure in the rear tires as well."

Jameson slowed coming out of turn three to make his way onto pit lane when Darrin clipped his right rear corner and spun him.

Jameson tried to correct it, and did at first, but the car came back around on him and sent him into the inside wall.

Both Kyle and I jumped up in the pit box to get a better look.

His car was smashed against the inside wall entering pit lane.

It was junk. There was no way *that* car was racing in Sunday's race.

"You okay, Bud?" Kyle asked.

Jameson didn't respond. He was already ripping his gear away. We could now see him pull himself from the car, tearing hoses off and throwing his gloves and helmet inside the car.

The paramedics were over there trying to get him to get in the aide car, but he was refusing.

Kyle yanked me forward. "Come on, I know what he's about to do."

Yeah well, I knew, too.

In instances like this, Jameson reacted first and then thought later, always had.

After today, it wasn't lost on anyone that Darrin Torres had never heard of the "Gentlemen's Agreement" in NASCAR.

There are written rules that you abide by as a driver and enforced strictly by NASCAR and its officials.

Then you have the unspoken rules, usually enforced by the veteran drivers, though all drivers are *expected* to follow them. And honestly, most veteran drivers have no problem letting a rookie driver know about the "Gentlemen's Agreement" when *they* feel *they've* forgotten.

The rules were simple really: If you're a lapped car, give room to the leaders. If you're a lapped car, don't block and don't challenge the leader. When bump drafting, use caution and never bump in draft through a corner. And finally, race with respect during practice, it was practice after all, not the race.

Like I said, Darrin had obviously never heard of this.

Kyle and I had just made it back to the garage area when we saw Jameson leaning inside Darrin's car trying to pull him out while Spencer and Aiden were in Darrin's crew chief, Frank's, face.

Kyle ran up to Jameson while I trailed close behind him. Kyle grabbed him by his racing suit, but with how angry Jameson was right then, it was going to take more than Kyle to pull him away. His expression was livid and like a bull, his chest heaved with deep breaths.

I grasped; this wasn't the right moment but I kind of giggled to myself at how he was acting like a bull in that moment which included his sexual stamina—ironic, huh?

"Get out of the car!" Jameson roared at Darrin who was currently taking his helmet off to get out of the car. "What the fuck was that?"

"You better be ready to finish the fight if you start one Riley," Darrin warned pulling himself from the car ready to throw down it seemed.

Before either of them could get to each other, and most of their team, two NASCAR officials were dragging them apart. News reporters hovered everywhere eating this up along with Chelsea and Mariah standing on the other side of Darrin's garage bay.

"I'm ready to finish this right now." Jameson pushed past Spencer throwing his arms up taunting. "C'mon Darrin, I'm right here. Let's see what you got," he added trying to provoke him further; not that it was really needed.

You could tell Darrin wanted to take the first swing but with a

NASCAR official standing there, he lowered his arm reluctantly.

"See you on Sunday, Riley," he replied curtly and turned to walk away with the rest of his team that had gathered around.

"Don't start something you can't finish," Jameson advised using Darrin's previous words against him.

When Jameson turned to me, it wasn't hard to understand the now malevolent grin he had plastered across his face. I knew then what Darrin was stirring up in Jameson, and I had a feeling Darrin was about to see a side of Jameson he never saw coming.

Alley was immediately in his face. "*You* and Darrin are wanted in the NASCAR hauler."

NASCAR hauled around a big red hauler where you were summoned if you'd been bad. This wasn't the first time Jameson had to go there to discuss his on the track conduct. And though he wasn't really a frequent flyer, they didn't call him "Rowdy Riley" for nothing.

Jameson shook off Kyle and Spencer and began walking at me, his unmoving eyes trained ahead. "Come with me, Sway." He grabbed me by the hand.

I was being dragged around a lot today.

On the way to the hauler, a reporter with ESPN shoved a microphone right in Jameson's face as he was trying to walk. "Jameson, we saw that you and Darrin had an altercation back there and on pit road. Can you tell us what happened?"

Jameson kept walking, but answered with brusqueness. "I don't know what happened," he told him unwilling to stop. "He was all over me during practice and when I pulled onto pit road, he spun me. I just wanted to see what his problem was."

Before Jameson could say any more, Alley was beside us advising him to keep his mouth shut.

"Decline to comment," she told him pushing him forward.

"They only want the truth," Jameson snapped, jerking away from her. "I'll give 'em the goddamn truth!"

I wasn't sure what to say to him so I said the first thing that came to mind, "Are you okay?" Alley walked away toward the hauler leaving us alone.

He huffed, turning to glare at me while we continued walking. "I just wrecked the car during practice." He threw his arms up in the air. "Now, my team has to get the back-up car ready to go before qualifying in two hours. So, yeah, I'm *fucking* great, Sway."

"Jesus," I balked. "Why did you ask me to come with you if you're going to talk to me like that?"

Jameson snorted. "I just ... look ..." He stopped walking and turned to me. "I'm sorry—I didn't mean to take it out on you."

I nodded, feeling myself close to tears. There were people walking around us, so I knew this was no time for us to be having an argument. But I also didn't appreciate this being taken out on me.

Jameson noticed as I was abruptly brought tightly against his side as he whispered in my ear. "I *really* am sorry. I'm just pissed that my team is the one suffering from this because Darrin is an asshole and seems to have something to prove."

I nodded again.

"You go ahead. I'm going to wait at your hauler."

Without another look, I turned and walked to the hauler where the crew was unloading the back-up car with the dented hood.

Jameson always reacted like this when angry. Anger first, lucidity later. I doubted that would ever change, so I never took it personally. It was just him—he didn't mean anything by it.

Not that it was okay to treat people like that, but I knew he needed to simmer down before he said something he'd regret.

With Jameson, he put everything he had into racing, and when someone threatened that, he reacted the only way he knew how. The only way I could describe this to someone was comparing it to a mother and their child. It's the exact same instincts for him.

If you understood his passion for racing, you'd understand his reactions.

Back at the hauler, everyone was hard at work preparing the back-up car for qualifying. Jimi was there now but wouldn't be staying since he had a race in Knoxville tonight.

"Where's Jameson?" I heard him ask Alley.

"Where else ... the NASCAR hauler," Alley answered, her Blackberry attached to her ear once again. "He'll be back any minute."

"Oh goddamn him," Jimi grumbled walking toward Kyle and Mason who were changing out the hoods. "Is he trying to set some sort of record for the amount of times he's in there this year?"

Gentry nudged me nodding his head at the hood.

"Shut up." I backhanded his shoulder. "Don't you have work to do?"

He never answered, just smiled twirling a wrench in his hand.

Gentry, was the type of guy who loved to make you squirm with embarrassment, kind of like Kyle and Spencer.

Let's just say he fit in well with these goons.

"What did he do this time?" Jimi asked looking to us for an answer.

"I didn't do anything," I heard Jameson's even tone coming from behind me. "Darrin started it," he answered sharply and began assisting the crew.

He still seemed angry, but his mood improved when he walked past me and winked.

Why am I so turned on by winking?

"*Jesus Christ*, Jameson," Jimi was pacing back and forth by now, as Alley filled him in. "I swear you need anger management."

"Do not." Jameson barked from under the hood but didn't look up.

"He's also being fined five thousand for that little stunt he pulled last night on the track," Alley added.

"What?" Jimi yelled over the shrill of the engine they'd just started.

Even now, Jameson didn't look up, but it wasn't hard to see the smile when he snuck a quick peek at me.

What was I doing?

Giggling.

"*What* stunt on the track?" Jimi growled at Jameson.

"It was nothing," Jameson eluded with a shrug.

Jimi wasn't accepting *that* as an answer so Jameson continued, "I took Sway for a ride around the track. I cleared it with Gordon first," he defended. "But ... I did a burn out. *Apparently*, I wasn't supposed to."

"You did what?" Jimi scorned—his face flushed with anger. "What would you have done if you wrecked out there? You could have killed her."

"I didn't though."

"You *never* think about anybody but yourself, do you?" Jimi was in Jameson's face; the rest of us watched their disagreement.

This happened often and usually ended with one, or both of them, yelling and then walking away.

Jameson threw the hammer he had in his hand against the back of the hauler. "Don't *ever* question my concern for Sway's safety!" he yelled in his dad's face. "I was careful."

Air tools and hammers seized as the paddock silenced.

Everyone stopped what they were doing and gaped at them, standing within inches of each other.

I knew Jameson would never actually hit Jimi, but I questioned it a time or two. Now was one of those instances.

Jimi shook his head, and backed away from Jameson. "I have a plane to catch." He turned sharply and walked away. This *also* happened often. "Try to stay out of trouble for one damn weekend."

Jameson ran his hand across the back of his neck and then looked my direction. Again, I didn't know what to do so I winked at him. Girls could wink, right?

I didn't expect it given his mood, but he winked back before turning to his torn up race car.

Emma walked up and sat down next to me outside the hauler. "Come shopping with me, I'm bored."

"And miss *this* excitement, not a chance." I leaned back in the chair and watched my hot head at work. It was almost as good as watching him drive the car last night.

"What happened?" Emma asked motioning to the car.

The crew and Jameson were frantically changing out the engine.

"Darrin wrecked him when he was entering pit road," I answered still staring at Jameson who was now bent over the fender providing me with a wonderful view.

"Seriously?"

I nodded, my eyes focused ahead.

"What an asshole!" She looked down at her phone in her lap and then grinned. "I heard you called Chelsea and Mariah lesbians."

I whipped my head around. "How'd you know about that?"

"Dana."

"Who's Dana?"

"Another pit lizard in love with Jameson."

"What? How did I not know about her?"

Emma waved her hand around dismissively. "She's harmless, a little crazy, but ostensibly harmless. She doesn't come around him though after Las Vegas. He found her in his motor coach one night and ended up calling the police on her because she refused to leave."

I laughed. "I would have liked to see that."

"Watch this." Emma's once amused smile took on a wicked edge. "Jameson?" she chimed toward him.

Jameson didn't look up but grunted, "What?" as he tightened bolts down.

"Dana says hello."

Slowly, he looked up at her, the color drained from his face as he stared at Emma with a wary expression.

We both burst into laughter, as did the rest of the crew working on the car. Emma was laughing so hard there were tears streaming down her face while she pointed at Jameson and laughed louder holding her stomach.

"Fuck all of you!" he shouted, slamming the door to the hauler.

Emma leaned closer. "The best part was she stole a pair of his underwear when she was in there." She burst into laughter yet again.

None of us saw Jameson again until it was his turn to qualify.

Kyle went inside to let him know and then went down to the garage, leaving me the only one there at the hauler.

I wasn't sure what he did in there for two hours, but he appeared to have taken a nap as his hair was in complete disarray when he emerged. He walked over to me and sat down in the chair Emma had been sitting in to tie his shoes.

"I thought you would have come in there." His voice was thick from sleep.

"I thought you could use a nap, and I was spending some time with Emma. She left to go get some dinner with Aiden."

Jameson accepted them being together, but it didn't mean he liked it by the look on his face.

"So you chose my sister over me?"

"You were being mean,"

"Was not," he argued.

"Oh, sorry, you were being such a sweet guy," I teased with a smile, rubbing his shoulder.

"That's better. Now …" He picked me up from my chair and set me on his lap. "I have to go qualify but after that …" The tip of his nose swept along my neck sending tingles down my legs. "I'd like to take you somewhere." He nuzzled me more, his face scratchy. His other hand slipped up the back of my shirt and traced circles over my bare skin.

"I have to check my schedule."

Jameson leaned back giving me a warning look. "*His* determined benefits, remember?" He arched an eyebrow.

"Wow, I don't even know what to say to that."

"Don't say anything, just go with me." He didn't give me a chance to respond before he was dragging me with him toward pit lane again.

Qualifying went better than practice. Jameson was surprised to find the back-up car was better than the primary car and ended up qualifying fourth for Sunday's race.

After taking a quick shower and putting on some shorts, we made our way to town.

Jameson refused to tell me where he was taking me. I asked if I needed to change out of my jean shorts and flip-flops, but he assured me I was dressed accordingly.

"Where are we going now?" I asked sometime after we picked up Chinese to go and got back in the truck.

He leaned his head back against the seat and slowly looked over at me. With a grin he said, "Somewhere alone, somewhere that I can have my way with you and *not* worry about someone walking in on us. Somewhere that I don't have to worry about breaking furniture or ... sticker burns."

"That only leaves this truck and the middle of nowhere."

"Exactly." He nodded gesturing to the blankets he'd grabbed before we left.

"So we're going to hump in the woods and eat Chinese food."

"No." He grinned. "We are going to hump and *then* eat Chinese food. We're not doing it at the same time. I think there's some kind of health code against that."

I laughed, shaking my head at him.

Soon we found ourselves in a wooded area where there was a clearing and a beautiful view of Long Pond.

"This is amazing," I told him, climbing into the back of the truck.

Jameson had already laid out the blankets. "I came out here last year when I was racing in the Busch series," he told me pulling me onto his lap where he sat on the tailgate, the faint sounds of "Wicked Game" hummed over the stereo.

"Really," I gave a sidelong gaze at Jameson. "Who was the lucky girl?"

He let out a soft chuckle against my shoulder he was kissing. "I told you, I haven't been with anyone in over a year. I came out here by myself. In fact, I actually spent the night texting you from this exact location."

I couldn't say anything to that.

What would I say?

He didn't give me a chance to think about it before he turned me around so I was straddling his hips, my legs wrapped around his waist. His lips skimmed along my collarbone and then back again before he removed my tank top as the song continued.

How could one song fit our situation so perfectly?

I was stumbling through this, falling deeper in love with this man, yet he remained clueless.

He honestly had no clue how madly in love I was, or did he? I had no idea how he felt—his guarded expressions gave me nothing.

"You're so beautiful, honey," he whispered before leaning in for the most passionate kiss I think I'd ever had.

When he pulled back to look at me his expression changed, softened even. His mouth opened as though he wanted to say something but he didn't, he just stared back at me with his hand rested against my cheek.

I wanted to say so much in that moment—it seemed fitting.

I wanted to tell him how much I loved him and how much I've always loved him, but just like him, I didn't say anything, I just gazed back at him. I could feel myself nearing tears so I leaned in kissing him again, and then removed his shirt.

Jameson laid back against the bed of the truck closing his eyes. I skimmed my fingers across the muscles in his chest, down the ripples in his stomach to the sharp lines of his hips.

Rocking my hips against him once, the friction of our clothing caused him to moan as he grabbed my hips securely with his hands, moving me the way he wanted.

I took everything he gave me that night, knowing I was falling deeper and deeper into whatever this was between us, but I also couldn't make myself care.

This was fun, this was exciting, and this was us.

Everything with Jameson and me was always so simple and easy that I couldn't think of a reason why this couldn't be, too.

There was a change occurring, I knew that. But I lived for the moment and enjoyed the simplicity of the undefined.

I knew the nagging feeling was an omen of what was to come, but I couldn't for the life of me stop.

7

Air Pressure – **You can adjust a car's handling
by raising or lowering air pressure in the tires.
There's a certain amount of flex in the sidewall
of a tire that acts like another spring in the
suspension. Increasing the air pressure will make
the spring rate higher. Lowering it makes the tire
softer.**

      The next morning, standing there staring at myself in a full-length mirror was a sight to see. My hair resembled Rob Zombie's; I had no idea how I was going to get those knots out. Seriously, it was some sort of cross between the frolic in the sheets and dreads. Nothing about it was sexy, though.

      My body *actually* had bruises on my upper arms, hipbones, *and* my ass. I couldn't remember a point when his grasp on me was too tight but it must have been, judging by the bruises.

      Jesus, you've been manhandled.

      Eh, I'm not complaining, it was a good time, bruises or not.

      I tried to remember how many times we'd bumped "uglies" in the past few days, but I honestly couldn't tell you.

      It wasn't really important to me, so I shrugged to myself and stepped inside the shower. It felt so good to finally take a hot shower.

      Rolling my sore neck around, the jets soaked blissfully over back. I was incredibly tender and aching everywhere from sleeping in the back of a pick-up truck last night, not that we really slept, but I was still uncomfortable. Not only would I require a therapist when these three weeks were up, but a massage therapist was beginning to pull rank as well.

Besides being small, his bathroom was luxurious. It had everything you would need and then some with the cream tile floors, black granite counters, glass shower door and mirrors everywhere. It's nicer than most people's homes—including mine. Not that I have a home of my own; I still lived with Charlie but this was *way* nicer than Charlie's house and a fucking mansion compared to that dorm I had lived in.

Once I stepped out of the shower, I heard some commotion outside so I opened the door thinking Jameson had returned from the drivers' meeting and could hand me a towel since I forgot.

Without thinking, I stepped outside completely naked. "Jameson, can you hand me a towel ..." My voice trailed off when I ran into him. "Oh, hey, is there a towel over there?" I asked but when my eyes met his, they weren't his.

"OH MY GOD!" I screamed, but Spencer screaming like a four-year-old girl and covering his eyes silenced my screams.

"I thought it was Jameson in here, not you!" He cried out tossing a towel my direction.

"Jesus Christ, Spencer," I wailed just as loud trying to cover myself with my hands. It would have worked if I had three hands, but I didn't. "You didn't think to knock?"

"What the fuck is going on in here?" Jameson asked from behind Spencer, his voice a blistering snarl as he stepped inside the motor coach, slamming the metal door. I never heard the door open but how could I with the volume of Spencer's screams?

Now let me take a moment here to really explain how this would look to Jameson.

I was standing next to the bathroom door, *completely naked* with my girly bits on display because when Spencer threw the towel, he was so freaked out that I *wasn't* Jameson, he didn't even throw it remotely close to me.

In fact, the towel was on my ceiling fan whipping around the room—and I say "my ceiling fan" because this particular ceiling fan, had housed a few of my undergarments in the past few days.

Spencer was now gaping between Jameson and me. Jameson, who was not even remotely amused, looked as though he was going to have a heart attack any second. Body shaking, fisted hands, he was a little worked up over this.

He *might* possibly kill Spencer.

"I ... I ... um ... shit," Spencer stammered, staring at me. "I thought it was you in here." He backed away holding his hands over his eyes. "I'm *so* sorry dude."

I will give Spencer credit, he really was trying not to look, but his hands kept coming away from his eyes so he could take a better look. He's a man; you couldn't blame him really.

I wanted to giggle, that's how inappropriate this whole situation was, but I decided that wouldn't be best given how worked up Jameson appeared.

"Spencer," Jameson growled slowly. "Get the fuck out *now!*"

I flinched at his furious tone.

Poor Spencer all but ran out of there, but before he got to the door, he reached for his hat, the whole purpose of him coming in here, but the hat was next to me. Naturally, Spencer looked at Jameson and back to me, wondering if he should just leave the hat.

"Spencer— GET OUT!" Jameson roared.

I swear the entire racetrack could have heard him. I actually covered my ears—it was *that* loud.

In the entire time I've known Spencer I have never seen him scared of Jameson, or anyone. Right now, he honestly looked terrified of him.

Once the door shut, Jameson reached for the towel on the ceiling fan and threw it my direction. "You might want to check who it is before you come out of the bathroom, *naked*. There's no privacy around here," his voice was low and bleak, but less furious. His eyes flickered to mine and then away. A moment later, his expression softened. "Please put some clothes on," he ordered walking out the door.

Well, that was interesting.

I know he had to get to driver introductions, but seriously ... I was naked. How can we *not* take advantage of that?

Oh, relax Sway. You just had sex less than four hours ago. It won't kill you.

Just as I turned around, the door flew open and Jameson stormed back in, locked the door, and started ripping his clothes off, stumbling around as he tried to rid them quickly.

When he got the majority ripped away, he stood there in front of me, breathing heavy. His eyes a dark jade color that smoldered with hunger. Reaching for the hem of his shirt, he pulled it over his head roughly, throwing it against the wall.

I didn't know what to do or say, so I just stood there watching.

Standing before me, naked, he finally spoke, "I couldn't just leave you in here, *naked,*" was his only response before he carried me toward the bedroom.

"I only have a few minutes," he grunted, pushing me up against the mirrored wall.

Facing the mirror, my chest smashed against it, they appeared larger. For someone who was barely a B-cup, this was a good thing.

"If you only have a few minutes, then you better stop looking at my boobs and fuck me."

His eyes narrowed at me and he winked. "Then hold on tight, honey." And then he flipped me around so my ass was pressed against the mirror and in the next second, he was sliding into me with a low fierce growl that actually gave me goose bumps.

The nice thing about a luxury Feather Lite motor coach was the mirrors. Now, with my back to the one mirror, I had a perfect vista view of Jameson's ass with my legs wrapped around his waist. If that wasn't a pit lizard's dream, I don't know what is.

This was another picture I wouldn't mind framing on the ceiling of my bedroom.

Jameson's hands gripped my ass, using the mirror to keep me firmly in place.

Never in my life had I ever thought a quickie would be considered one of the best sexual encounters I'd ever had, but *this*, was definitely in the top five now.

Jesus Christ, look at that ass, hard, round, muscular ... perfect.

I think I actually whimpered at that point shamelessly watching his ass flex with each thrust.

"I'm sorry ... I'm ..." his thick, gruff voice trailed when he tried to reach between us.

I knew what he was trying to do.

Capturing his hand with my own, I placed it back on my ass. "Only you." Wrapping my arms around his neck, I brought his mouth to mine.

That's all the encouragement he needed. He threw his head back and it was glorious, probably one of the best five minutes of my entire life.

Afterward, Jameson stayed there for a moment panting and kissing my lips, jaw, neck, and then my shoulders. "That was—"

"Amazing," I finished for him.

"I'll say." He smirked. "That wasn't very good for you though."

"Are you fucking kidding me?"

He looked surprised. "Huh?"

"That *was* hot!" I clarified pointing to the mirror behind him.

He glanced over his shoulder and then shook his head in amusement. "I feel ... like I should charge you for that now."

"I feel like I should pay you for it," I agreed and we both started laughing.

I looked around for my underwear while Jameson put his clothes back on. I found them on the nightstand, but again, they were ripped.

"Jameson," I held up the shredded underwear. "Stop doing this. I don't have any more underwear here."

He chuckled putting his Simplex hat on. "Ah ... it looks like Emma needs to take you shopping."

"I hate you for doing that to me," I grumbled in frustration.

The last thing I wanted to do was go shopping with *Emma*. I loved her but not enough to go anywhere near a department store, of any kind, with her.

"You don't hate me." He pulled me against his chest, his breathing still uneven. "I just gave you a *free* show."

"Whatever," I sulked, pulling away to put my jeans on without underwear.

Jameson watched me closely. "You're seriously out of underwear?"

"Yes, you asshole!" I held up the pieces of the black pair from last night. "These were the last pair since you ripped the other ten pairs I brought."

"You can't go commando," he stated firmly, as though it *wasn't* an option.

"What the hell do you expect me to do?"

His fingers raked through his hair. "I don't know." He threw his arms up. "I won't be able to concentrate if I know you have no underwear on. Put something on."

I was silent for a moment trying to think. "Fine, leave and then you won't know if I put some on or not."

He shook his head violently. "No, no, no," he quickly disagreed. "That makes it worse. Then I'll spend the entire race wondering if you're wearing any or not. You have to put something on."

"My God Jameson," I yelled and stomped over to his dresser to pull out a pair of his boxer briefs and slid them on, "Happy now?"

"Immensely!"

We left the motor coach after that with Jameson *immensely happy*, and me sporting his underwear.

As with any race weekend, the time just wasn't there and soon race activities were in full swing.

"Jameson, what do you think your chances are here for a win?" a reporter with SPEED asked him as we stood alongside his car prior to the start of the race.

"I think we have a shot at it, but it's hard to say. I didn't get a lot of practice time in this car since we crashed in practice yesterday. This Simplex Ford ran great in happy hour though. I think we could easily pull off a top five today." Jameson answered mechanically continuing to sign autographs for the swarm of fans huddled around his car on the grid.

I couldn't believe *how* many people were gathered around his car compared to the other drivers, yeah most of them were under twenty-five *and* female, but Christ Almighty this boy was popular.

You could barely move an inch without bumping into someone. I almost felt out of place, like I should have been asking for his autograph, but really, he gave me something better not more than an hour ago.

Jameson rarely looked up, just signed autograph after autograph. *I wonder if his hand ever got tired. I know something that never gets tired.*

The thought had me giggling next to him. With his head still down, his eyes darted over at me to see what I was giggling about.

Quickly, I looked away like I wasn't doing anything so he went back to signing his autographs.

One brave garage groupie was standing considerably closer than the rest and kept glancing at the way Jameson and I were standing together, I assumed. Either that or there was actually something wrong with her; no one stares that much.

But then when I thought about it, we were both leaning against the side of his car but what was even *more* obvious was the lack of space separating us.

The girl smiled looking at me. "Are you Jameson's girlfriend?" she asked diffidently, the corners of her mouth twitching into a wide smile.

Both Jameson and I looked up at her.

I choked on my own spit. Embarrassing I know, and Jameson chuckled at the shy girl's brashness.

Neither one of us answered, so she eventually left.

As I thought about what we were, what would I even say? Fuck buddies? The more I thought about it, the more I agreed with Jameson. It wasn't anyone's business what we were doing.

I found humor in another older gentleman hovering around for a good ten minutes asking random questions about the engine and what not. He had this handheld video camera with him, taping everything Jameson was doing.

It was actually a little creepy.

Eventually he said, "Say hi to the camera, Jameson."

Jameson finally looked up for a brief moment and then went back to signing autographs, his dark sunglasses covering his expression.

"Hi, camera," was his response, earning a chuckle from all the fans.

The strange man never left but continued trying to ask questions. "Hey, so can I ask you a question? I need to ask you a question."

Jameson looked up. "Ask the question then—I'm standing here," he snapped.

The guy never did ask a *direct* question and instead stood there astounded by the fact that Jameson actually spoke to him.

It was entertaining to me that here were people who were star-struck by my best friend, someone I've known nearly my entire life. It was a strange concept to grasp when you witnessed the rise to fame first-hand.

Reporter after reporter, fan after fan, hounded him prior to the race for autographs, handshakes, pictures, anything to take a piece of him away with them.

He handled it well. I could tell he was irritated but he did ... good.

I don't think it was ever the fans who aggravated him—it was the publicity of it all. Jameson was still a small-town boy at heart who wanted to race. All this media attention and the fans hanging on his every word were sometimes overwhelming for him. I honestly believe he handled it the *only* way he knew how.

Today was a little different though. When I say he handled it the only way he knew how, this usually involved his short temper getting the best of him.

Alley even noticed the change in his demeanor. "What's got him so calm? Usually he's told a reporter or fan to fuck off by now."

I shrugged; a heated blush crept up my neck to my cheeks.

Alley pushed me. "You're unbelievable." She looked down at her Blackberry. "I heard Spencer got a good look at your ..." her eyes raked down my body, "parts ... I've never seen him scared of Jameson before."

"Did you just call my girlie bits parts?" I asked amused.

"Shut up, I have a three-year-old at home," she chided. "I had to think of something to say after Spencer tried to call his penis his junk while we were potty training him."

"I feel bad for you sometimes," I told her patting her back.

"You *should* feel bad for me."

"Now, for the most famous words in racing ... gentleman, start your engines!"

Hot damn. I loved that sound.

My bones vibrated, my heart thudded loudly in anticipation.

I was already sitting on the pit box with Emma, Kyle, and Mason listening to the in-car audio.

"Fire it up, bud," Kyle announced to Jameson when Spencer put up his window net.

"Got it," Jameson fired the car. "Keep me calm today, Kyle."

"I'll do my best," Kyle answered.

They went on to talk about the car for a few moments and then Jameson talked to Bobby about drafting. Bobby, his teammate, had qualified second which put Jameson right behind him at the start of the race.

While the cars made their warm-up laps, Aiden got on the radio. "All right Jameson, you got two laps until the green."

"Aiden's right," Kyle said. "Two laps to go. Remember, watch your shift—don't spin the tires."

Jameson was quietly focused, he said little throughout the warm-up laps other than asking where his pit was and who he had to go around.

"Coming to the green here," Aiden announced. "Keep coming, keep coming ... green flag, green flag."

The cars roared past down the front stretch.

The downside to watching from the pit box was that you could only see what was in front of you and to the sides but on the back-stretch, you couldn't see anything unless the broadcasting station was following them at that moment. Most pit stands were equipped with televisions for this purpose allowing them to see what they couldn't ordinarily.

"Inside two ... inside one ... clear high ... ten cars at your door, middle two ... middle one ... clear low ... ten car high," Aiden guided him through the heavy traffic.

Everyone bunched up in the front, fighting for position.

Jameson managed to stay in the top five when the caution came out for a wreck in turn three. "Cautions out, cautions out—clear high,"

Aiden told him. "You're gonna have a few cars coming around on the inside, watch low."

"Who's it for?" Jameson asked the radio crackling.

"A shit load of cars. Watch low in four ... there's an ... engine lying out there on the front stretch ..."

"No shit?" Jameson chuckled.

"Yep."

"Aiden, can you see my right rear? It feels flat or maybe dragging. I'm not sure. I think I got into Tate a little on a restart."

"Uh ... where are you?" Aiden asked with slight panic.

"What?" Jameson sounded confused. "Are you serious?"

"Where are you?" Aiden's tone continued down the path of panic. "Are you on the backstretch?"

"Well yeah ..."

"Oh, I see you now."

"Well that's comforting that my spotter just lost me on the track," Jameson mocked. "How many times does this happen in a race?"

"So what do you think bud, how's the car?" Kyle asked, interrupting them.

"It's tight coming out of the turns, but it's not terrible," Jameson told him. "Check the right rear though since Aiden can't."

"It was one time, jeez," Aiden let out this apprehensive chuckle, as though he knew Jameson was less than amused that his spotter lost him on the track.

"Okay boys, pit lanes open—coming next time by. Let's do four tires, fuel, and a spring adjustment," Kyle advised the crew. "Keep coming, keep coming, watch your speed ... here you go ... three ... two ... one. Wheels straight, foot on the brake."

Jameson swung into his pit stall. I could see him in the car, handing the crew his water bottle and taking the replacement, flipping the visor up to rub his eyes.

"STOP!" Kyle jumped to his feet yelling, as Jameson went to pull out of his pit just as Darrin pulled into his pit stall in front of Jameson's. "Get him out of the way!" Kyle yelled to the crew.

The crew was screaming at Darrin's crew to push the car forward, but Jameson was losing positions fast.

Spencer was beating on the back of Darrin's car trying to get the crew to move, but they were busy performing their stop.

"C'mon! Tell him to get the fuck out of the way!" Jameson revved the engine steadily throwing his arms up. "Let's go! Move!"

If there hadn't been crew members in the way, I was sure he would have rammed into the back of him.

After about thirteen seconds, Darrin pulled out, but Jameson was now twenty-sixth.

This also put the two of them *right* beside each other on the restart.

"Jameson," Kyle warned, "don't do anything stupid."

Jameson didn't respond.

Here's the thing about Jameson's anger, there was no controlling it *or* preventing it. You just had to wait out the storm under cover. Knowing how he'll react is about as easy as predicting the path a tornado would take.

"You're going to be in some heavy traffic back there," Aiden advised. "Coming to the green next time by."

When the cars passed by on the front stretch, Jameson was all over the back of Darrin's car and silent on the radio.

"I'm serious Jameson," the warning in Kyle's tone was clear. "*Stay calm.*"

Again, Jameson was silent and I knew what was about to happen, as did Kyle.

"All right, you're coming to the green here. Watch yourself. You got the fourteen on the inside," Aiden said. "Here we go ... watch your outside. Harris has a run. Green**.**"

Jameson was on the outside of Darrin when the green flag was thrown; by the time they entered turn one he had dropped in behind him, but stayed right on his bumper. They stayed like that for a few laps when Jameson got a run on the backstretch with Paul behind him and went to the outside to pass Darrin.

Darrin saw him coming and blocked him right before turn three. There was so much chatter between Aiden and Kyle that you couldn't tell what was happening until you heard it.

Emma and I were watching on the monitor as Darrin pushed

Jameson up the track and in the wall, hard.

"In the wall, turn three, damage right side. Flat left rear and right rear."

"Bring it in," Kyle said. "All right guys, he's coming in. Four tires ... front splitter. Fix the damage on the left front and get him out. Anything you can't do in twelve seconds we'll get next time by."

"Watch your speed ... three ... two ... one," Kyle remained quiet watching the crew.

"Get the hammer out, pull that left front, Shane. Josh, grab the front splitter," Mason fired orders at the crew while they worked. "Spencer, pull the left rear out while you're there."

"Come on, let's go, let's go!" Jameson yelled revving the engine, slamming his fists repeatedly on the wheel for the second time today. "What the fuck are you waiting for? *LET'S GO!*"

Spencer yanked the jack out, waving to Kyle.

"Go, go, go! Clear all lanes!" Kyle shouted when they let the car down.

Emma was practically sitting on my lap now as we held each other tightly; talk about excitement.

Jameson made it out before the pace car came back around, staying on the lead lap. When the green flag flew at lap one twenty five, he was in thirty-eight with seventy-five to go.

Where was Darrin?

Third.

This had disaster written all over it. Jameson was the type of guy who didn't forget, and Darrin was about to see that side of him.

"This guy is such an asshole!" Emma screamed in my ear. You could barely hear anything over the noise from the cars. "Why doesn't NASCAR do something?"

"I know," I agreed. "Is he always like this?"

"No, *well* yes, every week it gets worse. He seems to be on a mission this weekend though."

"What's his problem? I mean, I know it has something to do with Mariah, but how is Chelsea involved?"

"Darrin thinks Jameson slept with Mariah ..." My eyes widened, Emma held up her hands defensively. "He didn't ... that I *know* of. He swears he didn't, and I believe him. Anyhow, after the race in Daytona, Darrin confronted Jameson about it. Of course, Jameson denied it and told Darrin to basically fuck off and called Mariah a whore. From then on, Darrin has had it out for him. Even back in USAC they had rivalry, but this is out of control. I'm not sure how Chelsea got involved but she is *somehow*. She is supposedly dating Tate, but I've never *actually* seen them together. It just didn't make sense how a guy like Tate Harris would date Chelsea Adams. Besides, not that this really makes a difference, but he's like thirty-four and she's twenty-two."

I listened to everything Emma had to say, wondering what they were up to with Jameson and how Tate, who gave Jameson his start, was involved.

I've met Tate on many occasions, and I never once got the feeling he was the kind of guy who would back stab Jameson. He was a nice guy.

Tate raced on the Outlaw Series with Jimi before he made his start in stock cars, so the fact that he knew Jimi made it all seem that much more impossible.

Not only that, but Tate Harris was the one who helped Jameson get the sponsorship from Simplex after he won the Chili Bowl. Knowing that, it didn't seem likely for him to be with someone like Chelsea.

Throughout the remainder of the race, I thought of ways to figure out Chelsea and Mariah, but I kept my eye on what was unfolding on the track.

By lap one seventy-two, Jameson was in thirteenth and moving through the field steadily. He was running lap times that would break the track record.

The caution came out with twelve laps to go and that single minded-athlete returned.

"Any changes, bud?" Kyle asked as the cars slowed down the front stretch as the yellow flag was displayed.

I watched as Jameson's black car fell into line behind Darrin.

"I'm not pitting," Jameson stated resolutely.

Rolling my eyes with a shake of my head, I knew damn well what was about to happen.

"You *need* tires," Kyle argued throwing a hand up. "You've been on the same ones for over sixty laps. Just bring it in."

"Not pitting."

Kyle ripped off his headset and threw it across the pit box. "God-damn him!"

There was no convincing Jameson to do something when he made up his mind but it didn't stop Aiden from trying as well. "I think you should get tires, Jameson. The top five cars are coming in, so should you."

"If I *wanted* your opinion, I'd fucking ask for it, Aiden," Jameson spat.

Aiden didn't say another word and sure enough, everyone pitted leaving Jameson by himself out there on used tires and a question-able amount of fuel.

When they lined up to take the green, it was Jameson, Bobby, Darrin, and then Paul.

I wanted to say something to him, but I also knew it wouldn't do any good. He wouldn't listen to me any more than he would listen to Kyle.

"Coming to the green here—watch your shift—Darrin has a run. Green flag, green flag," Aiden announced. "Cole's at your door, clear, fourteen has a run on the inside, at your rear ... still there ... still there, at your door ... clear." Jameson darted in behind Darrin leaving him in third in front of Paul in the twenty-four car.

He was all over the back of Darrin once again with eight laps to go and wasn't losing ground like we expected him to.

"I don't know how he's even keeping that damn car straight. He's riding on cords out there," Kyle told Mason, they both shook their heads.

He'd done this sort of thing before and we all knew what he was up to. It was obvious by the way they were bumping each other around the track this wouldn't end well.

ESPN was all over the coverage so we were able to see what was happening. Darrin and Jameson were tearing the two cars up and al-lowing Bobby to pull away to a two-second lead.

"*Jameson*, cut the shit and drive the fucking car!" Kyle yelled at him. "You're going—"

"Don't tell me to cut the shit when *any* run that I get on this ass-hole, he blocks me!" Jameson snapped. "I'm finishing what *he* started."

Jameson went high when Darrin was low so Darrin shot up the track in front of him.

Jameson never lifted.

He slammed into the back of Darrin on the second stretch coming out of turn two. Darrin fishtailed for a moment and then shot up the track into the outside barrier, his car spinning down onto the apron. Once it hit the grass outside the tunnel turn, the car flipped four times before it came to a rest in the infield.

His car was destroyed. Parts and sheet metal scattered from the turn across the infield and up the banking of the track. All that remained of his blue car was a roll cage and the engine.

Not a word was said on the radio by anyone except Aiden telling Jameson they had red flagged the race.

"They're stopping you guys outside turn two."

Darrin seemed fine. He got out of the car, stumbled slightly, rode to the infield car center where he was required to be evaluated, and then he was supposed to go to the NASCAR hauler.

The NASCAR Official in Jameson's pit motioned for Kyle to come down off the pit box. He did and when he returned he wasn't pleased.

"Bring it in, they're black flagging you," Kyle announced. "Take the car to the truck and then head to the NASCAR hauler."

"10-4," was all Jameson said.

He knew damn well what would happen if he wrecked Darrin intentionally, but I was also inclined to think he didn't give a shit right now.

In the drivers' meeting earlier today, they announced they wouldn't put up with retaliation of any kind. That was never something NASCAR condoned. Just as any sanctioning body, they were there to enforce the rules and that they did.

Though I understood the position NASCAR held in all this, I couldn't understand *why* Darrin wasn't penalized for the shit he pulled when he put Jameson in the wall in the beginning of the race.

He should have at least had a stop and go penalty.

The crew started loading tools and equipment as Emma and I headed to the hauler.

Jameson wasn't there yet, so we helped Alley field the media that was hovering by his hauler.

When the car pulled in, spewing steam and fluids, Jameson had already removed his helmet, gloves, and was working his belts as he shut the car off.

He was irate to say the least—not that I expected anything less of him. Like I said, I've seen this before over the years.

Sure enough, a news reporter was in his face before he even made it out of the car. "Jameson, can you tell us what happened out there? Did you mean to hit Darrin?"

Jameson was already walking toward the NASCAR hauler with the reporter tagging along.

Alley motioned for us to follow; we had to make sure he didn't do anything stupid.

"Can you tell us what happened?" the reporter repeated, shoving the microphone at him, fighting to keep up with his quick steps.

Jameson shook his head and snorted.

"What does it look like happened?" He threw his arms in the air. "He wrecks me in practice. He blocks me in my pit, and then he puts me in the wall. I got a run on him and he blocks me, again. I had *nowhere* to go."

"You and Darrin seemed to have it out for each other out there."

"You're so perceptive," Jameson retorted coldly walking inside the hauler, the door slammed shut behind him.

Alley stood outside with us. "This is not good. Why can't he keep his mouth shut and not react like this?"

I offered a shrug. There wasn't much else to say.

Kyle showed up and walked inside with a grim expression, he'd just been talking to Jimi and Simplex. I'm sure they had their concerns with their driver's actions today.

Twenty minutes later, they emerged from the hauler with two NASCAR officials who escorted each driver back to their transporters.

Jameson and Kyle didn't say anything, so we followed quietly.

Alley was typing away on her Blackberry, Emma was texting Aiden, and I watched Jameson's ass trudging back toward his hauler.

Now is not the time to be thinking about that, Sway!

I couldn't help it, I tried, but anytime I watched that ass, I *watched* it. Thoughts of the mirror had me smiling.

When we made it back to Jameson's hauler, he walked inside with Kyle and Alley.

Before the door even closed, Jameson was throwing tools. Kyle was yelling at him and Alley was actually *screaming.*

They hadn't loaded the car yet, so Emma and I sat down on the hood and waited for the storm to clear—it was going to be a long night.

We'd only been sitting there a minute when Emma looked back at the car with questioning eyes and then back at me.

"Is this the same car ...?"

"No. He wrecked that one," I smiled widely feeling the heat from the engine and my cheeks. "But it's the same hood."

"My goodness you guys are sluts."

"I know. Everyone keeps telling us that," I agreed, shifting my weight on the hood.

I had a damn hood pin up my ass reminding me that I needed underwear. "By the way, I need to go shopping tomorrow," I said under my breath. "I don't have any underwear."

Emma raised a questioning eyebrow at me and I knew she heard me. "Not that I'm opposed to shopping but why don't you do some laundry tomorrow?"

I looked away before I spoke because if I looked her direction I would burst into giggles that I'm actually telling someone this. "They're ripped."

"How did ..." she started laughing loudly. "Wow!"

"Shut up!" I tried to sound mean, but I ended up smiling at her. "So you'll take me?"

"You know, you could go ask Dana for a pair of Jameson's," she snickered. "I'm sure she has a few you can borrow."

"I'm wearing a pair of his right now."

"This just gets better and better," Emma replied, thoroughly amused.

Though I'd agree, it just keeps getting better and better, our *better* was entirely different. Before I could say anything more, Alley came out of the hauler with her Blackberry pressed to her ear.

She put her hand over the receiver. "You guys ready?"

"Ready for what?" we both asked at the same time, confused.

The door to the hauler was ajar, so I glanced inside. Jameson was leaning against the counter with his head bowed and his arms crossed over his chest.

"We're going to dinner," Alley said and continued talking to whom I assumed was someone with Simplex.

"Yes, he will be there ... okay ... the one on Pocono Boulevard ... yes ..." After glaring, she hung up, tossing her phone inside her bag. "Come on."

"I'll wait for ..." I began, but Alley yanked me along with them.

"No you won't. He'll meet us there and believe me ... you don't want to be around *that*," she pointed at the hauler, "right now."

Unwillingly, I followed and got in the Expedition with them.

"Where are we going?" Emma eventually asked as we pulled through the driver's compound and toward the infield.

"Jameson has a meeting with Simplex at Burke's Tavern & Restaurant in Pocono. I'm going there to make sure he doesn't do anything stupid and you guys are coming with me." Alley sighed and shook her head. "I'll be damned if I'm putting up with his moody ass all night by myself."

"Where's Spencer?" Aiden asked, getting in the backseat with Emma.

"With Jameson, he's supposed to make sure he gets there *on time*." Alley shook her head once again. "Oh, damn it—I should have had you do that, Aiden."

She was right.

Leaving Spencer in charge was a *very* bad idea. "See Alley, you should have let me stay. Now they are never going to make it. They're probably drinking beer right now," I pointed out.

Alley gave me a pointed glare in the rearview mirror. "No," she spat. "If I left you in charge, you two would be going at it up against a wall somewhere."

Both Aiden and Emma turned to look at me with amused expressions.

"She has a point there," I mumbled, pretending to play with my cell phone.

When we arrived at the bar, Melissa was sitting at a large booth with another taller man with dark hair, dressed in a suit.

Alley walked up to them, shook hands, and then introduced us. "Melissa ... you remember Emma, Aiden, and Sway, right?"

Melissa smiled politely and shook our hands again.

Alley pointed to the man, "This is Marcus Harding. He's the President of Simplex Shocks and Springs."

Marcus reminded me of an actor you would see on those *Matrix* movies with his jet-black hair and matching Armani suit.

We all shook hands and then took a seat around the table in the far corner of the bar.

Marcus cleared his throat, his voice stern like our high school principal, Mr. Lars. "Where's Jameson?"

Yep, he sounded like our principal and asked that same question frequently.

"Jameson's on his way. He had a press conference to finish up," Alley answered typing away on her Blackberry. "Jimi can't make it. He's racing in Knoxville and then catching a flight to Charlotte in the morning."

The waitress made her way over to take our drink orders.

When she looked to me, I answered before she had a chance to ask. "Shot of tequila, please."

Both Aiden and Emma looked at me once again. "If I'm going to sit here all night with *these* people," I motioned with a shift of my eyes to the *Matrix* Armani dude. "I'm *getting* drunk."

Another hour later and twelve, yes, count them, twelve shots of tequila, Jameson and Spencer showed up.

Jameson didn't appear to be in any better of a mood than the last time I saw him with the defiant stare he sported as he approached the table.

He looked cleaner, having showered I assumed, and looked like a walking billboard for Simplex, wearing his black and red Simplex hat, along with a black hooded Simplex sweatshirt and stone washed jeans.

I wanted to grab him and hump his leg like a Mississippi leg hound but that could be the tequila talking. I wasn't sure tequila knew what the fuck it was talking about these days.

Marcus and Melissa stood when they reached the table. "Jameson," Marcus greeted him with a firm handshake. "Thank you for meeting with us."

"Let's go to the bar," Alley ordered pushing us away. "Spencer, carry Sway and for Christ's sake, *don't* give her any more tequila."

I wasn't in any shape to be walking, that's for sure, but I wasn't about to be carried by Spencer of all people.

"Hands off, shithead," I snapped when Spencer reached for me. "You've already seen me naked today, no touching." Spencer raised his hands and backed away with that dirty smirk. I glared. "Don't make me hit you again," I warned when he stepped behind Alley.

I watched Jameson talk with Marcus and Melissa.

I had no idea what was being said, but Jameson wasn't looking all that pleased and neither was Marcus.

Jameson didn't say much aside from nodding.

After about fifteen minutes and another two shots of tequila I snuck from the bartender, Marcus and Melissa left.

After walking them to the door, Jameson approached the bar and stood beside me, our forearms touching.

My eyes flickered to him to find him staring at me. The bartender asked him what he'd like. Jameson didn't say anything. He pointed to the shot glass in my hand and held up two fingers, his gaze fixated on mine.

When the bartender returned with the shots, he placed them in front of us. We still hadn't said anything to each other by that point.

Jameson's eyes seemed different, but I couldn't place the difference. Maybe it was that defying edge again.

Slowly, he turned the bar stool I was sitting on to face him, the metal legs scraped across the floor.

Placing both his hands on my knees, he spread my legs apart to stand in between them. His right hand reached across me to grab the salt and then he leaned in and kissed my neck with slow wet kisses before dragging his tongue along my collarbone.

All this in a *very* public bar.

Before I realized what he was doing, he shook the salt on the place he kissed and placed the lime in my mouth.

After licking the salt away, he leaned back to take the shot, and then sucked down on the lime he'd placed in my mouth.

Holy mother of pearl.

Right there, in front of everyone, including his family, Jameson pulled the lime from his mouth and gave me another passionate kiss, similar to the one in the pick-up last night.

Ignoring Spencer's catcalls and Aiden's whistles, he attacked my mouth with angry kisses, his hands fisted in my hair welding my mouth to his.

I didn't know what to do or how to react, so I simply gave in and returned the passion.

Once I became lightheaded from the lack of oxygen, I pulled away, but his mouth never left my skin, instead it moved to my neck.

"Jameson," Alley warned after another minute. "There's a better place for this sort of thing."

Jameson ignored her, his arms wrapped firmly around my waist pulling me toward him and his camshaft pressed nicely against its crankcase.

I nearly fell off the barstool trying to get closer. My crankcase brought back her justifications and wiggled against him.

His hands immediately flew to my hips to stop me. "Stop that," he growled in a low husky voice. I didn't though. I did it once more to savor the feeling. "Unless you want me to fuck you up against this very bar, *stop it.*"

"That's one we haven't done yet."

"Don't tempt me," he stated firmly, his eyes hard and completely serious. "I'm really not in the mood to be challenged."

"Stop that you two," Alley nudged Jameson. "You're *in public.* Try and behave like normal civilized people and not like two hormone enraged seventeen-year-olds."

Jameson laughed stepping back.

"Yes, Mother."

I leaned forward to whisper in his ear, melting in the rich intoxicating scent of him. "Later?"

He winked and took the other shot.

The rest of the night passed in an absolute blur of tequila shots; Spencer singing "Bust a Move" with Jameson and Aiden as they danced around like complete idiots on top of the bar, and Alley yelling at all of us to behave.

We never did talk about what happened during the race or even after the race. Instead, we had a good time and behaved like the twenty-something kids we all were. You might think living a lifestyle with money and fame that Jameson could do what he wanted when he wanted, but that seldom happened with the obligations he had. But that night, he let loose.

I couldn't tell you what all occurred because once we left the bar, things spiraled out of control quickly when we found a strip of four bars in a row and decided to do a bar crawl.

The only thing I remember, besides Emma throwing up on Spencer at one point, was the last stop happened to be a tattoo parlor. Who in their right mind would put four bars in a row and then a tattoo parlor on the end?

That's just asking for trouble.

Brake Fade – The heat in the rotors of a car can reach five thousand degrees Fahrenheit and when the fluid inside the brake begins to boil, bubbles will form in the brake line and calipers. When this happens the brakes get softer and won't work as good as they once did.

My body was so completely exhausted from these last two weeks that I actually felt sick.

All things considered, this was a feeling I was growing accustomed to this last week.

Rolling over onto my back, I felt something hard and not the hard I was used to waking up with either.

Reaching underneath of me to pull out whatever it was I found a beer bottle. Groaning, I tossed it aside, only the thump it made didn't sound like the floor.

"Owww ..." Emma yelped.

What was Emma doing in here? More importantly, where is here?

Rubbing the sleep from my eyes, I attempted to decipher my surroundings, blinking vigorously until my vision improved enough to see.

I appeared to be in a hotel room, a very white hotel room. Squinting once again, my eyes adjusted slightly to the brightness.

My God, it's like an insane asylum.

I looked around for padded walls but saw none. At least I hadn't been committed last night.

Rolling over, I covered my aching head with a pillow.

No one else seemed to be in bed with me so I sprawled out, I could determine where I was later, sleep was far more important.

My head was hurting too badly for this bright ass room.

I needed darkness, lots and lots of darkness.

Who uses white paint these days anyway? Aren't people into the earthy tones?

Lying there, I noticed how incredibly sore I was below. This gave me a few concerning thoughts.

For one, my ass seemed to be fairly tender and I had some strict rules about the rear access. I hoped that wasn't the reason behind this particular soreness, otherwise Jameson was cut the fuck off.

With a heavy, but female sigh, I felt movement beside the bed so I turned over again to see Emma with her head resting on the bedside, staring at me.

"Nice tattoo, Sway," she whispered with a smug smile, her black spiky hair looked similar to a porcupine.

"What tattoo?" I turned over on my back to realize that it was the side of my ass that hurt. Not just any hurt, like *really* bad hurt, and burned.

Emma pointed south. "The one on your ass that says: 'Property of Riley.'"

Yes, she used air quotes.

I groaned loudly. "Not again!"

How was I ever going to explain "crooked lips" and "Property of Riley" to someone if I didn't end up with Jameson?

All the more reason to marry him.

Emma giggled and turned around to busy herself with a bottle of water.

I burst into laughter, and not just "ha, ha" that's funny kind of laughter, but piss on yourself laughter. I barely had enough control over myself to speak at the sight of the back of her neck.

"What?!" Emma asked hysterically. "What are you laughing at?"

Words couldn't be formed. I pointed to the back of her neck and fell back on the bed in a fit of uproarious laughter. I don't think I'd laughed that hard since the time Jameson and I branded those cows back in high school and mistakenly branded Spencer as well.

Concerned, and for good reason, Emma ran around the room screaming while searching for a mirror. Once she found one in the bathroom, I forgot all about my sore ass and laughed to the point that I actually had to squeeze my legs together to keep from peeing.

"OH MY GOD!" she screeched. "My dad is going to kill me!"

I threw my arms behind my head. "Nice tattoo, Emma."

She ran out of the bathroom and jumped beside me, shaking the entire bed.

"Sway, what am I going to do?" she stared at me wide-eyed. "Maybe it's a press on?" she considered, and then proceeded to try to wipe it off. "Holy mother ..." she winced, her eyes wider, if that was even possible. "That is *not* a press on."

"I could have told you that," I mumbled from under my pillow.

"At least yours is on your ass." She kicked me. "How am I going to cover this up? I should have never cut my hair shorter the other day."

"It's not that bad," I offered up. "Just get extensions put in your hair. Or wear turtlenecks."

"It's not that bad?" she repeated incredulously. "Are you fucking kidding me?"

I shook my head under the pillow throwing my arms up in the air dramatically. I really wanted to go back to sleep.

Emma ripped the pillow away glaring at me. "The back of my neck says: 'If you're close enough to read this, you better be pullin' my hair and spankin' my ass!'" Her eyes bugged out. "It *is* 'that bad,' Sway!" And yes, again she used air quotes. "It's like some ... horrible license plate frame saying you'd get from Trash R Us."

"I think it's funny." I giggled once.

"You would!" she snarled.

I sat up in bed and punched her tiny shoulder. "That was uncalled for, take it back."

She burst into tears. "I'm sorry. I'm just ..." she wailed louder. "I th-th-thought y-y-you h-h-had to be s-s-sober to get a t-t-tattoo?" she hiccupped. "Don't you?"

"Most places," I sighed. "But honey, what did you really expect from a tattoo parlor next to a bar?"

Rubbing her back softly, my poor little pixie Emma cried louder and crumbled in my lap.

At least her tattoo was nice writing, it was a pretty elegant script, not tacky like you'd think it would be by the phrase she inadvertently chose.

"Wake up you intoxicated whores!" Alley shouted deliberately as loud as possible slamming the door behind her.

Both Emma and I groaned, covering our ears.

She stepped inside the bedroom, dressed in a cream-colored business suit. "Nice to see you two among the living today."

"Why do you look so nice today?" I asked still petting Emma who was cradled to my chest like a baby kangaroo, *still* crying.

"Bitch please—I *always* look nice," Alley chided. "What's the matter with her?" she motioned to Emma.

I gave Emma a comforting squeeze and kissed her porcupine head. "She's upset about her tattoo," I whispered, because talking at a normal volume even hurt my head.

"Well *she* should have thought about that before *she* drank four Long Island iced teas and helped you finish off a fifth of tequila, now shouldn't *she*?"

"Jesus Alley," I balked, "harsh much? *She* was only having a good time."

"I don't feel sorry for any of you. *She*," Alley pointed to Emma who was now staring at the two of us in our heated conversation, "should have said no when Spencer told her what to write."

Emma snapped into action. "First of all, *she* is still in the goddamn room and *she* would like to be referred to in the first person. And second," her gaze narrowed at Alley, "Spencer did what?"

I was actually worried about Emma. The vein in her forehead was bright blue and looked like it was about to burst at any moment. Just to be sure, I poked it with my index finger. The vein squished under my touch.

"Where is Spencer?" Emma glared slapping my hand away. "I'm gonna kill him."

I sat back on the bed tossing the pillow over my face again.

Unfortunately, for me, my surprises for the morning were not over once I was lying there. It felt *awfully* breezy down below.

Reaching south, I checked out the situation and sure enough, I had no underwear on.

"Damn it," I mumbled to myself.

Now what am I going to do for underwear?

Maybe Jameson had some in here, or I could go commando because he's apparently not here to realize that I'm not wearing any.

At least I had someone's shirt on and a bra.

Then I thought, *where in the hell is Jameson?*

Emma, planning Spencer's execution, was scrambling around the room trying to find clothes to wear because she was only in Aiden's button down shirt and cowboy boots. Why she wore cowboy boots to sleep is beyond me, but, clearly, we weren't thinking last night judging by the tattoos.

"Where is Spencer?" Emma asked again pulling on her jeans she found near the door.

"I have no idea," Alley answered, not looking up from her Blackberry. "The last time I saw them they were puking behind the hotel."

"How do you *not* know where they are?" I asked confused. "Didn't you stay here last night?"

What in the hell happened last night?

"No," finally Alley looked up with an amused expression. "After Jameson puked in the Expedition for the second time, I booked this hotel room for you guys and I stayed at the Hilton down the street. I needed sleep and you guys ... well I have no idea *what* went on after you came back here. Obviously sleep didn't occur." She looked over at the wall and took a double take, her mouth falling open.

Both Emma and I followed her gaze to the wall and gasped as well.

And there, on the *very* white wall was a *very* large ... dick, spray-painted from floor to ceiling, complete with hairy balls and veins.

Hairy balls and veins weren't the worst part. The worst part was how *real* it actually looked. It was disturbing that someone could draw something that well with spray paint.

Eventually we averted our gaze from the monstrous dick on the wall and finally looked around the rest of the room for the first time. It seemed, in our discovery of the tattoos, we never noticed the pure insanity throughout the room.

There were probably a hundred beer bottles scattered throughout the room. Pillows were everywhere along with sheets, blankets, and the curtains from the windows.

You'd think a toga party was thrown in here or something. In the corner was a blown up bouncy house with what looked to be an entire grocery store's supply of unrolled toilet paper stuffed into it.

Next to it was an actual kiddy swimming pool with God knows what in it, but judging by the abundance of pudding cups throughout the room, I presumed it was pudding. At that point, I *hoped* it was pudding.

"I'm so glad I used Jameson's credit card and not mine for this," Alley replied stepping over some beer bottles and pudding cups.

"So you have no idea where any of the boys are?" Emma asked wrapping toilet paper from the bouncy house around her neck like a scarf.

"No, I said I didn't know where Spencer and Aiden were," Alley clarified. "Jameson is meeting with his team and Phillip to decide if they are appealing the fines NASCAR issued this morning." She threw the newspaper at me.

On the front page of the Pocono Record was a picture of Darrin's car upside down with a headline:

Rowdy Riley fined $25,000 for Aggressive Driving

NASCAR penalized Jameson Riley, driver of the No. 9 Ford Simplex car 60 points, fined him $25,000 and put him on probation through the end of the season for aggressive driving in the Winston Cup Series race Sunday afternoon at Pocono International Raceway.

Darrin Torres, driver of the No. 14 Wyle Products Chevy, who was involved in the incident with Riley, was placed on probation though the end of the year for aggressive driving, as well. The penalties issued Monday stem from lap 194 of the Gillette Fusion ProGlide 500, where Torres and Riley were racing for third place. Torres went up the track for a block on the second stretch when Riley hit Torres, wrecking him.

Torres's car hit both the outside and inside walls before becoming airborne in the infield. The accident collected at least seven cars.

"They will both be on probation through the end of the year." NASCAR Vice President of Competition, Gordon Reynolds, said.

Earlier this season, Torres was placed on three-week probation for retaliating against Riley in the Winston Cup race at Dover. In that race, the retaliation resulted in Riley being hit by Torres after the checkered flag had been thrown on pit road. Then we all know what happened in the Winston with the backyard brawl on the finish line where these two sparred.

"They have a history with each other dating back to their USAC days," Reynolds told us. "We had talked to both drivers after the Dover. And even though Darrin was put on probation, we had conversations with Riley about their relationship and told both of them that there needed to be boundaries on the track. Now we look at Pocono and you look at what we feel like was Darrin misjudging his corner and pit road space and then you look at the retaliation by Jameson coming out of turn two. It's out of control and effecting other drivers now."

Reynolds said the penalties are designed to keep the two drivers from retaliating in the future and affecting the other drivers, should there be any.

By losing 60 points, Riley is now 228 behind Torres with 23 races left in the championship.

The Riley Simplex Racing No. 9 team was also docked 60 points in the owner standings. Riley Simplex Racing has not decided whether to appeal and declined to comment on the penalties at this time but did have this to say.

When asked if Jameson would be commenting on the penalties, Riley Simplex Racing declined to comment.

Maggie Summers, a reporter with ESPN, caught up with

Jameson last night in downtown Pocono, the aggressive driving penalty was the least of his worries.

When asked about his thoughts on the race, his response was, "What race?" as he took another shot of tequila.

Gibson Racing will not appeal Torres's penalty, according to a statement released by the team earlier this morning.

"The incident at the end of Sunday's race at Pocono was unfortunate not just for Gibson Racing and the No. 14 Wyle Products Chevy team, but for all everyone," Torres said in the statement early Monday morning. "It didn't need to happen and that was one of our best cars. All in all, we support NAS-CAR's decision."

This was disgusting. This was ... I had no words.

How could they make it out to *just* be his fault?

"Can you believe the nerve of them?" Emma asked.

"What did he think was going to happen?" Alley reproached. "I mean ... he's not a child. Well ... that's debatable, but he *knew* what would happen when he hit Darrin."

She did have a point, but the way NASCAR painted the picture in this article, it made it seem that Jameson was doing all the retaliation and Darrin had no part of it.

"Was Darrin fined or put on probation?" I asked wrapping a sheet from the floor around my waist so I could use the bathroom and maybe find underwear.

If I couldn't, I was making a pair like the one Emma did with the scarf. They did that in the stone-age, right?

"Nope," Alley replied. "They're not going to fine NASCAR's golden boy."

"Unbelievable." I stepped over the kiddy pool to get to the bathroom. Emma looked in the bouncy house for her cell phone. "See if my underwear is in there!" I yelled over my shoulder.

Taking in a deep breath, I closed the bathroom door behind me, letting the sheet fall to the floor. I wasn't sure I wanted to see this but

I might as well get it over with.

It'd been a while since I examined my own ass. Not exactly expecting the size, it'd grown since the last time that's for sure.

Carefully, balancing myself on the counter, I surveyed my new artwork.

My God.

There, on my left ass cheek, was a square box with the words, "Property of Riley" imprinted in it.

The goddamn thing even had red along the outside edges as if it was meant to look like an actual branding with an iron. It wasn't tiny either; the tattoo almost covered the entire side of the cheek.

There goes my modeling career as an ass model.

I took a quick shower because God knew I needed it. I smelled as if I just came from a distillery in Guadalajara and my hair felt as though whatever was in the kiddy pool was in my hair.

Wrapping my sheet around myself, I walked back into the war zone hoping to find some clothing and underwear.

Emma and Alley were staring at the dick on the wall once again. It was as if they had some kind of obsession with it.

"Did you guys find the boys?" I asked joining them at staring at the wall.

It was sick how fucking real that looked.

Imagine the poor cleaning lady who has to clean this disaster. I bet she'll get a good laugh out of it, though.

"Yeah, they are getting some coffee up the street." Alley replied. "They're on their way back now, *with* Jameson."

"Is that a good thing or a bad thing?" I asked hesitantly. "How bad of a mood is he in?"

"What do you think?" her tone mocking. "When is it ever a good thing with him?"

Today was going to suck.

Alley left after a few minutes to fly back to Mooresville with Jimi to get Lane, which would leave Spencer traveling back with us.

Though this was a major concern for me, I was more concerned with Jameson's mood as it could either make or break the entire day and maybe even the rest of my time on this vacation from reality.

Still staring at the dick, I had a feeling Spencer was behind it.

It was something he would do, although I wouldn't put it past Jameson or even Aiden.

Aiden may seem like this polite, reserved southern boy from Pickard, Alabama, but he was far from that when you got a few beers in him, which was why he mixed well with all of us.

Thankfully, before the boys arrived, I found my jeans from last night but I was still wearing Jameson's t-shirt. I had no idea where mine was.

"Do you need these?" Emma asked holding up Jameson's underwear I wore last night.

"Where were those?" I stepped over a beer tower.

"They were in the closet, along with … part of your shirt." She shook her head. "I don't even want to know what happened in this closet last night."

"What do you mean part of my shirt?"

She held up half of the black tank top I'd been wearing last night.

"What the hell?" I shouted ripping it from her hand. "What is wrong with your brother? He has some kind of obsession with ripping my clothes off."

"He's got anger issues," she shrugged.

"And he bites me." The teeth marks from his latest bite were visible on the inside of my thigh.

"He was a biter in kindergarten," she told me. "He got sent home from school for it and spent a good part of first grade in timeouts, too. I see he hasn't grown out of it."

"What went wrong between you three kids? I mean, Jimi and Nancy are completely normal. Then you have Spencer who is just … insane. Jameson is borderline psychotic, and then there is you … the little pixie sister who tattoos license plate frames on her neck."

Emma shoved me inside the closet. "You're not any better. You can't even find your underwear." She sounded like a damn child. I was waiting for her to stick her tongue out.

"Because, *your* psychotic brother ripped them off like he was the Hulk," I pointed out and stuck my tongue out for good measure.

"We should go shopping."

I was amazed at how quickly her mood changed. A moment ago she looked like she was going to kill me for saying her family was strange, and now she was cuddled beside me in a closet with her head on my shoulder.

"Yeah, we should go shopping. I need underwear," I agreed. "Is he always like this?"

"Is who always like this?"

"Jameson, was he like this with all the other girls?"

"What other girls?"

"The ones he would sleep with. Did they have to go shopping all the time for clothing, too?"

Emma looked over at me and raised her eyebrows. "Jameson *never* has other girls around."

"Huh?"

"He doesn't bring anyone else around," she repeated. "Besides Chelsea in high school, you're the only other girl any of us have ever *officially* met."

"Really?" I played with my ripped shirt in my hands, hoping I didn't appear too transparent. "I thought ... I mean he used to be such a slut."

"Maybe the first year after you left for college, but we never met any of them and then when he started racing in the Busch series, it slowly trickled off and we never saw him with anyone. If he was with anyone, he kept it discreet."

He wasn't lying when he said he stopped sleeping around. Not that I thought he would lie to me about it, but it made me feel better coming from Emma who spent nearly every day with him.

"Don't tell him this," she whispered and I don't know why she was whispering. We were only sitting inches from each other and there is no one else in the room. "I think he's falling in love with you."

"I wish," I stated sarcastically.

"No, I think he is. You should have seen his face when he saw Darrin talking to you the other day. He looked ... jealous, like boyfriend jealous. I don't know, I've always *thought* he felt more for you than friends. Now his actions are the same."

"I'm not getting my hopes up."

Before Emma could say any more, the boys came barreling through the door.

And if I thought we looked bad I was wrong ... we looked like cover models compared to them.

Aiden's blonde curly hair was just as bad as Emma's was. You could tell he tried to tame it but it was still everywhere. He had no shoes or socks on and he was wearing Emma's shirt from last night. But what really caught my attention was *because* he was wearing Emma's shirt, and it was revealing about two inches of the curve of his hips, there was a tattoo plastered across his lower abdomen that said: Mount Up.

I giggled.

Then I looked at Spencer who came in behind Aiden. Again with no shoes or socks on *and* a Mohawk. He looked sick. His face was pale with dark circles under his eyes and his hands were full of *Rock Star* energy drinks.

And then Jameson came in.

Besides the fact that his hair appeared to also have the same pudding in it, as mine once had, it didn't look as bad as Aiden's. He was just as pale as Spencer but was dressed a whole hell of a lot better in his black suit, the tie loosened from around his neck with the top few buttons of his white button down shirt undone.

Holy Mississippi leg hound.

I don't think Spencer ever saw her coming as Emma all but flew through the air at him.

"You motherfucker!" she screamed jumping on his back like some kind of wild chimp. His *Rock Star* drinks crashed to the ground.

"What the fuck ..." he yelled back at her. "Oh God, stop screaming, my head fucking hurts."

Aiden *and* Jameson tried to pull her away but she never let up. She was like a Chihuahua that latched on and wouldn't let up until it shed blood.

In his attempt to get her loose, they stumbled together into the kiddy pudding pool. She finally let go, but sat there wiping pudding away and seething at him. "You're such a fucking jerk, Spencer!"

"What are you talking about?" he snapped back at her while also wiping away the pudding.

Aiden was holding Emma back and noticed what she was yelling about when her makeshift scarf of toilet paper fell loosely around her shoulders.

His eyes widened as he read it. "Holy shit." He turned her around to look at him, his eyes wide with panic. "You're growing your hair out."

"No shit," she snapped back and then pushed him. "Where were you on that one? You didn't think to stop him from convincing me to do this?"

"Like I was in *any* condition to stop anyone," he lifted her shirt that he was wearing. "If so, I would have never done this,"

Emma fell backward into the pudding pool again in a fit of laughter. Spencer and Jameson finally noticed Aiden's tattoo of "Mount Up," as well. Jameson had to lean against the wall to keep from falling over while his entire body shook with silent laughs.

I hadn't stopped giggling since they walked in. I was like the Pillsbury Doughboy.

Look, we have ridiculous tattoos, hehehe! Look there's pudding everywhere, hehehe! Look, there's a dick on the wall, hehehe!

Still laughing, I watched as the boys surveyed the room. They too looked surprised by the kiddy pool, beer, and toilet paper everywhere but were flabbergasted at the dick on the wall.

Seriously, I don't think you can grasp how large it was. To give you a mental picture, the ceiling in this particular room had to be at least fifteen feet tall. So if you have never seen a fifteen foot tall spray painted dick complete with hairy balls and veins on a wall—you're missing out.

Look, there's a dick on the wall, hehehe!

With my maturity level exceptionally low today, I couldn't stop myself. I was actually crying on the floor beside Jameson.

"Who drew that?" Emma finally asked pointing to it.

Aiden and Jameson both responded with, "Spencer," at the same time.

Spencer nodded arrogantly.

"It's pretty fucking awesome, huh?"

"No, what's awesome is going to be watching you explain your new haircut and the tramp stamp on your back to Alley." Jameson laughed.

"What tramp stamp?" Emma and I asked curiously.

Spencer started backing toward the wall so we couldn't see, but with the help of Aiden and Jameson, we managed to tackle him to the ground and pull up his shirt for a better view.

Right above his ass crack was "Insert coin to bust a move."

This was all too much to really believe.

I looked over at Jameson sitting against the wall still shaking with laughter. "How did you manage not to get branded in all this?"

Jameson's eyes flickered to Aiden and Spencer and then back to mine.

Before he could say anything, Spencer laughed a loud booming laugh that had all of us covering our ears. "He didn't. He got it worse than all of us."

Jameson smiled once and looked away, panic evident in his features.

"How did he get it worse? Emma asked jumping on Jameson. "What does his say?"

"Get off me," Jameson grumbled running into the bathroom slamming the door behind him.

All of us looked at Spencer for an answer but he shook his head. "I'm not saying, after the morning he had ... *he* can tell you what they say."

"What do you mean '*they*?'" I asked curiously.

"Like I said, *they*, now ask him." Spencer turned to his masterpiece on the wall. "*Goddamn*, that's talent." He nodded, pleased with himself and his art ability.

I heard the shower running so I decided to sneak in the bathroom to find out for myself what his tattoos said.

"Jameson?" I asked inching the door open hesitantly.

"Yeah," his voice muffled from the spraying water. Steam drifted in loops around me when the door closed.

"Can I come in?"

"Sure."

Making sure it was locked, I asked, "Are you okay?" as I leaned against the counter.

"I'm fine." Without seeing his expression, I knew by the tone, he was rolling his eyes. "Get in here with me."

"I already took a shower."

"Sway, I wasn't asking." He sighed. "Get in here."

Of course, the pit lizard in me started stripping away her clothes and stepped inside the glass shower—no need to ask twice.

Jameson was a sight to see with no clothes on and soapy water running off him everywhere.

He smirked, his own eyes wandering. When our eyes finally met, he winked. "Come here, honey."

Stepping forward, he wrapped his arms tightly around my waist pulling me against his chest.

After a few moments, my curiosity got the best of me. I had to know what those tattoos said. "Jameson?"

"Yeah," I watched as the water ran down his stomach.

"What does your tattoo say?"

"Which one?" He chuckled a nervous chuckle.

"All of them." Pulling back, I snuck a glance up at him.

His nose scrunched. "Well, one doesn't say anything, but strangely resembles these beautiful lips." He placed two fingers to my lips.

"I already know about that one."

He nodded.

"All right, well the other ones … let's see …" He pulled away from me, stood there and then looked down to the promised-land. "That one," he pointed to his right hipbone not more than two inches above his camshaft, " … says: *Sway's property*, and this one," he pointed to his left hipbone in the same position, "says: *Hands off*, and this one," he turned around and pointed to his ass where my lips were, " … says: *I told you, hands off, I bite.*" His eyes dropped. "I think that's all of them … that I can see."

The one on his ass was the funniest because the letters were placed right above the lips.

I started giggling. "What have we done?"

"*Obviously*, we weren't thinking last night."

"Well, that's debatable," I suggested, trying to imply I wasn't too upset about my branding.

He grinned widely. "What does yours say?"

"I didn't get one." I lied with a sly grin.

"Yes you did,"

"No I didn't."

"Turn around, Sway."

"No."

His eyes narrowed. "Sway, *turn around*."

"No."

He shook his head slowly. "You really shouldn't have said that." And he lunged for me. I was flipped around in his arms before I even had time to react.

He's quick.

With my ass pressed against his camshaft, he examined my new branding.

Sure enough, he burst into laughter. "It actually looks like they used an iron." His fingers traced the outline lightly—I winced. "Sorry," he mumbled moving his hands to my hips, pushing forward against me. "I like it though."

"I kind of do, too," I admitted shyly, looking down at my feet.

"Hey," he whispered. "Look at me, honey," he said when I kept turning my head away. His hand caught my cheek forcing me to look at him. And though I resisted out of embarrassment, when I finally did look at him, he smiled. "You can get it removed if you want." His stare was laced with vigilance as he gauged my reaction.

Shrugging, I told him. "I'll keep it."

He winked. "I'm *definitely* keeping mine." He actually looked proud.

"Really?"

"Why wouldn't I?" Now he actually looked offended.

"What are you going to do when you have **a** girlfriend? Don't you think she might have something to say about this?" I hedged.

He hesitated for a second before he spoke, his eyes dropping from mine. "It won't be a problem." His words didn't match his expression. He looked upset, maybe even uncomfortable that I said that.

Offering me a quick smile, he turned away to rinse the shampoo out of his pudding hair.

Fearing my own expression would falter, I decided to change the subject.

"Do you remember anything from last night?" I washed his back for him, running my fingers up his long lean muscles and over the sharp defined ridges of each shoulder.

His breathing caught when my hands reached around and followed the lines of his hip and down the inside of his thigh.

With my chest pressed against his back now, I could feel the quick rise and fall of each one of his strained deep breaths as though they were my own.

Jameson's hands moved from his hair to rest against the shower wall, his head fell forward against the tile when my hands found his camshaft and stroked it once.

This was the only distraction I could come up with.

"Huh?" he finally asked.

"What do you remember from last night?" I repeated in a low seductive whisper.

Jameson inhaled a shaky breath; I stroked him once more, this time squeezing my hand slightly.

"I ... uh ... not very much," he answered and then swallowed. "I remember the bar ... dancing with you in the middle of the street ..." I kissed his neck. "I remember the tattoo place, kind of, Spencer drawing his masterpiece, and bits and pieces of the closet."

"Why were we in the closet?" I questioned moving in front of him.

Not waiting for an answer, I pushed him against the wall; I dropped to my knees for a change.

Jameson threw his head back, knocking against the tile once again moaning when my lips found him.

Slowly, I drew him inside my mouth, earning me another moan of pleasure from him.

I was utterly amazed at how one minute we can be having a serious conversation regarding our feelings for one another, and then the next minute, we were having sex.

Jameson's hand wrapped tightly in my hair indicating his approval so I continued to suck, swirl, bob, and drag my teeth along his length. He didn't last long that's for sure. Within a few minutes of my dedicated ministrations, I could feel him try to pull me away.

Instead, I slapped his hands away, drawing him in deeper. Poor fellow, he only lasted another ten seconds before his head slammed back against the shower wall once again, groaned my name.

"Did you take a class on that or something?" he asked as he fell beside me.

"Yeah, Micro Polishing 101," I replied, splashing some water on my face. "I got an 'A' by the way."

He laughed pulling me into his arms so I was sitting on his lap, straddling him. His expression was, yet again, unreadable as he stared deep into my eyes. It was as if he was searching for an answer to a question, but I hadn't heard him ask anything.

"What?" I asked softly, embarrassed by the silence and slightly scared of what he was going to say or what he was thinking for that matter.

"Sway, I ..." he paused, his brow furrowed as he continued to stare at me with a nervous expression. His hand rose to cradle the apple of my cheek, his fingers brushing over my lips.

Blinking slowly, his stare faltered. Instead of finishing what he was going to say, he leaned in pressing his lips to my forehead once.

I leaned forward wrapping my arms around his neck pulling my body flush against his. His arms wrapped instinctively around my waist, cradling me to him. This embrace was different from the previous embraces we shared, it seemed ... affectionate?

Maybe Emma is right. Maybe my plan is working.

If it's not working, I truly hope there's a support group for pit lizards who get their heart broken because I'm going to need one after this.

While I was thinking this, Jameson's lips never left my wet skin, licking, sucking and biting my neck and shoulders. His mouth was soft, his lips were warm and the stubble on his face was coarse.

I soon realized while Jameson's need may have been met just moments ago, mine had not. Pressed against me, wet and ready, he was ready for rotation again.

Pulling his mouth from my neck, I brought it to my lips.

His mouth attacked me with frantic kisses. Reaching between us, he lifted me up so he could slide inside, with his signature low growl.

Gasping this ridiculously loud porn star moan when he entered me, his arms curled around my shoulders, pulling me into him with each avid thrust. His arms were thick and tense, the muscles flexing as he pushed and pulled me against him. His chest was a solid wall of muscle, rippling and defining with every movement he made.

Hot damn.

Arching my back in response to all this, his mouth found my nipples again as he started kissing and nipping at my chest.

It all felt amazing but Spencer had other ideas and started pounding his fist on the door.

Ignoring him, Jameson nipped across my chest, his nose swept between the valley, and the stubble on his cheek scraped across my sensitive skin. My moaning continued and earned me a chuckle from him.

"Fuck, you *really* like that, don't you?" Jameson asked in a low throaty voice.

"What do you think?" I moaned sarcastically.

He chuckled again. "You're adorable." He sucked my lower lip in his mouth biting gently.

Suddenly everything turned serious, our movements sped and we became determined.

"I just … can't get enough of you," he panted against my lips desperately searching for more. "You're all I think about … all the time, I can't stop."

"I know the feeling," I panted.

Without the slightest bit of warning, my whole body flushed with heat and I burst into flames deep in my belly.

"God that's so good, Jameson!" I screamed with absolutely no volume control.

He slammed me down on him harder.

"Shit," he growled out as the word "fuck" fell from his lips, and he buried his face in my neck, thrusting erratically into me until he was shaking.

Running my fingers through his wet hair, we both sucked in a labored breath.

After last night and as wonderful as this was, I had a feeling I was going to be incredibly sore real soon.

Before we could really come down from the endorphins settling nicely in our sex-crazed, tattooed bodies, the water turned freezing cold, and Spencer was nearly beating the door down.

"I fucking hate him sometimes," Jameson grumbled as we dried off.

"I know the feeling, sport," I agreed slapping his tattooed ass with my towel.

He gave me another grin before dressing in his suit.

When we opened the door, three questioning expressions greeted our flushed appearances.

I personally didn't think we were that loud, but their gazes told me otherwise.

Spencer grumbled to himself for a minute and then pushed Jameson out of the way. "I've had to piss for like an hour you assholes." He stomped into the bathroom slamming the door behind him.

This left Emma and Aiden still staring at us. Jameson and I both looked at each other and then back to them.

"What?" Jameson asked all defensively.

"Nothing," they both said at the same time and busied themselves with cleaning up the room.

Jameson looked around the room and laughed. "Don't worry about cleaning up. I already gave them my credit card downstairs. They said they'd take care of everything." His eyes flickered to the mammoth dick on the wall. "But, we should ... uh ... cover that up ... somehow."

Look, there's a dick on the wall, hehehe!

Aiden and Jameson looked around for some more spray paint while Emma and I gathered our bags. Once they found some spray paint, they proceeded to paint over it but not before they took about a hundred pictures of us posing by it.

Spencer joined in and was very sad that we were covering up his artwork. He pouted like his son would for a good twenty minutes.

Before heading back to Mooresville we stopped for some food at a local diner.

While eating, we started talking about what happened last night and who remembered what. As it turned out, it was hardly anything at all.

Jameson was sitting in front of me beside Spencer in the booth when I started giggling at how much he was eating. In a matter of ten minutes, he ate eight pieces of bacon, two slices of toast, a mountain of hash browns and now he was working on his egg whites.

I think he knew what I was about to say. Naturally most people in our circle knew my feelings on egg whites.

"Stop looking at me like that. Egg white are good for you," he offered up when he noticed my questioning glance. "Good protein. It would be good for your *energy* if you tried some." He winked, his fork drifting my way briefly as if to offer me a bite.

I personally thought egg whites looked like snot and refused to eat them but sure enough, I said exactly what I was thinking in that moment.

Smiling, I chewed the last of my toast as Jameson watched me with narrowed eyes. I think he knew what I was going to say.

"Well, uh, so is your *oil leak*," I gestured south with a wink, trying my hand at teasing him, "but you don't see me drinking *that* for protein and energy. Though I might try it sometime." I told him, and then winked.

Jameson, who was in the midst of taking a drink of orange juice, must have inhaled and then to compensate, sprayed orange juice all over his egg whites *and* me.

"You jerk." I glared wiping myself off. "I can't believe you did that."

"I can't believe you said that." Jameson said, wiping his own shirt clean of his breakfast.

"I can." Emma shook her head because really, that statement shouldn't surprise anyone who knew me.

"That was awesome," Spencer said through a series of snorts.

At least that's what I think he said. He did have an entire mouth full of food, so really, he could have said anything.

The rest of breakfast was quiet and surprisingly, I didn't say anything else to embarrass myself any further.

When we were finally in the car Alley rented for us, another minivan, Jameson finally spoke of his meeting with Simplex and his dad this morning.

"So you're on probation?" Aiden asked.

"Yeah," Jameson sighed looking down at his cell phone he was currently answering emails on. "I got fined twenty-five thousand and probation for the rest of the season."

"That's bullshit!" Spencer barked from the driver seat. "They know damn well it was *his* fault."

"Believe me, I know," Jameson agreed with a roll of his eyes. "But what else am I going to do? Phillip thinks it's in our best interest not to appeal the decision and just keep our nose clean for the remainder of the season."

"What do dad and Randy say?" Emma asked making herself a scarf out of a napkin she stole from the restaurant.

Resourceful little thing she was.

"Dad was too pissed to say anything and Randy, well, you know Randy, he did a lot of screaming. I'm not really sure what all he said," Jameson admitted. His eyes remained on his phone, but he shrugged once. "My head hurt too badly to argue with them, so I just sat there."

"So, what are you going to do about Darrin?" Spencer asked pulling into the airport parking lot.

"I'm going to find the motherfucker away from the track and finish what he started," Jameson replied, point blank.

You couldn't threaten a guy like Jameson Riley and get away with it. You couldn't try to control him either without pushback. That's something Darrin Torres was about to learn the hard way.

You see, the more you pushed him, the more he defied you. Back when he raced USAC, I saw this side of him more times than not and every time, his reactions remained the same. Defiance.

Blue Flag – The flagman waves this flag to indicate to a driver that a faster car is either approaching (steady flag) or attempting a pass (waved flag). If a driver is given this flag he doesn't have to do anything, just be aware and maintain the racing line, and avoid intentionally obstructing the faster car.

"I can't believe Alley rented this goddamn thing?"

"She's *your* wife …" Jameson pointed when we arrived at his parent's house.

"I feel like I'm driving a vagina on wheels."

"Like I said, she's *your* wife, dude," Jameson laughed. "And good luck with the whole," he motioned to his hair and ass. "Just … good luck." He patted Spencer on the back as we got out of the mini-van.

It was around midnight when we arrived at his parent's house in Mooresville. After last night, and spending the day with Spencer and Emma, I needed sleep.

As soon as Jameson and I got inside his room, we both fell on the bed tangled together, asleep within mere minutes.

When I woke up the next morning, I felt so much better. My ass still hurt from my new tattoo, but mentally and physically, I was feeling much better.

I swore to myself I would never drink that much tequila *ever* again. I'm sure that resolution wouldn't last though. I'd said that before, hell, I even attempted to sue them back in high school when I woke up naked in the back of my truck after polishing off a half bottle, okay, an entire bottle, by myself. Regardless, I was sure I didn't mean it, but I felt better already even if I was lying to myself.

Jameson was still asleep on his stomach so I decided to let him sleep. After showering and dressing in my new underwear I purchased, I made my way downstairs.

When I walked into the Riley's gigantic kitchen, I suddenly remembered how much I enjoyed cooking. Back home, I usually cooked for Charlie, but since I'd been on my pretend summer vacation, I hadn't done much but spread my legs.

That sounds horrible.

Making my way around their kitchen, I pulled out the ingredients to make Jameson some waffles—the boy was obsessed with them. His motor coach was overflowing with those damn Eggo waffles. I personally found them insanely delicious, too, but I wanted to make him a meal that didn't have me as an ingredient.

Not that I was opposed to that sort of thing, but we did need to find some balance as well as nourishment.

After the batter was done and the waffle iron was heating, I heard footsteps behind me—hoping it wasn't Spencer or Emma. I couldn't handle them again today so I warily turned around.

And there, in all his morning glory, Jameson stood, wearing only a pair of khaki shorts. With his insanely wild mess of hair; beautifully sparkly green eyes; sexy dirty smirk and his chiseled chest, my hot-headed dirty heathen was staring at me with burning, lustful eyes.

Hot damn.

He didn't say anything and placed his hands on the island and the counter trapping me in the corner of the U-shaped kitchen.

"Hi." My eyes stayed focused on his.

"Hi," Jameson replied, moving closer.

"I wanted to surprise you with breakfast in bed."

"My breakfast wasn't in bed, though, so ..." he grinned, shrugging his shoulders.

"If you would have *stayed* in bed," I said, pushing lightly against his chest, I grinned as well. "I could have surprised you."

Jameson shook his head slowly lifting me onto the counter with a soft grunt. "I wasn't looking for food," he clarified.

"What are you looking for then?"

"I think you know."

I tapped my index finger to my lips and looked up as if I was contemplating. "You were looking for waffles, weren't you?" I teased.

"No," he shook his head slowly looking around the kitchen. "Try again," he told me reaching for the honey bottle next to my arm.

"Honey?" I asked softly. "You were looking for honey?"

"I wasn't looking for honey …" his voice trailed off setting the honey aside and reached for the hem of my shirt. "But I found honey."

I grabbed his hands. "Jameson, your parents—"

"Aren't home," he finished pulling my shirt over my head. His hands snuck around my waist dragging me to the edge of the granite counter.

What kind of pit lizard would I be if I didn't whore moan and arch my back when I felt his already hard camshaft ready and waiting for me?

Not a very good one, that's for sure.

Staying true to par, I did whore moan and arch my back in response because damn, this boy was good.

Jameson's strong hands moved with determination up my sides and around my back to remove my bra. Slowly, he pulled the hot pink bra away and my nipples hardened in anticipation.

Throwing it behind him, he attacked my nipples. With each nip, I let out a whimper of pleasure and ground my hips against his, earning a moan of pleasure from him, too.

Jameson stopped, looking up at me from under his thick black lashes. "Are you opposed to being sticky?"

"I think *you're* the one with the issue with being sticky."

He smirked. "So that's a no?"

"Have you ever known me to be opposed to anything while my legs are spread?" I felt the need to point out.

"Good point." He grinned now. "You're going to need a shower after this." He reached for the honey bottle beside him.

Soon Def Leppard's "Pour Some Sugar On Me" was humming in

my head.

I really didn't know the words to sing them out loud but the entire situation was certainly playing out to the beat of the song when he leaned back, pulled my jeans off, and then reached for the whipped cream, shaking it with a quick flick of his wrist.

With his thumb, he popped the lid and winked. "You're sweet, but I think I'd like my Sway a la carte this morning."

"Is that so?" I giggled.

"Mmhm," Jameson proceeded to pour honey, whipped cream, chocolate syrup, and caramel sauce over my entire body.

Within minutes, I looked like a goddamn banana split.

Apparently, Jameson thought the same thing when he laughed. "Look at that," his head skewed to the side. "I've created the perfect dessert. My very own Sway banana split." He laughed again at his discovery, admiring his creation just as Spencer did with the dick on the wall.

What was even worse was that we were thinking the same damn thing, which was never a good sign.

This just proved Jameson was the other half of my brain, a theory our parents have had for years.

"Are you just going to stare at your dessert, or are you going to eat it?" I asked trying to be all super-sexy licking some honey from my arm but it didn't go down that way.

Instead, when I lifted said arm to lick it, I slipped on the sticky slippery granite counter and fell off the side onto the floor.

If that's not embarrassing, I don't know what is.

Jameson tried to catch me, but I had so much sticky shit on me, I slipped right out of his hands onto my tattooed ass.

Instantly we were both laughing.

In the process of the intended sexy lick-and-then-slip, Jameson was now covered in the same sticky sweet mess he covered me with, and currently trying to unbutton his shorts with honey fingers—not exactly an easy task.

After some effort, he managed to get the shorts down and proceeded to lick his Sway banana split.

I couldn't take my eyes off his because, holy Moses, it was sexy as hell.

Jameson knelt down in front of me where I was sprawled out pit lizard-style on his parent's cream tile floor, covered in sticky sweets.

"Gimme some sugar," he grinned bringing my foot to his mouth where he took his time at my toes, licking off the smeared chocolate and honey. I wasn't exactly comfortable with him licking my toes so I squirmed away.

Chuckling at my discomfort for that particular appendage, he moved up my calf to a dollop of whipped cream and a drizzle of caramel. "You taste good," his tongue carefully swept over me.

Ah, crap ... now I'm singing Trick Daddy's "Gimme Some Sugar."

His tongue darted out once more licking his way up my right thigh until he reached his destination but before his tongue met my ignition switch. He gave me a lopsided smile and bit the inside of my thigh.

I jumped.

"Did that hurt?" he asked in a low concerned gritty voice.

"No," I assured him. "Just ... uh ... surprised me,"

He chuckled licking the whipped cream, honey, chocolate, and caramel from my body before he continued his licking and sucking against my crankcase for some proper deburring.

Tongue. Lips. Hands. Fingers.

All of it, dedicated to my banana split and me.

Once his lips touched me, I lost all sense of time clinging to him desperately. The sensations were too much and I felt the sweet tension building within.

I'm not sure if it was being covered in sticky sweets that made this seem so intense, or if it was being with him over the past few weeks that were the reason.

Every day, every single minute of the goddamn day, I felt myself falling deeper in love with this man, if that was even possible.

I could feel a shudder rise deep within. It started at my feet, settling in my tummy, passing through me in waves. I knew I was panting, embarrassingly so, but couldn't make myself care.

"Oh God, Jameson ... I ..." I couldn't even form the words.

With a growl that bordered on a roar, he was up my sticky banana split body and sliding inside me with determined thrusts. I thought he was going to come by the way he was moving, but instead he pulled out, sat back on his heels to look at me, my banana split now covering his chest and stomach.

"I want to try something," he said pulling me up with him.

We slipped a few times because, Christ, there was a lot of whipped cream. Jameson had gotten slightly carried away when the whipped cream was out.

Once standing, he turned me around and bent me over the counter.

Hot damn.

Reaching for both my hands, he placed them securely on the edge of the counter in front of me.

"Honey, you're gonna want to hold on for this," he advised, his breath blowing across my shoulder, gasping slightly. "*Jesus,* you're sexy."

I giggled feeling him part my legs with his own. His hands traveled up my arms and over my shoulders where he stopped and pulled my hair to the side so he could place kisses down my neck.

Jameson's strong hands then traveled down my back and came to rest on my tattooed ass. Reaching between us, he slipped himself in, his hands gripping my ass tightly.

I think this is my new favorite position.

I looked around for a mirror but no such luck, so I looked over my shoulder back at him.

The moment I looked back at him over my shoulder, his eyes darkened and he lost it, *completely* lost it. His head fell back; his eyes closed as "Fuck, Sway" fell from his honey, chocolate covered lips.

Slumping forward, his arms wrapped around my waist. "Sorry ... I lost it when you looked back at me," he panted.

"It's okay. That was *amazing* ..." I went to turn around to face him, but slipped and once again fell to the ground.

Thankfully, Jameson had already pulled out because, Christ, we could have lost some important parts that way.

There we both were, lolling on the tile floor, covered in a sticky sweet mess and laughing at each other.

"Should we clean this up?" he asked, motioning to the mess

around the kitchen as he licked some chocolate from my finger.

"Probably, but—" I began but was interrupted by the sound of the garage door opening.

Jameson and I both gaped at each other in horror that we were naked, covered in sticky sweets, in his parent's kitchen.

This, by far, transcends anything that's happened in the last two weeks.

Luckily, Jameson reacted first reaching for any clothes nearby and throwing my shirt and jeans at me. Screw the underwear.

As I started to put on my shirt I realized that I was still covered in chocolate syrup.

Shit.

While I was trying to wipe it off Jameson stopped me. "Fuck Sway, just put your damn shirt on," he snapped staring down at my chest and all its chocolate glory.

"I'm covered in syrup and my tank top is white." My eyes focused between his legs. It was *very* obvious what we had been doing. "It'll just soak right through my shirt."

"Doesn't matter!" his voice was frantic. "They are opening the door. Put your shirt on and stop staring at me."

Pulling my shirt over my head, I forgot all about the chocolate and the fact that I wasn't wearing a bra.

Not only was I not wearing a bra, but I wasn't wearing underwear either. Nope, they were on the floor next to the fridge where Jimi was *now* standing.

He hadn't looked down yet; instead, his eyes were fixated on Jameson leaning against the counter—no shirt on, all sticky and smirking.

This couldn't have looked much worse.

Yep, transcends everything.

Jimi glared at Jameson. Still not on speaking terms, Jameson offered his own glare. "What the fuck happened in here?"

Nancy walked in setting bags of groceries on the counter about the time I picked up the whipped cream bottle from the floor.

Jameson, nonchalantly, tried to kick the honey away, but their eyes dropped to the floor as Jameson slipped and fell sideways against the stove.

I giggled.

What else was I going to do?

"Never mind—I don't even want to know." Jimi shook his head stepping into the kitchen. His foot stuck to the floor where he stepped. "Okay ... why is there fucking syrup everywhere? What the hell happened in here?"

By that point, I could hardly breathe I was giggling so much.

Jameson cracked under the pressure joining in with the giggles and ran his sticky hands through his hair, causing it to stick straight up.

"Uh ... we ... made waffles," Jameson finally answered holding up a burnt waffle. "Want one?"

"It looks like a bunch of fucking four year old girls made waffles," Jimi replied looking to me for an answer. I couldn't offer much more than a squeaked giggle snort and eventually a nod.

In the midst of all this, the chocolate had now mixed with the whip cream I was covered in seeping through my tank top. All this did was made it look like I was leaking chocolate milk.

Jimi averted his eyes to the floor, away from the chocolate milk, only to see my hot pink bra at his feet.

Let me rephrase my previous statement, this *could* look worse.

Nancy looked down when Jimi finally chuckled. "Clean this mess up." He was still laughing when he walked away.

"Jameson, my goodness, can't you keep your hands off poor Sway for one morning," Nancy chided pushing his shoulder and shaking her head slowly as though she was thoroughly disappointed in her son. "Here Sway; I'm sorry my son has no control," she apologized handing me my bra and then looked back at Jameson. "Clean this up, Jameson."

Tossing a towel his direction, she noticed his hip.

I giggled again when she grabbed him to get a better look. The tattoo was low enough that you couldn't see it ordinarily when he didn't have a shirt on but his shorts were unbuttoned and hanging rather low on his hips revealing the chiseled curve.

So there in plain view, running vertically up the cut line of his hip, were his tattoos on display for his mother.

Nancy shook her head again. "I don't know what I'm going to do with these kids," she mumbled mostly to herself. "I *really* hope you two get married someday since you can't stop humping in my house and branding yourself with each other's names." She slapped him on the chest. "Clean up."

"Yes, Mom," Jameson laughed and started cleaning up.

I reached for another towel to assist when Jameson leaned down near my ear. "Did my mom just say hump and marriage in the same sentence?"

"Yep!"

While we were laughing we overheard Jimi on the phone with Alley. "What do you mean he drew a dick on the wall ... you mean like a man dick ... *Christ*, I swear, these kids are not mine."

On Tuesday night we snuck out to Charlotte to watch Justin and Tyler test sprint cars. It was a change from the sticky sweet day mostly because we were clothed. I had the biggest bruise sprawled across my hip from where I fell from the counter but, other than that, the day was still providing laughs for us whenever we recalled Jimi's reaction.

Jameson and I sat there on the tailgate of his Ford F-250 watching the cars whip around the track, kicking up a cloud of dirt that hovered over it in a thick layer. After a few laps, the cars came back into the infield where Tommy took notes. Jameson made his way to them as Justin offered his feedback to Tommy.

Looking out over the track, I was reminded of how simple racing used to be for him. Now, it was far from that.

Jameson approached with a beer in hand. The corners of his mouth lifted slightly when he heard the sharp growl of a 410 sprint roaring to life. The sound really was addicting.

Securely seated next to me once again, we watched the car drift smoothly through the turns. My focus was more on Jameson as he observed the way the cars jerked sideways on the front stretch.

His long fingers grasped the neck of the beer bottle gauging a group of bystanders waiting for a glimpse of him. It seemed news spread that Jameson was here. Reality was waiting for him.

Instead, he looked beyond them bringing the beer to his lips. Before taking a drink, he sighed. "I miss this." He tipped his head toward the track.

I nodded, knowing my remarks weren't needed. He knew I understood. If anyone understood how he felt about dirt track racing it was me.

The bottle in his hand drifted my direction. "Want some?"

Shaking my head, I curled my legs up to my chest wrapping my arms around them as a breeze blew across the dirt. Times like this, I understood why I saw that vulnerability in him. He longed for a time when all he knew were sprint cars. Because it was where his dream of racing had formed.

I still saw that side of Jameson emerge racing in the cup cars, but now it was overshadowed by the drama of it all.

Aside from the day at track earlier in the week, Jameson had absolutely no free time during the day so that meant I spent my days with Emma.

By Thursday, I was contemplating killing myself as drastic as that sounded. I could only handle her for a few hours at a time before I needed a nap to recoup.

The only thing that made everything better was spending the evening with Jameson, wrapped in his arms, without an inch of space.

There were times late at night, after he'd fallen asleep, when I watched him sleep. I wanted to tell him how much I loved him, how much I wanted this to work, and how much I didn't want to leave next week.

Knowing I spent the last few years attending college so I would be in a position to help my dad, I had obligations now. Charlie needed me there to help.

As it was, he only had a handful of staff there to help. When you're running an entire track with only four people, you needed all the help you could get.

Once we arrived in Brooklyn, Michigan, Jameson, having put aside the events of last weekend's fine, was in race mode again and focused on racing. Being one of his favorite tracks, his mood improved.

Michigan International Speedway is a two-mile moderately banked D-shaped superspeedway. Some even refer to it as the sister track to Texas World Speedway because of its wide racing surface and high eighteen-degree banking. It's extremely fast with the average speed entering the corners at around two hundred and five miles per hour, which is due to its wide sweeping corners and long straightaways.

On Friday, Jameson had left to qualify, which left me with Emma, Nancy, Alley, and Jimi in the garage area.

"Emma, honey, it's like ninety-five degrees. Take that damn scarf off," Nancy said as she pulled on the bright red scarf Emma had been wearing since we left Pocono.

"No, that's okay," Emma tried to say but it was useless when the red scarf fell to the ground beside her. As luck would have it, she had her back turned to Jimi, giving her parents a full view of her Trash-R-Us token.

You couldn't miss the sharp intake of breath both Jimi and Nancy inhaled at the sight of their youngest child's neck.

Emma slowly turned around with panic-stricken eyes to meet Jimi's enraged eyes.

It took him a moment to be able to speak, but when he did the entire garage area turned and gawked.

"Emma Lynn Riley, *what* the fuck is that on your neck?" Jimi shouted.

Various members of Jameson's crew chuckled knowing what Emma had done last week. Though this was news to her parents, most everyone else knew about her tattoo.

Jimi flipped out and began yelling at the top of his lungs at poor little Emma, who then began to cry, and not just any crying, more like bawling.

"Dad ... calm down ... it's not that big of a deal." She made an effort to downplay it. "I'll grow my hair out. Why are you so upset?"

He gasped. "*Why* am I upset? You kids ... I refuse to believe that my DNA was a part of ... something like this." He was pacing across the concrete floor in the space where Jameson's car had just been. "First, we have Spencer who draws dicks on hotel walls and tattoos his ass. Then we have Jameson who obviously needs to be medicated or some shit, and then there's *Emma*, who tattoos her goddamn neck with something you'd see on a hooker!"

Nancy backhanded his shoulder. "Jimi, calm down! It's not that big of a deal."

"Not that big of a deal?" he seethed and then his expression changed. "I don't think they're my kids. That's it, I don't think they are ..." his voice trailed off as he stomped away.

Nancy attempted to comfort Emma and her obsessive crying. I stood there against the wall shaking my head.

There was never a dull moment around the Riley family.

Eventually Jameson returned from his qualifying run. He snagged the pole, naturally, so he was in good spirits.

As soon as he pulled himself from the car, Liz Clayton, a reporter with FOX Sports, was directly in his face. "Jameson, you got the pole, how'd you do it?"

Jameson leaned back against his car and chuckled at the inevitable question. "It was tough. I knew we got through one and two fast and uh ... I knew we were awesome getting into three. I had three lanes to choose from. The one I chose didn't really work, but ... I still ended up on the pole so I guess it *did* work. I felt like we were kinda tight in three and then I was a little free off, but it was because I hit the throttle too soon trying to get back to the line, it worked though." He gave a quick shrug. "It's nice for this whole Riley Simplex Racing Team. The guys did a good job, gave me an awesome car out there and to get the pole here at a track I love is awesome."

"Have you and Darrin had a chance to talk about last week?" Liz asked searching for a feature story.

Way to put him in a bad mood.

"No." His expression changed instantly, the casual tone no longer present. "We won't be talking about it. There's nothing to say."

Jameson walked away over to Kyle and Mason, who both had their clipboards going over notes.

Kyle congratulated him so I made my way over since he seemed to be smiling again.

"Congratulations," I said, hip-checking him.

"Thanks," Jameson replied giving me his lopsided grin he was so good at. "Do you want to get some dinner in a little while?" he asked checking his phone. "I have an autograph session but after that we can go somewhere."

"Sure."

"Nice run, Jameson," a man said from behind.

We both turned around to see Tate Harris and Andy Crockett, Tate's teammate, with Banner Racing, standing next to Jameson's car.

Andy Crockett was a name I heard a lot these days. He was another driver who was easy on the eyes and had racked up a string of wins earlier in the season.

"Thanks." Jameson reached for his hand to shake it.

Tate noticed me standing beside Jameson. "Oh, hey Sway. How have you been?"

"I'm good Tate." I smiled. "Nice to see you again,"

"Have you met my teammate, Andy Crockett?" Tate nudged Andy. "He drives the Number Six Miller Machinery car."

"It's nice to meet you." Andy and I shook hands while Jameson slung his arm around my shoulder, pulling me toward him.

Tate looked at me. "How's your dad feeling, Sway? Did he—"

He stopped short of what he was saying when Jameson cleared his throat and let out a half cough that sounded strange.

Huh?

Drawing my attention back to Jameson, he shifted uncomfortably beside me. He and Tate exchanged a loaded glance before Jameson smiled down at me.

"He's fine," I said softly not sure what that look was all about *or* why Tate would be asking about my dad, *or* why Jameson now looked like he'd seen a ghost.

"Yeah, so good luck tomorrow, Jameson," Tate said quickly and walked away with Andy.

"What was that about?" I looked at Jameson. "Why would he ask about Charlie?"

Jameson didn't answer right away and stared at me as if he was trying to make sense of what I just asked. "Uh ... I don't know. Maybe he wanted to know," he mumbled and then looked at the time on his phone. "Listen ..." He pulled me against his chest for a hug. "I have to get to the autograph session." He pulled away without another word and walked with Alley toward the grandstands.

What the hell happened?

I'm so confused.

Why would Tate ask about Charlie?

Being paranoid, I decided to call Charlie but, of course, it was Saturday night and he didn't answer.

When Jameson returned from the autograph session, he was still acting rather strange and cancelled dinner because he said he had a meeting with Simplex so that left me hanging out with Emma, Aiden, and Spencer while Jameson and Alley left with Jimi to meet Marcus.

We kept ourselves busy playing Wii Tennis for four hours straight, but that ended when Spencer got upset that Aiden and Emma were *supposedly* cheating and he threw the remote through Jameson's flat screen TV in his motor coach.

I did not want to be here when *that* was explained, but thankfully when Jameson returned, he was too tired to notice the TV.

On race day, Jameson returned to his hot-head self once again; I'm sure the fines and probation were now heavy on his mind from the constant media attention. They forget nothing.

Not long into the race, he took his vexations out on Kyle.

"Hey, you know what would be really helpful, Kyle?"

"What?"

"Just shut the fuck up and let me drive," Jameson seethed into the radio.

This had been going on for a while, Kyle and Jameson arguing back and forth. Darrin and Jameson were currently battling for first place in the final laps of the race. Jameson had led all but four laps so far and he damn sure wasn't about to give up the win now.

"If he has a run, let him go," Kyle ordered. "NASCAR is watching you."

"I'm just racing."

"Yeah ... right."

Knowing he was just instigating, Kyle finally stopped baiting Jameson and let him finish out the last few laps. He knew, as well as most inside the inner circle, the more you push, the more push back you get from Jameson.

"At your rear; at your door ... he's got a run," Aiden announced. "Cole's behind you."

"Cole?" Jameson called over the radio.

"10-4, what's up?" Bobby asked.

"Am I lifting out of three?"

"Not that I can see but I can't see anything with Darrin all over you," Bobby said. "I got an idea ... I'll get up behind and take the air off. *I'm* not on probation."

Bobby got behind Darrin, taking the air off him, allowing Jameson to pull away to a one-second lead.

"All clear, bud—coming to the white flag here," Aiden announced. "Hit your marks."

"Nice job Cole, fuck yeah," Jameson praised heading into clean air. "That's how you work together."

"Go get 'em dude," Bobby replied.

"Last lap here, drive out the windshield, and hit your marks. You got this, bud," Kyle told him, all the anger he had a few moments ago seemed to dissipate now that Darrin couldn't catch Jameson. Bobby was all over him trying to keep away, both of them destroying any chance at catching Jameson as they were using their tires up.

Emma and I were clinging to each other in the pit box once again. I had no fingernails left and Emma was biting her lips so hard they were actually bleeding.

Kyle and Mason stood as they came out of turn four to the checkered flag. "Nice job. Nice *fucking* job, Jameson!" Kyle yelled in excitement pumping his fists in the air. "Way to hang in there and battle back."

"Yeah!" Jameson screamed over the radio in his own excitement as he took the checkered flag. "Way to go, guys!"

Bobby and Darrin were still battling it out for second but Bobby pulled forward enough to come across the line about a foot in front of him.

"Nice job everyone," Jameson said in the cool down laps. "Cole, you're the man! I owe you one."

"Don't even worry about it. I'll finish second any day if Darrin doesn't win."

Jameson laughed.

Of course, my hormones were flaring when Jameson did a burn out right in front of us in the infield.

There's nothing this pit lizard loved more than burnouts. Well, now I'm lying, but they do get me going.

Once in victory lane, Jameson did his usual jump into his pit crew, his post-race interviews and posed for the insane amount of pictures.

We were walking toward the media center where he had the contender's conference when I finally got a chance to congratulate him.

"I'm so proud of you," I told him giving him a squeeze around his waist, his arms draped over my shoulder.

"Thanks, I think you're my good luck charm," Jameson said leaning over to kiss my head.

Alley, who was in front of us, pushed a group of reporters aside so we could make it through the crowd.

"Nah, it must be all the sex," I whispered. "It's relaxing you."

"It's definitely helping," he nodded giving me a squeeze, a soft chuckle fell from his lips. "I don't think I'm going to let you leave. I'll *never* survive without you."

"You'll be fine. I hear Dana's available."

He growled in my ear shivering. "Don't *ever* joke about that. She is fucking *crazy*."

"What are you going to do?" You couldn't miss the curiosity in my voice.

"Count down the days until I see you again," he answered immediately.

"Well, you—" I began, but was cut off by Darrin walking toward the media center.

Jameson's grip around my waist tightened when he noticed him.

Darrin noticed the possessiveness and let out a dark mischievous chuckle. "I'm not after your girl, Riley, I'm after you." His eyes shifted to me. "She's tempting though."

My hot-head reacted before I even realized what was happening.

"Stay the fuck away from her," Jameson snarled pushing Darrin against the doors to the media center, his forearm nudged under his throat. "I will only warn you *once*."

"Relax, Riley," Darrin said in a strained tone. "Like I said, she's not what I'm after."

Jameson pulled him back and slammed him against the metal doors again. "Are you threatening me?"

"No, I'm warning *you*," Darrin struggled against him pushing back.

Before Jameson could do anything else, crew members from both teams fought to drag Jameson back.

"Have you lost your goddamn mind Jameson?" Kyle shouted in his face. "What don't you understand about probation?"

"Get off me!" Jameson snapped pushing the door open to the media center.

The contenders' conference was hardly even about the race.

All the media cared about was the confrontation going on between Jameson and Darrin. They were eating this juvenile bullshit up and Jameson and his quick fuse weren't helping.

It was late by the time we were on the jet back to Mooresville, but I was surprised to see Jameson's family took a different jet home. Usually they'd fly together.

Jameson was quiet as I expected.

If I didn't know any better, I'd think he didn't win by the way he was acting. He seemed so different, but I also knew he had a great deal of stress these days.

"I need to leave next week after Sonoma," I told him lounging in the oversized captain's chairs. "I was going to fly home after the race."

He leaned his head back staring out the small oval window, his hands rested folded in his lap. "That's why we're going somewhere, alone."

"What do you mean, *alone*?" I asked shifting in my seat to look at him.

"Alone. No one knows but me and Wes, the pilot," he clarified glancing over at me with a grin.

An alarming amount of giddiness followed. You'd think I'd been asked to prom. "Do I get to know where?" was my first response.

"Nope, not until we're there," Jameson chuckled at my enthusiasm. "I can't take any risks. Personally, I'd prefer it if no one else catches us or sees us naked, *ever* again."

The last time with his dad getting a view of the fun bags, was the final straw for Jameson. So now, there we sat, my last week of the pit lizard's dream, on a jet to God knows where.

I was so excited I felt as though I was about to burst into giddy pit lizard delight flames. Thankfully, I didn't.

"I have one condition." Maintaining my image of control, I reached for my water next to me nonchalantly. "And it's an important one, so listen up."

"Yeah, what's that?"

"Where ever we are going, *no* clothes are allowed once we're behind doors."

Jameson started unbuttoning his white button down shirt yanking it aside. His hands rested on either side of the armrests on the chair I was sitting in. He was hovering now and I loved the hovering.

"Why wait until we get there, honey; let's start now."

Flat Spot – If a driver locks the tires up when stopping he'll grind a flat spot on the surface of the tire. When back on the track, a flat spot can cause a vibration that makes the car almost un-drivable.

I wanted to tell Jameson what had changed between us, but I hadn't. Thinking if I held out, I wouldn't have to tell him the change even occurred. My body betrayed my mind and, instead, it showed in every move.

The storm was losing strength outside, aside from the occasional crack of thunder and the steady pattering of the rain from the growling clouds. The ocean waves pounded against the rocks. With the French doors leading out to the open balcony, the occasional gust of wind whipped through the room.

For the second time tonight, the power was down. The only light in the entire condominium was coming from the candle lit beside the bed, flickering with the wind.

The candle cast a soft orange glow throughout the room as the glistening reflections of light caught the highlights in Jameson's hair; he hovered above me, making it shimmer in the darkness.

The surprise impromptu vacation destination was a condo he rented on the beach in Savannah, Georgia. The only problem was that a tropical storm was blowing through.

I had to admit, though, that it had made our few days there fun.

There wasn't anything to do but stay in bed; something we were good at.

So, there we were in bed again, but this time Jameson was different.

This was different as he moved languidly against me, his hips meeting mine with slow passionate movements. His kisses were different, slow, deep, and adoring.

We were *different*. Something had changed.

This wasn't about sex anymore. It wasn't just friends with benefits. What started out as simple three weeks ago was complicated as hell now. When I looked into his ardent green eyes, I knew he saw it, too. There was no denying the change.

I was savoring the warm sensation of his body moving with mine as the heat between us was creating a sheen of sweat as we slid against one another.

Despite the fact I was burning up, my entire body was trembling.

Jameson bent down to kiss my forehead and then leaned back to look at me, his features holding an emotion I couldn't decipher. His mouth opened as though he was about to say something and then his brow furrowed. Without finishing his words again, he pulled my mouth to his.

Here's the thing—the *really* shitty thing—I loved this man so damn much that it literally hurt inside, and yet I couldn't even tell him; I just couldn't.

I wanted to, but the words wouldn't form or when they would, my lips wouldn't speak them. What was I going to do, tell him the truth?

No, that was just ridiculous.

There were times when he had tried to tell me something as well but didn't, his words or thoughts falling short.

Jameson's mouth moved from my own, spreading kisses over my jaw and against my neck before he pulled back to look at me, his left hand moved from behind my knee to rest against my cheek. Unnerved by the tears forming in my eyes that this was going to end in less than three days, I turned away, watching the flickering of the candle.

How could I have let myself fall like this?

And, more importantly, where did the time go?

Those three weeks, well they were days now. And soon these days were going to be hours followed quickly by minutes, then seconds, and, before I knew it, my time in this fairytale I'd been living would be over.

And then what? What would any of this mean to him?

"Sway ... honey," his low timbre drew my attention toward him, his nose brushing over my jaw.

Slowly, I turned my head to meet his gaze.

When he saw the tears streaming down my cheeks, I felt him take a sudden intake of breath. Without saying the words, those tears told him exactly what I couldn't. They told him exactly how I felt.

They told him this wasn't just friends with benefits for me anymore—it never was. They told him what all these years as friends had been leading to. Those years and these last three weeks led up to this. I was in love and there was absolutely no way I could be "just friends" with him anymore.

I meant it when I said there was no going back.

As though he could hear the unspoken thoughts, he nodded his head once, his thumb sweeping over a tear, brushing it away.

I jumped in his arms when the thunder cracked, the wind picked up, pelting the window with rain. Just like the change occurring within us, the storm was changing, gaining speed.

"Please don't cry," he begged kissing my lips. "I'm sorry," he mumbled, his hands trembling as they caressed me. The trembling reminded me of the first night together in Charlotte, though this was entirely different now. "I'm sorry ... I'm *so* fucking sorry," he said again, his hand moved down my body, his eyes still locked on mine.

I couldn't look away; his eyes displayed for me what I thought I would never see.

It changed for him, too.

Leaning forward, his lips pressed to my neck, his warm breath flowing across my skin. "Non volevo cadere nel miele amore, mi dispiace," he whispered.

I moaned and his mouth found the sensitive skin on my neck, biting harder than I was expecting.

The release and relief were intense with my body melting into him.

"Sway," he whispered, lips urgent against mine.

Slowly his trembling fingertips found my cheek.

He was looking down at me, his features hardened with concentration maybe. I wasn't sure but moaned and he shuddered in response, closing his eyes and rocking his hips against mine.

"Oh God, Sway." His head fell against me just as he flexed forward. Running my hand down the long line of his back, his entire body seemed to react with more trembling. "I can't ... I'm ..."

Again, he didn't finish his goddamn words.

Despite my sedated feeling, it was really starting to irritate me that he wouldn't finish his words. That and him speaking in Italian, knowing damn well I don't speak Italian.

It took me four years to learn two words in Spanish so deciphering Italian wasn't in my immediate future.

"Jesus Christ ... the way you move ..."

I understood that he was distracted, but Jesus, finish a fucking sentence.

I really wanted to punch him in the face right then, but I didn't. That would probably ruin the moment. Remembering the mere days I had left, I didn't want this moment to end.

When he threw himself into his movements, I was distracted from my thoughts of punching him.

There was no holding back any longer. His entire body jerked in time with his release, his head buried in my shoulder as he held my body tightly against his.

He collapsed his entire weight on me, his breath hot and rapid on my neck. I stroked his back and shoulders, my own breathing and heart rate returned to a normal pace.

Exhaling heavily, he slid to one side nestling me against his chest. I liked the nestling. Nestling was good.

We laid there quietly staring at each other, listening to the sounds of the wind and the occasional crack of thunder. The soft sounds of our breathing mixing with the sounds of the storm filled the salty air between us.

What was he sorry for? What did he say to me in Italian? I have to know, it's driving me fucking mad.

"What did you say to me?" My words seemed to hang for a moment like the air between us seized.

"Huh?" His brow furrowed his gaze upon me, eyes guarded.

"In Italian, what did you say, and why do you never finish what you're going to say to me when we're ..." I motioned between our bodies.

His breathing increased and then he swallowed as though it was difficult to say. With my chin resting on his chest I could feel his heart beat quicken. "I ... uh ..." He pushed me gently from his chest and rolled to his side looking at me, his green eyes burning into my own. "Is this ... what is this between us?" he asked, his voice was different, low and anxious, wary even. His eyes searched my own for any indication he could get.

"Friends with benefits ... I *thought*," I responded quickly.

"Is that all it is to you?"

"Is that all it is to you?" I countered without answering.

He was quiet for an entire minute, believe me, I counted all excruciating sixty seconds.

I have rarely seen Jameson struggle for words. Until now.

When he spoke, I was surprised at how tense and unsteady his voice had now become. "No ... it's not."

My heart was beating a million miles an hour, thudding loudly in my ears. The blood was rushing rapidly throughout my body spreading like a summer wildfire scorching my skin. "It's not for me either," I agreed. "What did you say to me in Italian?"

His eyes closed and then slowly opened as though he was giving himself a pep talk. "What do you feel for me?" he asked softly, damn near inaudible.

"What?" My eyes searched his.

Still, I couldn't tell him.

He sighed softly.

"Sway, what is this for you? Don't tell me you don't feel something more for me. Don't tell me this is just sex anymore, because it's not Sway. I see it in your eyes. I feel it when you touch me. You *feel* something more for me."

"It *never* was about sex for me, Jameson," I stated as a tear slipped down my cheek. His palm reached for my face brushing it away with his thumb. I could feel the trembling in his hand return. "What did you say?"

"I said," he blinked quickly, his gaze falling to his hands. When his eyes returned, they were lustrous. "I said … I didn't mean to fall in love, honey." The shock on my face must have registered with him because he raced to add. "I'm sorry."

"You fell in love … with me?" I gasped.

I was expecting something along the lines of 'I like you more than friends' but not love!

He gave me a tentative, but uneasy smile.

"I did, I'm sorry." His eyes dropped. "I know that I can't be the man you need. I'm not *good* for you. I know that. I knew what I was getting myself into but I *had* to know. I had to know what it was like, to be like this with you, as though you were *only* mine; even if it was for only three weeks."

"Huh?" I looked at him as if I had no idea what he said.

I didn't have any idea what he said or at least I couldn't comprehend it.

I think my plan wasn't my plan at all and I was so confused that even thinking complicated this for me.

What just happened?

The confusion might have been because I was hyperventilating, and there was a serious lack of oxygen going to my brain once again.

"Are you okay?" he asked sitting up to look at me, his hand reaching out to touch my shoulder.

"I … how …" I drew in a much needed breath fumbling over my words and thoughts. "How long have you … um … loved me?"

"A while," he answered and placed a soft kiss on my shoulder. His fingertips danced lightly across the skin above my collarbone.

"How long?" I snapped.

"My grandpa used to tell me … you don't give up what you know to get what you don't know," Jameson said softly, his eyes dropped to our hands. "I guess he isn't always crazy. Sometimes he makes sense."

Not understanding how that had anything to do with this, I asked again, "How long Jameson?"

"I couldn't tell you, Sway." He shook his head and his hand fell from my shoulder resting against the bed. "I've tried to look back and pinpoint a time but I think it happened, gradually. Way before this started." He pulled me against his chest. "I think it started when we were kids and slowly developed over time. I avoided it for the longest time, pretending I didn't feel that way, but it got to the point I couldn't ignore it any longer. When I saw you in Charlotte, I knew I couldn't ... I just ... had to know. It was hard enough letting you go after Daytona. I had to do something."

"Jameson." I lost it.

Falling against the mattress in a heap, I bawled like a goddamn baby with Jameson frantically trying to comfort me.

"Sway, *oh God*, I'm sorry ... I shouldn't have said anything. Jesus Christ, I can't believe I fucked this up." He chided himself, "I knew I shouldn't have said anything."

"What?" I sobbed scrambling to look up at him. "You *shouldn't* have said anything? Christ Almighty, Jameson, are you blind?" I practically yelled causing his mouth to gape open.

"Huh?" It was his turn to look at me as if he had no idea what I said.

"Jameson," I shook my head and sat up to lean against the headboard. "I'm not mad that you love me. I'm mad that we wasted all this time because neither one of us had the brass balls to say it."

"Did you say brass balls and love in the same sentence?" he asked with a grin.

I slapped him across the face, not hard. "Pay attention."

"Sorry, I got distracted by you saying balls," he admitted with another grin.

"Seriously, you're like a fucking child."

He winked. "So you love me, too?"

"More than you can ever imagine." My head slumped at my admission. "It's the pathetic pretend to like the same flavor of ice cream or music, type of love. Break your heart type love."

He looked away when I said break your heart.

"See, I'm not ..." he paused. "We shouldn't be together, Sway."

"Why?"

"Because ...." He half shouted in a strangled voice, the muscles in his jaw tight. "You need someone who will be there for you. Someone who can drop everything and run to you when you really need them ... and you're *gonna* need him," he intoned, and by the look on his face, I had a feeling he meant something by that but he continued, "You need someone who can lay in bed with you on Sunday mornings. You deserve someone who can call in sick to work, only to stay in bed with you all day. I *can't* be that guy. As much as I want to be and as much as I love you, I'm *never* gonna be that guy for you. I just ... can't be."

"So this was really only about sex then," I deduced with a nod. "You knew nothing was going to change your feelings for me, that you weren't going to give us a *real* chance?"

"Well it sounds worse than it really is when you say it like that," he replied, his voice hard, "But ... yes. I know I can't offer you anymore than what we have right now."

Sometimes, honesty isn't the best policy. He could have lied right then and I would have been okay with that.

"You know ... don't worry about it ... let's just enjoy our last few days of the dream," I told him with a pathetic excuse for a smile, staring off toward the candles on the dresser.

He wasn't buying it but, eventually, he gave up trying and left me alone. It wasn't that he didn't try to get me to talk to him, but what would I say? He basically told me that there wasn't an option.

As much as I didn't want to admit it, I felt like he used me for his own pleasure. Yeah, he supposedly loved me too, but he knew damn well he wasn't going to offer me anything more than a friendship with him. I'd never be girlfriend status; I'd never be wife status. I'd always be this pit lizard with *his* determined benefits.

Really, though, how upset could I be about that when I used him for the same reason? I knew this wasn't going to change anything and I fell anyway. I fell hard into this crazy-irrational-break-your-fucking-heart-logic.

Support group, here I come.

The next day it was back to reality and racing. I was thankful for the distraction the race weekend could provide.

The rest of the evening in Savannah and this morning, we never spoke about what happened that night. It was probably a good thing because if I heard him say he loved me again, I'd start bawling just as I did that night.

Jameson was racing in Sonoma, California, at Infineon Raceway, known to some as Sears Point. It is a two-and-a-half-mile road course with a series of twelve complex twists and turns that go up and down hill. The track was noted for turns two and three that were banked on the driver's right, providing a challenge to the driver because ordinarily the turn would be on their left.

Jameson wasn't particularly fond of the track, as with any road course, but he managed to get the pole for the race so he obviously figured something out.

On Sunday morning of my last day of the pit lizard's crazy-irrational-break-your-heart dream, we were all sitting around eating breakfast outside the team's hauler when Jameson's phone beeped twice, letting him know that someone was calling him.

He glanced down at the screen turning his head sideways. "I'll be right back," he whispered to me and then walked inside the hauler to take the call in private.

All of us looked at each other in confusion and then went back to eating.

About twenty minutes later, Jameson stepped out with a calloused expression. Walking past Spencer at the door, he moved to sit next to me again.

I thought he'd continue eating because, let's face it, the boy could eat. Instead, he leaned back in the chair, his eyes fixated on his feet.

Concerned about the sudden change in his demeanor, I set my plate down on the table in front of me and leaned over to whisper in his ear. "Who was that?"

He didn't look away from his feet, only tilted his head in my direction and whispered back, "Charlie."

Why would Charlie call Jameson?

I nodded because *now* was not the time to discuss this with his entire team and family nearby. I thought we would get a chance to be alone sometime throughout the day, but on race day, it wasn't happening.

All the times I'd tried calling Charlie the last few days, he'd never pick up but yet he was calling Jameson?

Something was definitely going on. Even though I intended to find out, now just didn't seem like the most appropriate time to do so.

Walking with Jameson to the drivers' meeting, we couldn't make it two feet without a fan wanting an autograph or a reporter seeking an interview.

It's not like this was anything new (not knew), but Jameson seemed more annoyed with it this weekend than he had in the past. I constantly found myself wondering when I needed to interject before he snapped.

I stood outside the media center. Drivers, crew chiefs, and car owners were the only ones allowed inside for the drivers' meeting.

Once the meeting ended, his mood hadn't improved.

Just like the rest of the hounding media, the determined Ashley Conner caught up with him as we were walking back. I wanted to rip out her stupid black hair when she touched his arm to get his attention and I wanted to hump his leg when he cringed and quickly pulled his arm away from her.

"Hey, Jameson, how do you feel about today's race? You got the pole for the eighth time this year. Can you pull off back-to-back wins?"

Jameson and I kept walking with her following closely, but Jameson offered his standard answer he'd given every other reporter this morning. "I think we have a chance. You have to have lots of forward drive here. You can't be slippin' the tires. The track's gonna get slippery today, similar to yesterday during practice. We'll see how we are on the long runs. Hopefully we can be in position at the end to pull off another win."

Watching him today with all the demands reminded me of how

much Jameson gave up for this dream of his and how much his words to me last night were true.

I've watched Jameson for the past eleven years doing what he loved: racing.

I don't think anyone has ever realized how much of his childhood *and* now his adulthood that he's given up to follow his dream not to mention his social life. Growing up, he never attended school functions or played sports. It was always racing, *every* weekend.

During the off-season, he was preparing for the next season and working for his dad at his sprint car shop. He was learning everything he could about race cars. There was never a time when I could honestly say he was a normal kid.

All of his hard work had led him here, to his dream come true. But that dream, at times, had come with some hefty sacrifices.

He had commitments that most twenty-two-year-old's didn't have.

Even with all this, there was one thing that never changed about Jameson over the years and that was Jameson. He knew exactly what he wanted. I doubted most of us could say that about ourselves.

He was never what people thought he should be or told him to be, he was always Jameson. Cocky, arrogant, determined, focused, or whatever you wanted to call him, he *never* changed.

He knew who he was. Sure, there was that restlessness and vulnerability beneath, but that was something created by the lifestyle rather than him. Underneath it all was authenticity and a magic of a man becoming a legend his own way and he never doubted that.

I think that's *why* I loved him so much.

While most of us struggled throughout our teenage years to find our own identity or personality, Jameson never had to because he always knew himself. Since the moment I met him, he has been the *same* person. It didn't matter now that women threw themselves at him, that he made more money in a year than the entire town of Elma, or that he was a famous race car driver. He was still the same arrogant little shit I met when I was eleven, but, more importantly, he was *still* Jameson.

I wasn't sure what Jameson and Charlie talked about earlier, but since then, he was acting completely different. He always got a little strange on race day but this, his shifty sullen behavior, was a tad over-the-top if you asked me. During our summer traveling, I saw this side a lot, now it seemed fed by something else entirely. Back then, it was just trying to make it to the next race without breaking something, now it was trying to make it.

When I walked inside the hauler prior to the start of the race, his head was down. His elbows rested against his knees with his head in his hands, tugging at his hair. I'd never seen Jameson get nervous before a race but now he literally looked sick. His face was pale aside from the flushed cheeks, his right leg was bouncing nervously.

With a good amount of hesitation, I knocked lightly on the door before walking in.

The noise made him look up for a moment, but when he saw me he suddenly leaned out the side door and vomited all over the side of the number eighteen's hauler.

Oh my.

When he stood, unstable, he leaned against the side of the wall for support, picked up a wrench off the counter and tossed it from hand to hand. His eyes passed swiftly over me, focusing on the wall.

"Are you okay?" Timidly, I stood near the door. I wasn't sure if I should stay or leave.

Jameson didn't answer and instead nodded. Grave and tense, his jaw flexed, the muscles coiling.

I had half a mind to call Charlie again and see what he said to Jameson to change his demeanor so drastically. This time I'd be leaving a message.

"I have drivers' introductions," he mumbled walking past me without another word, dropping the wrench on the counter.

And then he was gone, and I was left wondering what I did wrong.

I could feel our relationship slipping away. I could feel Jameson slipping away after that night in Savannah and this, his reactions, confirmed it was happening.

For the first time in eleven years, I didn't know what to say to him. I didn't know how to be around him. For so long it'd always been so easy for us, simple.

But now, I didn't know where I stood in his life or if I even did anymore. This seemed like such a one-eighty from where we were a few nights ago when he told me he loved me.

How could he tell me he loved me and then act like this?

Jameson said little when I was standing at his car with him on the grid after introductions. Not knowing what else to say, I simply hugged him, wished him luck, and walked away.

From my place on the pit box, I watched as Chelsea Adams strutted her way over to his car with those long beautiful legs.

I almost vomited right there.

Jameson's head was down when she approached, adjusting his belts. Chelsea bent over, shifting her weight to one leg, effectively sticking her ass out and leaned inside the car. His helmet was off, but I couldn't see his expression when he looked up at her.

Kyle leaned into my shoulder. "Don't pay her any mind."

I wanted to listen to him, I told myself to listen, but when have I ever listened to myself?

Chelsea tilted her head to one side as though she was waiting for an answer from him.

After a moment, I could see Jameson nod his head once and then watched her strut away.

My eyes locked on the devastation. It was like a bad car accident I couldn't look away from, fixated on the bloody carnage of my broken heart.

When Chelsea was out of sight, Jameson looked in my direction and then quickly looked back to his belts.

Suddenly his eyes returned, as though he hadn't realized it was *me* that was looking at him.

In that moment, his eyes said it all.

Jameson was right; he would never be what *I* needed and I'd never be what *he* needed.

I never understood that part, until now. I wasn't the only one he was referring to. He didn't need some track promoter's pit lizard daughter following him around. Sure, he needed me as a friend but he didn't need the complication we now had.

My stupid emotions got the better of me.

Judging by Jameson's tortured expression, I knew he saw the tears streaming down my face even from fifteen feet away.

Shaking his head slowly, his eyes fell closed.

I could see he was breathing heavy. After a moment, he continued his routine by placing his ear buds in, helmet, and then locking the steering wheel in place. Once he motioned for Spencer to raise the window net, I looked away.

I couldn't believe how in one afternoon, everything between us had changed. Everything I felt for him was still there, but everything had changed in an *everything* type of way.

I also knew that anything that happened—didn't matter.

Well it did, but still, he needed me, and I *knew* he did. He needed me because for the past eleven years, I was *always* there for him. I was there waiting to pick up the pieces should they fall apart. But the thing was, despite whatever happened, that wasn't Jameson—he wouldn't fall apart.

Not like I could at least.

The race didn't go well. Jameson said little throughout the race until the handling got so bad he couldn't keep the car on the track.

At a track with twelve complex turns, that wasn't a comforting feeling I'm sure.

"I'm slippin' all over the place. I can't keep it straight," Jameson announced halfway through the race. "We gotta change something."

"Other than the slipping, do you feel anything else?" Kyle asked looking over lap times with Mason. "Any adjustments you want made?"

"I don't know what's going to help," Jameson told him. "It's hot out here, the tires just slip. There's no grip anywhere."

Jameson's car was extremely loose once the track heated up.

When the track heats up from the tires creating friction, it begins to feel slippery as oil is released from the asphalt as its temperature increased from the friction created. Two things happen at that point: you have no grip for one, and the tires become malleable as tiny pieces of rubber are torn away from all that friction. Eventually all that rubber laid down will counteract that but there's a period when nothing helps.

Only eighty laps into the race, he hit the wall coming out of the second turn.

"Heavy damage to right rear quarter panel," Aiden announced.

Moments passed as they assessed the car on pit road until Kyle announced the news.

"Take it to the truck."

Jameson hadn't said anything yet on the radio and judging by his earlier mood, I didn't think he would.

Stepping down from the pit box, the crew loaded up, and I made my way back to the hauler.

When Jameson pulled the car in, I could see the grim expression plastered across his face. He would take a huge hit in the points for this DNF, but I also knew that wasn't his *only* concern at the moment. Whatever had been on his mind before the race was still there.

When he drew himself from the car, he threw his helmet across the hood and stomped inside the hauler without looking at anyone, slamming the door behind him.

What followed was a stream of loud, ear-splitting crashes.

Jameson was like a ticking time bomb at times, combined with his hasty personality, it could make for a deadly combination at times.

Kyle shook his head leaning against the car while the crashes dissipated, his arms folded over his chest. "He acts like a goddamn child at times."

"I'll talk to him," I suggested leaving Emma and Kyle outside.

I peeked my head inside the door hesitantly, unsure if I would be hit with a flying object.

"Jameson?" I called out searching for him.

I found him slumped on the floor against the cabinets. With his head bent forward, his knees were raised, his hands resting on his knees with a piston in his right hand.

With his gaze fixated on the piston, he spoke, "You shouldn't be in here right now, Sway." His voice surprised me, he sounded irate, a tone he rarely used with me.

I didn't listen though. Instead, I sunk down beside him on the floor, looking over the wreckage in the hauler.

Parts, paper, and tools were scattered across the tile floor in the aftermath. Water dripped from the counter where he'd smashed a gallon container that was sitting there.

Watching the water drip forming a puddle, I jumped when I heard the door open.

"Jameson?" a familiar nasally voice called out.

Seriously?

We both looked up to find Chelsea sticking her head inside.

I almost grabbed the piston from Jameson and threw it at her.

"Are you ready?" Chelsea asked looking at Jameson.

He hesitated for a brief moment before replying, "I'll be ... there in a minute."

I looked over at him, on the verge of tears once again.

He stared back at me, his expression unreadable and then his eyes fell back to the piston.

That's why he nodded? He agreed to go with her?

Chelsea smiled at Jameson again. "I'll be waiting." She turned and glared at me before walking out.

"I'll let you get to ... *that*," I choked, tears threatening to overtake me. I felt as though my heart had been lynched right then.

Jameson closed his eyes, shaking his head, unable to answer. His breathing was heavy and uneven. Similar to earlier today, he looked as though he was going to vomit. He swept his trembling hand across the back of his slick neck. I could literally feel his body trembling next to me.

If I wasn't so upset right now, I would be concerned about his physical condition, but no, I *didn't* care. Well I did, but I didn't.

Trying to hold on to some dignity, and telling myself not to cry,

I rose from my place on the floor beside him and felt his hand grasp mine when I started to walk away, his warm fingers grazed mine.

"Sway," his voice cracking as he tugged on my hand. "Don't go, *please* honey."

I couldn't look at him. "Why? *Why* should I stay?" Emptiness was lingering, and I struggled not to fall to my knees before him.

"I ... don't want you to go. Not like this."

Still refusing to look his direction, teetering on the edge of control, I maneuvered my hand away from him to lean against the counter with my back to him. My head fell forward against the cabinets. "*Why*, Jameson?"

A silence spread throughout the hauler waiting for him to answer. The only sounds were my silent sobs and Jameson's heavy breathing behind me.

What surprised me, the piston he was holding flying across the hauler striking the wall beside me, the metal wall indented on impact?

"Fuck, Sway," his voice was harsh with an emotion I couldn't identify. "What do you *want* me to say? Just fucking tell me what you want to hear and I'll say it. I'll say whatever you want me to!" he pleaded in a desperate but brusque tone.

That statement right there brought me back to reality. And though I wanted to hear he loved me and wanted me to stay, that wasn't going to happen. It wouldn't mean anything if I had to tell him to say it.

"That's the problem, Jameson." My eyes fell closed. "I shouldn't *have* to tell you."

I couldn't stop the sob that broke through. He tried to reach for me again but I shook him off and made my way out of the hauler, stepping over the piston lying at my feet.

It hurt every muscle in my body to walk away.

It was unnatural for me, something my muscle memory for him was against, forced even. When I reached the door, I could feel the burn of his anguished eyes on me.

Once the door closed behind me a string of loud profanities followed by another loud crash of tools hitting the walls of the hauler.

It wasn't a few tools—he was destroying everything that was left of it. All you heard was deafening cracks of metal hitting metal while he ripped everything apart. That ticking time bomb had detonated.

Do you ever wonder when the exact moment was that your life turned to shit? I did.

I was certain I was in that moment right then.

Aside from the time I lost my virginity in the back of a truck at a dirt track, this was what I referred to as "rock bottom."

Crying uncontrollably like the broken-hearted pit lizard that I was, I stumbled across the paddock toward the drivers' compound and Jameson's motor coach.

I walked past Kyle on the way there, so now he was tagging along behind me trying to convince me to let him give me a ride to the airport.

Fighting the nausea and panic, they seemed to be balancing each other out and keeping the other from overtaking me completely.

When I realized I had no way of getting to the airport by myself, I agreed to let Kyle take me. After all, I could hardly navigate walking right then, driving didn't seem like a good idea.

"Are you okay, Sway?" Kyle's eyes looked over me, searching for any sign of damage. "Did he hurt you?"

"No. I'm fine," I tried to speak calmly, but I swayed in place. I couldn't tell him that physically I was fine, emotionally, not so much. "I need to leave."

I stepped outside the motor coach after getting my bags to see Darrin walk past and linger near the Expedition, waiting.

Kyle was already inside the truck so I had to pass by Darrin, alone, to get to the vehicle.

This day just keeps getting better, doesn't it?

Right before I was about to open the door, I heard his dark vexing laughter. "You didn't think he'd want you around with Chelsea around, did you?"

Without thinking, my dirt-track-raised-instincts shined like I was the center of the solar system. I didn't hesitate for one second. I stomped over to him, dropped my bags at his feet, grabbed him by the shoulders and brought my knee hard between his legs, and I think I felt his balls crunch.

"You didn't think you'd be able to use that dick forever, did you?"

I countered, laughing the same dark vexing laughter and trotting my brokenhearted pit lizard ass back to the car leaving him moaning on the ground.

When I got inside the car, Kyle was laughing so hard he could barely speak. Eventually he strung together, "That was awesome," and then followed up with a concerned gaze and, "Remind me never to piss you off."

Pulling through the gates, I saw Jameson getting into a black SUV with Chelsea. Not that I really gave it much effort, but I couldn't help the sobs that broke through when he glanced back at me. I knew he couldn't see me behind the blacked out windows, but I saw him and that alone was enough.

I felt bad for Kyle, having to drive me to the airport while I cried like a baby, but he was a trooper and let me be. Every time he tried to help or comfort me, I sobbed harder so he finally gave up and just let me cry it out.

I had no idea this would feel so horrible when I decided that night in Charlotte to do whatever this was. The pain, the regret, and the sadness that I felt, was overwhelming.

The most compelling part about it was that given the chance, I'd do it all over again right now if he asked me to.

I hated how he consumed my thoughts. I hated how every decision I made was with him in mind. If you've never had someone control you this way, without knowing, you couldn't understand how I felt and how much it bothered me to feel that way.

So my crazy-irrational-break-your-heart-logic *was* crazy-irrational-break-your-heart-logic after all. It was one hell of a vacation, too. My crankcase had seen more align boring and press forging in those three weeks than ever before. I couldn't say I regretted doing any of it because I didn't. I don't regret anything that happened, it was the best three weeks I could have imagined. I wished he would see that I was enough for him and that he didn't have to ask me to stay. I would have stayed just to be with him, but I wasn't what he needed.

Maybe Chelsea was what he needed, someone without obligations back home—someone who could be there for him every weekend.

Damn you crazy-irrational-break-your-heart-logic. Damn you.

Now I needed to go find that support group for pit lizards who got their hearts broken because this one, currently crying her eyes out on a plane back to Washington, was broken-hearted.

I didn't care that the entire plane was staring at me like I'd lost my mind because really, I could give a flying fuck what they thought.

When the passengers next to me started putting in their headphones, I really wanted to stand up and shout something completely inappropriate like, "Jesus Christ, I have crabs, give a girl and break!" But I didn't.

Instead, I sat there and sobbed my broken heart out, occasionally blowing my nose really hard and asking the woman next to me to hold my snotty tissues.

That's what she deserved for putting headphones on and acting like I didn't exist.

Once I arrived back at the Sea-Tac Airport, I was walking to get my bags when I passed by a sports bar with highlights of today's NASCAR race.

Naturally, I stopped, broken-hearted or not, I wanted a glimpse of him.

I caught the last half of the highlights. "While Bobby Cole went on to win the race, his hot-headed teammate, 'Rowdy Riley,' didn't fair so well in the race or the hit he took in the race for the championship. FOX Sports tried to catch up with Jameson after the race but a representative for the team said that he declined any interviews."

They cut to a view of his hauler. "It appears this hot-headed rookie took his frustrations with today's DNF rather hard and out on his team's equipment. It was reported that Jameson destroyed the team's hauler not more than fifteen minutes after this afternoon's race when he wrecked in turn two, causing some thirty thousand dollars of damage in equipment."

Knowing I was behind the temperament, I stopped listening after that. I also knew my heart was in about a million pieces right then, but I couldn't help but want to be there with him.

It had only been four hours since I last saw him and I was already tempted to fly back to him and tell him I'd be anything he wanted me to be as long as I was with him.

You're pathetic Sway, absolutely fucking pathetic. Go find your support group.

Back in the state of constant rain, I hardly noticed the steady rain with the steady stream of my own waterworks.

I found my truck quickly. After all, it was the only 1979 primer red Ford pickup in a lot full of Lexus' and Mercedes'. My poor little red dragon had been sitting here for three weeks. I was actually surprised she even started.

I turned on the radio, hoping music would relax me, but it didn't, because the first thing that came on was, once again, ESPN news. What was even more surprising and had me moments away from calling Jimi was their breaking news.

"This just in, after Jameson Riley reportedly destroyed his team hauler and personal motor coach in a fit of anger after this afternoon's race, he didn't stop at that. He was apparently arrested prior to getting on his private jet in California to return to his hometown of Elma, Washington."

Say what?

"The charges haven't been released but it's been rumored that he was arrested for suspicion of sexual assault against a young woman, Chelsea Adams, a former high school sweetheart of his."

Immediately I called Emma, who answered on the first ring, more than likely waiting for my call.

"What the fuck happened since I left?" I shouted before she even had a chance to finish her greeting.

"Sway?"

"Yes, it's Sway." I wasted no time throwing out the questions. "What happened? Why was he arrested?"

"He was arrested," she stated in a soft voice, sounding frightened.

"For fuck's sake, Emma, I *know* he was arrested!" I shouted. "What's the matter, what happened?"

Emma was quiet for a moment. "We don't know what happened." She sighed. "Chelsea and Jameson left the track together. None of us saw him for about three hours. When Ethan dropped him off at the jet, the police showed up and said he was under arrest for sexual assault. Jameson didn't say anything to us but by the look on his face, I'm not sure what he did. I've never seen him like that, he wasn't Jameson."

"Emma?"

"Yeah?"

"Was he coming to Elma?'

"Yes."

Marbles – These are bits of rubber scrubbed off tires when cornering. They gather in outside of the turn, and if a car goes wide into this area it will lose grip.

Over the years, my life had been shifting and now, I didn't know who I was anymore unless I was with Sway.

When your life is one long range of sleepless nights, demanding obligations, and vain women, veracity was something you cherish. Something you need.

I had that with Sway, always had. Also, that wasn't something I wanted to give up either.

That was until Charlie had me keep a secret for him, a secret that had the power to destroy all of us but, more importantly, Sway.

"Jameson, it's Charlie."

"Uh … hey, Charlie," I answered hesitantly, knowing why he was calling.

He cleared his throat. "I'm not calling to lecture you about my daughter, though I should."

"All right."

Charlie thought my intentions were wrong, and I thought his intentions were wrong. We didn't see eye-to-eye most of the time.

"What I'm calling about are the negotiations for the track."

I swallowed hard. I knew this was coming soon, but I didn't think it would be this soon.

"Oh … did Phillip draft the paperwork for you?"

"He did, thank you. Tate has the paperwork for you to sign since he was here last weekend."

"All right …" I sighed, "How long?"

He gave his own deep sigh. "Six months … maybe less." You couldn't miss the sadness in his voice. He didn't want this anymore than I did.

It felt like Mike Tyson punched me in the stomach as I slid back against the wall in the hauler, letting my head fall forward. "Does Sway have any idea?"

"No," he answered immediately. "I'd appreciate it if you didn't say anything. Tate said he let something slip last weekend. I'd like to tell her myself. She deserves that much."

It pissed me off to no end that he hadn't told her yet anyway. This is not something you keep from your only daughter who lost a mother at six years old.

"I understand," I choked, on the verge of tears. We may not see eye-to-eye, but I still loved him.

"She's coming home Monday, right?"

"Actually, her flight leaves tonight after the race. She wanted to be home before the Northern Sprint Tour and the Outlaws."

"I appreciate that. I need her here with me." He paused, and I could tell he was choking up. "For a long time, I thought you were using her, but I see it. I know you love my daughter. And I know how much she loves you."

I was quiet. I didn't know what to say.

"Jameson … are you okay?"

"Yeah, I just … I want to be there for her, but I can't." I had so many obligations I couldn't get out of.

"I know the feeling," he agreed.

"When are you going to tell her?"

Maybe if he knew when, I could make a trip to see her and help her through it.

"I'm not sure yet … it's not the type of news you spring on someone the moment they walk through the door, you know."

That conversation replayed in my head constantly.

The thought of Sway being without both her parents was literally making me sick. The thought of Sway being without me was literally making me sick.

So the moment she walked inside the hauler prior to the race I *literally* got sick.

First, I told her I loved her, then, I told her we couldn't be together, and now when she got home, her dad was going to tell her he wouldn't be around much longer.

If that's not fucked up, I don't know what is?

Charlie was diagnosed with metastatic brain cancer a year ago. Sway was in college at the time, focusing on getting her degree, which Charlie pushed because of his illness. He wanted her to take over the day-to-day operations of the track when he was gone. I thought it was selfish of him, and he thought I was selfish for not providing Sway with the relationship she deserved.

A few months ago, I received a call from him stating that he wanted to meet with me and discuss some things. Worried something was wrong with Sway, I caught the next flight out and was in Elma later that night, where he told me he was dying. I freaked out, almost punched him in the face for leaving Sway when he was the only family she had left, but then the anger subsided and the grief set in. I'd known Charlie since I was seven, and over the years he'd become just as much of a father to me as Jimi.

He'd continued treatments over the last year, all without Sway's knowledge, but now the treatments had run out. The cancer that started in his brain had now spread to the rest of his body.

Charlie had begged me not to tell Sway because he wanted to tell her himself. But how do you tell your only child you're dying?

It's not a conversation you bring up at the dinner table ... and with Sway already losing her mother at such a young age to cancer as well, Charlie was having a hard time with it. So instead of dealing with reality and preparing her for the loss, he prepared her future, the future *he* wanted for her. As you can see, I was defensive and fairly grouchy when this topic was brought up.

But really, could you blame me?

When I flew out to see him in March, he asked that I take over ownership of Grays Harbor Raceway from him. Charlie knew he'd need to sell it. Sway wouldn't be able to handle running the track and ownership all at once.

The plan was for me to take over ownership, and Sway would run the day-to-day operations with the help of Mallory and Emily, with Mark Kelly continuing as the track facilitator. There were a handful of maintenance guys, but other than that, there wasn't a lot of help around. Not only that, but Charlie didn't have the financial capability to hire more; I did though. With everything he had put into that track, he wanted and deserved for it to pass into capable hands.

I didn't have time to deal with the operation of an entire raceway, but I damn sure wasn't about to let the track *and* the people down who had given me my start, so I agreed.

I was completely against Charlie insisting Sway take over the operation of the track, but he was convinced this was what Sway wanted. Part of me blamed him for the reason why I couldn't be with Sway. Instead of thinking of his daughter's happiness, or my happiness, he came up with the plan for her.

The only other people who knew Charlie was sick were Mark Kelly and my attorney, Phillip Clemons. Tate and a few others had noticed how sick he was, but Sway hadn't.

Sway was obtuse to a lot of things in this world. She was just like her mother at times but that was Sway; crazy, irrational, caprice natured Sway, who I was madly in love with. I hardly recognized myself without her. I was so confused for so long, wondering what was real in the life that I was living that I never looked at what was right in front of me until she left Daytona in February.

She was there when my career began, and I had no doubt in my mind Sway would be there when it ended. I had chosen this profession to follow my dreams and, in exchange, it felt as though I was sacrificing my sanity to do so, not to mention my personal life; I had no personal life and the personal life I wanted, I couldn't have, or at least I thought I couldn't have.

I don't know when my relationship with Sway went from platonic to something more, but to this day, I could vividly remember the numbness and emptiness I felt when she was no longer there every day. When I met Sway, how could I have known that years later our lives would be intertwined to the point of co-dependency?

Co-dependency is a strong word when you think about it. Normally I'd associated it with some sort of chemical dependency and, really, that's *exactly* what Sway was to me. I felt the same blissful high when she was around and the wretched withdrawal when she wasn't.

When Charlie insisted that she go back to college and become an adult, as he put it, I saw how much it hurt her to leave but she did it anyway because he had asked it of her. Knowing why she did it, how would it be okay for me to do the same and ask her to stay?

Selfish, right?

Well, I did something even more selfish by asking her to stay with me for three weeks, and then telling her that "friends with benefits" was all I could offer her.

I *honestly* thought that was all I could offer her, and I *honestly* thought that was what she wanted from me. I couldn't ask her to give up everything and follow me around like the pit lizard everyone thought she was to me.

What I failed to realize was since Sway's first sexual experience, that was all she had ever been to men and now, I demeaned her in the worst way.

Sitting there in my car, getting ready for the Sears Point race, I couldn't focus on anything but Sway needing me when she went home, so when I looked up, hoping Sway would come by once more prior to the race but saw Chelsea, I was shocked. I'd seen her around the track, but hadn't actually spoken to her since the day I left Elma five years ago.

"What do you want?" I seethed. We didn't exactly part on *good* terms back then.

If there was one person I hated most on this earth, it was Chelsea … well, Darrin, too … and let's not forget about Mariah. All right, so I hated a lot of people, but for good fucking reason.

"Oh, Jay, don't be like that," she uttered skimming her fingers along the window net of my car. "I know you missed me."

I cringed, she made my skin crawl. "Don't call me Jay for one," I snapped refusing to make eye contact with her, "and what the fuck do you want? Get off my race car, you'll taint it."

"I have some paperwork to give you." She smiled. "Tate said he needed me to give it to you. He has to fly to Nashville tonight."

My pessimistic nature got the best of me as I glowered at her.

"All right," I agreed with a good amount of hesitation. "I'll meet you after the race."

She smiled. "See you then."

Wary of her intentions, I watched her walk away, making sure she didn't go near Sway. The way she strutted made me choke back bile that I was ever involved with her.

Though my gut was telling me otherwise, I really hoped it wasn't a ploy to get me alone. This had bad news written all over it, but I needed that title transfer and, more importantly, I needed it without Sway's knowledge. If she knew about the transfer then she'd know something was wrong with Charlie. For one, I promised him, and two, I really didn't want to be the one who told her.

When Chelsea was out of sight, and I knew she hadn't stopped at the pit box where Sway was, I looked away, but quickly looked back when I saw a wide pair of emerald bemused eyes staring back at me.

What felt like a knife stabbing me in my chest, was seeing tears streaming down her cheeks from fifteen feet away. I was breathing heavy. I felt as though I was going to have a heart attack any second if I didn't get out of this car right then and run to her.

Thankfully, Spencer stuck his head in the window and brought me back to reality. Wanting to comfort her, I'd already undone my belts to get out.

"You got this dude," Spencer bumped my fist with his own. "Be smart out there."

I didn't say anything, but motioned for him, with a flick of my wrist, to raise the net as the gnawing feeling deep inside my chest began to ease.

Knowing what was on the line, I *had* to get focused. I couldn't afford another mishap on the track after last week, let alone another DNF. As it was, I had already slipped to fourth in the standings with the dock in points.

"Jameson, it's Aiden. Watch your temps today. Cole's already saying his are high. But I guess ... *well*, just see how it goes ... you know what you're doing."

Here we go again. Aiden could never actually say what he needed to.

When I met Aiden Gomez, I had no idea he was borderline insane but what spotter wasn't? I also became aware very early on that he was physically incapable of deciding on anything. Simple tasks like what he might have for breakfast took him a good thirty minutes some days. It drove me insane, but it also provided me with entertainment when we traveled. I'd instigate it by adding fuel to his internal debates. When he'd ask what I thought, I'd answer him with a question; he hated that.

This was why he's only twenty-three and already has an ulcer. He can't make a decision to save his fucking life.

The bottom line was, when you were on the road as much as we were ... you needed the entertainment where you could get it, and we got it with Aiden.

In addition to my instigating, I convinced him to do things that would ordinarily piss most people off, but he usually did it without question. This provided Spencer and I with ample amounts of entertainment. It'd usually start with Aiden saying something along the lines of, "I don't want to piss anyone off."

Then I'd say, "Let me worry about pissing people off."

He'd smile and say, "You're off to a great start."

The thing about Aiden was, even though he was borderline insane, had an ulcer, couldn't commit to something as simple as what kind of eggs he would like, and didn't want to piss anyone off, he was exactly what our team needed. If not because we needed a spotter, then at least for entertainment purposes. I wasn't exactly thrilled he was dating my sister, but regardless, they made it known that wasn't up to me.

"All right bud, watch your shifts. You're coming to the green this time by," Kyle announced, as I led the field down to the green.

I got such a rush of adrenaline behind the wheel; it really was an indescribable feeling. And it's not a feeling I've felt anywhere other than in a race car. For me, there was something about being behind the wheel of an eight hundred horsepower car that gave me power. A power I had nowhere else but behind the wheel. It was addicting ... to say the least.

About forty laps into the race, the track was changing fast. I had no front grip and was currently using Cole through the curves to not hit the wall or slide into the sand pits. His car was fast and I doubted that he wanted to be battling for third with me, but Cole was the best teammate a driver could ask for.

"I'm slippin' all over the place; I can't keep it straight," I told Kyle. "We need to make a change."

"Other than the slipping, do you feel anything else?" Kyle asked. "Any adjustments you want made?"

"I don't know what's going to help. It's hot out here—the tires just slip. There's no grip anywhere." I was sweating like a motherfucker in the car, and all I could think about was Sway and the *way* she looked at me when she saw Chelsea walking away from my car.

How many more times was I going to break that woman's heart?

My distractions engulfed me as I went into turn two around the half-way mark.

I tried to correct it but ended up fishtailing and slammed into the outside wall coming out of two.

"Goddamn it, son of a bitch! Let's add one more fucking thing to my already *fucked up* day!" I hollered.

"Heavy damage to right rear quarter panel," Aiden announced.

Limping my way back around to the pits, the guys assessed everything. "Something broke on the rear," I told them.

"Sway bar," Mason said. "Gentry, grab a new link. Shane, check out the lower control arm."

"Uppers bent into the header," Shane said. "Lower broke off completely."

"Take it to the truck," Kyle said brusquely. "There's no time to fix it."

He caught an untold amount of heat from Jimi *and* Simplex when we didn't finish well.

I can't wait for tomorrow to explain this one.

Every Monday, we had a team meeting to discuss the race with management (my dad and Uncle Randy). It wasn't exactly the high-light of my week when we didn't place well, nor was it for Kyle.

Loosening my belts, I started throwing shit around the inside of the car, ripping hoses away; anything to make me feel better and, let's face it, when I am pissed I throw things, I've never grown out of the terrible twos.

I was fucking livid by the time I pulled the car in front of the truck. Most of the crew was already there with the same dejected look they always had when we didn't finish well

How much worse can one day get, really?

I didn't make eye contact with anyone when I got out. I was vaguely aware of the fact that Sway was leaning against the side of the hauler as I slammed the door shut.

Reaching for anything I could get my hands on, I threw it against the wall. Not only had I single-handedly wrecked a race car that could have been salvaged with a few minor adjustments, I got news that Charlie only has around six months to live, and I would soon be the owner of a racetrack.

But, the motherfucking cake topper of it all was that I told Sway I loved her and then broke her heart. On purpose.

You deserve a medal for the Biggest Jackass of the Year.

Sliding back against the wall, I was ready to vomit any second when Sway stepped inside.

"Jameson?" her shaky voice was timid.

"You shouldn't be in here right now, Sway." I warned. Though I'd never hurt her physically, I didn't want her to see me like this. As it was, she'd bore the burden of my temper enough.

Of course, she didn't listen, why would she? Sway did what she wanted, and when it came to me, she'd do anything, I knew that.

Sitting there in silence beside her, I was moments away from tell-ing her that I couldn't do any of this without her and I needed to be there when Charlie talked to her. I would literally walk away from all this for her. But would that really be what she wanted, or needed?

"Jameson?"

I looked up to see Chelsea standing at the door.

She smiled at me and the bile returned. "Are you ready?"

Oh God, what if Sway thinks I'm going with her because I want her?

I couldn't tell her why I was going with her. If she knew about the transfer, she'd know something was wrong with Charlie.

"I'll be ... there in a minute," I quickly said to avoid telling Sway anything.

My eyes focused on Sway's, wide with pain. I looked away unnerved by the fact that once again I broke another piece of her heart.

Would there be anything left soon?

Throwing the piston in my hand at Chelsea was moments away from happening, as I tossed the cool metal back in forth. It was tempting.

"I'll be waiting," her voice was like nails on a chalkboard.

"I'll let you get to ... that," Sway choked out when the door shut.

The heart attack feeling returned once again. I swallowed over the lump in my throat, trying not to vomit. My entire body was now shaking ... I was a fucking mess over this woman.

My heart broke when I saw tears in her eyes. I held my breath waiting for her response knowing it wasn't going to be what I wanted.

Sway started to get up; unconsciously I reached for her hand.

"Sway," my voice was failing me. "Don't go, *please*," I begged. I wanted her to look at me, maybe then she'd see that I didn't want Chelsea but she refused, making a vital effort not to see me.

"*Why?*" her shoulders shrugged. "Why should I stay?"

"I ... don't want you to go," I admitted. "Not like this."

She let go of my hand and leaned against the counter, her back still to me. "Why, Jameson?"

I have a temper, that's no lie, but when it came to Sway, and letting her go ... I knew no bounds. I lost all bearing and threw the piston toward the wall.

"Fuck, Sway," I tried to control my voice and keep from yelling at her, but it was useless. "What do you *want* me to say? Just fucking tell me what you *want* to hear and I'll say it. I'll say whatever you want me to!"

In that moment, that's what you choose to say? Fucking idiot.

"That's the problem, Jameson. I shouldn't have to tell you." She sobbed and walked out.

My terrible twenty-twos shined. I reached for anything within reach and smashed it. When I ran out of things to throw, I destroyed the cabinets, computers ... anything I could. Knowing it was wrong, I tried to stop myself, but I couldn't.

Nothing made sense to me. Why did it have to be this way? Why couldn't she have everything she's ever wanted? Why couldn't she have her parents? Why couldn't she have me?

Those were the constant questions I asked myself. And the most important, why couldn't I have the dream and the girl.

I struggled with this for a long time after Charlie had told me, but why her? Why Sway, and why did I have to fall in love with her and complicate her life even more? Why couldn't we have just been friends?

The problem was, for two people like Sway and me, the bond couldn't be *just* friends. The intensity was *so* strong it wouldn't be fair to be with someone else. There was absolutely no way either one of us could have given ourselves to someone else entirely. No matter what we did, there would always be a part of both of us that belonged to the other.

I fell back against the wall, my own sobs overtaking me. I never cried, but this ... what I did to Sway, drove me to complete hysteria. I was a blubbering fucking mess on the floor. I wasn't sure if they were tears of sadness or tears of frustration. Either way, I was feeling both emotions so strongly in that moment it was hard to decipher which was stronger.

My eyes were red, my face pale, my hands bleeding, and my heart was broken as I made my way over to Tate's hauler. Chelsea was there waiting. She had changed into a short black dress with matching heels that made me want to vomit again.

"Finally," she stood and huffed. "What took so long?"

"Where's the paperwork?" I asked, petulantly burying my hands in my pockets.

"Follow me." Biting down on her bottom lip, she motioned with her finger as she strutted away.

"No, no, no," I shook my head refusing to move toward her. "You said you had paperwork for me. I'm not leaving *with you*."

She laughed bitterly. "You either follow me, or you don't get the paperwork. I know you *need* that paperwork." She smiled iniquitously. "So I suggest you follow me."

I tensed, my jaw clenched tightly. I needed that title transfer. If I didn't get it from her, I'd have to fly to Elma and get it from Charlie—which wasn't really an option since I needed to be in North Dakota tomorrow for a meeting with Simplex to discuss sponsorship for my sprint car team.

I sighed heavily, following her. "Fine."

Once we got to the car, I looked around hesitantly. You know that feeling you get when something is wrong?

I was getting that one, with a big flashing sign telling me this was a trap.

"Where are we going?" I asked when the car started moving.

Some overly large dude was driving, so there I sat in the back seat pressed up against the door because I refused to get any closer to her than I already was.

She smiled without answering.

I was so fucked.

"I got what I wanted," she crooned softly crossing her legs in my direction when the car stopped in an open field. "Now, how about we catch up?"

A quick look around confirmed no one in sight but an open field with dead grass and a few abandoned barns in the near distance.

"Where the hell are we?"

She shrugged with a smile. "I just wanted to be alone with you," she answered with another seductive smile. "You know you want me, Jameson."

I started coughing and choking before I stopped abruptly, glaring at her.

"Sorry, I was choking on some bile," I told her with a smug smile of my own.

"Oh don't be like that." Chelsea moved closer.

I reached for the door handle while the driver locked it. "You can either play nice ... or I'll have Peter there," she motioned to the driver, "help me detain you."

She was practically on top of me now. "Get off me!" I snarled each word distinctively pushing against her.

She pushed forward, pressing her chest in my face. "I only want to play."

Yet again, I lost it reaching for her upper arms. "I mean it Chelsea—get the fuck off me before I throw you off."

She glowered for a moment; a sinful smile grazed her lips. "Have it your way, I got what I wanted."

"What are you talking about?"

"*Sway*, she believes that you left with me."

"What?"

"Darrin told her we left together ..." her voice trailed off. "It's exactly what I wanted."

My heart was pounding in my chest with anger, and not just anger, but outright rage as I processed what she said.

"You see, Jameson, I have a plan," Chelsea intoned. "I want you back, and I'll stop at nothing to do so. You were meant to be with me ... so if your precious Sway gets in the way ... I can't say that she won't get hurt." She let out a dark laugh. "It's a pity she won't have any family left after Charlie's gone. She's going to need someone."

I suddenly felt the rage boiling inside me. I was absolutely furious that she had deceived me but, more importantly, she had let Sway believe a lie. Not that I hadn't already lied to her but, Christ, she's been through enough already.

The adrenaline coursed through me, burning like acid.

I responded as I always did.

Within a second, I had my forearm pressed to her throat; her body was constrained against the seat with me hovering over her. "Whatever you have planned you deceitful fucking bitch, it will *not* work."

"It's already worked," she strained. I had my arm pressed so tightly to her throat she could barely breathe. "She thinks we left together. That's all I wanted. I can't say the same for Darrin and Mariah, but I only wanted *you* in all this. I wanted *you* back."

"You'll never *have* me," I growled back jerking her forward as though I was going to kiss her. And just before my lips touched hers,

I slammed her back against the seat.

"You never *had* me in the first place," I snapped.

The Vin Diesel fucker in the front seat pulled me backward with little effort and threw me to the dirt ground. I didn't try to get up; the dude was big as fuck and could kill me in seconds if he wanted, I was sure of that and wasn't willing to test the theory.

Chelsea stepped out of the car approaching me, the tiny pebbles in the dirt crunched beneath her heels. Kneeling beside me, her voice was sharp and vengeful. "It's a shame you can't see we were meant to be together," she breathed. "You'll see." Rising, she strutted back to the car.

So there I sat, in the middle of the desert, waiting for someone to pick up their goddamn cell phone, so I could get them to come get me. I started walking back to the track, well I thought I was, I couldn't be sure though. I had no idea what direction it was.

I dialed Spencer, Aiden, Tommy, Alley, Kyle, and then resorted to calling Ethan, Harry Sampson's crazy kid who bought lawn mower spark plugs for my race car one time.

Thankfully, he picked up. "Dude, where in the hell are you?"

"Disneyland," I answered, "Come get me."

He was quiet for a moment, probably trying to decipher if I was lying or not. "How'd you get to Disneyland?" he stammered.

And to think I hired him.

"Ethan, fuck, I'm not at Disneyland!" I snapped. "I'm in the middle of nowhere ... I think I'm on Tolay Creek Road, though." Searching my surroundings, I saw a street sign ahead and began walking toward it.

"How did you get out there?" Ethan was still confused, which wasn't all that surprising. After all, he did think lawn mower spark plugs would be fine for a hundred thousand dollar race engine. "Your car is still at the track."

"Ethan," I sighed. "Just come get me. I have to get to Elma tonight."

Another hour later, he finally picked me up and headed to So-noma Sky Park where the jet was waiting.

Ethan tried asking what happened, but I ignored him.

I had to figure out a way to get that title transfer without Sway knowing, or at least before Charlie told her. Sway wouldn't want me to take on such a huge responsibility of track ownership, but if it were already done ... she wouldn't have a say. I also had to figure out a way to get her back and find out what in the hell Darrin, Mariah, and Chelsea were up to. Oh, and I had to run a sprint car team and be the NASCAR Rookie of the Year like everyone expected me to be with racing in my blood.

To say I had a lot on my plate right now was the understatement of the fucking millennium.

Even with all of this, all I thought about was Sway. I knew I was wrong to lead her on the way I did, but I had to know if she felt the same way about me. And when she told me she did, I freaked out because the last thing I wanted was her to feel the same way ... it made it that much harder to end it.

I realized I made no sense at all and that I fucked things up beyond belief, but that seemed to be the only thing I was capable of doing.

Sway always implied that she was crazy and irrational, but I was just as crazy and irrational. We were perfect for each other.

When we got to the airport, I noticed a patrol car parked beside the jet and knew it couldn't be good.

"What did you do?" Ethan asked motioning to the police car. Two officers were now standing threateningly beside their cruiser when I got out.

"Nothing," I mumbled and trekked toward the jet.

"Mr. Riley?" a shorter, blonde-haired officer asked.

"Yes," I answered adjusting the strap of my bag on my shoulder.

He stepped forward reaching for my hands. "You're under arrest for sexual assault of Chelsea Adams."

I laughed maniacally shaking my head. "You have to be fucking kidding me?"

Spencer and Aiden made their way over when they saw the officers put the handcuffs on me.

"I'm afraid not, sir," he answered, adjusting the cuffs. "She's been admitted to the Sonoma Valley Hospital."

What the fuck?

"Dude!" Spencer yelled. "What did you do?"

"Nothing, call Phillip," I ordered.

I was fingerprinted, had blood drawn, my picture taken, asked if I wanted to give a statement to the officer, to which I told him to fuck off and now here I sat in a holding cell with some guy named Chester waiting for Phillip or my dad to come bail me out.

With my one phone call, I chose to call Charlie.

"Charlie ... it's Jameson."

He laughed. "Should I be worried that you're calling from jail?"

"No ... It's nothing I can't handle, just a misunderstanding. Listen ... I never got the paperwork from Tate."

"Yeah, he called to say he's sending it back. Something about you assaulting his girlfriend," Charlie laughed again. "So I guess I could send it to Phillip for you?"

Why is he laughing, how is this funny?

"No, I'll come there."

He laughed yet again. "Did you forget you're in jail?"

Right.

"I mean when I get out. This is just a misunderstanding," I sighed. "What did Tate say?"

"Well he's not too happy. He screamed a lot and said he couldn't believe after all he's done for you that you would assault his girlfriend." He was quiet for a moment. "You know, Tate has connections with Simplex. Why would you risk something like that?"

"I didn't do anything!" I yelled, instantly forgetting who I was talking to. "Sorry, Charlie ... I'm just ... Sway thinks I left with Chelsea because I wanted her."

"I see."

"Is she home yet?"

"Yeah," his voice seemed concerned for good reason. "She went straight into her room."

"Will you tell her … never mind. I'll tell her myself."

"That's probably a good idea. See you soon kid." He laughed. "Well, I hope so."

He was just like Sway with the fucking laughing.

Laugh it up, chuckles.

I know he had some sort of satisfaction that I was in jail.

I sat in that cell the *entire* night, Chester and me, since my dad refused to post my bail.

I learned a lot about Chester last night. He was a drunk, his only family was his dog, and he kept it that way because he couldn't speak. He loved NASCAR, and, more importantly … me.

"You're Jameson Riley!" Chester exclaimed jumping up and down when I entered the cell.

Now if you've never seen a two hundred and fifty pound man jumping up and down, you're not missing much, let me tell you. I feared for my life.

"No, I'm not," I told him, backing away toward the corner of the cell near the questionable toilet. "You have me mistaken for someone else."

"Yes, you are." He smiled and showed me a picture of us at a race. "I met you before."

I agreed that it was me, since I feared for my safety and all.

He forced me to sign his chest, and I will say forced because he pinned me to the wall until I did. He later informed me he was going to have my signature tattooed on him.

The dude was whacked out of his goddamn mind. I never did figure out why he was in there, not that I could have understood the toothless bastard anyway.

I'll tell you something else I realized … I had a real problem with the Sonoma County Sheriff's Office after that night.

Who thought it'd be a good idea to put me, an extremely good-looking race car driver, in a cell with *this* guy? It was complete stupidity in my book.

What kind of operation were they running here?

When I was released, I asked how much his bail was set for and the charges. Maybe I could be a nice guy after all and give this wacko a break by posting his bail.

The clerk laughed at me, "Oh, Chester ... he's in here weekly."

"Seriously," I raised my eyebrows as I signed the release papers.

"Yeah," she leaned in closer, her brown eyes amused. "Male prostitution," she said winking.

"Right," I nodded. It made a lot of sense from our conversations last night. I looked over at Phillip, my attorney, "Don't ask."

He patted me on the back laughing. "Your dad is waiting at the airport." He paused, looking over my appearance. "I once flew to Germany for a girl."

"How'd that work out for ya?"

He smiled, "Don't ask."

"Find out what the hell they are up to," I ordered as we walked outside the jail. "I'm not sure what it is, but it's not good."

The bright morning sun shocked me at first after spending the night in a dark cell. I took a deep breath of the warm summer morning. It hurt, but not my lungs, it hurt deep inside my heart because for the first time in three weeks, I didn't wake up in Sway's arms.

"Will do kid, now take care of yourself. I'm out of town for the next few days so ... try not to get arrested."

I shook my head. "I'll try not to."

An hour later, I was on a plane with my dad, of all people. Not the person you want to bail your ass out of jail, believe me.

I'd been listening to his ranting since we left Sonoma, and I had a feeling it would be this way until we reached Olympia, and then, of course, the drive to Elma.

Thankfully, he agreed to let me fly to Washington today, and then I had to leave first thing in the morning, fly to North Dakota and meet with Simplex. Then, I fly to Loudon for a press conference and then the race weekend began again. It was an endless cycle.

The only problem about flying to Elma was that he was coming with me as he wanted to look over the paperwork Charlie was having me sign, and I had a feeling that he wanted to be sure that I made it back to North Dakota tomorrow.

Phillip assured us Chelsea didn't have shit on me. She claimed I assaulted her, which I did, but she also claimed I forced her to give me oral sex.

Yeah, that never happened.

The Vin Diesel dude claimed he witnessed the entire thing and feared for his safety, so he did nothing. He had at least a hundred pounds on me, maybe more, so I doubted the charges would hold.

My biggest concern was Tate. He was good friends with Marcus, president of Simplex, so if Tate said pull my sponsorship ... Simplex would pull my sponsorship.

I had to think of a way to get to Tate without Chelsea and explain this. Also, Tate was a friend of mine. I couldn't have him thinking this lie. I may be an asshole most of the time, but I valued the relationship I had with him. After all, he did give me a start in NASCAR.

"You've got more talent behind the wheel of a race car than anyone I've ever seen, but you're fucking it up with this goddamn attitude of yours." Jimi poured himself another shot of whiskey.

Here we go again.

"Jesus Christ, Dad, give it a fucking rest already."

I couldn't take much more of this shit. First, he makes me spend the night in jail with Chester and now I get this four-hour long lecture after I told him everything that happened, including the shit I didn't want him to hear and promised Charlie I wouldn't.

"I won't give it a rest. When are you going to get your shit together and be the man I raised you to be?"

I finally looked at him dumbfounded. I knew I'd missed various parts of what he said that I personally felt didn't pertain to me, but how was this related?

"Huh?"

"With Sway," he huffed. "Jameson, you're going to lose it all if you don't pull your head out of your ass and admit to yourself that you love her and want to be with her."

"I've already lost her, and I don't love her," I lied.

Though I didn't want to admit it, I fucking loved that woman so much it hurt to breathe without her next to me.

"Cut the shit!" He threw the newspaper he'd been looking at across the cabin. "You've loved that girl since you met her. I honestly thought you two would come around sooner when you decided to complicate matters by sleeping with each other. But no, you're still as dumb as you've always been when it comes to women." He sighed and looked over at me.

You know the look, the one that says *I'm about to tell you something important so you had damn well better listen*, yeah, that look.

"You *can* have it both ways, son. It's all about balance. You need a woman who can understand the sacrifices you've been forced to make and she's *that* woman. She's always been that woman for you. Any man worth his salt will stick up for what he believes is right, but it takes a better man to admit when he's wrong."

"What the hell did that last statement have to do with anything, and why are you quoting Andrew Jackson?" I asked laughing.

"Do you pay attention to anything?"

"I do when it makes sense," I chuckled. "That didn't make sense."

"You're a fucking idiot, and I'm ninety-nine percent sure, you're not my child," he chided, returning to his whiskey. "You don't even look like me."

Could I have it all?

My plan was to see Charlie, sign the transfer paperwork, find Sway, tell her I'm sorry and then beg her to take me back.

I wouldn't beg her to take me back as my friend with benefits though. I wanted more. I wanted her to be my girlfriend and eventually my wife.

Okay, well now you're getting ahead of yourself there, sport.

First, get her to forgive you for being the President of Dick's International. Then you can think about marriage.

I didn't care, though. If Sway said, "marry me" right now, I'd fly to Vegas and do it tonight.

I didn't care any longer that we lived across the United States from each other, or that we might not see each other very often. I *had* to be with her. Only her.

If these last three weeks or these last twenty-four hours had taught me anything, it was that I loved Sway more than anything. At this point, I would stop at nothing to prove that to her. She needed me whether she knew it or not.

At least, she was going to need me soon, and I would be there for her.

Looking back to all the times I thought I didn't need her seemed so stupid now. It wasn't that I *wanted* to be alone. I honestly believed no one ever *wanted* to be alone in life. But I was scared in the beginning.

What if I laid it all out there, and she didn't feel the same way? Then what?

What if it didn't work out, and she wasn't my friend anymore?

The heartbreak and not having her around wasn't something that I could deal with. After Daytona was a prime example of that. Losing Sway was not an option.

I could have it all.

With Sway, *we* could have it all. I could prove it and if there was one thing I was good at, it was proving something I believed in.

I realized what had changed within me after she left.

The truth was, I'd give it all away to have someone love me for me and feel the way I felt during those three weeks.

Was that really so much to ask for?

Well, probably, but I didn't care anymore. I wanted more than just a taste.

Firewall – This is a solid metal plate that separates the engine compartment from the driver's compartment of a race car.

In my twenty-two years I realized a few things: some simple, some not. The most important, in some unexpected ways was that your life could change in an instant.

Most of the time change was often unanticipated in our lives so you're never prepared for it. Because of that, the outcome was typically never what you'd hoped. And when the floor gives out, you found yourself trapped in the shattering aftermath, struggling to piece the broken and blurred edges of your life back together. Some of us run for change. Sometimes running causes more damage. Some people endured it, and well, some hide from change fearing the unknown or the change itself.

It's only natural.

Personally, I've never been one to run from anything in life. Charlotte was a prime example of that. Throughout most of my life, I've had a *do or die* attitude about most things.

To hear that my father was dying of brain cancer was almost too much to tolerate with an already broken heart. I was sure therapy could only help so much before medication would be my only answer.

I sat there in the living room of our home while Charlie and his girlfriend, Andrea, told me he was dying.

Now the only reason they were telling me this was because I ran across some legal documents on the counter that morning when making breakfast including a title transfer of Grays Harbor Raceway to a one, Jameson Anthony Riley, of Mooresville, North Carolina.

"How long?" I asked, my voice just above a whisper. The tears hadn't stopped since I saw the name Jameson Anthony Riley. "How long did they give you?"

Charlie looked at me for a long moment; his voice broke as he uttered the words, "Six months ... or less."

Shaking my head violently, I tried to comprehend what he was telling me, but I was beyond handling anything.

I was numb, and the one person I wanted here with me wasn't.

Charlie moved to sit next to me. "I know this is hard, baby." He leaned in placing a kiss to my temple. "I wanted to tell you so many times, but how do you tell your only child that you're dying?"

I nodded, knowing he never intentionally wanted to hurt me. Hurting me was the last thing he wanted to do. I understood completely why he had reservations for not telling me. Here was a man who had to bury his childhood love at twenty-five and raise their only daughter by himself. Of course he had reservations about telling me.

"Having Jameson take over ownership of the track was to ensure it stayed in rightful hands," he added. "He's young and knows how to run a business."

This track meant everything to Charlie and me. It was our life. When his world was shattered by the death of my mother, this track pulled him together. It gave him a reason to go on and brought us together in a time when we needed each other most. I had a feeling this was also Charlie's way of ensuring that I had something to distract me. I'd be too occupied with the operation of the track to grieve his death.

Nodding again, Lucas and Logan, Andrea's six-year-old twin boys, barreled into the room. Andrea had moved in recently to help take care of Charlie, and her sons came along.

"Why is she crying?" Logan asked taking a seat on his mom's lap. "Did your boyfriend dump you?" He smiled at me. This wasn't a smile you'd see on a six year old ... it was an evil smile.

It was something similar to the Joker.

In that moment, I did something completely juvenile and stuck my tongue out at him in sheer desperation.

This went on for a while—the little shit tormenting me and Andrea trying to get him to leave me alone. He didn't, and soon his brother, Lucas, joined in until I was at the point where I was going to snap their tiny little heads off. So I grabbed some Jack from the cabinet and headed for the track.

This track had helped me through so much over the years, and I knew I'd find peace there with Jack Daniels. Jack never let me down; he was always there for me.

An hour later, Jack definitely didn't let me down.

You realize what your life has become when you're sitting inside a sprint car in the middle of the day drinking Jack Daniels directly from the bottle, and talking to it like it was your best friend.

Some might wonder why there was a sprint car just sitting at the track with no races going on. One of the local drivers had been practicing today. I snuck inside his car and, well, one look at me and he said he'd be back later.

Poor bastard probably felt bad for me.

I felt bad for me.

In between shots, I could hear the gravel crunching beside me, and then a heavy dramatic sigh of disappointment.

"Is that you, Jack? Why are you disappointed in me?" I stared at him wondering what he could possibly be thinking, running my fingertips down his dark label.

"Judging by that bottle in your hand, I'm assuming he broke your heart?" I looked up and saw Alley, at least I thought it was she, my vision was a tad obscured.

At this point, I could have been hallucinating.

"Jack didn't do anything," I laughed attempting to stretch my legs. "He's a poor innocent bystander." I stroked his neck in reassurance, so Alley didn't offend him.

Alley sighed again ripping him from my hands. "Not Jack, Jameson!" She stepped back to look at me. "Whose car is this?"

"I don't know ... I'm in a car?" My head lulled to the side feeling the results of Jack.

Looking around, I realized she was right. No wonder I was so scrunched.

Before I became a permanent fixture, I decided to extract myself from the car. Once I was out, I fell to the gravel and dirt beneath me.

Alley picked me up—at least I thought it was she—it smelled like her.

Leaning against her, if you classify putting all of your weight on someone as "leaning," we walked. At least I thought we were walking. I needed a lot of assistance just to put one foot in front of the other. It seemed Jack did a number on me, too.

"So what did he do?" Alley asked.

I reached for Jack again, but she pushed my hand away. "Who?"

"Jameson."

"He did exactly what you thought … he used me for *his* determined benefits," I admitted. Dragging my feet through the dirt, my white flip-flops turned an ugly brown as we passed through the pit entrance. "How did you find me? Why aren't you with Lane?"

"Lane's here. He's visiting with Andrea, Charlie, and the twins." She laughed. "Those are some interesting kids she has."

"They're assholes. I almost punched the little one in the face this morning after he came out of my room wearing my thong underwear over his pajamas."

Alley chuckled, but said nothing.

"How did you know where I was?" I asked, looking up into her anxious eyes.

"Charlie told me that you came here," she said resting her head against mine. It was a sweet gesture, not like Alley.

"Did he tell you … ?"

"Yeah, sweetie, Andrea told me tonight that Charlie had talked to you. I'm sorry."

I felt warm familiar tears slip down my cheeks.

After about an hour, no doubt from Jack's influence, I spilled my guts. "I hate that they kept it from me. I hate that they lied to me. I hate that Jameson knew and didn't tell me but, most of all, I hate that I'm not upset. I'm not upset that they didn't tell me. I can't find it in me to hate either one of them because … I love both of them more than anything, and to be mad at them would be a waste."

"I know," Alley agreed. "I would be hurt if my dad kept that from Spencer or me. But I understand your feelings here." We were sitting against the maintenance shed right outside the pit entrance when she reached for my hand. "What did Jameson say?"

"I haven't talked to him since I left Sonoma. I think he's in North Dakota ... if he got out of jail that is." My voice was bitter despite me not being mad at him.

"He was released this morning," Alley laughed. "Jimi made him spend the night in jail."

"Oh," was all I said.

I also hated that he hadn't even called. I mean, I know we parted on ill terms, but just because we had one fight didn't mean I stopped being his best friend.

But, then again, he *was* in jail.

"Do you think he did what they charged him with?"

"No," she replied without hesitation. "I had a meeting with Simplex this morning and briefed them on everything. There is no way in hell he sexually assaulted her, *no way*. Chelsea claimed he assaulted her, which, from his statement with Phillip, he pushed her off him. So, yes, that could be considered assault because, let's face it, Jameson is never gentle. But she also claimed he forced her to give him oral sex," she raised her hand when I gasped. "He didn't."

"I wonder what she's out to prove."

"Jameson said she wants him back."

"Well, he's a free agent so ..." I hated saying that, but I would never be more than his pit lizard with his determined benefits. He made that clear.

"He's not a free agent, Sway, and he *never* was. Jameson loves you; he always has. I knew that when I first met you two on that plane ride when we were kids."

"Then why did you not want us together?"

"Because ... Jameson had a lot of growing up to do, and if you hadn't noticed, he's a fucking child with anger issues. He should be medicated."

I drew in a heavy breath. "Why do I love him? Why am I ready to forget everything just to hear him say he loves me?" I whined.

Alley laughed again. "Sweetie, *that's* love. Why do you think I stay with Spencer? Yeah, our three-year-old son is more mature than he is, but Spencer has always been there for me. When you love someone, you love them for who they are, not for who they could become or who *you* think they should be. You love them *and* their faults."

Alley was right. Yes, Jameson kept a secret from me, led me to believe we could have a relationship, and then quickly put it to an end when he found out my feelings were the same as his, but even with all that ... I loved him. I loved the cocky, arrogant, crazy Jameson, with his extreme anger problem and his dirty heathen talking. I loved him for who he was, regardless of his faults. So despite the fact that he said we couldn't be together, nothing changed. I still loved him.

I'm so pathetic!

"Where is Jameson now?" Intending to get up, I hunched forward, but realized I'd been sitting there too long.

"Here ... but, I'm not sure where." She grunted, heaving me up with her. "I flew out with Lane. We leave tonight for Loudon. Jameson has to be in North Dakota for a meeting with Simplex tomorrow morning. They are thinking of sponsoring his sprint car team, but now they want to discuss *his* sponsorship."

"How come?"

"Tate and Marcus, the president of Simplex, are *good* friends, which is how Jameson and Riley Racing got the sponsorship in the first place. Tate was not pleased that Jameson supposedly assaulted Chelsea. So what did he do? He called Marcus and told him to drop the sponsorship without even talking to Jameson about it, so now Jameson has to tell his side of the story." Alley led me toward her rental car.

"Where are we going?"

"You need to get some sleep, sweetie." Her phone beeped once and she glanced at it quickly before smiling. "Let's go."

"Can I at least have Jack back?" I reached for the bottle still in her hand.

"No." She jerked it back.

"Why?"

"Because someone else is waiting for you." She smiled half-heartedly, tucking the bottle away. "You need to be sober for this conversation."

We drove the mile down Highway 8 until we made it back to my house.

Once she pulled in the driveway, she looked over at me. "I'm going to head inside." Her eyes looked past me at the chain-link fence along the side of the house.

I followed her gaze and was met with the last person I thought I would see in that moment.

Jameson.

Standing there, leaning up against the fence, it was evident by the dark circles under his bloodshot eyes that he hadn't slept. He ran his hand through his mess of hair repeatedly.

He was waiting for me.

When I saw him, the tears immediately returned.

I wasn't mad that he didn't tell me, nor was I mad about what happened in Sonoma; I couldn't be. I loved him regardless of what he did, and as unhealthy as that may be it was the truth.

With my mom's death, and now Charlie being sick, that proved to me that I couldn't take this life I'd been given for granted. I couldn't waste time on being upset or regretting the past.

What good did that do me?

When you had lemons ... make lemonade ... right?

Stepping from the car, his hands were in his hair. I knew then, by looking at him, he was hurting inside just as much.

Jameson never wanted to hurt me, nor did he *want* to keep a secret from me. I knew my best friend and that was not something he would have *wanted* to do.

He didn't move from his place against the fence. Shifting his weight, he looked down at his feet when he noticed me standing beside the car. The restlessness that was visible in Charlotte had returned. Only now it was easy to see that the restlessness was a loneliness this lifestyle had created for him.

I trudged over to him, staring at my feet with each heavy step. My face was red, swollen and pathetic looking, but I'd been through hell today ... who gave a shit how horrible I looked.

Once I reached him, he sighed heavily and nodded his head once, as if he was giving himself some sort of pep talk.

When he spoke, it was low and soft. "I know you hate me ... and I hate myself for it." The despondence in his tone unnerved me.

"I don't hate you," I answered immediately wanting to punch myself for sounding so fickle, romance novel, dumb heroine with no spine, but it was the truth. I didn't hate him. I never would. "I could *never* hate you."

Jameson's lips twitched slightly into a half smile. He opened his mouth as though he was going to say something, but then he sighed and looked down again. He was nervous.

Wanting to comfort him, I sat down on the ground beside him. It only took a moment before he slid down the fence, our shoulders touching. Of course, the pathetic-in-love pit lizard in me leaned her head against his hard, warm shoulder.

Just as instinctively as our bond was to the chain-link fence behind us, his head leaned against mine.

"There's so much I wanted to say and do in this moment, but ... I froze. Now I don't know what to say, *or* do," he whispered into my hair placing a kiss on the side of my head, his voice riddled with repentance. "I'm sorry."

"Let's just sit here for a little while," I suggested.

I didn't want to go back inside right away. Fresh air would do me some good. For one, if I saw Charlie, I would burst into tears again and two, I had no desire to see the Lucifer twins. It was also evident by my appearance and the spinning ... I had a little too much to drink.

Jameson noticed quickly when I hiccupped and laughed. "Have you been drinking?"

I must have been swaying more than I thought because when I tried to look at him, he was slanted. "Just a little." I squinted trying to make him stand straighter. Didn't work.

"How much is a little?" he asked, giving me a funny look.

"I had a few shots," I told him. "Or maybe it was half a bottle. I actually have no clue."

"There's a big difference between a shot and a half a bottle." He gave a weak smile. "But it looks to me like it was more like a half a bottle."

"Could have been a whole bottle," I said, glancing toward the road when my dad's neighbor arrived home. "I don't really know. Alley stole it."

He nodded in response, but said nothing more. I was glad he didn't. I didn't need a lecture on alcoholism right now.

We sat there for what seemed like days but was really only around an hour before the sun started setting. The cool air felt good against my flushed cheeks, a relief from the intensity surrounding me.

I decided we'd sat here long enough without speaking, and on top of that, my ass was soaked from the wet grass or I peed myself. I was certain I'd known if I had pissed myself. I'd been down *that* road before.

"Are you taking over ownership because Charlie asked you to? I mean ... you don't have to. I know how much responsibility you already have."

I felt him shake his head. "No, I *want* to. I don't ..." he paused, drawing in a shaky breath. "I can't leave this all to you. I want to be there to help you, and I don't want the track in the hands of just anyone. I became who I am today right here in this town, *with you*. I can't turn my back on it now."

It made sense. If Jameson or even Jimi didn't take over ownership, we'd have to sell the track. I couldn't do it by myself and Mark couldn't either. Knowing this, Charlie had thought the decision through. Jameson was young, determined, and business savvy. He was perfect for the job.

"I didn't ... I didn't leave with Chelsea to upset you," he told me. "She had the title transfer I needed to sign, *well*, so I thought she did."

"So you didn't sexually assault her?"

"No," he balked. "Well, I pushed her off me, but nothing *sexual* happened."

I nodded but didn't say anymore.

Jameson shifted, drawing me into his warm comforting arms. Turning, I faced him looking deep into his eyes.

I saw it then, for the first time. The regret, the love, the guilt, the stress, everything that defined him was there. It was where that rest-lessness and that vulnerability stemmed from. He carried so much on his shoulders at such a young age. How was track ownership going to help any of this?

"Jameson, I don't think you should take over. Maybe Jimi—"

His warm, calloused fingers silenced me. "It's already done, Sway." He shook his head soberly as though he never entertained the idea of *not* taking over. "I'm the new owner of Grays Harbor Raceway as of two o'clock today."

"Jameson," I breathed. "How is this going to work? I—"

His fingers silenced me yet again; he blinked slowly, not liking the reminder that this was a difficult situation. Then, with the same slow blink, the pain in his eyes hardened into that fire I always saw in him. That determination to prove to everyone he could be more than Jimi Riley's son was there again. Only now, he was determined to run with what was handed to him. "I *can* do this ... but I can't without you, honey."

"What?"

"I *need* you. I know that I've made some mistakes ... okay, that's a lie. I've fucked up big time, but I can't breathe without you next to me. It literally fucking hurts without you."

"You're so romantic." I laughed at his use of the "fuck" word.

"I know ..." he agreed with a small smile.

"I need you, too," I replied softly. I wasn't lying. I needed him now more than ever.

He surprised me when he said, "You don't though, and I *don't* deserve you."

"You're what I *want*."

"You shouldn't," he warned. "I'm not good for you. I'm selfish, arrogant, have extreme anger issues, and I act as though I'm stuck in a two-year-old child's body ..." he raised an eyebrow at me. "Should I continue?"

"No, I get it." Looking down at my feet, I watched my toes slip through the damp blades of grass. Avoiding looking at him, I didn't want to see the rejection that I saw in Savannah. "We can't be togeth-er. We shouldn't be together."

"I think you misunderstood, honey." He placed his large hand against my cheek. I closed my eyes at the feeling of his warm skin touching mine. "I'm not what you *need*, but I'm too goddamn selfish to let you go again." He paused as he waited for my eyes to meet his. "Do you have any idea how hard it was to watch you walk away, knowing I broke your heart intentionally?"

"Probably the same as having it broken," I replied sarcastically.

His eyes flashed with that same emotion I saw so often over the last three weeks, and it finally made sense.

Jameson did feel the same but he didn't *want* to feel that way. He was right, this lifestyle wasn't ideal, but it happened, and though it was creating that restless loneliness for him, he still wanted something more.

Regardless, I had to know if he *still* felt the same way. The fickle dumb heroine in me spoke, "Do you still love me?"

Jesus that sounded so stupid.

"How can you even ask me that?" He looked deep into my eyes, his voice cracking. "I don't think I've ever loved someone this much in my entire life. It actually hurts. You have my heart and soul. I'm willing to do whatever it takes to be with you."

I wanted to hear him say it. He'd just bared his soul, but I thought he knew by my expression that I was waiting for it.

Fumbling with my own, his hands found mine in his lap.

When my forehead leaned against his again, his eyes closed, and I watched as two tears slid slowly down the side of his face only to have him shake them away. "I'm sorry for everything. I don't want to do this without you."

"Then don't," I whispered wiping the tears from his face.

Losing my control once again, I cried ... pathetic broken-hearted pit lizard cried, when I saw how emotional *he* was over this. All this time I had no idea he felt this strongly for me.

And though I felt broken, this time it was different because slowly I could feel those broken pieces being glued back together with Jameson super glue. He loved me, actually *loved* me, and *wanted* to be with me.

"Sway, please," he sighed as his fingers traced my lips—his head shook from side to side. "Please forgive me."

I could feel the soft skin of his lips against my own, waiting for me to respond.

"Do you think we can make this work?" I choked on my tears. Twisting back, I took in his expression, one of a man looking for redemption.

"I know we can," he said, brushing the hair that had fallen in my eyes, tucking it behind my ear. "I love you ... that's all that matters."

"Are you going to crawl up to my window now and rescue me like my knight in shining armor?"

He scrunched his nose in that adorable way he always did. "Well, I was never good at climbing, and I'm slightly afraid of heights so ..." He offered a lopsided grin. "Would you settle for me getting down on my knees and begging for forgiveness?"

"Eh, don't worry. I won't make you climb or beg." I stood reaching for his hand. "When do you leave?"

He frowned, standing tall before me. "In the morning." Brushing off his jeans, he took my hand. "I have to meet with Simplex in Grand Forks, North Dakota, tomorrow, and then I need to be in Loudon on Wednesday."

We began a slow walk toward the house, lingering in the shadows of the wraparound porch with a sense of dread. "That sucks."

Jameson nodded. "It does." Pulling me against his side, he slung his arm over my shoulder. "But we'll be okay. Together."

I looked up at him; he was looking down at me with his beautiful smile. "I'll do whatever it takes to make you see that this will work."

"That could be fun ..." I teased, attempting to make light of the stressful day.

"You're adorable."

Laughing lightly, I stopped on the front steps leading up to the door.

"Are you coming in?"

"I was hoping you'd ask." His voice was shy. "I didn't get a hotel room."

"Well, it's a little soon to be moving this fast ... I mean, we just started dating. I'm not that kind of girl, you know." I tried to hide my smile, but it was a futile effort.

Jameson laughed freely before stepping toward me.

"Honey," he gave me a slow wink wrapping his arm around my shoulder. "I wasn't planning on stealin' home or anything."

"Well, that's a shame," I teased back, opening the front door.

Once we stepped inside, the chaos began. Charlie was sitting on the couch watching baseball, Andrea was making dinner, and Logan and Lucas were running around the living room playing tug-of-war with my bra.

At least they picked one that looked decent ... little shits.

Their eyes shot up when they saw Jameson and ran at him full speed. "You're Jameson Riley!" They both shouted and clung to his legs.

"Uh," Jameson looked slightly panicked. "I guess I am."

"Boys, at least let Jameson come inside!" Andrea yelled from the kitchen. "Hey, Jameson," she greeted Jameson dragging her shithead children away.

Jameson leaned over to whisper in my ear, "They're adorable."

"Please tell me that you didn't refer to the Lucifer twins as *adorable*?"

He looked confused. "Lucifer twins?" Raising an eyebrow, his amusement showed and then he smirked.

"Yes, those kids are assholes." My bra whizzed past me to Lucas. "I'm *positive* their father is the devil."

"They can't be *that* bad. They're just kids." The smirk still hadn't left his face.

Lucas ran past us in the other direction with my bra on. "*Really*?" I pointed at Lucas. "Do they take your tampons and use them as rafts for their GI Joes in the bathtub or wear your bras?"

"Well, no." Jameson shifted his stance seeming thoroughly entertained by this.

"Exactly, they're annoying as shit. I have no idea how I'm going to live here with them."

I'd only been around them for less than twenty-four hours and getting my own apartment was looking like a top priority for my week.

Andrea made spaghetti for us, which was delicious.

Most of the dinner talk was about the track, and how Charlie would prefer the operation to be handled.

When Logan started shoving his noodles up his nose, I decided to excuse myself to my room, *with* Jameson.

Grabbing some leftover spaghetti and a bowl of milk for Mr. Jangles, my cat, we departed to my childhood room.

After getting Lucas off my bed, I placed the food on the floor and sat down on my bed. I couldn't figure out why Lucas wanted to sleep on my bed ... creepy little weirdo.

Jameson slowly stepped inside closing the door behind him, the sound of the door locking echoed throughout.

I was relieved he locked the door. With the twins around, thoughts of getting a deadbolt were high on my list.

Mr. Jangles was on the bed so I tried to push him off only to have him push back.

"Mr. Jangles, you're such a jerk sometimes. You need to share." Flicking his kitty tail at me, he jumped down to his own bed on the floor finding his food dish.

"What is that?" Jameson motioned toward Mr. Jangles looking slightly terrified of him. "Seriously, what is that?"

"It's a cat." I glanced at him with an *Are you really that stupid?* expression. "What does it look like?"

"*Well*, if it didn't have so much hair I'd think it was a small child." His eyes narrowed trying to make sense of him. "What in the hell do you feed him, McDonald's?"

I laughed, curling my legs up around my chest, leaning back against the wooden headboard. "No, spaghetti and milk."

"Maybe you should cut back on the carbs," Jameson suggested, taking a seat next to me on the bed. He observed Mr. Jangles watching him scarf down his spaghetti in disbelief. "Jesus, Sway, this thing eats more than I do."

"Be careful what you say around him." Mr. Jangles crawled onto the bed so I covered his ears. "He's sensitive about his weight," I whispered, scratching his overly large back. "Have some compassion."

"Well, we wouldn't want to offend Mr. Jangles, would we?"

"No, we wouldn't."

Jameson smiled looking down at me from under his thick dark lashes. "Why do you call him Mr. Jangles? Why not a normal name, like kitty?"

"Jesus, I was drunk at the time, give me a break. And kitty was taken if you hadn't noticed already," I huffed annoyed.

After a moment, his head tipped toward me, a faint smile took over. Despite what he'd been through, or what we'd been through, he was here for me right now when he knew I needed him. And when I looked at him now, his doubtful expression gave him away.

Taking a deep breath, I melted at the warm, clean, musky intoxicating scent of Jameson lying next to me. Cradling me to his chest, his warm arms wrapped around my waist. I leaned back to look at his serene, peaceful face and kissed him.

With his arms already around me, he easily slid me on top of him. Everything seemed so familiar, but yet so new and thrilling. His lips were soft but moved fiercely—he felt the change, too.

I wanted to feel him. I wanted his skin against mine, but when my hands traveled down his stomach and started to pull his shirt up, he stopped me.

"Sway, wait ..." he said breathlessly.

I smiled against his lips shaking my head and his grasp away. "I want to."

"No, Sway ... I'm not messing this up this time." He sighed, moving me to his side but kept his arms around me. "I love you, and I'm doing this right, this time."

"What have you done with the Jameson I know?" I tapped on his head.

He grinned playfully his shoulders straightening. "I'm all grown up now."

"Pfft ... hardly ... so doing this *right* means we can't have sex?"

He chuckled softly at my boldness. "No, we can't," he brought my lips back to his for a slow, lazy kiss and then pulled away, "because I'm going to take my time with you and show you I deserve you ... show you how much I want you." He kissed me again and swept my hair away from my neck so he could kiss down the side. "I'm not going to fuck this up," he stated.

"Hmmm ... So that means we won't see each other for around three weeks and we *can't* have sex? That sucks," I grumbled.

Jameson laughed. "Shouldn't I be the one mad here?"

"Yes, I'm surprised you're not ..." I reached my hand between his legs quickly before he could pull it away. He threw his head back and groaned as I performed some reciprocating motions over his jeans. His camshaft had *other* plans for him. "See ... he's mad at you," I pointed out.

"I'm no longer ruled by my dick, Sway," his words came out half-strangled. "We need to wait." Reaching for my hand, he placed soft kisses on the inside of my palm. "We just have to."

The rest of the night we held each other, *still* fully clothed.

Believe me, I tried again, but he was set in his ways. I almost got him to surrender when I started dry humping him when he was sleeping. He woke up, rolled me over, and continued the motions until he reached for his zipper and snapped out of his trance.

He really was different. He wanted to do this right, and he was going to prove it.

Damn it.

I was all for doing this right, but no sex? That just seemed dumb to even consider.

Sometime in the early morning as the sun began to peek over the dense trees surrounding the house, I woke up. Jameson was on his side facing me, still sleeping.

I couldn't sleep, so instead I lay there trying not to wake him.

Here I was, less than twelve hours ago thinking my life was over and hearing the news that my dad was dying. Then Jameson showed up and my world shifted again. Something I'd been holding onto for so long was now mine, and now something I never thought would be taken from me would soon be gone.

One thing was certain: I couldn't agonize over this. Charlie wouldn't want that at all. He would want all of us to act as though nothing was wrong—he didn't want the reminder.

To him, to all of us, life needed to be normal and that's exactly what I would do, for him.

The next morning Jameson left for North Dakota, and I walked back into the house after saying our goodbyes, sad as ever that I wasn't going to see him until the Northern Sprint Tour was in town … three weeks away.

Once he left, I noticed a note he left on my pillow.

You are where my heart belongs.
Jameson

It looked as though he signed an autograph for me. Smiling to myself, I sent him a text message thanking him once again.

Looking over the note, it finally made sense to me. That uneasiness, vulnerability, the restlessness, the way he kept his distance at the bar that first night and the way he stared at the ceiling after we had slept together. It was because of this, the conflict he felt over the decision. The bigger picture here, and what I never really understood, was me. I was the link he needed, the connection between where he came from, and where he was going. I grounded him back to where it all began and reminded him of why he was chasing his dream. I couldn't take all the credit, but I knew the place I held in all this now.

Talk about a revelation.

Charlie was sitting in his chair watching television when I walked into the living room, so I sat down on the couch and watched with him.

I hated baseball but I wanted to spend some time with him.

"Sway, I think you should go to Loudon this weekend," Charlie told me sometime after the third inning began. "Jameson needs you there."

I was confused. "I thought you needed me here this weekend?"

"I only need you here for the bigger events. This weekend is just regular season races." He glanced over at me. "If these last few days have taught me anything it is that I will not stand in the way of your happiness anymore, you *deserve* to be happy. You deserve to be the twenty-two-year-old that you are."

I felt relieved to hear him say that. My entire life I had to live way beyond my years and some days, I just wanted to be a careless twenty-two-year-old who didn't have to worry about a father who was dying of brain cancer, a boyfriend who I wouldn't get to see all that often, not to mention, the General Manager of a racetrack.

Hold the fuck up. *Did I just say boyfriend?*

Is that what he was to me now?

Lucas strolled nonchalantly into the house eating what appeared to be mud out of his hands.

Personally, I wasn't all that surprised.

Charlie eyed him closer as Lucas walked back outside again with his mud. "What the fuck ... was he eating mud?"

I glanced back at Lucas and then to Charlie again, shrugging my shoulders before slurping my mocha. "It appears that way."

"What is wrong with those boys?"

I laughed. "You know Dad, they're six years old. You really shouldn't expect so much from them."

Wedge – This is the weight from corner-to-corner of the weight of the race car. If you increase the weight on any corner of the car, it will change the weight of the other three corners.

I would have given Sway anything she wanted but that wasn't what this was about anymore. She had no idea the influence she had on me and the ability she had to completely destroy me.

I told myself I'd never let someone else have that type of power over me, but she did, and I trusted her completely with that power.

I wanted to do this the right way. The way I should have done it in the beginning. I wanted to rediscover her, slowly, and in the most intimate ways. Ways I've always dreamed about. I wanted to know her, all of her. In turn, I wanted her to know me in ways I'd never let anyone before.

I fell asleep wrapped around Sway enjoying the fact that she wasn't going to push me.

When I awoke the next morning to my phone buzzing, I found that heifer of a cat, lying on my stomach.

Jesus Christ ... it feels like a damn child is sitting on me.

I went to push him away, but instead he dug his claws into my bare stomach causing me to wince in pain. I didn't like cats, I just didn't. I would never harm one, it's not like I was some serial killer or anything who started off by killing animals. I just didn't actively care for them.

"Let go ..." I whined, trying to pull him off.

What the hell was his deal or name for that matter? Sway told me what it was.

Mr. Jingle ... Mr. Jungle?

"Mr. Jangles ... leave him alone," Sway moaned reaching for the cat, ripping out my skin as she did so.

Right, Mr. Jangles.

My phone continued to buzz, so I reached for it knowing it was Emma.

"Well?" Emma quietly asked me. I could tell she was smiling on the other line.

I groaned. "Why are you calling me?"

Rubbing my eyes, I drank from the bottle of water next to the bed.

"How did it go?" It sounded like she was chewing on something. She did that to piss me off knowing I hated the sounds of people eating. "Did you convince her to take your sorry ass back?"

"Do you always have to be so annoying?" I whispered, I didn't want to wake Sway. "I have to go, though, my flight leaves in two hours, and I still have to make it back to Olympia."

"We are talking when you get to Loudon," she ordered.

"Whatever."

"Bye, asshole."

Sighing, I quietly rolled over dropping my cell phone on the floor. Sway was still asleep, curled around Mr. Jangles.

I watched her for a moment, realizing how lucky I was.

"I'll take care of you," I breathed softly brushing her hair off her face and kissing her forehead. "I promise."

I hated leaving her, especially after last night. We'd talked for hours about what would happen after Charlie passed away, which I knew bothered her.

No one wanted to have both their parents gone at the age of twenty-two, or any age for that matter. Sway never displayed hate or resentment for anything that'd happened throughout her life, she took it as it came and made the best of the situation. I envied her so much for being able to do that. Some thought she was crazy, but that was

Sway.

Most could learn a thing or two from her.

So many times I got asked the question, "How do you do it at such a young age?"

I assumed they were referring to the lifestyle I lived and all the commitments I had, but their cagey expressions toward me said something along the line of, "You're fucking it all up, aren't you?"

I got this from everyone, too—the media, the fans, my family, and now my sponsors, who shelled out millions for me to race; they all questioned me.

That wasn't exactly the image I wanted them to see, but in actuality, I didn't think I was fucking up. Sure, I'd made some questionable decisions so far, but I *was* in control, so I thought.

"Mr. Riley, can you tell us what your involvement is with Chelsea Adams?" Marcus Harding, President of Simplex Shocks and Springs, asked as I sat across a table from him.

I'd flown to Grand Forks, North Dakota, of all places to meet with Marcus and the Vice President, Bill Helm, to discuss possible sponsorship of my sprint car team but, alas, here I sat discussing my recent involvement with Chelsea. I really wanted to say: "What the fuck does this have to do with sponsorship?" but I knew how involved Tate was with Simplex. Being a family-owned business, personal relationships were something they valued, as they did with Tate.

So I kept my thoughts to myself.

I cleared my throat before answering, "My only involvement with Ms. Adams was to retrieve legal documents she supposedly had for me. When I went with her, she indicated she didn't have them."

"Did you sexually assault her?" Marcus asked, his hazel eyes probing and accusing.

Wanting to get my point across, I maintained eye contact with him as I responded, "I would prefer to answer that for you but, unfortunately, I've been advised by my attorney that since this case is still under investigation, I'm not *allowed* to discuss specifics."

"I'm sure you'll understand then that we cannot discuss further sponsorship obligations until these charges have been settled," Bill advised with hard gargoyle eyes. "We *will* continue to sponsor you, for now. But please keep in mind that we do not condone this type of behavior, nor do we appreciate the aggression you've been displaying on the track. That's not an image we want portrayed."

I took a deep breath attempting to control myself.

Why the fuck they couldn't tell me this over the goddamn phone had me seeing red. I barely had enough control to continue speaking in a normal civilized manner. Inside, my blood was boiling.

I wanted to snap, but instead, I said, "Yes, sir, I understand," through a clenched jaw. "Thank you for meeting with me."

I didn't say anything else. Though I was seething, I didn't trust my tongue not to keep me out of trouble. My mouth had gotten me into enough hot water over the last few weeks.

Phillip had advised me that it was in my best interest not to discuss specifics with anyone and I agreed. It wasn't their business to begin with. He was working with Chelsea's attorney to come up with some kind of agreement regarding the charges brought against me. She told the police that I assaulted her and forced her to give me oral sex. She even went as far as to say that I held her head down while she did so, causing bruising, which she had. I never touched her aside from holding my arm to her throat. The bruises she had were on the back of her neck. I had a feeling Darrin was involved, and I wanted to figure out what the hell he was trying to prove.

With everything that happened, I knew something was going on, but I also had a job to do, a sprint car team to run, and a girlfriend who needed to know how much I loved her.

I tried once again to contact Tate but, of course, it went straight to voicemail. So, I left yet another message: "Hey dude, it's Jameson. I need to speak with you, call me, *please!*"

Tate had been avoiding my phone calls since that night in Sonoma, and I had an inkling he would be for a while. The fucked up part about it was we'd been friends for three years now. How he could believe that deceitful bitch over me was appalling. What's worse was that he had the nerve to call Marcus without even speaking to me about it first.

Who does that?

Still fuming over my interactions with Bill and Marcus, I was now on the way to Loudon, New Hampshire, *with* my dad—not exactly my idea of fun.

He was once again giving me his insight, whether I wanted it or not.

He only had a few hours before he needed to be in Nebraska for a race tonight, so he *insisted* on flying with me. Like I said, this was not my idea of fun. It wasn't that I didn't like my dad; it was that I didn't want to hear what he had to say today, that's all.

Quietly keeping to myself—looking over paperwork—I moved on to signing autographs for the Dartmouth Children's Hospital, trying to avoid conversation that would likely result in the *any man worth his salt* speech again.

Hell, I was still confused from the last one.

Avoiding him the best I could, my silence was over quickly.

"What the fuck!" Jimi yelled across the cabin toward me.

Why he was yelling when we were not more than three feet from each other wasn't my main concern. The vein pulsating in his neck was far more troubling.

"How did you do twenty-five thousand dollars damage to a *fucking* golf cart?"

"What?" My eyes didn't move from the posters.

I already knew the look I was receiving. It was the same look I got when I threw the baseball through his car windshield, while driving, because he wouldn't let me have a Happy Meal. It was the same look I got when Spencer and I glued Emma to the wall of her bedroom and left her there for an afternoon. And it was the same look I got when I took my sprint car out for a spin on the high school's running track *during* the homecoming football game.

"Do golf carts even cost that much?" he wondered, and then shifted his eyes back to me. "You need to grow up!"

I laughed, feeling his penetrating gaze upon me. "Spencer wrecked the other one," I defended finally looking up.

It was the same look.

"I expect that from him, *well fuck*, I expect that from you too but regardless, stop it." His eyes bulged again. "I'm not okay with this."

"I won't wreck any more golf carts."

His eyes narrowed for good reason. "Or haulers ... and motor coaches."

"Or haulers and motor coaches," I agreed with a grin attempting to lighten his mood.

"Don't get cute, I'm not amused." He let the corners of his mouth twitch into a smile but corrected it quickly. "You need to be medicated."

"Do not."

"Yes ... *yes,* you do." He tossed the bill from Glen Brooke Golf Course at me, walking to the rear of the jet grumbling again about getting a DNA test done on us.

In my head, I silently added up everything I'd been charged with in the last few weeks as far as destruction went ... $25,000 for the race, $34,000 for the hauler, $16,000 for the motor coach, and then the $9,000 for the hotel room. My eyes focused on the recent bill from the golf course, $26,000. I was certainly no math whiz, but that was a hefty tag.

Maybe I did need to be medicated?

It was either that or I would be going broke.

When I arrived in Loudon, it was a whirlwind of press, appearances, and interviews. That was just on Wednesday. After a *very* long fourteen-hour day, I was finally in my hotel room and missing my girl like crazy so I decided to call her.

She answered on the first ring, greeting me cheerfully, "Hey there, handsome!"

"Hey, beautiful," I rasped, my voice was shot. "How was your day?"

"*Ooohhh,*" Sway giggled. "Someone had a long day, but I'm digging the voice."

"I've missed that giggle, honey."

"I've missed you. I had to spend the day with the devil's spawn. Little fuckers shaved Mr. Jangles," she seethed. "He looks like the bear off that *Great Outdoors* movie—you know the one with the shaved ass?"

Laughing, though I was the only one laughing, she continued to tell me about her day. When I lay back on the bed, I felt something under me. Reaching behind me, I fished out a package addressed to the Jameson Riley Fan Club.

Emma must have dropped it off so I opened it and out spilled about a hundred envelopes from what looked to be fan mail. Skimming through a few, Sway told me how Lucas also pierced Mr. Jangle's ears with safety pins while Mr. Jangles purred away.

"I'm not sure who should worry you more, Lucas for doing it, or Mr. Jangles for not scratching the shit out of him," I teased and gasped loudly when I realized that *all* these letters were from Chester—the male prostitute from jail.

Afraid of the contents, and feeling slightly nauseated, I shoved them all back in the bag and placed it on the floor a good ten feet away.

I may, or may not have, covered it with a blanket, as well.

"I'm not sure who to be worried about either, but I'm gonna say the Lucifer twins." Sway agreed. I made my way back over to the bed. "A couple hours ago Logan brought out my vibrator and proceeded to play *Star Wars* with Lucas while we ate dinner."

I was silent for a second trying to comprehend what exactly she said when I heard Sway take a deep breath.

"What's the matter?"

"I just ... miss you." Her tone was desperate. "And they're making me insane."

"I miss you too," I whispered in a low voice that I knew would calm her down. "*Now,* back to this vibrator ..." Then I let the full force of my voice loose on her, knowing the effect it could have.

"You're not allowed to use that voice if we can't have sex," Sway warned.

"You know," I whispered purposefully. "Just because I said we can't have sex ... doesn't mean we can't have phone sex ... and I *really* wanna talk about this vibrator you have," I hedged.

Sway moaned loudly. "You're killing me." I could hear rustling on the line and imagined she was lying on her bed, already feeling the tightness in the pit of my stomach in anticipation.

"What are you wearing?" I asked in a deep voice that sounded funny to me with how gravelly I'd become. "Come on, honey; don't get shy on me now."

"Nothing," her voice softly flowed through the line.

"Wow, that was fast," I replied.

"I just got out of the shower. Logan got glue in my hair, so I spent the last hour in there trying to get it out," she sighed. "It will be a miracle if I don't kill them."

"How about you focus on something else," I suggested removing my clothes and getting in the bed. "Like me. Back to the vibrator. How long have you had it?"

Sway blew off my questions about the vibrator as if she never mentioned she had one in the first place. "That sounds like a swell idea ... what are you wearing stud?"

"Nothing, now."

"Ah, I'm good," Sway giggled. "Two minutes into this and I already have you naked."

"You have no idea what you do to me," I groaned as my hand slipped under the sheets. "Now this vibrator ... where'd you get it?"

"Why don't you tell me?" Her voice was dripping with sex.

Throwing my head back against the pillow, I found it hard not to fly across the states and show her exactly what she was doing to me. "Fuck, Sway. I miss you so much. I wish you were here with me right now."

"Do you have a fantasy?" she asked. I could tell this was turning her on; I knew my girl well.

"Besides fucking you on the hood of my race car?" I answered immediately. I'm sure my arousal was evident in my thick tone. "You know, I fantasized about that one for years."

"Oh, fuck me!" she panted.

My one thousand square foot hotel room was filled with our breathy moans, panting, and dirty talking. It felt wrong, and it felt as though I was slipping back into what we had before but, in the reality of it all, that was Sway and I.

I had no doubt in my mind that once Sway was here in my arms, I would show her how *this* was different, how *we* were different, over and over again.

The next morning when I woke up, I was met with Spencer in my bed. Yeah, that happened and sadly, this wasn't the first time it had happened.

Jumping back, I reached for the blankets since I was, in fact, still naked. "What the fuck are you doing in here?" I barked at him.

"Alley kicked me out of the room," he mumbled, rolling over to go to sleep.

"So you came here ... what would make you to do that?" I pushed him off the bed and reached for my jeans on the floor. "I don't like you anymore than she does."

"Dude!" Spencer grumbled when I showed him my bare ass. "I don't need to see that!"

"Stay out of my room then," I yanked my jeans on. "Why'd she kick you out?"

I don't know why I was asking, it's not like I actually gave a shit why she was mad at him. After all, this was a daily occurrence.

"She's *still* upset about my new haircut."

I laughed, rummaging through my bag to find a t-shirt and socks. "That's what you get for letting Aiden cut your hair, dumbass."

Though it took some convincing, I got Spencer to leave, and made my way to the track to start the race weekend. It was going to be a long one without Sway here.

With the restraining order on Chelsea and her glued to his hip, I struggled to get Tate alone the last few days between practices and qualifying. I couldn't go anywhere near him with Chelsea there.

At the drivers' meeting, she wasn't around so I tried my luck there.

Never being one to beat around the bush, so to speak, I walked up to him when he was with Bobby and Paul. Seeing me standing there, Bobby and Paul left, leaving Tate and me in the corner of the media center.

"What do you want, Riley?" Tate glowered, his arms crossed over his large chest. The light colored shirt he was wearing made his dark eyes appear darker. "What?"

I stared at him for a moment. Once I was standing there face-to-face, I had no idea what I wanted to say. Eventually I settled on, "I want you to hear *my* side of what happened."

"I already know what happened." He turned to walk away.

I grabbed him by the arm—his face was hard to read. "No, you don't," I said on the defense. "You know *one* side of the story."

"Enlighten me then," he challenged, stepping closer.

Tate wasn't as big as that Vin Diesel motherfucker, but he wasn't pint-sized, either. I briefly wondered if this was a bad idea, but decided to stand my ground anyway. I would not be accused of something I didn't do.

"The *only* reason I went with her was because she told me that you gave her the title transfer for Grays Harbor." I looked directly at him making eye contact this time. "When I left with her, she had *other* plans in mind. When I denied her advances, she got upset. End of story."

"Where'd she get the bruises from?" Tate asked with a sour edge to his voice. I had an inclination right about now that he did not intend to believe me regardless of what I said to him.

"I have no idea. I pushed her off my lap, but I never touched her neck and sure as shit never forced her to suck my dick."

He hesitated for a brief second before speaking, "Stay away from Chelsea," he growled and walked away.

Well that went well.

Knowing my inclination was now correct, I was about to go after him to give him a piece of my mind.

Fortunately for me, Kyle appeared and shook his head. "Don't." His eyes were caveat. "Just let Phillip handle this. If you get involved any further, it could interfere with the case."

Leaning against the back wall, Gordon, the Director of Competition, began the drivers' meeting. Standing there, I realized Kyle was right. I needed to forget about it for now and let Phillip do his job. Not being the type of person to sit back and do *nothing* made this a feat in itself. I had to be in control and right now—I wasn't.

Darrin walked in with his crew chief, and both glanced in my direction. Keeping my calm, I looked the other way.

I couldn't tell you what it was between us, but it started back in USAC when he wrecked me for no reason. From there, I guess you could say the rivalry was born. We never did talk back then. Our first conversation came around the time I was testing in the cup series over the winter and went something like this:

"So you're the badass USAC driver everyone talks about ... you don't look so badass now," was his *kind* way of greeting me.

"I've had my moments," I responded signing a few autographs as I walked toward the paddock that winter afternoon in Daytona.

"Guys like you have it easy. Your father funds everything for you."

Guys like me? He had no idea how much time I spent racing as a kid. Since I was old enough to walk, it's all I've ever wanted. Constantly training and focusing on what I thought was important. The long hours, the time spent traveling, how I never really had a childhood, the things I gave up ... Sway ... he had no fucking clue what it was like for me.

Luck ... sure I had that on my side at times, but I worked hard for everything I have.

"Yeah, I have luck, but I've worked for everything I have." I told him matter-of-factly, walking away.

"Yeah ... right," he muttered and walked away himself.

As you can see, we never really got along.

During the meeting, they talked about the usual topics, pit lane safety, caution flags, and then a few changes in race format with a competition yellow this week due to rain yesterday.

And then it was on to aggression, something they weren't happy with. Gordon and NASCAR made it clear they wouldn't tolerate any retaliation on the track, and any driver caught up in retaliation of *any* kind, would be suspended for a minimum of one race from this point forward in the season.

I respected NASCAR's position as a governing body for the sport. But I had a problem with how they enforced these rules at times. This one, the retaliation, was total bullshit if you asked me.

NASCAR had turned into some kind of marionette with the way they tried to suppress everything. They were sure quick to advertise the fights they didn't condone though. The one of Darrin and me in the infield after the Winston still plays when they advertise the next race. Funny enough they penalized us both for that, but they were making money from it.

Seemed stupid if you asked me.

Personally, I say if you want to punch a driver in the face because he pissed you off, well then, punch him. They did it in hockey and look at how well that's received. It's not like they didn't want to see the fights, they wanted to, believe me. Everyone wants to see that aggression.

Fans wanna see the good ol' days when the drivers went at it in the infield of Talladega. They wanted drivers who showed emotion; they wanted *real* people.

I agreed this needed to be done in moderation. Retaliation as an act was a very fine line. The way I saw it, you need to be held accountable for dirty racing. If you race dirty, you had better be ready to defend those actions; that was my theory at least. Most racers I knew raced that way. And, well, Darrin, he knew nothing about this apparently. He had no problem racing dirty, but when it came to answering the bell, he acted as though he had done nothing wrong. That's where my problem was with him.

After the drivers' meeting, I made my way back to the motor coach to put my racing suit on and get some food. Last night I wasn't able to get in touch with Sway so I tried once more but it went straight to voicemail. I thought for sure that I'd be able to get in touch with her since it was my birthday and all, but no such luck. Part of me wondered if something was wrong with Charlie but she would have called … I hoped.

Before long, as with any race day excitement, I found myself standing outside my car waiting for the pre-race ceremony to begin. Leaning to one side, my legs crossed over appearing relaxed. Conversation around me shifted to the way I was leaning against the car. The guys on my team nicknamed my pre-race stance to the "Rowdy Way," as though this was an intentional stance for me and actually meant something. To me, it didn't really mean anything. It was just how I relaxed before the race.

I'm not sure when I began leaning against my car that way. A handful of other drivers did it as well, maybe all with a different meaning, or maybe it was comfortable for them, too.

As far as when it started for me, it may have happened back when I raced sprint cars. At times, you found yourself waiting on pill draws, putting heat in the engine or simply waiting for your feature race to begin. So I leaned against my car. In a sense, it was a resting position. But, in time, that's where the "Rowdy Way" was developed, and though I never consciously did it, I became known for it and news reports tagged a name to it as if it was some kind of intimidation measure.

When drivers walked by I casually stood there, leaned against my car. And, maybe, if I was honest with you, it could have been a way for me to deliver a message to them. A curious indifference that told them they would never get to me.

But I'm not that honest. It's just a way of relaxing, right?

Reporter after reporter made their way over to me along with a few hundred fans who'd been granted pit passes. By my casual stance leaned against my car, it silently told them Darrin didn't bother me. NASCAR didn't bother me. In reality, I could have been lying, but that's the message I delivered.

Sometime during all this, I looked up in the midst of the people hounding me for autographs and my eyes focused on Ashley.

I wanted to run from her but couldn't, so instead I gave a fake smile as she asked her questions.

Ashley Conner and I had an encounter back when I was racing in the Busch series. And I say encounter because to me, that's all it was, though Ashley seemed to have other ideas about that.

"Another pole for you Jameson, what do you think your chances are here to pull off another win? You wrecked last weekend, do you think you can pull through this time?" Ashley flashed a trained seductive smile and attempted to be flirty by tossing her black hair around.

Immediately, my eyes dropped, avoiding her. The last thing I needed would be to give her the wrong impression here and let her think I was interested again. I wouldn't even say I was interested before; she was just a means to scratch an itch. An itch I no longer had.

"We've had some ups and downs the last couple weeks with this number nine Ford Simplex car, but I think we pulled some things together." This was my standard answer most of the day. "I think we've got a shot at the win here. Cole is fast, as well, so we'll see how it goes. The clouds make a difference here—it can change the track drastically throughout the race."

Ashley thanked me, her cameraman walked away, but she stayed near the car.

"So Jameson ... I was wondering if you'd like to grab some dinner tonight after the race." Her voice grew soft and persuasive.

Still not looking at her, I leaned my head toward her, but continued to sign autographs. "I don't think so Ashley."

"Oh, come on. We haven't been out in months."

"Try years, not months, and my answer is still *no.*" I finally looked over; her blue eyes sparkled with desire. "I'm seeing someone."

Ashley's eyes narrowed. "Jameson Riley doesn't date, *remember?*"

I recalled telling her those exact words at one time. "I do now," I barked back, turning to some fans who had gathered beside my car.

This pervasive curiosity into my personal life and who I was or wasn't dating annoyed me. All I've ever wanted to do was race, but with that came everything else. Sacrifices.

If there was such a thing as hell on earth, I was in it without Sway. I hated being without her and to make matters worse, I hadn't been able to reach her on the phone prior to the race. So now there I sat, running in twenty-second position with a car that could easily win the race, all because I didn't hear her voice and she wasn't here with me.

What the hell had this girl done to me?

I couldn't get her out of my mind. I couldn't escape the sound of her voice, the feel of her touch, the smell of her skin, and I vividly remembered the way she felt under my hands, against my body, the way she tasted. I was a mess without her.

I'm pathetic, *really* fucking pathetic. After the race, I should call her and ask for my balls back.

To make matters worse, I started humming "Purple Rain," which wasn't helping, so then I started belting out the lyrics at the top of my lungs. All this did was remind me of a time when Sway was with me.

"How's the car handling?" Kyle asked. "Did the wedge help?"

Instead of answering him, I belted out the lyrics as loud as I could. Aiden laughed, knowing I'd lost it.

"You've lost your mind." Kyle laughed.

"I know," was my only answer because I had, in fact, lost my mind.

"Get your shit together Riley, and win this race for me," a soft voice ordered over the radio.

My face broke into a wide smile at those words. "Sway?"

She came for me. My girl came for me. If I didn't already love this woman so much, I just fell in love all over again.

"Nope, it's Mandy Moore, now stop butchering Prince and bring me home some candy," she giggled.

"That I can do, honey."

After that, I was on a mission to show my girl I could win this one for her. I became the same hasty version of myself I could be on the track.

"Come on, bud. *Stay* focused," Kyle insisted as I was ranting continuously about the slower cars in front of me. "Be patient."

"Yeah, right," I mumbled. "Give me lap times."

"Twenty seven last time, even with the leader."

My heart was pounding vigorously as I battled with Harris for ninth. My car was awesome, but I couldn't get out of the traffic and Tate wasn't giving an inch of room beside me. Not that I expected him to.

"The ten is outside—keep low," Aiden advised me as we came out of three. "At your door, still there, still there,"

"What the fuck is his problem?" I grumbled when Tate once again bumped me coming across the backstretch. "I give him room and he pushes right back." I glanced over as he flipped me off.

Real mature, Tate.

"He flipped me off."

"What did you expect him to do?" Kyle asked. "He thinks you're messing around with his girl. Just drive through the windshield, bud. Don't pay any mind to him."

"Cole ... you got me? Am I lifting?" I felt like I was lifting too soon allowing him to catch me in the corners.

"Yeah, 10-4 Riley, wait longer coming out of four. He's holding back, but when you lift he's right there."

"I can't wait any longer ... I'll be hung out to dry." I huffed.

"GET DOWN, get down, fourteen spinning in turn two, stay low,"

Aiden cut us off. "Caution's out!"

I saw Darrin in the wall as I drove past, smiling to myself.

Darrin's car was junk, which made me smile wider. He was walking toward the aide car when I passed by and, like the child I could be at times, what did I do?

Flipped him off.

Now who's immature?

"What do you think, bud?" Kyle asked. "Any changes?"

"I'm tight coming out of two and three. Maybe free it up, but other than that, I'm good. If I could get past Tate, I could get up there with the leaders."

"All right, let's do four tires, air pressure adjustment, down a round, and fuel," Kyle ordered. "Pit road's open ... watch your speed, keep coming ... keep coming ... here you go. Three ... two ... one ... wheels straight, foot on the brake."

It seemed silly for him to say that, I knew to do all those things, but in the rush of everything on pit road, those little reminders were appreciated.

The crew went to work as I watched the rest of the field come by in the pits. I had an excellent pit stall right before the entrance to the garage, leaving the stall directly in front of us open—it made it easier on the exit.

"Spencer, watch the right rear. Gentry, tear the tape off the front ..." Mason shouted orders at the crew as I took a drink of my water. The inside of these cars easily reached over a hundred during a race, and could leave you incredibly dehydrated toward the end.

I was there already, believe me.

The front left tire changer reached over the windshield yanking the tear-off and then scraping along the nose of the car to brush away any debris that gathered. If kept there, it raised the engine temperature because it blocked the air vents on the bumper restricting the airflow.

Keeping my right foot securely on the clutch, my left foot slipped from the break when the jack let go and moved to the throttle revving the RPMs in anticipation.

"One lane, one lane ... hard, dig dig, dig!" Kyle yelled as I jostled out of the pits, other drivers doing the same all trying to avoid a colli- sion that could ruin our day. "Nice job! That's *how* you do it!"

"Fuck yeah, guys." We gained four spots on the pit stop. "That's how you do a pit stop—you guys are awesome!" I told them feeling hopeful.

No doubt about it, I was amped. Not only did this put me ahead of Tate, but I had only six cars in front of me, and I knew none of them had *anything* on my car today.

"Coming to the green this time by," Aiden announced.

"How many laps left?"

"You'll have forty to go when you take the green."

Forty to go and six cars to pass ... I could do that.

During pace laps, my mind went back to Sway. How awesome would it be to have Sway here and win on my birthday?

When I took the green, I was on a mission. I said little, only ask- ing for lap times occasionally. This was my way of seeing how close I was running to the lap times on the leader. With twenty to go, I was running in second and battling with Paul for the lead. Getting a nose under him, he put up a good fight for a while.

"Paul's spotter came over," Aiden said. "He said go high, and Paul will let you go."

"Yeah, right?"

"No, they think they've got a problem, engine maybe."

"He's smoking now," I replied and went high.

Sure enough, Paul's engine blew coming out of four, but thank- fully didn't bring out the caution.

"How many laps now?"

"Fourteen to go," Kyle told me. "Hit your marks and stay focused. You're running lap times a second faster than the rest of the field."

I went back to singing "Purple Rain."

"Two to go this time by. It's all clear in front of you. You've got a 2.1 second lead on the forty-eight," Kyle said when I passed the start/ finish line.

I was quiet again aside from the rumble of the engines. It was the only way I could focus on hitting my marks I set and keeping the car straight. The last few laps were also the crucial ones because drivers tended to get carelessly aggressive, me included.

When the white flag was displayed, Sway came on the radio again singing in her best Prince voice.

"You are so adorable," I crooned back at her when she finished and as I came out of turn four to the checkered flag, I yelled, "This one's for you, honey!"

The emotion of the last few weeks got to me as other drivers who passed waved and congratulated me.

So much had happened with Sway, Charlie ... everything. I knew that Sway's favorite part was the burnout, so I did an extra-long one until the smoke was so thick I couldn't see, and I was sure the engine let go.

Once I made it to victory lane, Sway was waiting for me along with my mom, Emma, Alley, and Lane. When I pulled the car in and killed the engine, Kyle stuck his head inside and ruffled my hair. "Nice fucking job, bud!"

"Thanks for giving me a good car, and great pit stops. It's a team effort, *always*," I reminded him.

Most thought it was all on the drivers but, really, every person within a race team contributed to a win. From the engine specialist, to the tire specialist, from the crew chief, to the pit crew, it was a team effort, and if all those aspects lined up, your team was unstoppable. We were unstoppable. They could fine us, challenge us, or whatever else, but I knew then we were unstoppable as a team.

Taking my time removing my gear, I tried to gain some composure again. When I pulled myself from the car, my team roared to life, beer sprayed, cameras were flashing, but I only wanted to find my girl.

Glancing over my shoulder, I saw her making her way over to me with a huge grin that mirrored my own.

Once Sway reached me, I wrapped her into my arms for a tight hug. "Thank you so much for coming," I whispered in her ear pulling back to kiss her.

I didn't care that the entire world was watching this on television or that there was a crowd of people gathered around, I only cared that my girl came for me.

She was choking back tears when I pulled away so I gently brushed them away with my trembling hand and drew in a shaky breath, holding back my own emotions. It'd been one hell of a week.

Sway smiled again. "Happy Birthday, baby!"

"Thanks," I grinned. "You've made it the best yet."

Reporters were hovering, wanting their interviews so I shifted Sway to my side, keeping a firm grasp around her waist when Neil with ESPN asked his questions.

"First off, Happy Birthday!" he told me patting my back. I leaned into him because everyone was still screaming around us making it difficult to hear him. "So tell us, how'd you pull off your fourth cup career win?"

"We had an awesome car all day. I couldn't have asked for a better car here. The crew did great there on the last stop and got me four spots, which helped. I really need to thank them on this one. Not only do they give me excellent pit stops, but these guys never stop." Shifting my weight toward Sway, I continued on, "When I get to go home they are still at the shop getting ready for the next race so I owe this to them, truly I do. I need to thank my sponsor, Simplex, for standing behind me. They allow me to come out here each week and compete for the win, so thank you." I took my hat off and bowed my head to Melissa standing near us to which she gave me a wave. Turning to Sway, I winked. "I'd also like to send a quick hello to Charlie Reins. He helped me get started in racing, and I owe a lot of my experience to him for letting me race even when the track was closed for the season," I said with sincerity at the camera. "Thanks, Charlie."

Sway couldn't hold back the tears any longer; I felt her shake beside me.

Cradling her closer, I leaned over to kiss the top of her head.

"We hear you're the new owner of Grays Harbor Raceway as well," Neil evoked. "How did that come about? Was this something you've been planning for a while?"

"No, it wasn't planned, but the opportunity kind of fell into my hands, and I couldn't pass it up." I didn't dare say anything about Charlie being sick on national television.

Neil patted my back. "Well, congratulations on the win and the new ownership, birthday boy."

Soon the rest of the family made their way over to congratulate me as well. The next two hours were spent between pictures, kissing Sway a tad inappropriately at times, the contenders' conference, more kissing, and now finally we were back home in Dirty Mo celebrating the win and my twenty-third birthday.

Oh, and more kissing.

I thoroughly enjoyed spending time with my family and team, but I wanted to be alone with Sway, so around one in the morning we finally made it upstairs to my room.

The moment we were alone, I captured her in my arms and carried her over to my bed. I'd been waiting to get her alone all day, so I almost forgot and let my hormones lead me.

"There are some things you need to understand," I murmured against her neck, tracing my nose along her jaw as we lay on my bed. Slowly, I removed the last bit of her remaining clothing.

She giggled when I tossed it aside.

"You listening?" I ran my tongue along the column of her neck. "Don't get distracted on me now."

"I can't … focus when you whisper like that," Sway confessed arching her back against me. "I need you."

"I'm not going to fuck you, Sway," I whispered in a low gravelly voice I knew would send her over the edge, taking my lips away for just a second.

"But, you said—"

I placed my fingers against her soft lips. "I'm going to make love to you, and I'm *not* going to stop until you've passed out."

She giggled.

Raising her chin, I forced her to look at me. "No laughing during this … you'll … bruise my ego."

"Well, we wouldn't want that, would we?" she giggled yet again.

"No, we wouldn't." I smiled leaning back on my heels to remove my shirt, tossing it on the floor.

I watched as her eyes took in my bare chest. Her hands started at my shoulders and made their way over my chest muscles and down toward my hips where she unbuttoned my jeans.

Once she removed my jeans, she straddled my hips and began to move against me, with no clothing between us it was easy for her to slide against me.

Sway moaned at the contact and arched her back. It took every ounce of self-control that I had to one, not flip her over and fuck her senseless and two, not blow my load before we even got to the good stuff.

I had to get her to slow down, so I took a firm grasp on her hips, halting her movements. "Sway," I panted. "Honey, you're going to make me come if you keep that up."

Gently I rolled her over covering her body with my own. Her hands clung to my shoulders as I began entering her.

Her back arched against me and her head fell back into the pillows, a gasp escaped her carefully parted lips, her palms pressing against my back urging me forward.

Hitching her leg higher on my hip, I paused, trying to regain some sort of composure and not come instantly when she whimpered, clutching my shoulders. "No."

I had to stop for a minute and regain control; it was too much.

"I'm not stopping, honey." A shuddered breath escaped me as I fought the urge to move. "I just need to … calm down for a minute."

She said nothing, but smiled at my confession, her fingers threading in my hair, a reminder she wanted everything I was giving her.

Some would think knowing a guy like me that I would be completely in control at a time like this, and that I wouldn't be scared to death about what was happening between Sway and me. But if you thought that, you didn't know me very well. I was hesitant, fumbling and terrified of making love to someone like her. There had never been a point in my life where I had ever *made love* to someone and I wasn't really sure how.

So much had changed between us. This wasn't fucking anymore and this wasn't friends with benefits. I needed to show myself to her in the most intimate ways, and that really did scare the shit out of me.

Can I even do this? Can I show her that side?

She watched me moving above her, her eyes never leaving mine. I'd like to say that I was composed and relaxed but I wasn't. Nope. Far from that actually. My body was trembling all over, my breathing was shaky, my heart pounding.

You'd think I'd never had sex before, but really, I'd never had *this* type of sex before. This was completely new to me.

Melting into her touch, that's when I finally told her. "Honey, tell me," I begged her, breathing in sharply. "Please ... tell me ... you love me. Tell me this is right. Tell me—"

"I love you," she whispered against my lips as hers brushed over mine, so soft, so right. "It's right. We're perfect. This is perfect."

She reassured me as our bodies moved together. Our eyes stayed connected the entire time. There was a hunger in her eyes, but there was also trepidation.

The fact that she seemed just as nervous assured me this was new to her, too. It was relaxing to know that she'd never been *this* way with anyone.

Closing my eyes at our movements, I relished in the sensation of her warm body beneath me, our bodies moving slowly in the most intimate way.

Bending forward, I kissed her forehead and pulled her closer. I was going to hold on to her as long as I could.

Before long, I couldn't hold back. I was losing the battle quickly and Sway was determined to push me.

Frustrated, she squirmed beneath me trying to speed my movements. "Go ... faster ..." she moaned, arching her back. "Faster."

My stomach tightened in preparation. "I can't ..." I grunted reaching for a tighter hold on her. "If I go faster ... I'll come."

"I will, too ... just go faster ... *please*," she begged with a whimper. *How can I deny her?*

I couldn't stop now, my forehead fell to hers and it was over. I completely lost any will I had and let go when she begged me. I couldn't even focus; my body was shaking embarrassingly, along with my heavy panting. I was a mess.

The rush consumed everything, the pleasure, the reminder that she was finally mine, left me breathless. Not more than a mere second later, Sway was moaning my name. Thankfully, my bedroom is on the third floor and no one could hear us up here, with the sounds coming from this woman you'd think I was killing her.

When the sun began to rise, basking the room in a soft orange glow, I pulled Sway closer.

She sighed contentedly and snuggled in. Sway had this way of worming herself into my arms in the middle of the night without me noticing, but when I awoke, I was always surprised at how close she was ... not that I was complaining.

"I don't want to screw this up," I suddenly blurted out running my fingers through her dark hair.

"What?" Sway twisted in my arms to look up at me. "What are you talking about?"

Tracing my fingertips lightly up her shoulder, and then over her collarbone I told her my fears. "This ... I don't want to screw up what we have. I fucked it up once and I can't do that again. Now that I know what it's like with you ... it would kill me if I lost it."

"Okay, so don't," she ventured, kissing my lips. "And don't be so dramatic. It wouldn't *kill* you. I might, but *it* wouldn't."

I laughed lightly but knew she was missing the point to this.

"You do realize that I don't know what I'm doing," I hinted waiting for her to understand. "I'm not sure how good I'll be at it. Maybe you could just not expect anything real fancy or fairytale like."

She giggled shaking her head, her arms wrapped around me.

"What's going on with you?" she soothed, running her hands up and down my spine; her gentle touch was relaxing but not enough.

"I guess I'm just scared." I mumbled into her shoulder. "I feel like I have a lot to live up to."

It took her a moment, but she giggled again.

I needed to make her see.

"Okay ..." I sat her up to face me, my hands moved to her face. "I've *never* been in love before. I don't know how to be a boyfriend and have a career at the same time." I paused looking at her nervous expression. "I don't know what to do."

"You've never been in love? What about ..." she began.

I shook my head quickly, interrupting her. "I didn't know what love was back then ... I was seventeen. But looking back at it now, no, it wasn't love at all, not even close. Chelsea, all those other women, they didn't mean anything to me."

She was looking at me so earnestly that I fell in love with her that much more.

"So …" I continued with a smirk. "I have no clue what I'm doing, but I'm willing to try for you. I may fuck up along the way, probably *a lot*, but I want to do that with you … as your boyfriend."

"Does this mean we're going steady?" Sway asked between giggles.

She is so fucking cute.

I laughed freely. "I think it does, Joanie."

"Kiss me, Chachi."

Fresh Rubber – Slang for a new set of tires.

I woke up to the soft sounds of Jameson playing his piano. I hadn't heard him play in years and, at first, I thought I was dreaming. Propping myself up on my elbows, I looked at the piano situated in the far right corner of his massive gray bedroom.

I had to laugh at his décor. Everything in the room was white, gray, or black.

Total man pad.

He even had an intake manifold in the corner of his room.

When my eyes found him, I sighed contentedly and was reminded of how happy I was that this dirty heathen was my Chachi.

And my Chachi was currently serenading me.

His head bowed as if in submission to what he was doing, his long masculine fingers glided over the ivory keys. I was entranced by how he moved on the bench, his head bent barely looking up. It was a beautiful combination with dulcet tones of the piano.

He'd memorized "Shame On The Moon" over the years; it was one of his favorites and Jimi's. Who didn't love a little Bob Segar though?

There are no words to describe how Jameson played. I envied his talent. His eyes were closed, and it was easy to see how much passion he had for playing, as he did for racing. I could feel it in my bones.

After a few moments, he began singing in that low, rich voice.

His fingers picked up pace when the song went into a climb, his head leaned back, belting out the lyrics, and I could feel my eyes stinging with tears.

Listening to the words, I could tell why he chose this particular song.

He was telling me he was scared *but* ready.

Jameson played the chorus for a good ten minutes while I observed in admiration that someone could have that much natural talent in everything he did.

When he began to sing again, his voice was lower than before, almost a whisper, drawing me in. When he finished, his head hung, and he sat there running his fingers gently over the keys. His hands stilled on the keys, a discordant cadence echoing in the room.

Without wearing a damn thing, I strutted my no-longer-pit-lizard bare ass over to him, to show him a thing or two about talent.

I wonder what I would call myself now since I couldn't really be considered his pit lizard. Clearly, I was *way* more now.

Pit lizard girlfriend ... Joanie girlfriend ... pigizzle ... ha, ha, ha ... good one Sway.

You're now a pigizzle. I told myself.

Jameson's head remained down, but when he heard me giggle at my pigizzle-self, I saw the corners of his mouth twist into a smile. Placing both my hands on his bare shoulders, I ran my fingers softly over the ridges in his defined shoulders, feeling his muscles flex as his hands caressed my legs.

Turning on the bench, he looked up at me through his long dark lashes, his green eyes burning. It wasn't hard to see the change that occurred in us ... in him. His once nervous eyes were now filled with love and adoration.

He loved me, you see.

"Good morning, beautiful," Jameson whispered against my stomach, trailing kisses from the prominent ridge of my hip, over my belly button and along the other hipbone. Sweeping his tongue up toward my rib cage, he nipped at the skin as he did so.

My entire body trembled despite my demand for it not to, earning a chuckle from him in response. I hated the way my body was so responsive to him; I couldn't hide anything.

With a wink, he picked me up, carrying me over to his large king-sized bed, lying me down. He pulled away, but only to remove his shorts, and he was back to worshiping my body, with his hands, his mouth, his tongue, and, of course ... his glorious camshaft. There was no dirty heathen talking last night, but it returned this morning ... *ohhh,* did it return.

What started out sweet and caring quickly turned minutes later when I told him it was great and all, but I wanted my dirty car-talking heathen, damn it. More importantly, I wanted to be fucked.

You asked and you received.

With another wicked smirk, he flipped me over so I was on my knees in front of him and wrapped his hand around my hair, gently pulling me back against his chest.

"Jameson ..." I moaned as he pushed inside.

He took a firm grasp on my hip with the hand that wasn't tangled in my hair bringing his soft wet lips down on my shoulder, biting and kissing his way along the top of my collarbone.

The teasing and biting continued for a few moments, but when I was starting to shake, I had to put an end to it. I needed this and I needed it now.

The moment I felt him inside of me, I never wanted it to end. It was like I couldn't get enough of him. I knew being with him physically would be unlike anything we'd ever experienced together, but now it was so much more than before. His intensity was evident in every kiss, every touch, showing me this was different, showing me the love he had for me.

"Just fuck me already!" I blurted out when he continued with his slow movements.

"Are you ready for some align boring 'cause I'm not holdin' back any longer. These bearings need aligned, *properly,*" Jameson grunted, his hips meeting mine slowly at first, but I could feel a change coming.

"What does no holding back mean?" I asked slightly confused. I never thought Jameson held back anyway.

What will this mean?

In my head, I was envisioning whips and chains or some shit so I turned to look back at him with wide eyes. I'm all for the dirty talking and rough sex, but I was slightly terrified of any S & M. I once watched a porno that involved this and couldn't sleep for a week thinking that shit was something only serial killers did.

"What I mean is ..." He squeezed my ass, "... there are times when I'm going to make sweet love to you ... slowly and with more passion than you ever thought imaginable." Jameson then moved my hair to the side kissing along my neck slowly. His hand tangled in my hair once more and he tugged with enough force to make me want to scream. "And there are times when I'm going to fuck you until you *beg* me to stop."

Why am I suddenly excited as hell to see which one I'm getting today?

Of course, my excitement must have shown on my face because Jameson suddenly chuckled, his laugh marred by his heavy breathing.

"Which service are you offering up today?" I arched my back against him, keeping my eyes locked with his.

Jameson smirked. His eyes were half-opened watching me. His gaze darkened, burning my skin as it ran over my body. "Guess which one ..." he ground out through his clenched jaw as I swiveled my hips against him, causing him to moan.

The dirty talking tapered off as did any talking for that matter. Jameson's third floor bedroom was filled with nothing but his grunts, my whore moaning, and sounds of Prince in the background.

We were starting to have an obsession with Prince.

Afterward, a few minutes passed as we lay there, until his phone started buzzing next to the bed.

He leaned forward, kissed my forehead, and then reached over me to his phone. "I'm sorry, I have to get up. I need to be in LA later today for a commercial for Simplex, and then I have to fly to Memphis to meet ... my *biggest* fan."

I looked at him, confused. He sat up running his hand through his mess of hair peeking back at me.

"Your biggest fan?" The dread in my voice present, I was praying this wasn't some woman.

"Uh … yeah … he's a five year old little boy who has leukemia," he told me. "He's being treated at St. Jude's in Memphis and I was his wish."

"His wish?"

His eyes dropped to his lap and his hand ran across the back of his neck. "Well, he has leukemia and well, he's dying from it, and his wish was to meet me. He wanted to be a race car driver when he grew up. St. Jude Children's Hospital got in touch with Melissa and asked if I could come out to spend the day with him."

I didn't realize I was crying until Jameson brushed the tears away. "I never meant to make you cry," he whispered.

I shrugged slightly, trying to avoid his questioning stare.

Gently, he tugged on my hand and my eyes meet his, sighing when I saw his eyebrows rise in question.

"No, it's okay … I just … there's always so much sadness around, you know? I hate that there are children out there who can't even live to see their dreams come true or fall in love," I said softly, my arms sliding around his neck, bringing his lips to meet mine. He responded and kissed me softly.

"I know what you mean, honey." He cradled me against his chest. "I know what you mean."

I was about to get up when he stopped me, tugging on my hand.

"You could come with me, if you want," he suggested. "I'm sure Axle won't mind."

"His name is Axle?" I smiled, thinking how perfect of a name that was for a little guy who loved racing.

Jameson chuckled. "Yeah, it's cute. He wanted to be a race car driver … it fits, huh?"

"It does." Sitting on the edge of his bed, I nodded. "I don't think I'm going to go."

"But you—"

"No, his wish was to spend the day with you," I shook my head in reassurance. "That's what he deserves."

"Thanks, Sway, for everything." His eyes held mine intently. "For coming yesterday, for last night and this morning … just … *thank you.*

I wish I could tell you how much it meant to me, but I don't think I could without sounding trite," he said with so much sincerity, it made me start crying again.

Jameson left for Los Angeles and then Memphis, so Emma and I flew back to Washington. Emma hadn't been home to Washington since the last winter so she was enthused as hell to come along. Though I'd never admit this, I was excited to spend some girl time with her.

Alley was going to come along, as well, but Lane ended up getting the flu so she stayed home with him.

I wanted to be in Daytona this weekend with Jameson for his race, but his schedule was packed that weekend and wouldn't allow much time for me anyway. So I decided to fly home when he left for California. It'd also be good for me to see Charlie again, and Emma was anxious to see the crazy guy, as well.

The only problem with Emma coming along was entertaining her in Elma, Washington. We didn't have much there to offer a crazy shopaholic. No malls, no fancy department stores, hell, we barely had a grocery store. All of this meant I had to take Emma to the mall before we made it to Elma.

She insisted on the Tacoma Mall ... I'm not sure why anyone would want to go to the Tacoma Mall but, alas, there we were walking into every goddamn store they had. She bought shoes, underwear, dresses, and God knows what else.

I had a hard time focusing on anything, between Emma whirling around me, texting Jameson, thinking of Jameson, missing Jameson, and wanting to be with Jameson. I didn't get nearly enough alone time with him like I wanted. I was a pathetic pigizzle.

The thought of calling myself a pigizzle had me laughing while I enjoyed my iced mocha and followed Emma around, who was, once again, trying on another pair of god-awful red boots. Where she would wear those was a mystery to me. But when she said that Aiden had a fantasy with her in red boots, I ran away to the pretzel stand.

While quietly enjoying my buttery, salty goodness, Emma came skipping back with another bag from Macy's and plopped down beside me on the bench.

"So ... I ... made us an appointment," she whispered looking the other direction, avoiding eye contact.

There's one thing you need to know about Emma, when she knows you'll disagree—she avoids eye contact.

Forcing the little shit to look at me, I grabbed her face. "What kind of appointment Emma?"

I had to ask because when we were in high school she once made an appointment for us to get our ... let's just say they're some things even close friends don't do together, I don't care how *close* you are with them. A line needs to be drawn. I now had a line, and Emma was sure to step a foot over it any time she saw an opportunity.

"Justwaxingthatsall," she said quickly, her words scrambling together in her rush not to reveal.

"Come again?"

"Waxing," Emma replied through squished lips and my firm hold on her.

"I don't need any waxing ... my bits are nice and trim."

"Vajazzling," she blurted out flinching back like an abused dog. "What?"

"It's vajazzling ... it makes the goods sparkle."

"I don't want the goods to sparkle."

Yes, you do ... admit it ... you're intrigued by this.

Who wouldn't want their crankcase to sparkle?

"Yes, you do." Her eyes were bright with excitement. She knew she was wearing me down. She now had a leg over my line. "It'll be fun."

"How does it sparkle?" Now I was avoiding eye contact.

Why have I never heard of this?

In my head, I was thinking of flashing lights or some shit like that. The thought of anything electric down there wasn't comforting—unless, of course, I had control over it.

Emma smiled triumphantly. "You'll see." Her expression was something similar to ... well ... someone who'd just gotten her way.

Am I going to regret this?

Yes ... it was Emma's idea—it couldn't be good.

"Look at that girl's tattoo ..." someone snickered behind us as we gathered our bags. "Jesus."

Since Jimi and Nancy found out about Emma's tattoo, she stopped hiding it and rebelled against everyone by showing it proudly.

In a blink of an eye, Emma grabbed my mocha and chucked it at the teenage girl who snickered at her Trash-R-Us token. She had horrible aim, so the cup only went a few feet and fell to the ground, spilling my five-dollar mocha all over the marble floor of the Tacoma Mall.

"Can you believe the nerve of her!" Emma shouted, not attempting to keep her voice down. "Some people!"

"Um—" I was about to say something when my phone vibrated.

It was a text from Jameson that read: ***Hey beautiful. Missing you right now. Axle says hello and I quote: She's hot! Chachi***

I laughed and sent one back.

Hello, handsome. Missing you too. Tell Axle thanks, I think. Joanie

A few minutes later, my phone buzzed again with a media message of the cutest picture ever. Jameson was kneeling beside Axle. They both had helmets on, but what caught my eye was that they both had the biggest grins on their faces. Jameson appeared relaxed and content with him. Little Axle, with his huge brown eyes, was looking over at him with such veneration it made me start crying, again.

Thanks for making me cry!

Soon he replied with: ***Sorry, honey, I didn't mean to. Axle wanted you to see a picture of him. Gotta go race now, he thinks he can beat me. Love you.***

My curiosity for vajazzling got the better of me. An hour later Emma and I were lying on the table, in separate rooms, getting vajazzled.

The entire process was strange and rather uncomfortable. Especially when the tiny Asian woman ripped out my beaver pelt and began adhering diamonds on it. When burning a hole in her forehead with my stare didn't work, I spread my legs and went with it.

When she was finished, she handed me a mirror to observe her meticulous handy work.

I wasn't sure what freaked me out more during the entire process, her wide grin when I'd scream, or the fact that my legs were now spread with a mirror between them.

Instead of worrying about that, I focused on the situation below. *Wow.*

Examining my crankcase, she looked sparkly. She'd been turned into a shiny, sparkly, smooth, vajazzled crankcase, complete with a checkered flag and a number nine.

Hot damn if I didn't look good.

I was tempted to click a picture and text Jameson, but I refrained. He was with children today. Then I thought I needed to reveal this Holy Grail extravagant masterpiece in person. Maybe even with fireworks.

When the tiny Asian left, carefully I put my clothes on. I didn't want any diamonds to fall out in fear they would ... get misplaced. The thought made me cringe of having anything sharp make its way inside my crankcase.

Emma was standing in the lobby waiting for me. Just as I was about to ask her what she got, she pulled me into the bathroom, dropped her pants and bared her goods to me.

"Christ Almighty, Emma; I didn't need to see that!" I wailed, diverting my eyes away from her horseshoe she had designed on her girly pad. "You could have *told* me what you got. This isn't show and tell."

Pulling her jeans up, she reached for the button of my jeans. "Hey, I showed you, now you show me."

"No way. *Not happening.*" Slapping at her, I backed away, "Never, No!" I shook my head violently. "Not in this life time." It was becoming pretty obvious Emma was not concerned with my lack of show-n-tell.

"*Sway*, I showed you. That's not fair," she whined crossing her arms in front of her.

I wanted to back away farther, but I was now straddling the toilet in my attempts to escape.

"I do not care!" I shouted, sprinting from the bathroom with her trailing. "I never said this was an all-skate."

"At least tell me what you got," she insisted, catching me once I made it to the lobby doors.

I couldn't help the smile that grazed my lips when I thought about my checkered flag crankcase. Fortunately, she couldn't see it since I was running away from her. "A checkered flag with the number nine," I answered quickly making my way through the parking lot.

My running didn't last long; I was completely out of shape. Soon I was panting, wheezing, and holding my side in pain.

"Oh, that's sweet. You should send him a picture." Emma held up her phone. "I already sent one to Aiden."

"I'm not sending him a picture," I chided, helping Emma put the bags in the back of the red dragon. "He's at St. Jude Children's Hospital today. I'm not sending him a picture of that while he's entertaining children. That's gross."

"What's he doing at St. Jude's?"

"There's a five year old boy, Axle, whose wish was to meet Jameson."

"Oh." I could tell it bothered her, as well. "Jameson donates a lot of money to that particular hospital. I can see why he'd want to spend some time there."

Making my way through Tacoma traffic wasn't the highlight of my day. When we got to Olympia, I headed for caffeine.

"Where are we going?" Emma asked.

"You threw my coffee away, so you're buying me more." I smiled. "You should think of getting some, too," I hedged. She had no idea what she was in for with the Lucifer twins.

Rolling with my advice, Emma did get coffee and then we were cruising down 101 toward Elma country and cow shit.

With Emma's dancing rocking the truck from side-to-side, I turned down the music once we were back on the freeway. "What do you think Chelsea, Darrin, and Mariah are up to?" I asked.

Emma was all keyed-up after that. She wanted to be a lawyer at one time, so solving a mystery was right up her alley. That and she watched entirely too much CSI. "Well," she began with much exaggeration, "I think Darrin used Chelsea in an attempt to get Jameson in trouble. You know, trying to prove he's like some sort of bad guy who goes around assaulting women." Emma paused taking a drink of her mocha. "Darrin's pissed that Jameson is one of the best drivers out there—he's competition for Darrin. I *really* think all this is Darrin's doing. It has to be. He's hated Jameson from day one. I mean, you remember their USAC days together."

"Do you think Tate is involved?"

"No, I don't. I think Tate is in denial. He would never do that to Jameson purposely; he's being fed lies by Chelsea—I'm sure of it."

I was quiet for a few minutes merging onto Highway 8. Then it hit me ... if we found someone who was close to them maybe we could see what they're up to. "Do you know anyone who's friends with them?"

"The only person I know who hangs around them is Dana. I don't know that she's friends with them, though." Emma took another drink of her mocha. "Dana doesn't go to every race; she's an obsessed fan. I don't even think she has any family on the series."

"I wonder if we could get her to, you know ... help us."

Emma giggled. "Jameson would *kill* us."

"What he doesn't know ... won't hurt him." I waggled my eyebrows at her.

The last thing I wanted to do was cause additional stress for Jameson. He had enough already. If there was some way I could help him resolve this whole Darrin issue that would mean less stress for him and less stress for me.

When we arrived back at Charlie's house, I was in the middle of putting my bag in my room when Emma came in with a grimy expression on her face. We'd only been there for five minutes, so I assumed this expression had *something* to do with the Lucifer twins.

I watched as she pulled the red boots she bought from a Nordstrom bag, only they weren't red anymore. They were now charcoal and burnt.

My thoughts were confirmed. It was Satan's spawn. Unless Aiden's fantasy involved a fire fighter, those wouldn't get him going.

"Ah, yes," I grinned. "I see you met the Lucifer twins."

"*Met them*?" Her eyes bugged out. "They set my boots on fire!"

"They've done worse … look at Mr. Jangles." I pointed to his shaved ass. "He will never be the same."

"I was wearing the boots when they set them on fire, Sway." Emma tossed the boots on the floor. "Who the fuck are those hoodlums?"

"They're Andrea's twin boys." I gave her a wide smile. "They *live* here."

"You're shitting me, right?"

"Nope, not shitting you."

"I'm not staying here with them." She placed her hand on her hip giving me a pointed glare. "I refuse."

"Yes. You are," I demanded. "If I have to stay here, you sure as shit have to."

Mr. Jangles walked over to Emma and started rubbing himself up against her legs. She glanced down and then took a double take before jumping on my bed. "What the fuck is that?" she squealed in horror.

You'd think she saw the devil or something.

I looked around for the devil—I wanted to have a discussion with him about his children and their behavior.

"What is wrong with you guys?" I shouted a few octaves louder than necessary. I felt bad for poor Mr. Jangles—it's not his fault he was overweight. "He's a fucking cat!"

"What do you feed him, McDonald's?"

I shook my head and laughed. "You are so much like Jameson."

There was never a dull moment having Emma and the Lucifer twins around all under the same roof. On Wednesday, they shaved Mr. Jangles the rest of the way and made him look like a lion, keeping a ball of fur on his tail, fur on his feet, and then the long fur around his face. He looked like an overly obese lion.

Having no hair did nothing for his figure, that's for sure. The shaving combined with the safety pinned pierced ears, made him resemble some biker dude's cat, not my fluffy, white, long-haired Mr. Jangles who loved me and his spaghetti. I half expected him to whip out his switchblade and shank me in my sleep.

Thankfully, he did not.

On Thursday, they filled balloons full of Hershey syrup and threw them at Emma and me while we lay in the sun. That same day, we also found out that the ceiling fan in the living room was not strong enough to hold a dog's leash while Logan was attached to the end of it.

Although, it *was* strong enough to hold a can of red paint and spray it throughout the room, causing it to resemble some kind of scene out of the series, *Dexter*.

On Friday, Lucas put marbles in the red dragon's gas tank causing her to make an extreme amount of noise while driving.

Logan also decided Mr. Jangles needed a bath.

After all, he was covered in red paint, so he put him in the washing machine on spin cycle.

There are two things you need to know about this. One, a normal cat will throw up twice their body weight … when dizzy. Two, a Mr. Jangles- sized cat will throw up roughly ten times his body weight … when dizzy … give or take an ounce.

Like I said, there was never a dull moment.

Soon it was Saturday, and I was getting a little jittery as to what the next few days would bring. The last two nights of racing at Elma were cancelled due to a summer storm blowing through.

Unfortunately, Daytona wasn't having the same storm, so Jameson was racing while I was stuck with Emma *and* the Lucifer twins.

Charlie and Andrea snuck up to Lake Quinault for the weekend to spend some time together. Long story short, this left us alone with the devil's spawn.

It wasn't exactly pressured upon us to watch them or anything. Feeling bad for them, we volunteered to watch the shitheads, which was why we were now picking out movies and buying a shit load of junk food in hopes they would pass out in a sugar-induced coma. It worked on Lane.

Did that happen?

No, that would have been entirely *too* easy.

Emma and I were curled up in the chaise lounge in the living room, together, watching *Poltergeist* because Emma insisted we watch scary movies since it's stormy outside. I think her brothers dropped her on her head when she was a baby because this logic was stupid to me.

I was not enthusiastic about watching a scary movie to begin with. The last time I watched a scary movie was *The Exorcist* with Jameson, and I ended up sleeping with my bedroom light on for a goddamn month. And let's not forget my phobia of preachers after that.

I hated clowns, too, and just a few minutes into this horrid movie, I *really* hated them.

By the time Carol Anne said, "They're here," Emma was sitting on top of me, viewing the movie through my fingers as they covered her eyes. I wasn't doing any better with my baby blanket wrapped around my head.

Yes, I still had my first baby blankie ... don't judge me.

When Robbie was pulled under the bed by the clown, we screamed. But not nearly as loud as we screamed when the Lucifer twins coaxed Mr. Jangles into the room.

It was a suspenseful part of the movie; you knew something intense was coming any minute. All of a sudden, the shaved obese lion with safety pinned pierced ears, Mr. Jangles, came flying through the air landing on top of us.

We screamed bloody fucking murder.

I'm not gonna lie, I screamed as if I saw the devil himself.

I should have asked him to take his kids back.

After the screaming fit, the twins disappeared for good reason. I'm sure they gathered that their lives were in jeopardy.

The storm gained strength. Wind blew, power was lost, and it rained, a lot.

All this with Emma, the Lucifer twins, and me *alone* in the dark.

To say we were scared of the dark was an understatement ... we were *petrified* of the dark. It might have something to do with the fact that we watched *Poltergeist* but that's unimportant.

"What if it's Carol Anne?" Emma whispered in my ear. She was close enough that her breath tickled my neck. She couldn't have gotten much closer. After all, we were wrapped around each other.

"I fucking hate you for making me watch that movie," I seethed through my teeth, scanning the dark room for any sign of the devil's spawn. "Where in the hell are those Lucifer twins?"

All we heard were their evil giggles throughout the two-story house. If that's not creepy, I don't know what is.

Their giggles were quickly silenced when a loud crash came from outside, followed by heavy footsteps. The little creepers weren't giggling anymore … nope, they were clinging to our legs like Gorilla Glue.

Whoever would be walking around outside in this weather was crazy. That confirmed my fears that it could be some kind of deeply troubled axe murder. No one in their right mind would be out in this.

"Sway, what was that?" Lucas whined and, even in the dark, I could see how wide his eyes were.

I honestly couldn't say I felt sorry for the little shit, not after what he pulled during the movie with Mr. Jangles.

"It's probably your father rising from Hell to teach you a goddamn lesson," I snapped, prying him from my leg.

"Sway, that was a little harsh." Emma punched my shoulder. "He's *just* a child."

"A child my ass." I may have been a tad on the rude side right then, but I was, in fact, just as scared as that six-year-old. "Did you forget what they did to your boots?"

Another loud crash came from outside near the spooky tree that strangely resembled the one from the movie.

Tomorrow I would be cutting that down. I never noticed how scary it was until now. Or maybe it was the movic.

More banging followed, along with barking dogs that I didn't know the neighborhood even had. The wind picked up and blew the back door open. I thought for sure that only happened in movies before the characters were gutted.

What did we do?

All of us screamed at once and ran in opposite directions.

Thankfully, Emma ran the direction of the gun cabinet.

But did she grab one? No, that would be too easy. Instead, she ran right past it to the kitchen. I ran after her, well wobbled. I had two of Satan's spawns attached to my legs.

In my attempts, I smashed into Emma, knocking us all to the ground.

Glancing at the object she had a death grip on, I laughed. "A house full of guns and you grab a *fork*?"

"I panicked, all right ..." her voice shuddered. "I panicked."

"So you grab a fork? Why not a knife that was right beside it?"

Emma glared. "I p*anicked*!"

"Clearly."

Lucas was trembling in my arms about the time Logan wrapped himself around Emma like a human scarf.

"Sway ... w-w-what's out t-t-there ...?" Lucas asked.

It was at that moment that I actually started to feel a little bad for them. I mean, yes, they are shitheads, but they're just as scared as we were, possibly more.

"Don't worry, it's nothing—" I was cut off by yet another howl of wind and another loud crashing noise.

What the hell was out there?

Both boys clung tighter to us as we backed up against the wall in the kitchen behind the table. Somehow we felt safer with chairs in the way, creating a diversion, let's just hope we didn't die in this version.

What if it is Carol Anne? I thought to myself.

All my thoughts went back to my theory of needing a man around. As old fashioned as that sounded, I was a firm believer now. It was their job to protect and these six-year-olds with us were providing *no* protection. I didn't have the heart to tell them, given their current state of terror, if they couldn't "man up" at a time like this, there was no hope for them.

"Emma," I whispered shakily, repulsed at how freaked out I'd become over a stupid movie. "Go see what's out there."

Emma did a ridiculous gasp-gulp thing that made me chuckle. "Me?" she asked pointing to herself with distress. "Why do I have to do it, why not you?"

"You have the fork," I pointed out. "I clearly can't protect myself as well. You, on the other hand, could fork 'em."

"That's bullshit!"

Another loud crash came from the back of the house and someone stepped inside, the floor squeaking with each wet step they took.

Emma, driven by fear I assume, screamed like a little girl, held the fork up and ran for the perpetrator, all the while—*still* screaming.

There was squeaking from the water on the floor, screaming and more screaming. She crashed into the said perpetrator, knocking them both to the ground.

"What the fuck!" the man cried in pain, but I knew that voice. How could I not ... no one else had that rich raspy, but velvet, voice N*o one.*

"Jameson?" I asked hesitantly, Logan and Lucas started giggling.

"Yes it's me ... *what the hell*?" he grunted in pain. "I think you hit bone ... *goddamn it,* Emma!" he continued to scream in pain on the floor.

I quickly scrambled over to him, and though I couldn't see clearly with the lack of light, I could vaguely see the outline of Emma's weapon, impaled in Jameson's bloody right shoulder.

"Emma!" I screeched reaching for a flashlight. "You *stabbed* him."

"Like I knew it was him," Emma defended. "He should have said something!"

"Said something?" his voice took on a panicked edge but remained harsh. "*Fuckkkkk* ... this hurts ... damn you, Emma," Jameson slammed his fist on the ground and then moaned in agony having jarred himself.

"Maybe we should take him to the hospital. I think I did hit his bone ..." Emma admitted quietly, backing away from Jameson who was screaming again because Logan pushed on the fork.

"Get him away from me!" Jameson growled fiercely my direction. My arms instinctively reached out to Logan, fearing for his safety. "Stay away from me."

"Why are you all wet and muddy?" I asked, examining his shoulder.

He winced as I felt around his wound. It was bleeding, but not terribly—probably because the fork was still in there. Once it was pulled out, I was sure this would need stitches.

"If you haven't noticed ... it's fucking raining out."

I could tell he was pissed, but he didn't need to be mean with me. I wasn't the one who stabbed him.

"Why are you yelling at me? I didn't stab you!"

Jameson gingerly rose from the floor using the wall for support, panting. "I'm sorry ... G*od*, it hurts so fucking bad," he groaned, holding up his forearm with his left arm, careful not to let the weight of it pull on his shoulder.

"I think we should pull it out," Lucas suggested, jumping up in a chair he pulled over. "Can I do it?" he asked, bouncing, his eyes wide and excited. "Please, can I do it?"

"Don't fucking touch me," Jameson seethed, backing away from him. "*Don't* touch me!"

"Okay, both of you," I motioned to the boys. "No one touches Jameson. He's got ..." Eyeing his protective injured stance, I settled on, "anger issues."

Emma moved closer to Jameson, but he backed away. "Jameson, I'm really sorry. Like, *really* sorry. I thought you were Carol Anne."

"Who the hell is Carol Anne?" he snarled, still not letting any of us close to him. He reminded me of an injured animal who wanted nothing to do with humans. I wondered, though briefly, if he'd crawl off to die alone.

"From *Poltergeist*," said Emma with a careless, but still timid, shrug.

"That's a fucking movie ... it's make-believe you shithead!" Jameson snapped. "I swear to God, Emma, if I can't race ... I'm stabbing you."

"That's a little harsh," Emma replied.

"No one is doing any more stabbing!" I yelled, breaking up their silly fight and needing to collect my thoughts. I couldn't focus with all this yelling and accusing. "Let's go, Jameson. I'm taking you to the hospital."

"No, no, no ... you're not leaving me here alone with them!" Emma objected pointing at the Lucifer twins while they tormented Jameson.

"Fine," I groaned. "All of you get in the car."

"*No!*" Jameson interjected immediately. Just the very thought had made his face pale, or so I thought. "I'm not going anywhere with Stabberally over there ... fuck no." He shook his head violently. "No fucking way."

"Don't be a jerk," Emma smacked Jameson on the shoulder, the bad shoulder. "I didn't mean to stab you!"

"Oh, son of a bitch!" Jameson screamed dropping to the floor. "Get the fuck away from me, Emma! I will pull this out right now and stab you with it if you touch me again."

"Why are you being so mean to me?" she asked, getting in his face again. "I said I didn't do it intentionally."

Jameson stepped forward as though he was actually going to take revenge on his little sister.

"Enough!" Stepping between them, I motioned for everyone to get out of the house. "We are *all* going to the hospital. Now get in the car, right now."

At this point, I assumed that I looked a little like the Exorcist or something similar because no one questioned me again. We all piled in Charlie's Expedition and began our journey to Grays Harbor Community Hospital.

Jameson moaned the entire way about how bad it hurt, as the kids and Emma egged him on. I wanted to warn him that this was probably the *best* part of it. Just imagine how he's going to feel sitting at Grays Harbor Community Hospital for hours waiting for them to pull their heads out of their asses long enough to help us, but I didn't.

I could only handle one bad situation at a time.

Around three in the morning, we finally arrived at the hospital and the Lucifer twins were out cold in the back seat, along with Emma, so we left them in the car.

Jameson was pleased.

He insisted I go inside with him, so I did. He insisted I stay right beside him because he was convinced he was going to be attacked somehow, so I did. He insisted I go back with him when the triage nurse was looking over him, so I did. But when he insisted that I go to the vending machines to get him Skittles, I drew the line. Not that I wouldn't get him Skittles but he was being a *huge* baby about this entire situation. It was just a fork. If it was a knife, I may be a little more sympathetic. Maybe.

Jameson sat there complaining about Emma stabbing him, the kid next to him sneezing on him, and the avid NASCAR fan who grabbed every brochure from around the hospital and had him sign it.

"How long does it take to get seen?" Jameson grumbled as he adjusted himself in the chair next to me again. "This is unacceptable. We have been here for three hours. My God, I've been *stabbed*, how is that not an emergency?"

"Try four. It's Grays Harbor Community Hospital, what did you expect?"

"I don't know … " He laid his head on my shoulder. "It hurts."

"You're such a baby." It might have been rude, but I went ahead and said it anyway. "It's a fork, not a knife."

"Let me stab you with a fork and then we'll see how much of a baby *you are*," he retorted glaring and then his expression softened as that familiar smirk appeared. "You know … I've always wanted to do it on an exam table," he told me, waggling his eyebrows at me. "Wanna be my naughty nurse?"

"No," I stated firmly, even though this image was already present. "We are *not* doing it in here. How does your mood change so fast? I think you may be bi-polar or something."

He grinned wider at his attempt to soften me.

I was not softening.

"No!" I shook my head at him trying not to reveal my own smirk.

The avid NASCAR fan returned with yet another brochure for him, and Jameson snapped. "Dude, come on. *Seriously*? You can't see that I'm injured and signing autographs is slightly difficult?" He motioned with his head toward the fork still sticking out of his shoulder.

The man shrugged, handing Jameson the brochure.

He reminded me of a taller version of Jack Black, only he was not funny. If anything, he was annoying. I mean really, did he honestly think this was an appropriate time to be asking for an autograph?

"Jameson Riley?" a nurse called out, a folder tucked under her arm.

The man walked away when Jameson pushed the brochure back at him and said, "Go away."

All things considered, I couldn't blame him for denying the autograph.

"*See*, we can't do it, they're calling your name," I smiled and kissed his cheek.

Helping him up, we walked behind the counter to the nurse who smiled at Jameson. "Hello, I'm Debbie Sloan, your nurse." She reached out and touched his forearm. "So what are you here for?" Debbie asked once we got inside the room, adjusting her stethoscope around her neck and clicking her pen.

"You're fucking kidding, right?" Jameson asked, not amused.

Debbie giggled, clicking obsessively.

"Yes, sweetie. I'm kidding." She opened his chart. "So let's see, you're Jameson Riley ... wait ..." Comprehension quickly followed. "As in the race car driver?"

Jameson, who had been staring at the exam table, imagining God knows what, met my eyes for a moment and then went back to Debbie. I could tell by that quick glance, he was a little apprehensive about answering.

Shifting in the chair, he answered with a nervous chuckle. "Um ... yeah, I'm him."

"Oh, wow. How exciting! My daughter would kill me if she knew we were treating Jameson Riley." Debbie reached for her notepad. "Can you sign this for her?"

Poor guy, he could never escape this.

I could tell he was irritated that he couldn't even get treatment without people bothering him for an autograph.

"Yeah, sure," Jameson reached for the paper. "What's her name?"

"Dana, she's obsessed with you. She's been to like seven races this season." Debbie giggled. "Now that I've seen you in person ... I *see* the attraction." She honestly appeared to be undressing him with her eyes.

It wasn't lost on Jameson, that's for sure.

He stood backing against the door.

"You ... um ... what's your daughter look like?"

Does he think he knows her?

"Here," Debbie shoved a picture forward.

One glimpse at it and Jameson was out the door running to the car all the while muttering, "No fucking way ... nope ... not happening." He looked back to make sure I was following him. "Let's go, Sway. I'm not being molested at a damn hospital."

Running after him, I caught up about the time he reached the car. "Jameson ... what about the fork?"

He stopped suddenly, took a few deep breaths in preparation, and then reached over and yanked it out. Then fell to the pavement, screaming in pain.

Though blood was pouring from his shoulder, I completely lost it in a fit of inappropriate piss-yourself laughter. I laughed because this headstrong, cocky man, who could handle anything, couldn't handle this obsessed fan or her nurse of a mother, so he resorted to extracting the fork himself.

"Why didn't you do that in the first place?" Lucas grumbled rolling down the window. "I could have slept in my own bed, *jerk*."

Still giggling, Emma rolled down the other window enough for her head to peek through. "What's going on, are we leaving?"

"Jameson was afraid of the nurse, so he pulled the fork out." I motioned to Jameson who was still sprawled out on the pavement. "See."

He looked like he was about to vomit. He looked like an injured animal, his face completely white, his brow furrowed, scowling with his jaw clenched tightly as he curled into himself.

"I wasn't scared of the nurse ..." he moaned loudly bringing himself to his feet. "That's Dana's mom!" he pointed at the hospital. "No fucking way I'm letting her touch me."

Emma pointed toward him laughing hysterically, and the Lucifer twins looked at us as if we're all crazy.

The entire ride back to my house Jameson sulked. Emma randomly started laughing every now and then, and the Lucifer twins continued to poke at Jameson's shoulder, asking him repeatedly if it hurt when they touched it.

He ignored them for a while, but after twenty minutes, Jameson finally turned in his seat, glaring at them. "I don't care if you're six years old. When this fucking car stops, I'm getting out and I will rip your tiny little arms off! Then what? Huh?"

Neither said a word as they gaped back with wide panic-stricken eyes. So did I.

I never thought anything would make those little shits speechless, but that's what Jameson was going for.

Jameson sighed heavily and turned around to stare out the windshield.

There wasn't a sound the rest of the trip.

When the car stopped in the driveway, the Lucifer twins ripped their seatbelts off and ran in different directions toward the house, followed by Emma. I was tempted to run with them, but didn't.

Jameson and I remained inside the Expedition. After that tantrum, I wasn't about to be the first to speak.

Slowly, he tilted his head at me. "Was that harsh?"

"Yes … I'm terrified of you now." I looked over at him for the first time since his temper tantrum. "So are they."

"Good … little fuckers."

"Oh … calm down. It's *not* that bad." I remembered his previous words to me when he first met the Lucifer twins. Surely, his perception of them had now changed.

"Not that bad?" he asked incredulously. "You have to be fucking kidding me! First, my engine blows up ending the race for me after only fifty laps. Then I fly six hours to see my girlfriend, in a fucking wind storm that puts Hurricane Ike to shame …"

I sighed dramatically.

"Okay, well it's not nearly that bad, but you get my point." He waved his good arm around. "Then I come to rescue her like her **a** knight in shining armor, like she wanted, and my fucking sister stabs me with a fork. *Then*, the nurse at the fucking hospital is Dana's mom. Yes, that's right. Dana, the stalker's, mom!" He threw his bottle of water across the inside of the truck. "I have a fucking right to be harsh."

It was now time for drastic measures.

"If I show you my boobs, will you calm down?" I offered.

He was silent for a good thirty seconds. "Maybe," he motioned with his hand for me to lift my shirt. "Show me and let's see."

Flipping up my sweatshirt, it worked as it always did.

When Jameson started to drag me onto his lap, I had to stop things. "No, we are not doing it in my dad's car and you're bleeding."

He chuckled lightly but continued to molest me. "So many rules now—no exam tables, no cars—what happened? You never had rules before."

"I don't have rules ... there are just some things I *won't* do. One is not having sex in my dad's car and two is not having sex while you have a fork stuck in your shoulder in a hospital."

"How about we continue this in your room?" Jameson suggested, pushing his hips to meet my hand that he'd placed directly on his camshaft. "I'm injured, I need care."

"We need to get a bandage on that."

My thoughts shifted to some good tender loving care I was sure I could provide him. Suddenly, I was nervous about the reveal of my crankcase's wax and shine, so I blurted out the first thing that I could come up with.

"Are you sure you can get it up? I mean, you were stabbed with a fork ..." My mouth, similar to my crankcase at times, was making all kinds of justifications as to why I *couldn't* have sex with him when honestly, it came down to my bling pad.

How exactly do you reveal this?

His eyebrows rose in question. "I was stabbed in the shoulder, not the dick, Sway."

"Prove it ... I don't think you can," I challenged. "You could have a lifter problem now?"

What the hell? What happened to your justification?

"Are you questioning my ability here?"

I tapped my finger to my lips, "Yes."

"That's it!" He grabbed me by the ass swinging the door open. With no doubt a good amount of pain, he carried me all the way to my room, threw me down on the bed, and covered my body with his own.

His hand under my chin forced me to look at him. "You're in for a *long* day."

Pit Stall – This is the area along pit road where the car will make a pit stop during the race.

Jameson was asleep on his stomach when I made my way out of my bedroom. We had a long night.

It was now the Fourth of July and we'd planned to go camping up in Dayton Peak. For good reason, the Lucifer twins would not be attending this fun-filled event.

Aiden had flown in late last night and, walking past the guest bedroom they were currently occupying, I plugged my ears in case I inadvertently overheard something I didn't care to hear.

It could happen and *has* before.

Spencer and Alley were going to come, but Lane still wasn't feeling well so they stayed home.

Jameson was only in town until Tuesday afternoon and then he headed for Joliet, Illinois, for the race at Chicagoland Speedway. This only left us with two days after the stabbing occurred.

He kept his promise yesterday, too. I didn't do anything but spread my legs. Though I'm not sure how, he never noticed my vajazzled bling pad while doing this. The Holy Grail had yet to be revealed. I had stage fright. I was actually getting a little nervous for her unveiling to occur.

What if he didn't like it?

I wasn't sure how easily that shit came off and the thought of it being ripped off seemed like cruel punishment that I was not going to allow. But, then again, I hoped eventually it came off. How would I explain this at eighty years old? Then I thought, at eighty, no one would have their head down there anyhow. So that dilemma had been solved.

Making my way to the bathroom, I splashed some water on my face along with some of my favorite Banana Boat After Sun lotion. Just the smell brought me back to our first summer together on the road, when sunburns were a daily occurrence. It was another memory of mine that made this all feel real.

Grabbing some pop tarts from the kitchen, I scurried back to my room before anyone saw me. I really didn't want to see the Lucifer twins any time soon. They still tormented the fuck out of me, but ever since Jameson threatened to rip their arms off, they steered clear of him. I contemplated threatening them as well, but I knew they wouldn't take me seriously.

Jameson had yet to wake up when I made it back to the bedroom with two cups of coffee and blueberry pop tarts. I kept myself busy while he slept off his pain medication that I had given him last night when he complained that his shoulder was killing him. The two things I needed to do today were pack for camping and cut down that tree. I must have woken up four times last night, envisioning that tree tapping on my damn window.

It had to go, that's all there was to it.

I heard footsteps behind me and turned seeing a naked Jameson making his way over to me. My eyes focused on his glorious camshaft as he approached me, watching it and then feeling like a complete pervert for doing so.

Jameson, of course, chuckled softly, wrapping his arms around me. "See something you like?"

"No ... " I lied.

"You're a horrible liar." He dove in, kissing along my collarbone and up my neck, along my jaw until his lips met mine.

I kissed him back until the wind blew once more, the tree scratching against my window.

"How are you with a chainsaw, sport?" I asked, pulling back to look at him.

"Please …" he said dismissively rolling his eyes. "I can run anything with an engine." His hand came down to my crankcase suggestively.

My eyes remained on his, pointing to the *Poltergeist* tree outside my room. "Cut that motherfucker down!"

He laughed. "You want me to cut down a tree?"

"Yes, lumberjack," I mocked. "I want you to cut down a tree."

"What did that tree ever do to you?" he looked at the tree and then to me with a touch of curiosity. "And how will I rescue you like your knight in shining armor without the tree?"

"Is that why you were so muddy?"

His eyes dropped. "Yeah, I fell."

My reaction was to giggle hysterically, kind of like when he yanked that fork out. It was adorable that he tried, but also incredibly funny to me.

He growled and then picked me up, throwing me against my mattress. "What did I say about this giggling?" His body pressed against mine, trapping me.

"Not to," I squeaked out between giggles, arms and legs flailing to get loose.

"Exactly," he sat up, straddling my hips, his hands pinned mine securely, ensuring I wasn't going anywhere.

Stuck underneath him trying to wiggle free, he only squeezed tighter, just as a python would, crushing his prey.

"Now what are you going to do?" Jameson asked in a husky voice. I could tell this little wrestling match was turning him on.

Struggling was pointless; Jameson had nearly a hundred pounds on me. "I'm not going to giggle anymore." Another small giggle escaped my lips before I slapped my hand to my face.

"That's right." He nodded haughtily. "Now, is that a blueberry pop tart over there?" His eyes motioned to my nightstand.

"No … it's strawberry," I lied knowing blueberry was his favorite.

"You're lying."

"No, I'm not … I *only* have strawberry."

"Why does your breath smell like blueberries then?"

"I have blueberry tooth paste."

Jameson scrunched his nose. "That's ... disgusting."

"No, it's not," I smiled showing my sparkly white teeth, praying there wasn't any blueberry pop tart in them. "It's delicious."

"If I find out it's a blueberry pop tart, you're in *trouble,*" he warned.

Once his grip on my arms was free, I ran. I ran for all I was worth. I heard his laughter behind me with the pop tart in his hands, but I kept running until I collided with Lucas in the living room.

"Oh ... sorry," I mumbled, helping him up.

He scowled, grumbling something along the lines of "watch where you're going," and plopped down on the couch with Mr. Jangles.

How rude.

"There you are," Jameson grabbed me from behind wrapping his arms around me—I could smell the blueberries on his breath. "*You're* in trouble."

"Ugh ... " Lucas grumbled. "Didn't you two get enough yesterday!" He draped his blanket over his face.

"What was that, Lucas?" Jameson still hadn't forgiven them.

Lucas didn't say anymore, but pulled Mr. Jangles on his lap, for protection I assumed. It's not like Mr. Jangles offered all that much protection these days. He may sit on you, but as far as defense mechanisms go, Mr. Jangles had none, other than his thirty-five pounds. Now if you were, let's say, a mouse, you were shit out of luck, he'd crush you.

It took a really long time to get ready to go camping.

For one, Jameson did, in fact, cut the tree down, but when it landed on the red dragon, I cried.

I got that truck when I turned sixteen, and she'd treated me well. Yes, she would sometimes stop running on the freeway, and occasionally leave me stranded, but she loved me. We had some good times together. Those "good times" did not include the time I lost my virginity in it to Dylan Grady. Dylan was not my best decision, and one of those times I could really look back and say, "That's where you went wrong."

After destroying the red dragon, Jameson looked as though he was going to cry himself when he realized his lumberjack skills were seriously lacking.

"I'm so sorry, honey," Jameson whispered in my ear, sitting on the tailgate with me. "So sorry," his arm draped loosely over my shoulders.

The red dragon was junk now. The tree landed right across the cab of my primer red 1979 Ford F-150. Poor ol' girl.

"S'okay," I hiccupped as another cry broke through.

Jameson lifted me onto his lap. "How many more times am I going to make you cry?" Shaking his head in disappointment, his gaze was fixated on the broken branches surrounding us.

"Really Jameson—it's fine. I needed to get another car anyway."

"It's *not* okay, Sway." His head bowed. "I'm buying you another one."

"You're *not* buying me a car, Jameson."

"You don't have a say in this, it's already done." He pointed to the road at a silver car parked at the end of the driveway. "It's yours."

"Where'd you get that?" Squinting into the bright sun, I could faintly see a Subaru. "That wasn't there earlier."

"I rented it when I got here," he told me. "When I killed red dragon, I called Subaru and bought it."

"Why?" I looked up at his sad eyes.

He shrugged. "I can be an asshole, but I refuse to be an asshole *all* the time."

"What is it?"

His eyes lit up. He loved talking car. "It's a Subaru Impreza STI. Awesome on the dirt,"

"Are we taking it camping?"

"Precisely why I rented it, well, bought it, now."

"Neato."

I still hadn't forgotten about the red dragon, but this was a nice distraction. And, let's face it—I was easily distracted, just like my heathen.

We walked down the gravel driveway to the car that was parked under the birch trees. It was pretty, shiny silver, and had a turbo.

Running my hand over the hood, I thought of my pit lizard days on the hood of Jameson's race car.

My eyes shot up to his when he chuckled.

Winking, he bit down on his lower lip and was by my side in a second. "As much as I want to try out this hood ... we need to get up to Dayton Peak soon."

Damn him.

Loaded with tents, sleeping bags, more junk food than any one person could possibly need, and more beer than any one person could possibly need, we made our way through Shelton toward Dayton Peak.

Once we hit the dirt roads, Jameson stopped the car letting the engine rev a few times. His eyes darted over to me when he changed the song playing on his iPod to The White Stripes, "Icky Thump."

"Hold tight, guys," he warned, revving the engine twice before slamming it into first gear, his head bouncing to the beat.

The back tires spun spraying gravel and dirt over the surrounding pine trees.

Emma screamed, Aiden laughed, and I was in carnal lust, naturally. Watching everything he did—it was hard *not* to be turned on.

Just like in his race car, the way his agile hands maneuvered the steering wheel, the quick movements his feet made shifting gears, the muscles in his forearms that flexed with each shift. All a turn on. As we went sideways drifting around the corner, he belted out a verse from the song.

I laughed out loud, Emma screamed again, and Aiden laughed.

Driving the way he did a sprint car, he pushed the car to the very edge of each corner before throwing the wheel the opposite direction.

I could tell by the smirk plastered across his face that he missed this. He loved racing in NASCAR, but Jameson would always be a dirt track racer. It was in his blood. His grandpa had raced. His dad raced. It was all he had ever known.

It didn't take long to reach Dayton Peak with Jameson driving.

Unloading the car, Emma was trying to carry the beer over to the fire when she dropped a few.

Aiden had his arms full so she looked at Jameson, who was peeing on the side of a tree.

"Jameson, I need help!" Emma yelled from behind the car balancing boxes. "Please."

"No," he answered. "Leave me alone. You stabbed me."

"He holds grudges, doesn't he?" Emma looked at me.

"Not really, but you did *stab* him."

Though it took some time, we eventually got everything unloaded. The night fell into our usual laughter we found around the fire. Aside from a few instances of sibling spats regarding a *recent stabbing*, everything went well.

The storm from the other night still lingered, making for a rainy, windy night but that didn't stop us from having fun.

From our campsite there was a spectacular view of the Puget Sound area. It was the best place to watch fireworks on the Fourth. From Seattle, Bellevue, Tacoma, and Olympia, you could see it all.

Jameson and I sat on the other side of the campsite from Emma and Aiden. Jameson wanted *no* part of being next to Emma or hearing them make out, which they were doing frequently.

"Do you remember the last time we were up here?" Jameson whispered in my ear. Nuzzled behind me, his warm arms wrapped around my chest waiting for my reply.

Snuggling in, I clutched the blanket around us as a breeze blew through, the crisp Northwest wind encircling us. "Yeah, we were sixteen."

Jameson chuckled lightly in my ear, his two-day scruff tickling my cheek. "You were *so* beautiful that night." His arms squeezed me once. "The way your hair shined against the fire, the way your green eyes looked almost black with the night."

"Did you get that from a Hallmark card?"

"No, I was *trying* to tell you that I loved you longer than I've realized." He exhaled, kissing my ear, his warm breath scorching my cool skin.

"You had feelings back then?"

"I didn't know it, but I remember wondering what it would like to be with you." He cleared his throat. "That sounded bad … I uh … I've always been … *very* attracted to you. From the moment I first saw you, I may have been eleven, but I've always thought you were the most beautiful girl who I've ever met."

I laughed. "Really, you have?"

"Yes." He nodded. "I guess I didn't realize the attraction went beyond physical attraction. I'm slow."

We watched the fireworks die down, but one thing led to another and we were no longer watching fireworks, but creating our own.

The passionate, gentle Jameson was out tonight. He was affectionate and tender with touch and words. His actions were dawdling, ardent and attentive.

Once inside the tent, everything turned erotic.

There was something about being in the dark. I couldn't see him, but I heard his movements, his sexy whispering, his steady strained breathing, and soft grunts as we continued where we had left off outside.

Slowly, he began sliding my panties down my hips. Though I couldn't see him, I felt his tongue against my inner thigh and then at my crankcase.

"What the fuck?" Jameson yelled jumping back. "My ... lip ... is bleeding."

I wasn't even thinking, *clearly*, or else I would have recalled my trip to the mall before I let Jameson go down on me in the dark—bad idea. I guess I should have thought about the sharpness before I went and ripped out my beaver pelt to add bling.

"I got ... vajazzled," I replied softly, relieved it was dark so he couldn't see how completely embarrassed I was about this whole situation. Just in case he had night vision, I flopped my arms over my very flushed face.

To make matters worse, Jameson turned on the lantern beside the air mattress. "You vaj ... what?" He looked at me with confusion, wiping blood from his upper lip. Dropping his eyes to the bling, he positioned the light to observe my masterpiece.

Slowly, a smirk appeared.

"You ... I ... uh ..." The smirk grew wider leaning down between my legs for a closer look. His fingertips softly grazed over the vajazzled crankcase bling. "Is that a number nine?"

Nodding was all I could do. I was too embarrassed to speak—didn't stop the giggles, though.

"When did you do this?" Still hovering above me, his voice was a soft whisper in my ear. "And I love it, by the way. It's sexy as hell."

Oh God, there's that whispering again.

"Tuesday ... when Emma and I were at the mall."

"How did I not see this yesterday?" he wondered.

"You were a *little* preoccupied."

Grinning, Jameson recalled the amount of align boring that took place yesterday. "Well, looks like I need to show this ..." his fingers brushed over the flag, "some attention. After all, you did go to the trouble to ... um ... get my number."

Turning the lantern off, he went back to work.

I couldn't take much more of it and within a few minutes I was frantically yanking him up my body. Willingly with a growl, he was exactly where I wanted him to be.

It must have been the illusion of privacy, or the darkness providing obscurity, but everything seemed heightened. I didn't last long at all, but just as I reached my release, Emma screamed.

"Jameson ..." Just speaking was difficult let alone getting him to focus. His hips continued to meet mine with erratic movements. "We should see ... what that was."

Jameson grunted in response, his hands moved from around my shoulders to my ass letting me know he had no interest in stopping. "*Oh God,* Sway ... so close ..." his gravelly voice confirmed my theory.

Emma screamed again. "What the fuck is that, Aiden?"

Did Jameson stop then? No, but he did increase his pace again.

"Jameson ... we should ... stop." I pushed again on his chest only to have him shake his head. "Emma might need help."

Apparently, he didn't like that answer because I felt him rise from my upper body, but he didn't pull out. "I do *not* fucking care," he snapped, and then leaned back down to continue his movements.

I could tell by his gritty voice that he was beyond annoyed that she was interrupting us when he was so close.

"Hey, Jameson, you might want to come out here," Aiden warned.

There was something unusual in Aiden's voice that drew Jameson out of his sexual stupor.

"Son of a bitch," he pulled away reaching for the lantern. "Why does this always happen? I can't even fuck my girlfriend anymore without someone wanting something from me."

I snuck a glance at his face, throwing my clothes on. Flushed with anger, he was breathing heavy and he still had a *big* ... problem.

I giggled. Naturally.

"Nothing about this is amusing, Sway," he snapped, unzipping the tent. "Stop laughing."

Yes, it *was* funny.

Once outside the tent ... you couldn't *help* but laugh. Aiden and Emma were standing on the roof of the Subaru while a skunk hovered around their tent.

"Are you fucking kidding me?" Jameson shouted at them throwing his arms up. "You called me out here for a goddamn skunk ... unbelievable!" He turned to go back inside the tent. Only problem was Pepe Le Pew's girlfriend was now making her way inside our tent.

Before I even realized what was happening, Jameson was dragging me through the woods, away from the campsite. We didn't go far, partly because it was so dark you couldn't see and the other, well, Jameson needed something and he needed it *now*.

He wasted no time at all in removing my jeans, picking me up with one arm and wrapping my legs around his waist. Carrying me forward until my back pressed against a tree. Frantically, his other hand fumbled with the button of his jeans.

I shivered in anticipation. This was so incredibly sexy.

His face was set in a scowl, the light from the full moon defined his flushed cheeks.

His movements were nothing as they were watching the fireworks, or in the tent. They were rough and aggressive, it actually almost hurt, but I wasn't complaining. Not that I was into the S & M shit, as discussed, but I could get down with the aggressive press forging.

Wrapping his arm securely around my waist, he pressed me rather hard against the tree trunk. His hands were everywhere, all at once, as was his mouth. Desperately kissing, sucking, and biting every inch he could reach.

My bare ass was rubbing against the tree, causing not-so-friendly chafing and splinters, but I didn't care, this was hot. The only noises that were coming from Jameson were a stream of grunts and heavy panting. Within minutes of this starting, it was apparent it was ending soon.

"Oh God, Jameson ... that's *so* hot ..."

"Are you? I ... need ... *please* ..." Jameson grunted in my ear. Before he even finished his incoherent words, I could feel every muscle in his body go rigid.

He held me in place for a moment and then slowly let me down.

"Ouch," I whined when the splinters made themselves known.

"I'm sorry." Jameson reached out running his fingers lightly over my cheek, his eyes searching mine. "I wasn't very gentle, was I?"

"I liked it," I admitted with a giggle, but stopped when I heard leaves crunching and branches breaking. "What was that?" I asked in a whispered voice, reaching for Jameson.

He must have heard it, too, his grip around my waist tightened and he pulled me hard to his side frantically, looking for the source of the noises.

When we spotted it, I nearly pissed myself.

Jameson's head tilted to one side, his eyes on mine. "Great," he muttered, turning back to the animal.

"Jameson ..." I frantically breathed in his ear.

"Sway," he whispered back. "Do *not* move."

Standing in front of us, not more than a hundred feet away was a cougar. Not just any cougar. This was a hungry cougar ... looking for food. Crouched down in the hunting position, I was sure he was currently looking for Jameson and Sway food.

You know that predatory look an animal gets when it's getting ready to attack?

We were getting that look right then, fierce glowing eyes, *and* that intimidating crouch.

"Sway, stay still," Jameson warned again.

I didn't think I was moving, but apparently, I was.

I was shaking. But could you honestly fucking blame me?

"I'm *trying*!"

"Now is *not* the time to argue."

"I was trying to point out that I was, in fact, *trying* to remain still, but there was a cougar looking directly at us like we're his next meal."

"Stop talking," Jameson turned to glare at me. "You'll attract him."

"Don't tell me to stop talking. I was explaining myself. And if you haven't noticed," I gestured to the animal, "he's already attracted to us. He's getting ready to eat us."

Jameson opened his mouth to say something more than likely just as irritating, but stopped, turning his attention to the cougar. Leaning his head contemplatively to the side, his eyes remained on the cougar. "You attracted him with your moaning. He wants you," he accused with a cocky smirk I didn't appreciate.

"Me?" this time I shouted, "Maybe it's a female, ever think about that? I wasn't the only one moaning," I snapped. "By the way."

"Really?" He challenged, raising his eyebrows in question. "You're going to argue with me when there's a two-hundred pound predator looking to make a meal of us?"

"I will when you don't make any sense. I'm not to blame for it hunting us." I remained glued to his side through the entire argument. "You were the caveman dragging us out here. This is *your* fault."

"I could have finished in the tent, but no, Emma and Aiden were scared of a fucking skunk and now look." He waved toward the cougar who was now sitting, no longer in a crouched position.

I giggled. It was clearly not the time to be giggling, but our arguing has caused a deadly animal to stop, mid-hunt, to watch. That's funny to me.

Jameson gave a quick glance at the cougar and chuckled softly, then leaned down near my ear. "Start walking backward toward the car, but keep up the arguing. It's distracting him."

"Her! It's a girl. Look at her, she's eyeing you."

"Stop it," he gave me a repulsed scowl, "talk about something else."

"Like what? Is there actual protocol for what to discuss when your life is threatened by a vicious animal?"

"No, but I don't want to talk about a cougar looking at me like it wants to mate with me. That's disgusting."

"You know," I stepped over a log with the help of Jameson. "Some men like cougars."

"Sway," he glared over his shoulder. "Change. The. Fucking. Subject!"

"No."

"Goddamn it, *why* are you always so stubborn?"

"Because it's funny to me that you're freaked out that you attracted an animal with your bestial noises."

By then, we were almost at the car. I could see Aiden and Emma sitting in the back seat. "I wasn't making bestial noises, was I?"

"Yes, not that I'm complaining ... I'm just saying that's *why* the animal came out to play."

"All right, that's enough." He smacked my ass. "Get in the car, slowly."

The cougar followed but made no attempt to chase us. I think she was more curious than anything, *and* attracted to Jameson.

Once we reached the door, we both jumped inside the car and locked the doors. Briefly, I thought, obviously a cougar can't open the door. You never know though.

"Is that a fucking cougar?" Emma screeched from the back seat, climbing in Aiden's lap. "Oh my God!"

"No, it's a German Shepherd." Jameson scrunched his nose and looked around. "What the fuck is that smell?"

It was strong and Jameson and I both immediately started gagging.

"Don't be a dick!" Emma slapped his injured shoulder. "It's Aiden, and it's not his fault."

Jameson spun around in the seat, his expression furious. "If you fucking hit me again—I will shave your head when you're sleeping and burn all your clothes!" He looked at Aiden. "Why do you smell like that?"

Emma answered for him. "He was sprayed by Pepe."

"Get out, you stink." Jameson motioned for him to get out.

"There's a fucking cougar standing outside!" Aiden yelled. "I'm *not* getting out."

Emma slapped the back of Jameson's head. "Don't talk to him like that."

Jameson started to climb in the backseat, as if he was actually going to attack his sister.

I grabbed his arm before he made it over the center console. "Christ Almighty, you two act like children." Once he sat back down, I sat back drawing my legs up. I had a feeling we were going to be here a while. "Just stop it."

"She started it," Jameson mumbled, staring out the window at the cougar who was sitting outside.

I wasn't sure when he said, "She started it," if he was referring to the cougar or Emma. The cougar seemed to have some sort of predilection toward him. And Emma, well there were no words for her.

After a few minutes, I began to realize the smell was unbearable.

"Aiden," I whined feeling as though I would die if I had to continue to smell him *any* longer. "At least take your pants off or something."

"What?" Jameson snapped coldly, glaring at me.

"For the smell," I explained quickly. "If it's on his pants then maybe it won't smell so bad if he puts them outside."

"She's right," Jameson nodded, turning to Aiden behind me. "Take those fucking things off and throw 'em outside."

Aiden shrugged reaching for his belt. Jameson turned around and looked at me to see if I was looking.

I giggled again; I was amused that he would actually think I would want to see Aiden naked. He looked away and started the car so Aiden could lower the window.

"Leave the windows cracked," I suggested as I fanned my nose. It really did smell *that* bad.

Aiden threw his pants out the window and quickly raised it back up, leaving it cracked for some much needed ventilation.

"We should leave. It's like three in the morning now and none of us have gotten any sleep," Emma whined.

"We can't leave all that out there. It's littering."

I wanted to go home as well, but leaving tents, numerous beer bottles, and food in a national forest was not a good idea.

"Sway's right," Aiden said. "They could arrest you for something like that."

I looked over at Jameson, who'd remained quiet during this. He was gazing at his pet cougar, who was staring right back at him.

"Are you okay?"

"I'm fine," he mumbled, refusing to look at me. "I want to go home."

"Then get out, clean up the mess we made, and we can leave," Emma suggested, kicking the back of his seat and jolting him forward.

"You get out and clean it up," Jameson said quietly. "You don't have a cougar giving you ogle eyes."

We all started laughing, *except* Jameson.

Hours passed, and it became more entertaining to me that this was actually happening.

Here it was—five in the morning—we'd been in that damn car most of the night with a cougar right outside Jameson's window and Aiden, who smelled like God knows what.

Another two hours later and we were still captives.

"It's like it has some kind of obsession with Jameson," Aiden said at one point. "It just stares at him. It's weird."

The cougar hadn't moved. She just sat there, perched outside Jameson's window, eyeing him.

Jameson, well, he was beyond annoyed with the whole situation. Not only was there a cougar sitting outside his door, but he had to pee, *badly.*

Emma, being the annoying sister she was, took every opportunity she could to make this worse for him by talking about water, water-falls, running water ... anything with the notion of water, or the trickling of water.

I could tell he was moments away from whipping it out and pissing on her.

Emma sighed contently, propping her bare feet on the back of Jameson's seat, bouncing her legs, and shaking his seat. "Ha, I got the last beer," she announced cracking it open. "Sucks for you guys."

I wasn't sure if she was trying to bounce the pee out of him or just annoy him to the point of insanity.

"Emma," I shook my head giving her a sidelong gaze of you're-not-really-that-stupid-are-you?

"What?" She honestly tried to act as if she was doing nothing wrong, continuing to bounce her legs.

Jameson snapped.

He ripped the beer bottle from her hands, unzipped his pants and peed in the bottle. When he finished, he offered the beer to her with a grin. "Drink up."

"That's disgusting!" Emma chided. "I didn't need to hear you pee."

"I don't fucking care. You're lucky I didn't piss on you." Jameson laughed. "You would have fainted at the size of my d—"

Slapping my hand over his mouth, I said, "Jameson, *stop*."

Another hour later and nothing had changed.

At one point, the cougar had licked the window taunting Jameson and creating quite the uproar from the rest of us.

Jameson quickly put an end to our amusement when he held up the beer/pee bottle and threatened to pour it on us if we didn't shut up.

I had a feeling between the race, the stabbing, the red dragon, and *now* the cougar ... Jameson wanted to go home, as in Mooresville, far away from Washington all together.

None of us were really paying any mind to one another. Jameson was playing with his iPod, I was picking off old nail polish, and I had no idea what Emma and Aiden were doing.

"Hey," Jameson looked around with a sudden zest to his voice. "Where'd the cougar go?"

We all glanced around the clearing only to find she was gone.

"Finally," Jameson groaned opening his door, but quickly closed it when we realized *what* replaced the cougar. "Oh, Jesus."

A black bear. Yes, a fucking black bear.

"OH MY GOD!" Emma shrieked in horror crawling on Aiden's lap. "Drive away Jameson, drive!"

"We can't leave, Emma," he told her calmly. "Just be quiet. If we're quiet, it'll go away."

"Not likely," Aiden chuckled. "He found your Twinkies, dude."

We both looked toward our tent to find it rummaging through our food and, more importantly, Jameson's Twinkie stash.

"Oh, damn it," he groaned in disappointment, resting his head against the steering wheel. "I've been craving those for like a year."

The next two hours were spent watching the bear eating all of our food, listening to Emma scream any time it got close to the car. The bear sat on the hood of the car and then finally left when it smelled Aiden's pants.

Good times.

Although fearing the arrival of more animals, we eventually got out.

Once the animal kingdom left, Emma and I packed up what remained without the help of Jameson and Aiden who were doing "man things" ... or so they said. This consisted of shooting beer bottles with the shotgun they brought, and lighting the rest of the fireworks, while it rained on us.

Too bad that shotgun was in the tent last night. It would have come in handy for the cougar, or the bear, or Emma, if Jameson had his way.

Finally, we were all piled back inside the stench-infested Subaru and were ready to get the hell out of this cougar-bear-skunk forest.

"Let's get out of here." I was wet, my ass had splinters, and I was cold. I wasn't fond of any of those things and particularly not together. "I'm done with these animals and this rain."

Jameson let out a sarcastic laugh and attempted to start the car. The engine clicked.

"Uh, the battery's dead."

"You've got to be kidding me!" I panicked. "What do you mean *it's dead*?"

"What do I mean?" he laughed. "I mean the battery's dead as in the *battery* is dead!"

"My God," Emma whined from the back seat. "Why is it dead?"

We've all had enough, that's for sure. At this point, I don't know if I will ever go camping again.

"How can I explain this differently?" Jameson let out a frustrated sigh, leaning his head against the steering wheel. "The battery is dead, and a car needs a battery to start."

I sighed frustrated. "How did this happen?"

Visions of being stranded up here flooded my brain. I imagined being one of those tree-hugging hippies and never shaving my legs or armpits again. Though never shaving again was alluring, living in the woods was not—especially after last night.

"Clearly, something was left on and drained the battery." His gaze shifted to Emma.

"I didn't think having one light on would drain the battery."

Jameson and Aiden messed with the battery for a good hour, but no luck. It wasn't starting without jumper cables and something to "jump" it with. Two things we did not have.

We ended up calling a tow truck, but had to walk down to the main road to help them back here; we were in the middle of fucking *Deliverance*.

"Jesus Christ, Aiden, you stink!" Jameson grumbled downwind from him.

He had to put the skunk jeans back on because the bear ripped apart our other clothes as though he was a gerbil or something. Emma was very, very upset about that … something about destroying a two-hundred-dollar pair of jeans.

Insanity if you ask me—Emma *and* the jeans.

"Don't you think I know I stink, asshole," Aiden walked a good thirty feet in front of us down the gravel road. "It's on my skin. I can't get it off."

"I'll get it off when we get back to Sway's," Emma assured him. "Tomato soup should work. I'll wash you clean."

I knew she was trying to provoke Jameson, and Emma knew damn well how to do it with twenty-one years of practice.

"Shut up!" Jameson kicked rocks at them. "I don't need to hear that shit."

It was at that point when I'd met my max with those two. They never stopped arguing all night and frankly, I was sick of it.

"Both of you shut up," I gave my own childish kick of the rocks. "I'm not going to deal with any of your bullshit today, understand? We are going to behave like normal human beings!"

They didn't behave like normal human beings, though. There was no way we could. We were, in fact, four people, who'd been forced to sleep in a car, inches from one another because of a cougar, a bear, and Aiden's skunk. Normal was not an option.

Emma started in again, and I was about to pummel her tiny ass when Jameson's phone rang.

Jameson looked down at the screen, his eyebrows furrowed. "That's strange." The phone twisted with his fingertips, he seemed to contemplate answering it.

"What?" we all asked eagerly, praying it was the towing company.

"It's Tate," Jameson told. "Hello … yeah …" There was a long pause and then Jameson started shaking his head with a smirk. "No … I'm sorry, but I can't say I didn't warn you this would happen … yeah, my senior year … I walked in on her and my brother's best friend."

What?

Looking to Emma for answers, she shrugged and jumped on Aiden's back.

A few minutes later, Jameson started talking again. "I appreciate the warning, but I can handle myself … okay, see you on Wednesday." He hung up the phone and looked over to me, nodding with that smirk again.

"That was Tate." He held up his phone. "He walked in on Darrin and Chelsea. Looks like the whore's back to her ways."

We all began walking toward the road again as Jameson continued talking, "He tried to warn me that he overheard Darrin talking to Frank about how he's looking for revenge." He shook his head.

"Jameson," Reaching out to his shoulder, I stopped walking. "I think you should listen to them. Darrin is out of his mind."

"Sway, I can handle it," he assured me with that defiant stare I knew so well. "It's nothing I haven't dealt with before. I've been racing since I was four … I've *been* threatened before."

"I know … I think there's something more to it this time."

His arm slung around my shoulder. "It's adorable when you're protective." He bit down on his lower lip, and I knew where it was heading again.

"No," I held up my hand, walking away. "I'm not doing it in the woods again."

"There you go with the *rules* again." He kicked at the rocks again.

"So many rules."

"I still have splinters in my ass," I reminded him. "So yes, I have a fucking rule now. No trees. And did you forget what happened with the cougar?"

That shut him right up.

"Is that why you and Chelsea broke up?" I asked after a few moments of silence when my curiosity got the better of me.

He was quiet for a minute as though he was deciding *what* he wanted to say or maybe how to say it. "That ... among other things." His eyes focused in the distance. "We just weren't right for *each other*." I knew by the way he emphasized each other, he meant me.

"I, for one ... am glad you guys broke up."

"Me too," he agreed, kissing my head.

It took a long time, but eventually the tow truck came, towed away the skunk Subaru and took us back home.

Jameson and I sat on the tailgate of the red dragon letting the Subaru ventilate and trying to avoid the Lucifer twins.

"We are *definitely* not buying that one." He pointed to the car. There were scratches all over it, the hood was dented and it smelled. "That car is awful, if not for the smell, but the luck last night."

"No doubt," I agreed. I loved the way he said we; it made me feel like we were a *real* couple. Not that we weren't a *real* couple now, but sometimes, I liked that little bit of reassurance that he was referring to us as we.

After all, we were going steady, and I was his Joanie.

16

Restrictor Plate – This is a thin metal plate with four holes that restrict airflow from the carburetor into the engine. Teams use it on larger tracks to reduce horsepower and keep speeds down.

Jameson and I were heading into a busy month of racing. Sitting there on the tailgate of the smooshed red dragon, we discussed the next few weeks and how often we'd get to see each other.

He was scheduled to leave tomorrow afternoon for Joliet. Then after the race Saturday night, he had to fly to New Richmond for the World of Outlaw race, then to Lima, Ohio, for an appearance, and then he had to be back here next Thursday for the start of the Northern Sprint Tour.

It would be a busy two weeks, that's for sure.

"Let's go to dinner," Jameson said abruptly, jumping down from the tailgate. "I'm hungry."

That sounded like a good time. Aiden and Emma were already heading home to Mooresville, which meant we would be alone. Even better.

"Where do you want to go?" We didn't have much to choose from here in Elma, Washington. We had the Rusty Tractor and that was about it.

"Ranch House," Jameson answered, nodding his head. There was one thing Jameson loved almost as much as racing and that was barbeque. "I haven't been there in years."

"Nice choice."

It didn't take long to get there, maybe fifteen minutes, and with Jameson in tow, we got a seat right away. It paid to have a super-star for a boyfriend—you never had to wait in line for anything. Even though I held a certain amount of reserve for this ability to be served right away because of your social status, I'll admit, it had its perks.

"What are you going to order?" I asked, sitting across from him at a table in the corner.

The Ranch House was a small barbeque restaurant on the side of Highway 8 in Olympia. They had the best barbeque around, no lie. And I would *kill* over their potato salad any day.

"I think I'm getting the beef ribs," Jameson replied with a big smile, rubbing his belly in anticipation. "Definitely, the beef ribs."

"You're showing an awful lot of excitement for food."

"I just spent the night in the woods with no food." He gave me a folly glare. "I'm hungry. And did I mention that bear ate my damn Twinkies?"

"Yes, you may have mentioned that a *few* times already."

Jameson, giving almost every person in the restaurant his auto-graph and talking racing with all the men, occupied most of the time waiting for our food.

In my mind, it was hardly a date. I've grown to realize that this would be our life, though. It would always be this way for us, and I understood that as I had grown up around this type of public adora-tion with other racers and had seen it first-hand with Jimi.

At times, I felt bad for Jameson, though, as it can't be easy. He knew when he chose this as his profession that this came with the job. At least he could still go out in public—most celebrities couldn't even do that these days.

One particular man had been standing there talking to him for fifteen minutes while Jameson's food was getting cold.

He gave him his time to talk and then very politely said, "It was nice meeting you, sir, but I'm actually on a date here with this beauti-ful woman." Jameson stood to shake his hand. "I should show her the attention she deserves," he said with a wink toward me.

"Oh—sorry," the man apologized with sincerity. "It was nice meeting you, Jameson. Good luck this weekend at Chicagoland." He turned to me. "I'm sorry for disrupting your evening, ma'am."

I waved my hand around. "It's no problem," I told him with a mouth full of potato salad, hardly attractive.

Jameson laughed.

"You're adorable," he said softly and began eating his ribs.

Once he began, I couldn't focus on anything other than him eating. The way he licked his fingers, the incredibly sexy way he chewed. *Hot damn.*

It was like some sort of food pornography.

I wanted to jump across the table, hump his leg, and then lick all that sticky barbeque sauce from him.

And I'll be damned if he didn't know exactly what he was doing with the smirk on his face. He knew all right.

"How's your brisket?" Jameson asked licking barbeque sauce from his thumb.

"Stop doing that," I glowered at him, taking a bite of my brisket.

He smirked licking the other thumb. "Doing what?"

"You're distracting me. All I can focus on is you licking your fingers."

Jameson leaned forward, his breath blowing across me when he spoke. "Are you imagining what all my tongue can do for you?"

"No, not at all," I lied calmly. "I'm enjoying my meal."

"Bullshit," he called my bluff. "I know you find this hot." He ran his sticky barbeque finger over my lower lip. "You bite down on your bottom lip when you're horny."

"Do not," I stated, releasing my bottom lip.

He chuckled softly leaning back in his seat and placed his napkin on the table. Jameson glanced around the room, then turned his head to the side and smiled again. "I've got something to distract you."

The perverse pigizzle in me wanted to drop to my knees under the table and see exactly what he had to distract me. I refrained only because this was his favorite restaurant, and I'd like to be allowed to return.

Taking a slow drink of water, trying to distract him and myself, I asked, "And what would that be?"

"When are you going to marry me?" His green eyes smoldered.

Say what?

I instantly started choking on the water I had ingested; I was choking to the point that my face was the devil's ass again as I gasped for some much-needed air.

Jameson moved next to me rubbing my back. "Breathe, honey ... just breathe."

"I ..." *cough.* "Am ..." *cough.* "Trying ..." *cough.*

The entire restaurant gawked at me. And though they all seemed genuinely concerned, it was still incredibly embarrassing. I wanted to crawl under the table and hide.

Jameson wrapped his arm around me, leaning into my ear, effectively blocking everyone's view of me.

It was a simple gesture that I appreciated very much.

"I didn't mean to scare you," he whispered, "and that *wasn't* my proposal. I may be a jerk, but I can be romantic. I want you to know that I am going to marry you, someday. I have every intention of spending the rest of my life with you."

"Did you get that from a Hallmark card?" My voice was hoarse from all the coughing.

"No, those are my feelings," he responded with so much sincerity that I started crying. In the middle of the damn restaurant, with Jameson's arms wrapped around me, I was bawling.

"Come on, honey," Jameson hugged me closer. "Let's get out of here. I want to take you somewhere special."

"Not the woods," I responded instantly. "Please not the woods."

"No ... not the woods ... I'm not sure I will *ever* go camping again."

"Me either."

"Where are we going?" I asked when he pulled off Cloquallum onto a private dirt road.

"We are going to the first place I kissed you."

I was quiet for a moment trying to recall the first time we kissed. There were a number of occasions growing up when Jameson and I had locked lips. Back then it never led to anything—just kids being kids and experimenting.

"Where was that?"

Jameson's hand rose to his heart. "I'm hurt you don't remember."

I watched curiously as we drove through Elma, wondering which time it was.

There were a few kisses that I distinctively remembered, but I remembered my first French kiss most of all, because it was with him. We were thirteen, and we had spent the day swimming out at Summit Lake. Now I don't even remember how it happened, but we saw Spencer kissing his girlfriend at the time, so we decided to try it. I thought it was strange, wet, and sloppy.

When Jameson turned down his parent's old driveway, I remembered instantly where our first kiss took place.

I hadn't been there in a while, not for a couple years at least. They kept the house in Elma, but his aunt Mary was living there now. The grass that was usually kept cut short during the summer was now overgrown shadowing the long paved driveway. The tree we used to climb near the gates was still there, hanging across the creek as it always had.

No one appeared to be home, so Jameson drove out back to the quarter-mile clay track where he had learned to race, and the place where we spent the majority of our summer breaks growing up.

"Now I remember," I told him, getting out of the truck.

We stopped by the water barrels we had used as the flag stand back in the day when Jameson turned toward me.

"I was standing right here ... we had met about a month before." He smiled. "You were the trophy girl and I, of course, won."

I laughed, remembering the silly little games we used to play back here when he was home. Nothing mattered back then, but when you're a kid, *everything* mattered.

Little games were your entire life—the reason you got out of bed in the morning. A kiss wasn't just a kiss back then, it was all you thought about because to you, that *was* your world.

I learned quickly not to take everything to heart back then, and I felt comfortable enough around Jameson that I could *just* kiss him and not have it mean anything to me.

But I'd be lying if I didn't say that it made my thirteen-year-old world to have someone like him around—someone who I could be *me* around.

That's why I cherished my friendship with him so greatly—I could be me.

Jameson's eyes focused on mine. The smells of summer surrounded us, blending with the rich scent of the clay from the track, reminding me of all those summers out here.

Smiling up at him, I said, "You told me instead of the trophy, you wanted a kiss."

He pulled me against his chest and his arms slid around my waist. "I didn't wait for you to answer me, I kissed you." His lips were about an inch from mine. "I was afraid you wouldn't let me."

"I would have, and I *did* let you."

His lips twitched into a small smile. "Yes, you did."

Leaning forward, I captured his warm lips with my own.

He kissed me back and then pulled away. "I didn't mean to freak you out at the restaurant. I meant it, though," he admitted. "I *will* marry you, when you're ready."

"What if I said I was ready right now?"

"I would call Wes and have him fly us to Vegas." He actually looked serious, which scared the shit out of me. "Let's do it now."

"You're lying."

"No, I'm not," his face grew solemn. "I mean that, Sway. I love you, and I would marry you tonight if I had it my way, but I don't think *we're* ready for that."

"You're right, we're not. You've got issues."

"I know," he agreed. "But at least I'm not the crazy one. I'm the angry one."

"So we got an angry one, and a crazy one ... what happens if we ever have a kid?" I asked.

"Maybe between the two of us the kid will come out normal."

"Possibly, but *highly* unlikely."

"Oh well, being normal is overrated. It's much more fun being crazy and angry." He dove in for another kiss, this time it wasn't an innocent kiss like when we were eleven.

It was a kiss that had intention and meaning behind it. He was telling me with one kiss, that I was his, forever.

We'd been sitting on the water barrels for about twenty minutes, talking about the races we had on this track when Jameson surprised me yet again by his comment. "Do you want kids?"

"Huh?" I had no water to choke on this time, only my breath.

"I … just … I don't know … thought we should talk about things like that, you know, where we want our life to go?"

I laughed at how nervous he seemed all of a sudden.

"I do want kids, someday." I snuggled against him, peeking into his vibrant green eyes. "But, more importantly … I want them with you."

Jameson smiled. "Good."

"Do you want kids?"

"Yes, with you, I do."

"Well, it's settled then." I clapped my hands together. "We fly to Vegas, get married and then start on the kids."

"I'll call Wes right now."

I climbed on his lap, straddling his hips. "I have a better idea—let's get started on the kids first. It's a much better plan at the moment."

Jameson reached for the button of his jeans. "You read my mind, honey."

"Let's at least make it back home." I kissed his lips once more before standing. "We wouldn't want to attract any more cougars."

"That's not funny." He glowered at me. "Don't joke about that."

Jameson left on Tuesday morning for Joliet, Illinois, leaving me alone at home. I needed to spend some time with Charlie and I knew, by the way he was acting, that he didn't have a lot of time. It seemed that overnight his personality was changing, which was actually entertaining if you didn't let the fact that he was dying bother you.

Charlie had always been a fairly reserved man who rarely cussed and didn't let anything bother him. Now, he cussed like a truck driver and got riled up over everything. I found this quite humorous because it was usually the Lucifer twins provoking him and not me.

On Wednesday, they threw a baseball through the kitchen window to which Charlie almost had a heart attack. His expression was something similar to the time I pierced my lip in my Madonna stage

... fear, anger, and then rage.

"I don't care how it happened!" Charlie shouted the same way he did to me at that time and then realized the entire kitchen was full of soap. "What the hell happened in here?"

I stared blankly at all of them wondering when his head was going to explode.

"You said you didn't want to know," Logan hid behind his mom with wide frantic eyes.

"That was before I saw the soap." His eyes about bulged out of his sockets. "Now I want to know, what the fuck happened?"

It was shit like that all week. I think the twins actually provided entertainment for Charlie, if not for him, it sure as shit was entertainment for me. For once, I wasn't the one setting him off, and the twins had found their new target.

On Friday, I was on my way to the grocery store for Charlie when Andrea insisted I take one of the Lucifer twins. I had my own thoughts on this, and it'd be a miracle if I *didn't* kill one of them. Despite my concerns for committing the homicide of a six-year-old, I smiled and said, "Of course."

"I don't want to go with her!" Lucas wailed to Charlie.

I don't know what made him think I *actually* wanted to go in public with him anyway. I was completely against this.

"This is so stupid." Charlie grumbled with a roll of his eyes looking over at me. "Do you even want to take him with you?"

"No," I admitted, but smiled despite my anger. "Not really. I don't want to take him anywhere."

"There you have it," he said, turning to Lucas. "She doesn't want to take you anywhere either."

Lucas immediately brought out the tears.

"He's mad at me!" he wailed once again, but this time with a tremendous amount of water and snot coming from his nose and eyes as he climbed inside the Expedition with me.

"Stop it!" I yelled as he buckled himself in. "Stop crying."

"I can't help it, and you can't tell me not to cry!" he yelled back, completely losing any composure he might have had earlier. "I can cry if I want to!"

"I'm not concerned with you crying, *believe me*," I told him. "My only concern is with the snot coming out of you. Where does it go? On your hands? Your shirt? Your pants? Where is it all going?"

Lucas hiccupped. "My sleeve, I guess. I can't help it."

I looked down and sure enough, his sleeve was slimed like Turner from *Turner and Hooch.* "That's no good."

And then he started crying again because *his* snot was on *his* shirt. I didn't have the heart to tell him all this crying wasn't making me like him anymore. In fact, I didn't like him at all right then.

Amazingly, we made it back from the store, *both of us*, alive.

But I swore that was the last time I would take him anywhere with me.

On Saturday morning, I went out to get the mail. Mostly junk mail, but one letter from the Washington State Department of Licensing stood out, so I opened it. Charlie was sitting in his chair watching NASCAR qualifying while simultaneously reading the paper, which was his usual Saturday morning activity before leaving for the track.

"Dad, what is this from the Department of Licensing?" I held up the envelope.

"How the fuck should I know," he grumbled, straightening his paper with a flick of his wrists. "You opened it. What the hell does it look like?"

I looked down at the letter. "It says here that you hit another car. What are they talking about? Did you get in an accident?"

As if this was war, he finally looked up from the paper, his eyes narrowing from across the room. "Are you shitting me? I didn't hit that car, *they* hit me. There's a difference."

"What do you mean they hit you?" I stared at him, slightly perplexed because the letter said the car was parked at the time. I had a feeling I knew exactly where this was going but played along. "How can a parked car hit you?"

He got up throwing the paper on the chair. "It's *exactly* what I mean. I didn't hit that car. End of story."

"Apparently it's not the end of the story," I laughed. "They're taking your license away. You shouldn't piss off the Department of Licensing. They have a certain amount of power over us."

He didn't say any more and stomped to his room mumbling incoherent profanities at the Department of Licensing.

You know what I love? Crazy people. They were so entertaining to me and made me feel better. And I mean in the sense where everyone was like me. A little crazy.

Picking through the rest of the mail, still laughing at Charlie, my phone vibrated on the counter. I glanced at the number and smiled instantly.

"Hello, handsome," I answered, balancing the phone on my shoulder. "How are you?"

Jameson sighed contently. "God, I miss you, honey." I could literally hear the longing in his voice. "You don't have any idea how much I hate not having you here with me."

"Oh, I have a pretty good idea. How's qualifying?" I looked over at the TV to see what position he got, but couldn't distinguish the numbers.

"I qualified tenth, not very good, but not bad either." The muffled noises of engines broke through before I heard the raucous voices and then Spencer's laughter.

"You'll do fine," I reassured him.

"I know," he sighed again. "It's not the same when you're not here with me."

"Only another week and we get to see each other."

"I'm looking forward to it." He let out another long sigh. "It's the only thing that keeps me going right now."

"You're such a cheese ball." I giggled again, taking some left over pizza out of the fridge. "What will people think of you now, all domesticated and shit?"

"I know, but I love you. And I don't give a shit what anyone thinks." Louder noises echoed in the garage. Kyle was telling him he was needed, but he ignored him for the moment. "Phillip called …"

"Yeah, what did he say?" Placing two slices of the pizza in the microwave, I had to lean against the door to keep it closed. Yet another thing Lucas broke this week. "How'd the pre-hearing conference go?"

"Chelsea didn't show." Jameson gave a relieved chuckle. "Her lawyer said she's dropping all charges."

"That's great, Jameson. Now we have to worry about Darrin."

That was a huge relief. The last thing Jameson *needed* right now would be for his fans to think he was some kind of asshole who went around sexually assaulting women.

"You let me worry about Darrin," he stated firmly. "I don't want you involved in this."

The last thing Jameson *wanted* was for me to get involved in his problems, particularly when it came to Darrin. But, as I said before, when it came to Jameson, this pigizzle knew no bounds.

Since I wasn't able to attend the race that weekend, I settled for watching it on television. Jameson's engine blew up for the second weekend in a row after only seventy laps.

The camera shot to him pulling himself from the car. He sat on the edge, his head resting against the roof for a moment before he swung his legs around.

I wanted, so badly, to be there in that moment. He looked disappointed in himself, though it had nothing to do with him.

I continued to watch until they interviewed him, smiling once I saw his face on television. Even though he was upset, it was still good to see him.

"Jameson," the reporter caught up with him as he exited the garage. "Looks like you were giving the team feedback there. Can you tell us what happened?"

He sighed heavily, running his hand across the back of his sweaty neck. "I had about four laps there where I thought something was wrong, but I don't know; it just blew up. It was running two ninety most of the race so it was only a matter of time."

"This is the second week in a row you've blown up, with yet another DNF. How is this affecting the team's morale? Do you think it has something to do with the engines at Riley Simplex Racing? Or maybe with Harry Sampson?"

"This has *nothing* to do with the cars we are provided each week *or* all the hard work our engine specialist, Harry Sampson, puts into the testing of these Ford engines provided by CST Engines," Jameson snapped back. "We have excellent cars and engines. This is obviously something else entirely." Before Jameson could say any more, Alley was dragging him away.

The engines weren't the problem and with his grandpa building them for his team and Harry maintaining them, I knew what he was insinuating with that comment. I had a hunch he was right.

Darrin.

It was hard to imagine Darrin would be able to get near the car at the track. There was usually always someone from the team nearby but it *wasn't* impossible, either.

If Jameson was right about Charlotte and the fuel additive, it definitely wasn't impossible for Darrin or his team to be fooling with their engines, too.

As his pigizzle and my duties as such, I decided to try and make him feel better by sending him a picture.

Would it make you feel better if I showed you my boobs?
It took a while to get a response ... exactly forty-three minutes.
Maybe. Show me and let's see.
I attached the picture to the text and clicked send, feeling slightly childish sending a picture of my boobs through a text message. It was another eleven minutes and I hadn't heard anything so I sent another one.

Did it work?
Another three minutes later, he finally responded: ***Sorry ... I had to take care of a problem you created, but Spencer wouldn't leave.***
Are you good now?
YES!
Wow, that was quick. I laughed, snuggling into the couch and enjoying the teasing.
You have no idea.
Don't worry, only a few more days and I will be taking care of it.
Looking forward to it, I miss you and love you!
Same to you, handsome.
The time away from Jameson flew by, and soon we were together again. Only problem was, I wasn't exactly feeling dapper.

I hated throwing up, truly I did. I had a strong feeling this was why I was in a really bad mood. Bitchy and exhausted, I felt like crying with all this added stress upon me. That could have had a hand in it, but it could also be that shark week (my period) was on its way; I assumed. I always got extra emotional and tired.

The other draining stress was that Jameson and I didn't know the first thing about running a racetrack. The lack of knowledge was becoming evident when Mallory was telling me how to do a job I'd been training to do since I was a kid. I knew how to do my job, but I didn't know how to be a General Manager, as well.

"Sway, you're never going to guess who's here!" Emma ran up to me throwing her hands on my shoulders.

Emma *and* Jameson were both here for the weekend for the Northern Sprint Tour. Although Jameson was *not* thrilled about Emma tagging along, he should have thought about that before he went and put her in charge of his fan club.

My stomach was still rolling as I stood there staring at her. Maybe I shouldn't have eaten that second corn dog ... or the nachos.

"Who?" I asked, focusing on her excitement instead of the rolling in my stomach.

"Dana ..."

"No way."

*What in the hell was she doing in Elma? This w*as my first thought, but then I knew the answer to that. She was stalking Jameson.

"Yep ... let's go talk to her." Emma yanked me along toward the concession stands. "Do you think she'll go for it?"

"I'm sure she's going to want something in exchange." I thought about it for a second. "Maybe like a picture or something."

"Yeah," Emma snorted, "of his ... ahem ..."

"Not happening," I stated firmly. "I'm the only one who sees the camshaft from here on out."

Stopping next to the bathrooms, Emma nodded to the coffee stand under the grandstands. "There she is. That's her friend Sadie standing with her." She pointed to the one with blonde hair.

"Which one is Dana?" I just now realized I'd never seen her before.

"She's the one with brown curly hair. She did have blonde highlights the last time I saw her in Charlotte, but it appears she's trying to resemble a certain someone." Emma looked at my hair, playing with a strand. I slapped her tiny hand away.

Dana had dyed her hair the *exact* same color as mine. Nudging Emma forward, I told her, "Go talk to her."

She stepped forward and then reached for me with a nervous expression. "You're coming with me."

I really didn't want to meet Dana right now. I didn't feel good, and I had Mallory making me crazy today, and then Jameson was all kinds of stressed out, which, in turn, stressed me out.

We stopped right in front of them.

"Oh Emma, hey, how's ..." Dana looked at me and stopped talking all together, scrutinizing my entire body.

I felt like she was undressing me; not that she wasn't. I knew what she was doing—she was comparing herself to me. I would've done the same given her position.

"Hey, Dana," Emma smiled. "This is my friend, Sway."

I wanted to bare my tattooed ass to her and say, *"Yep, that's right. I'm Jameson's!"*

That'd be one hell of a first impression—wouldn't it?

I reached for her hand instead. She didn't seem like the stalker type. She was pretty, brown hair, blue eyes, slender form, and some enormous fun bags.

Dana smiled politely at me. "Nice to meet you," she motioned to the blonde girl next to her, "This is my friend Sadie."

"Do you live around here?" Emma asked, smiling widely at me. I was receiving a lot of smiles.

"Yeah, I've always lived in Elma." Dana's smile widened. "I actually went to high school with you guys."

Emma and I both looked at each other. "Oh," we both said after a few moments of awkward silence.

I don't ever remember seeing her in school. Although, I hardly paid attention to anyone who wasn't in the Riley family. It's not like I actually knew who even went to school with us.

"So Dana ... um ... we were wondering if we could ask you a few questions," Emma stepped closer to her trying to remain discreet.

"Private things."

"Oh, sure," Dana seemed eager to be talking to any member of Jameson's family. "What do you need?" Her eyes lit up.

"How well do you know Darrin and Mariah?"

"Pretty well. Mariah is my cousin."

Both Emma and I gasped.

What were the chances of this shit?

"Seriously?" I blurted out.

"Yeah, I mean, we're not close or anything." Dana's eyes narrowed at me. "But I know a *few* things," she hinted.

"And what would you want in return for these, *few things* of knowledge?"

Please don't say a picture of his camshaft.

Dana was quiet for a minute her eyes glazed over. "A date ... with Jameson."

I laughed out loud.

"Um ... Dana ... I don't know if that's something Jameson would agree to," Emma replied, elbowing me in the side. "You did *steal* his underwear."

"I guess you don't want to know that bad then," she countered, clearly not amused by my sudden onset of the giggles.

Emma and I both exchanged a loaded glance in between my giggling.

I nodded. "Fine, but let me talk to him first."

Dana gave Emma her cell phone number and then walked away.

"Emma, he's never going to agree to this. That woman," I pointed to Dana walking away, "is fucking crazy." I shook my head walking toward the office where Jameson was. "After the stabbing, I suggest you run, like fugitive-style. Only pack what you can carry in one arm," I suggested.

"Make him agree, it's our only option," Emma ordered rolling her eyes and began to walk away.

I only made it up one step before her hand grasped mine. "As much as he annoys the fuck out of me, I love him, and I refuse to let Darrin hurt him," Emma told me. "We *need* answers."

I still felt nauseous, and *this* wasn't helping. Not only was my stomach bothering me, I *did not* want to tell Jameson he had to go on a date with Dana because I was trying to find out answers. Answers he *did not* want me finding out. But if I didn't, and something happened to Jameson, I would always wonder if I could have stopped it.

Everyone was hard at work preparing for a night of dirt track racing when I walked into the announcer's booth.

Jameson was standing in the corner with Mark going over the schedule for the events tonight.

When his eyes met mine, he quickly made his way over to me by the door.

"Hey, are you okay?" Jameson kissed my forehead, his arms wrapped around me. "You don't look so good."

"I'm fine," I eluded. I really did look like shit, and I *felt* worse than shit. "Just tired."

He took me into the private office off the announcer's booth. "Are you sure you're okay, honey? Are you horny or something?"

"No ... well ... actually yes, but that's not why ..." I tried to make something up but drew a blank and went with the truth, well part of it anyway. "I don't feel very good tonight. I think it was that corndog I ate."

Jameson scrunched his nose disgusted. "That's what you get for eating a corndog."

We laughed and talked about the schedule for the night and stole a few kisses before heading back outside to the announcer's booth.

"Oh ... by the way, you are going on a date with Dana." I cringed, waiting for his protests, "on Sunday."

"I don't think I heard you." His hand came up slamming the door shut. "What was that?"

"You're going on a date," I repeated, "with Dana."

"You can't be serious." His eyes were hard and not pleasant at all. "*Please* tell me you're not serious."

I stood there, waiting for him to agree, while he stood there, waiting for me to tell him I was joking.

"I'm serious, Jameson. It's the only way to get Dana to tell us what Darrin and Chelsea are up to."

"I thought I told you to stay out of this?"

"You did, but we *have* to know."

"Going on a date, with Dana, is not worth knowing!" he shouted. "No fucking way. Not happening. Ever!"

"Jameson," I sighed heavily. "Just *please* ... I don't like this anymore than you do."

"I highly doubt that or you wouldn't have agreed to whore me out!" he barked back as he shifted his weight from one foot to the other. "I feel cheap."

"Whore you out?" I pushed him back against the wall, trying to be intimidating, clearly not achieved by the smirk. "Listen," I grabbed his face between my hands. "I'm not going to sit back and wait for Darrin to hurt you ... I will find out what that fucker is up to. So if Dana is our only option, you take her to dinner."

"You're okay with me going out with another woman?" he questioned, for good reason.

"*Fuck no* I'm not okay with it, but what choice do I have?"

"You could let me take care of this myself and not get involved." He glared, challenging me to say something else.

It was clear he didn't want me involved. But, then again, that *what if?* was blaring so loud, I couldn't see past it to *not* make him do this.

I grumbled, frustrated, "Just go out to dinner with her." I stepped back creating distance from his glare. "Emma and I will be there to make sure she doesn't try anything."

The silence that followed made me nervous before he finally caved.

"Ah, Christ." Jameson stared at me with obvious doubt. "I swear to God, Sway, if this goes badly, I'm holding you *and* Stabberally responsible."

There was a loud knock on the door. "Hey, Jameson," Mark poked his head in. "I need you for a second."

Jameson nodded to him, and then looked back to me. "No longer than an hour. I'm serious, I'm fucking timing it." He pointed to his wrist heading to the door. "One hour."

This had bad idea written all over it, but what other choice did we have?

I didn't have one. I refused to sit back and wait for Darrin to pull his next move on the track for the simple *what if?* factor.

I sent Emma a text letting her know that Jameson agreed, and then walked out of the office to find Mallory again.

The rest of the evening was spent with Mallory and me arguing over silly inconsequential things like what the schedule would be for the ticket booth or when to close the beer garden down.

Jameson spent most of his night arguing with track officials being slow to throw out a caution or being slow cleaning up a wreck.

Being a racer himself, he wasn't exactly the person you want yelling at you to throw a caution. They had their own ideas about the way things should be run, and it wasn't always the right one.

Throughout the busy evening, we may have seen each other twice since our Dana conversation and both occasions, he was yelling at someone.

It was a relief I wasn't behind the yelling, but I knew this was going to happen; I warned him. He didn't need all this superfluous stress added to his life; he had enough going on as it was.

When the races were finished for the night, I finally got to see Jameson. It didn't take long before Emma needed him to sign some autographs for the little midget series.

After that night, I had a feeling this was the way race nights would be from now on at Grays Harbor.

"Where is he?" Emma asked coming into my bedroom Sunday afternoon, the day of the date with Dana. "He didn't run away, did he?"

"In the bathroom," I answered, not looking up from my book. "He's taking a shower."

She plopped down on my bed. "Is he still mad at me?"

"What do you think?" I raised my eyebrow at her.

"Ugh ..." she groaned. "He's overreacting."

"Is he?" I laughed. "Emma, you made reservations for him and Dana at Sorrento's."

"So ...?"

"It's one of his favorite places, not to mention he is going with Dana." I finally looked at her. "You're tainting his memory of the restaurant forever now."

"We're going to be right outside." She rolled her eyes. "It's not like a *real* date—she knows that."

"Does she?"

Emma giggled with a touch of mischief. "I told her it wasn't a date ..." My glare had her confessing. "Okay, okay ... I told her it was a date, but she knows it's nothing more than a "friend" date. I told her that you're his girlfriend."

That still didn't make it any better.

Emma and I were going with him, but Dana didn't know that. We were supposed to hide out in the kitchen while they were on their date. I hated calling it that, but that's what it was, for her sake. Dana needed to think Jameson was going on a date with her so she would tell him what Darrin was up to.

Jameson, on the other hand, was convinced she was going to try to rape him or something, and to say he freaked out when Emma made reservations at Sorrento's was an understatement ... he went apeshit.

I heard my bedroom door open and Jameson walked in with only a towel wrapped low around his waist.

"What are you doing in here?" he asked Emma.

They scowled at each other for a moment. "Talking with Sway," Emma finally answered.

My eyes were drawn south and stayed there. He was showing entirely too much skin for me to focus on anything else.

"You've got five seconds before I'm completely naked," Jameson warned, tugging on his towel. "Four seconds ..."

Emma screamed in horror running to the door.

"Works like a charm," Jameson smirked, walking toward the bed. I set my book down wrapping my arms around his waist when he made it to the edge of the bed. "What do I wear?"

"Nothing revealing."

"Obviously," he held up a black Simplex long sleeve shirt. "How about this?"

"Don't wear black."

He threw the shirt back in his suitcase. "Why, what's wrong with black?" he asked confused.

"You look ... incredibly *hot* in black, it makes your eyes stand out. I don't want her drooling over you."

"Right, no black then," he agreed, rummaging through his bag. "What color looks the worst?"

"Wear that one," I pointed to the navy blue Oakley shirt. He picked it up, pulling it over his head and then sat down beside me. "And don't wear your cologne."

"I wasn't going to," he said with a chuckle. "I only wear that for you."

My shoulders slumped forward. Jameson must have noticed because the next thing I knew, he pulled me onto his lap.

His hand moved under my chin. "This was your idea, *remember*?"

I sighed forcing a small smile. "I know ... it doesn't mean I like the idea."

"Does that mean I don't have to go?"

"NO!" Emma yelled from behind the door. "You're going!"

"I asked my parents for a dog ... and *that's* what they brought home," Jameson said pointing to Emma who was now inside my bedroom with her hands covering her eyes.

"Shut up, Jameson." She reached forward to punch his shoulder. "Now get in the car. You're going to be late."

He laughed sarcastically. "We wouldn't want that, would we?"

An hour later, Emma and I sat there crammed in the corner of the kitchen at Sorrento's in downtown Olympia, watching Jameson and Dana.

Every time Dana tried to touch him in some way, Emma giggled hysterically as though this was a comedy club.

I did not. I wanted to run out there and rip her hair out.

"You're enjoying this, aren't you?" I asked adjusting my position on the floor. My ass was starting to fall asleep.

"You have no idea," Emma grinned evilly as she stuffed another bread stick in her mouth. The guys working in the kitchen were kind enough to let us sit back here and also kept handing us food. I didn't have the heart to tell them we were like dogs, and if you fed us we might never leave.

"He's going to kill you," I told Emma with a mouth full of food. "Just so you know."

"I don't care." She laughed. "This is a hoot."

Dana, once again, reached for his hand over the table. Jameson jerked it back quickly and glanced around the restaurant, probably looking for us. I felt bad for him sitting across from her and her gazing unabashedly at him.

His discomfort was noticeable with the way he was fidgeting and how his knee was bouncing uncontrollably. All signs were pointing to an angry Jameson. Another telltale sign was that he had barely touched his food.

He hadn't spoken much as she seemed to be doing most of the talking. I did notice his mouth moving a few times though, so I assumed that he was answering her questions.

"Does she talk a lot?"

"You have no idea." She smiled. "That's what makes this *so* entertaining. How much you want to bet she wore his underwear tonight?"

I shook my head in disbelief. "He really is going to kill you."

Emma reached for her phone and sent someone a text.

"Who are you texting?" I asked adjusting my position again.

"Spencer," she answered. "He thinks this is hilarious."

"I bet he does."

"Where's he going?" Emma asked looking up as Jameson walked past.

"Maybe he's going to the bathroom ..." I guessed and snuck over to the door to see. "Stay here, I'm going to make sure he's not running away."

If he were running, I'd probably run with him at that point.

I followed him as he walked into the men's bathroom.

Jameson jumped, taking a sharp intake of breath when I hopped on the counter behind him, watching him pee.

"Thank God," he breathed in relief. "I thought you were Dana."

"Nope, just a jealous girlfriend."

Jameson turned around to wash his hands. "What the fuck would you have to be jealous of?" he asked incredulously reaching for the paper towels. "Have you not seen *that* out there? She fucking crazy, certifiably insane."

"Oh, it's not *that* bad."

"Not that bad?" he seethed, stepping between my legs, pulling my hips to the edge of the counter. "In the last thirty minutes she has told me her entire life story. We went to high school together and I smiled at her once in the halls. That she has a life-sized poster of me above her bed that she does God knows what to every night." He shivered. "She told me that she has five pairs of my underwear, one of which she's wearing, right now, and she named her dog after me." His face went pale. "Sway, she knows some *really* strange things about me."

"Like what?"

"Did you know that my favorite pizza is pepperoni and pineapple?"

"Is it?"

"Apparently it is. She read it in a magazine, so it must be true." He rolled his eyes. "How much more time do I have to spend out there?" Jameson brought his lips to mine once. "I can't take much more of this shit. She actually asked me if it was true that I have a huge dick."

"No," I giggled and snorted. "She didn't?"

"YES!" he shouted.

"What did you say?"

"I told her it was none of her fucking business." His eyes got a strange look to them. "She asked if she could have a picture of it."

I laughed hysterically to the point that Jameson was holding me up, so I didn't fall.

"You're worse than Stabberally!" he snapped, pushing my shoulder. "Stop laughing, right now."

"I'm sorry, it's not funny," I told him, trying to breathe and kiss him once more to keep my smile at bay. "Has she told you anything?"

"No, this is pointless." His head slumped forward. "I asked, but she said we'll get to that. I don't want to do this anymore."

"I'm sorry." I jumped down with a renewed sense of security. "I'll make it up to you tonight."

"Fucking right you're making this up to me." He smacked my ass. "And not just tonight ... you and Stabberally owe me, *big time*."

Jameson left first and after a couple minutes, I made my way back to the kitchen.

The next thirty minutes were spent with Dana slowly moving closer and closer to him. Jameson drank an insane amount of water so he could sneak away to the bathroom every five minutes, and Emma paid a waiter to keep offering wine to Dana, the most expensive wine, since Jameson was paying.

"He really is going to kill you for this," I pointed out.

"I don't care." She shrugged carelessly. "It's entertaining. Spencer and I have a bet going for how long it takes for her to try and kiss him."

I rolled my eyes yet again. "Now I know why he wishes he was an only child."

We really hadn't been paying attention in the last twenty minutes when all of a sudden we heard glass breaking and then Jameson's voice raise.

"Get off me!"

We turned immediately to see Dana on top of the table with her arms around his neck, tightly, holding on for all she was worth.

"Just one kiss, please?" she begged. "Just one!"

"No. I mean it, get off me or I call the cops right now." Jameson reached for his cell phone in his jeans. "Let go, Dana." He pushed her away, holding his phone in the air as a warning. "Stay away."

Breathing heavy for a moment, she then lunged for him again.

Jameson was quicker this time and ran at the exact moment she lunged for him, barreling through the kitchen doors.

"No fucking way I'm going back out there. I'm leaving." I could tell by the grim, set look on his face, this was not up for negotiation.

The date is over.

Emma's phone beeped while they argued. "Oh," she said, looking at the text. "It's Dana." We all turned and watched as Dana walked out of the restaurant. "She said that Darrin wants to end your career. He will stop at nothing until he's taken everything you have."

A silence spread over us, even the cook beside us said nothing.

"Ask her why Jameson?" I ordered pointing to the phone. I was not accepting that as an answer. "Why is he so focused on Jameson?

What about the other drivers?"

The cook offered Jameson some bread dipped in garlic oil, which he took and scarfed down like Mr. Jangles eating spaghetti. Apparently, his appetite had returned.

Emma typed away as we waited for some type of response.

Jameson, after eating his bread, stood beside me wiping his neck off from where Dana touched him.

Apparently, that wasn't enough for him so he grabbed my purse and dug out my hand sanitizer. After examining the label for a brief moment, he dumped the entire bottle in his hands, rubbing it all over his neck and face.

Curiously, I watched him, both amused and then concerned at *how* much he used.

That couldn't be good for his skin. I may not have mentioned this before, but Jameson had some obsessive-compulsive tendencies when it came to anything touching his skin. He once took a bath in alcohol when he thought he had a rash. Yeah, he's weird.

Emma's phone beeped again, silence spread for a second time. "You're the only competition for him and he doesn't deal well with that."

"I don't take well to being threatened," Jameson barked, walking toward the door after Dana got in her car. "I'm tired of this bullshit."

I don't know if it was the fear of Jameson being hurt or all the smelly Italian food, but the breadsticks Emma and I had been eating came back up once we reached the parking lot.

Jameson gave me a contemplative scowl once we were in the car. "I want you to stay out of this. I mean it, Sway, stay out of it."

Could I do that for him? No, probably not.

I wanted to stay out of it, but with anything related to Jameson, I couldn't *just* stay out of it.

17

Dirty Air

JAMESON

Dirty Air – The rear wing of the car in front tends to push the air higher, creating low-pressure pocket directly behind the car. At high speeds, down-force can be disrupted if you follow another car too closely. When that happens, the car following won't be able to steer very well and is said to be in dirty air.

I watched my reason for breathing lying there in bed sound asleep.

She was beautiful, stunningly so, with her cheeks flushed, her lips pushed out into a pout. Other than her cheeks being flushed, she looked rather pale.

I was starting to become concerned by her appearance, and the throwing up. Since Saturday night, she'd thrown up every day. At first, I thought maybe she had Lane's flu or food poisoning from those mystery corndogs they served at the track, but things weren't adding up.

Sway looked different, her face was glowing, and her funbags, as she called them, were huge. She was cranky and *extra* bitchy toward the Lucifer twins—not that I disagreed with that part.

She stirred beside me, and I wrapped my arms around her waist as I slid her snugly against my chest. Gently I reached up and pushed a few stray strands of her hair out of her face and then kissed her forehead.

I hated mornings like this, the ones where I would be forced to leave her in a few hours instead of staying in bed with her all day. This was the main reason why I avoided a real relationship with her for so long. She deserved someone who could be there when she needed him. But, then again, I was too selfish at this point to let her go.

I continued to pepper her face, shoulders, arms, anywhere I could reach, with slow, thorough kisses. In a way, it was as though I was attempting to show her enough love to last her until I returned.

Sway's eyes flickered open with a smile. The curtains danced from the warm summer breeze swirling through her room.

There was nothing between us but the morning air when I covered her body with my own. She smiled when my lips touched hers and I reached below the sheets pooled around my waist, moving between her legs. It was such an intense feeling I got the moment I would enter her body. Every muscle and every nerve ending would tense in anticipation, waiting for the moment.

Her sparkly green eyes met mine. "Good morning," Sway mumbled against my lips.

"Good morning, honey."

And it *was* a good morning, because for now, we were here together. I could forget all about my commitments. I could forget all about having to leave later today. Instead, I focused on Sway.

"I love you," I whispered against her shoulder.

The sun continued to rise, casting a warm glow throughout her bedroom. I looked over at the clock knowing my time here was ending soon. I needed to meet Wes at the Olympia airport in a few hours.

"I need to get up," I groaned running my hands through my hair. I propped myself up on my elbow to look down at her. "I have to be in Sarver, Pennsylvania, tonight."

"Where do you have to go next?" Sway asked rolling over in my arms to look at me.

"I have a busy two weeks." I tried to think back to my schedule. "I fly to Sarver today, then to Indy on Thursday. On Monday next week I have to be in Orlando for a commercial. Then I fly to Pocono again. After that, I think I have a few days free before I need to be in Watkins Glen." I touched her face gently. "After Bristol, I have a two-week break. Maybe we can sneak away for a few days together, you and me," I grinned.

A smile flickered across Sway's lips. "That would be nice."

Running my fingertips over her warm flushed cheeks, I thought about how sick she'd been. "How are you feeling?"

"Uh ... okay, I guess. I'm actually hungry." She sat up in bed, pulling on my t-shirt from last night. You could smell bacon being cooked in the kitchen downstairs. "Let's eat before you leave. Andrea cooks a bitchin' breakfast."

"Sounds good to me," Kissing her once more, I made my way to the bathroom for a quick shower as she headed downstairs.

Once dressed and my bag was packed, I joined her at the kitchen table. Emma was up now, sitting beside Sway, eating. I pushed her off the stool when I walked past, stealing her bacon as I did so.

"You're such an asshole!" Emma snapped, picking herself up.

My eyebrow arched in response, challenging her. "Really ..." I laughed. "I'm the asshole? Do you not remember *anything* from last night?"

That shut her up immediately.

Fixing a plate of food, I took notice to how much Sway was eating. Her plate was piled with food and she seemed to be holding it down, which was a good thing.

"I think you have a tape worm or something." I took a seat next to her. "Where does all that food go?"

"In the toilet," Emma laughed. "It's not like she'll hold it down."

Sway's nose scrunched at Emma but continued to scarf down her bacon and eggs. Sure enough, ten minutes after she was finished she ran to the bathroom. I was about to go after her when she slammed the door shut.

"Will you stay here this week?" I asked Emma, setting my plate in the sink. "I'm worried about her." Leaning against the counter, Logan came strolling in exchanging a glare with me.

Emma gave me a strange look while Andrea smiled at me. "Yeah, I'll stay with her." She held out her hand. "Can I have your credit card?"

"What would make you think I would *ever* hand you my credit card?"

"For payment," she set her plate in the sink. "If I'm staying here, you *should* reward me."

"Your reward will be me not going home and burning all your favorite clothes for the shit you've put me through," I responded, patting her before making my way down the hall to check on Sway.

"Are you okay?" I asked softly opening the door. Sitting on the edge of the bathtub, Sway slumped against the wall beside the toilet.

"Yeah, I think maybe I have the flu." She fumbled with the hem of her shirt to avoid looking directly at me.

"Hmm ... I guess Lane had it." I felt her forehead. "Maybe you caught it from him somehow."

I really didn't think it was the flu. I had a feeling it was something else, but didn't say anything. Seeing those very same symptoms in Alley, all the signs were pointing to her being pregnant.

When Alley was pregnant with Lane we were all still traveling around together in my truck, which made for some interesting trips.

There were times when I was moments away from volunteering to ride on the roof rather than sit next to a hormonal Alley for sixteen hours a day.

I didn't want to freak Sway out, so instead I smiled reassuringly at her. "Maybe you should ... go to the doctor," I suggested, pulling her up into my arms. "Just to make sure you don't have something else."

"Yeah, I think I will this week."

The thought that she might be pregnant, with my child, had me glowing as much as her. I wasn't ready for kids, but if they happened, they happened. I knew Sway was on birth control pills, as I had seen them the morning after we first slept together. That right there made this even more confusing to me. If she was on the pill there was no way she could be pregnant, right?

Maybe she does have the flu.

Ugh ... my cell phone beeped twice, reminding me of the real world waiting for me.

"I have to go." I kissed her forehead. "I'll call you when I get to Sarver."

With a few more lingering kisses, *after* she brushed her teeth, I headed for Olympia to begin my busy two weeks without Sway.

As with any time away, my focus then was solely on racing.

"The car is shaking real bad. My shifter is vibrating like a son of a bitch. I wanted to see if it was all of us?" I asked Cole around lap two twenty of the Brickyard 400.

This week had flown by with my numerous commitments and now here I was, on race day, trying to piece together an ill-handling race car. It could have been worse. The last two races the engine had blown way before lap two hundred, so I guess in all actuality, we were doing good if you considered running eighteenth good.

I didn't.

"It's all of us," Cole finally answered. "I can barely get the car in fourth without slippin' off the shifter."

I used to love Indy, but lately, it only served back memories.

Last year, I raced in the Busch Series and pegged the wall in turn three, nearly sending me to the hospital with a concussion. The year before that, I raced here in a USAC midget and flipped it seven times on the backstretch.

This track hated me.

There was still a chunk missing from the outside barrier where my car landed upside down on it during that USAC race.

Somewhere around lap three hundred, we were doing better, *until* the caution came out.

Kyle came over the radio after the pit stop. "Too fast entering, come back in bud."

"What?" I slammed my fists down on the wheel. "You have to be shitting me? I came in on fifty six like I have the entire goddamn race."

"I know," Kyle replied. "Harris and Cole are being held, too,"

"It's bullshit!" I yelled back heading back to pit lane for my stop and go penalty.

Between air pressure inconsistencies, track changes, shoddy pit stops, a handful of cautions for debris, the entire race went this way and I wasn't surprised to see I finished thirty-second.

If I kept this shit up—we could forget about any chance at the championship. As I sat right now, with four DNFs, I was now fourth in the race for the championship, not good in my mind.

With a new team I understood the time for transition, but this was out of our control. I still felt we were unstoppable, but I also couldn't see past the frustration in the heat of the moment.

When my anger passed and I had gained some composure, I walked back to the motor coach to gather my bags and head to Orlando.

Bobby stopped me, his expression similar to mine. "Hey dude, how'd you finish?"

"Thirty-second," I mumbled pulling my sweatshirt over my shoulders and began walking again. "It was rough out there."

"You did better than me; I ended up thirty-eighth." Bobby kept step with me. "I wanted to talk to you about Darrin."

"Oh yeah," I turned to him. "What about?"

A few lingering fans at the entrance to the drivers' compound pushed forward for autographs to which we signed.

"I've heard some things in the garage … looks like he's out for blood this time."

"What are you talking about?" I asked grimly, tired of this shit. Everyone wanted to warn me about Darrin, but had nothing to warn me about, no hard evidence as to what he had planned.

"He wants to end your career, Jameson."

"Oh," I said sarcastically, stopping outside my motor coach, "and how does Darrin plan on doing that?"

"By wrecking you …" Bobby's brown eyes held nothing but worry. "Listen, Jameson," he shifted his weight, deciding on his delivery, "I'm not one to get caught up in this bullshit of he said-she said, but when it comes to my teammate, a person who I have the utmost respect for, I pay attention. I *know* Darrin—I've known him since my days racing quarter midgets. You're not the first person that he's threatened their career with. And if he succeeds, you wouldn't be the first person whose career was ended *by him*." His expression was blank, his eyes gauging me.

"Who?"

"My best friend, when I was nineteen. We were racing out of Knoxville Raceway. Darrin and Kasey had been battling all season in the Silver Crown Series."

"Kasey O'Neil?"

Bobby nodded. "The race wasn't taped so no one knows *really* what happened, but I was behind Kasey the entire time." Bobby took a deep breath. "I watched as Darrin purposely clipped his left rear."

Spencer walked out of the motor coach, leaning against the side as Bobby continued, "When Kasey's car finally came to rest against the guardrails, there was nothing left. The roll cage failed and was crushed on top of him." Emotion welled up in his eyes before collecting himself quickly. "He died on the way to the hospital from massive head injuries."

"I heard about him," Spencer said. "His dad races on The World of Outlaw series with our dad—Langley O'Neil—right?"

Bobby nodded. "Yep." He shifted his feet and then looked at me again. "Just be careful." He stared at me with obvious doubt in his eyes. "I thought he hated Kasey, but Kasey was nowhere near the driver you are. I've never seen someone do the things you can do in a race car, Jameson."

"What do you suggest I do?"

"I suggest you steer clear of him." Bobby's eyes shifted to Spencer who snorted. "If you run into him on the track, let him go. It's not worth it."

"I will not pull back," I replied undeterred. "If he wants to end my career, let him try. I'm going to race him the same as I race any other driver out there."

Bobby shook his head, frustrated. "I'll see you in Pocono." He patted my back, shook Spencer's hand, and then walked toward the helipad.

Here's the thing: I've encountered cocky drivers before, and what I learned most was to ignore the situation. The more you knew, the more frustrated and involved you became with them, and the more you failed to concentrate on *why* you were racing in the first place.

Once I landed in Orlando, I tried calling Sway, but it was almost midnight her time so I assumed she was probably sleeping.

Aiden and Spencer came with me to Orlando and brought Lane. Once we landed, he was complaining about being hungry. Having a hungry three-year-old, at three in the morning, was something none of us were willing to deal with.

That was how we ended up at an Applebee's in the airport.

"Can you believe this fucking service?" Spencer complained looking over his shoulder. "It's an airport, I'll give them that much, but seriously, I asked for a beer like an hour ago."

"Keep your voice down," Aiden hushed him when an elderly lady balked at his reaction. "You're offending people." Aiden's eyes dropped back to the menu. He'd yet to figure out what to eat. After all, this decision usually took hours for him.

"They're offended? Jesus ..." Spencer snapped. "It's not like I pissed in their potatoes."

Ahh ... it's good to be around the boys.

"Jameson," Spencer began, slouching to one side of his chair. "What do you think of what Cole said?"

Resting my elbows against the table, I ran my hands through my hair and then along my jaw. "I ... don't know. I get that everyone is trying to warn me, but I'm not going to stop racing because some jealous fucker can't get over the fact that his girlfriend wanted my dick ..." my voice trailed off when I realized Lane was present. "I mean penis."

Spencer laughed. I had a feeling that Lane was used to this because he never looked up, continuing his coloring.

"I don't understand *how* Darrin gets away with half the shit that he pulls on the track," Aiden added, pouring himself a glass of beer from the pitcher the server finally brought over. "It's like NASCAR looks the other way."

Placing the hot wings in the middle of the table, the waitress focused on me. "Is there anything else I can get you, honey?" She pushed her tits together, leaning forward.

"No, that's all." I smirked when Spencer and Aiden started laughing.

Knowing Spencer was moments away from embarrassing me, I turned my head to Lane. "What are you coloring, buddy?"

His answer was to push a red crayon in my hand. A clear indication that I was to color, I assumed.

The waitress didn't leave. Instead, she bent down to my ear and whispered, "Here's my number, call me later. I'm off at ten."

I pulled back to look at her nametag. "Jen, is it?"

She nodded with a flirtatious smile; her hand rubbed my back.

Dropping the crayon, I reached for the note she placed in my pocket and handed the note back to her. "I have a girlfriend."

"She doesn't have to know," was her response.

Aiden made a disgusted snorting sound and Spencer grinned.

Lane, who'd said little since his tantrum getting off the plane, piped up in his little chipmunk voice. "Yes, she does, I'll tell her. I love my auntie Sway." He never even looked up from his coloring.

There wasn't a straight face around our table as we laughed at Lane. Jen left.

I didn't think he could hear her, let alone understand what she was implying. Though Spencer acts stupid, he is not. I was beginning to realize Lane was the same way.

Eventually the conversation drifted back to Darrin when our food arrived.

"You know who his aunt is, right?" Spencer asked Aiden who couldn't understand why Darrin wasn't being held more accountable for his behavior on the track.

"No, who?" we both asked.

"Deanna Reynolds."

Reynolds? I only knew one Reynolds that would make for ... that would mean Gordon was Darrin's uncle.

"No shit?" I choked on my beer. "How did you find this out?"

"The power of Google my dear brother," he nodded his head arrogantly. "You'd be amazed what is available on the internet."

"Wow, I'm impressed." I took another drink of my beer. "You're actually kind of clever."

"I am *really* clever. People think I'm stupid, but I'm really not." He shrugged. "Shit, have you seen Lane?" He started looking for his son, who we thought was still coloring beside us.

Alley really should have thought twice before she allowed us to take Lane with us. But, then again, she should be able to trust his father at some point. I'd like to think Spencer had grown since leaving Lane at the grocery store and bringing home the wrong child.

When we found him, I burst out laughing. Lane was peeing in the corner of the restaurant. A waitress with wide-eyes was telling him he shouldn't do that.

Lane's response, "I can't read signs. I'm three." He shrugged. "How'd I suppose to know that the bathroom? I had to pee."

Aiden nudged my arm watching Spencer try to explain *why* his son was peeing in the corner of the restaurant. "Do you think that's why Darrin hasn't been penalized?"

"He *has* been penalized for his actions," I clarified, pouring myself another beer. "Just ... not enough." My eyes shot up when I heard my name announced in the distance. "He won't stop until I've given up. But I'm not going to."

Aiden stared at me warily. "Jameson, be careful."

My name was said again, this time by another group of people near the entrance of the small restaurant. I knew then my time here was up, or at least my quiet time here was at an end.

"I didn't get where I'm at today by being vigilant, Aiden."

I understood *why* everyone was warning me, but I would be damned if I was going to let Darrin Torres push me around or end my career—a career that I worked so hard for and sacrificed so much for.

The night fell into a steady pace of signing autographs and posing for pictures. Somewhere in between all this, my attention shifted toward Spencer and Lane.

It made me think of Sway, wondering if she was, in fact, pregnant. I wanted to ask Spencer what Alley was like, but I knew what that would turn in to. I had no intentions for brotherly bonding right now. It'd probably be more embarrassing than informational, especially with the intuitive Aiden around.

Staying in a hotel room with two beds, three adults, and a three-year-old was not exactly the best experience I'd ever had, including the night I was stalked by a deadly predator that had every intention of mating with me.

Never again would I do that, both camping in the woods and sleeping in the same room with these crazies.

Between Spencer's snoring, Aiden's concern for Darrin and his general quirkiness, and Lane saying he had to pee every five minutes … I wanted to rip my fucking hair out.

I finally had to say, "Listen, when you have to pee, just go."

It was as though he had a bladder the size of a goddamn hummingbird.

I wasn't wild about his lack of bladder control, and felt as though we'd made a connection about when to go and when not to around midnight.

All that went to shit when he took my advice of "just go" literally and peed in the goddamn bed.

When Wednesday rolled around, I was, once again, back to racing and grateful not to have to be around them all day.

Instead, I was back in Sarver racing sprint cars with Justin West and Tyler Sprague.

Lernerville Speedway was a 4/10 mile dirt track located right outside of Pittsburgh, Pennsylvania. Being back on the dirt reminded me of the good ol' days when Sway was with me every day.

When speaking with her throughout the week, she avoided my lingering questions all together. I threatened to fly home if she didn't tell me what was bothering her, but again she changed the subject to something inconsequential. I had a gut feeling she knew she was pregnant but was afraid to tell me.

So many times, I typed out the text message to her, asking if she was pregnant but erased it when I realized that was stupid.

You don't ask something like that through text messages—even I knew that.

As soon as I landed in Pocono later that week, race day was there before I knew it. Media, sponsor obligations, and team meetings filled my days.

I qualified second, behind Darrin. This meant that we both visited the NASCAR hauler prior to the race where Gordon explained that they would not tolerate any bullshit on the track today.

I chuckled to myself that here Gordon was telling his nephew this. If only I'd known that months ago, all this would have made much more sense.

Darrin was hardly a *good* driver. Sure, he could drive; there was no way to make it to this level without the ability, but he didn't have it in him to be a champion in the series and he lacked a serious sense of sportsmanship.

I tried calling Sway before the race but it went straight to voice-mail, once again. The Modified Nationals were last night in Elma so I assumed she had a late night.

Making my way toward the grid for driver introductions, I saw Alley approaching me, in tears.

Alley never cried.

She slipped her Blackberry in her pocket before she approached me. Wrapping my arms around her, I attempted to comfort her.

"What's wrong?"

"Jameson ... you can't go out there today." She choked on her tears, her eyes held worry.

"What?" I pulled back, holding her at an arm's length. "What are you talking about?"

"Mariah ... she ... told ..." She blinked quickly. "I overheard her on her cell phone ... in the bathroom." Alley wiped her eyes with the sleeve of her Simplex sweatshirt. "He's going to wreck you."

"It wouldn't be the first time," I mumbled with a sigh. "Look, Alley ... I get that everyone is concerned, I really do, but this is *my job*. If I don't go out there and do what Simplex and my dad are paying me to do, we lose sponsorship. That means ... I lose my ride and you're out of a job, too."

"I know but—"

"I have to get to driver introductions." Holding my hand up, I began to walk away. "Just let me handle this, *please*. Stay out of it."

Alley followed, nodding. Watching her, I could tell something else was wrong; her body language was different. This wasn't about Darrin. Her eyes flickered to mine once and then quickly at the ground.

"What are you not telling me?"

She grimaced, looking away. "Nothing, Jameson." Alley reached up, her arms snuck around my neck for a hug. "Be careful. We'll talk after the race."

"No, no … what is it?" I forced her to look at me. My stomach fell as I thought something might be wrong with Sway. "Is everything okay with Sway?"

"Sway is fine." She met my tortured expression quickly diverting her eyes. "Axle …" her voice trailed off, and I knew what she was telling me.

He died.

Nodding, my eyes fell to my feet and I began to walk away. I thought I heard her mumble an "I'm sorry," but I couldn't be sure over the loud thumping in my ears.

An hour later and one trip to the bathroom to compose myself for interviews, I was standing next to my car, doing pre-race interviews, trying my hardest not to get emotional over that little boy who fought so hard to make it.

Ashley approached me as I leaned up against the car with Spencer.

Spencer being Spencer attempted to embarrass me. "Hey Ashley, how's the vertical smile these days?" He laughed, slapping me on the back.

"Ask Jameson, he'd know," Ashley snarled back.

"Uh … no … I would not," I interrupted their bantering. "Is there something you want, Ashley?"

Ashley turned on her faux smile, glaring toward Spencer. "So Jameson, you're starting second … how's the car?" She shoved her recorder in my face.

"I think we should do good," I answered methodically. "It's the same engine from the car we used here a few months ago."

We couldn't use the car because that was destroyed, thanks to Darrin. Looking out at his car, it finally dawned on me *why* Darrin chose Pocono to supposedly wreck me.

I wrecked him here in June.

Kyle walked up once Ashley left. "Hey," he patted my back, "let's get ready. Keep focused."

How the fuck was I supposed to stay focused?

I couldn't get in touch with Sway, which always threw me off. Axle … I couldn't even say it … Darrin … fuck.

Putting all that aside, I had a job to do. I went through my ritual, putting my ear buds in, then helmet, gloves. Spencer bumped my fist and wished me luck, as he did before *every* race and raised the window net.

Every Sunday and the occasional Saturday night, when I fired up my cup car, Spencer was the one who put my window net up, always had been and would remain. In time and by habit, it was sort of our ritual dating back to the days when I raced midgets and sprint cars. He was always the last person I saw before pulling onto the track.

"All right bud, stay focused," Kyle told me once I had the radio connected. "Keep your head clear. You can do this. We have an awesome car today. Show us what you got."

"I'll do my best guys," I responded once he gave the order to fire up the engine.

The race was tedious for the first half until Darrin found me again. Once the green flag dropped, I passed him fairly quickly, but now he was back, or maybe he was there all along waiting for his moment.

Having led the last hundred and sixty laps, I damn sure wasn't about to give the lead up easily.

"Clear low … outside rear … at your door … rear … clear," Aiden helped me through the lapped traffic; Darrin was all over the back of me. "Caution's out … stay low … sixty car is spinning in two … in the grass. Watch low, there may be some oil down."

"What do you think?" Kyle asked when the pace car pulled ahead of me. "Changes?"

"Uh … maybe a round out of the rear, other than that … we're good."

"Okay," Kyle then gave the orders to Mason. "You heard him. Round out of the right rear, make a slight air pressure adjustment, four tires and fuel."

Keeping my eyes on Darrin's pit, the team scrambled to make the changes in less than twelve seconds. Knowing Darrin was going to try something, I had to be on guard for anything at that point, including pit road.

"One lane ... hard ... hard!" Kyle yelled. "Nice job, way to dig."

I got out first, but Darrin was right behind me. During the pace laps, he nudged me once. I looked in the mirror to see him flip me off, an indication maybe of what was to come.

"Remember what I said, stay focused," Kyle warned me. "Forget about him."

Once the green flag was out, Darrin was attached to my bumper. There wasn't an inch of space between the two of us. To make matters worse, I was loose, really loose. I had to pull away as he was taking all my grip from the rear tires.

"I have to get him off me. I can't keep this thing straight," I told the boys. "He needs to back the fuck off."

"He knows he can't get around you," said Kyle. "That's why he's doing it."

I tried to remain calm, I really did, but I was about ready to blow my fucking lid ... I'd had enough of his shit.

"This one's for Kasey," Cole announced over the radio darting up beside Darrin, clipping his left rear. It didn't spin him, but it got him loose enough that he fell back to fifteenth, allowing me to pull away.

"For Kasey," I agreed, grabbing high gear coming out of the tunnel turn.

After that, my car was unbelievably fast. Any turn, I could choose any lane I wanted and it stuck. Laps passed, drivers challenged, but the confidence in my car and my ability was there. A race, any race really is never *just* a race. It's a battle of endurance, skill, desire, but most of all, want. I wanted it.

"It's all on you now, bud."

"Well ... sit back and enjoy the show then," I told them knowing that want was outshining everything else.

Before I knew it, I was taking the checkered flag.

"YEAH!" I screamed. "Great job, guys! Way to keep me focused, thanks!"

"Nice job!" Aiden said, followed by another from Kyle.

All I could think about the moment I took the checkered flag was that little chocolate brown-eyed boy who wanted to see a live race more than anything.

At times like this, while my dreams were coming true, it was hard to imagine that some never got a chance to even visualize a dream let alone have it come true.

Loosening my belts to relieve the ache, I drove around the track for my slow victory lap waving to the fans gathered near the fence.

Pulling down on the apron in the tunnel turn was not something I usually did, but I did a burn out just as I did when Sway was in the car with me that night I took her for a ride here. My smile broke through thinking of her reaction that night.

Smoke poured through every opening in the car, the radio cracked in my ear, broken chirps and muffled voices. One seemed to be Spencer yelling, but I couldn't decipher his words.

When the smoke from the burnout cleared, I stalled the car. With my foot on the clutch, I fired it up again, revving a few times.

"You copy, Spencer?" I could hear the roaring of an engine, but it wasn't mine.

I turned my head to the left ... everything went black.

18
Cylinder Head SWAY

Cylinder Head — The cylinder head sits above the cylinders on top of the cylinder block. It closes in the top of the cylinder, forming the combustion chamber and is sealed by a head gasket.

I was having pleasant dreams, but staying in a house with the Lucifer twins and Emma, those dreams were short-lived. I understood *completely* why Jameson was jealous that I was an only child after spending this much time around Emma and those goddamn twins.

"Sway ..." an annoying voice chimed in my ear. "Get up!"

"No, leave me alone." Ignoring the voice, I rolled over to snuggle with my Jameson pillow, wishing it were he and *not* Emma in the room. Was that really too much to ask for?

"Come on, I need to go to the store." She pulled on my arms. "Come with me."

"Why do you have to go to the store?" My arms flopped back on the bed.

"Ugh ..." she sighed loudly, "Aunt Flow is in town."

Aunt Flow?

Oh yeah, her period; I always referred to it as shark week.

With little effort, I went back to sleep, but the persistent little shit wasn't having it. She continued to annoy the ever-loving fuck out of me for the next thirty minutes by putting toothpaste on my face until I woke up.

"You're *so* annoying." I sat up in bed, and I could tell that I looked like the living dead by the way she was staring at me. "What?" I wiped the minty fresh from my nose.

Her eyebrows rose in question. "Are you okay?"

"Yes, why wouldn't I be?"

"You just ... look like shit."

"Bitch!"

She laughed. "I wasn't trying to be mean, you look ... sick."

"I don't feel good." Slumping back against my bed, I rubbed my eyes, "and apparently look like shit."

My senses seemed heightened and not only did I smell minty, but I smelled ... popcorn ... burnt popcorn. "What's that smell?" My eyes focused on her appearance; her very bright appearance. "Why are you all orange?"

Emma rolled her eyes. "Believe me, I'm not impressed either."

I waited patiently for her to indulge, but she didn't, so I pulled her hair. "Why are you orange?"

"Do you have to be so goddamn violent?" She huffed, pushing away. "Listen, I played with fire and got my ass burned."

"What?"

"*My brother* ... you know that asshole boyfriend of yours ... *well*, he filled my lotion with sunless tanner before he left." Her shoulders slumped. "I'm assuming as a payback or something. After I realized what he did, I thought maybe it wouldn't look so bad, but then it kept getting more orange and now I smell like burnt popcorn. Mr. Jangles was licking me all night. Long story short ... I'm a salt lick for your pussy."

"You're so strange."

"You're telling me." Emma lay down beside me, scrutinizing me with a wide grin. "Why don't you feel good?"

"Fuck if I know, maybe I have Lane's flu." I turned to look at her. "Why are you still here, don't you have fan club shit to do?"

"Jameson made me stay," she remarked, her grin still wide. "He said I was to make sure you were okay and now," she gestured toward her skin, "I realize why."

"How long have you been feeling like this?" Emma placed her tiny clammy orange hand against my forehead.

I slapped it away, baring my teeth. "Stop touching me. You stink."

"Sway," Emma smiled as though she'd solved a crime, "is there a chance you're pregnant?"

What?

I just had my ... okay, well when was shark week?

The real revelation came to me a good two minutes later. I hadn't had my period since before I left for Charlotte.

Oh my God! I haven't had a period in seven fucking weeks!

I jumped out of bed with alarm. "Emma!" I yelled. "What the fuck am I going to do?"

She began jumping up and down on my bed reaching for my stomach. "Is there a little Jameson in there?" she cooed, pressing her head against stomach. "Hello, little fella."

I pushed her backward. "Stop that!"

"Sorry," she apologized, undeterred by my harshness, "I'm so excited. Let's go get a test. I want to be there when you find out."

"Emma, I *can't* be pregnant right now." My mind was going through all the reasons why this wasn't a good thing and filing them all away in the *you're-fucked-file*. "With Jameson gone all the time, Charlie, the track ... this is the *last* thing Jameson needs right now."

"If it was the last thing he needs," Emma scooted toward the edge of the bed, "why was he so careless?"

"I, um ... shit ... I don't know." I threw my hands up. "What am I going to do now?"

"Jameson has *always* been like a walking billboard for a condom ad." She placed her hand on my shoulder. "He knew damn well what he was doing. Did he ever use a condom?"

"I think ... well, the first time, but after that he didn't."

"Did you tell him you were on birth control pills? Did you guys have that discussion?"

Now that I think about it, we never did. How could we be so stupid? He never asked if I was on the pill, why would he not?

Oh God, what have we done?

Moments later, I was puking with Emma holding my hair.

Another forty-five minutes later, we were in the aisle of the Olympia Top Foods grocery store looking over pregnancy tests. We drove to Olympia because I didn't want any one in town to find out. With Elma being a small town, people talked.

Looking over the tests, I couldn't believe the selection they had. It was overwhelming.

"Which one do I get?" I asked Emma, who was currently slurping down her second mocha. "Stop drinking those. That's why you're so short." I ripped her drink out of her hand and began drinking it.

"Hey," she reached for it. "You can't drink caffeine anymore, and I can't get these on the East Coast. No one makes coffee like the Northwest."

"I can't have caffeine?" I asked incredulously. "Why the hell not?"

"Nope, or sushi or chocolate ... there's a whole list of things Alley couldn't eat when she was pregnant with Lane. It's not good for the baby."

"Well, fuck, it's like you have to stop living."

"Pretty much," she agreed and threw all the pregnancy tests in the cart. "Let's go."

Emma went on to explain the details of Alley's pregnancy since I wasn't around for much of it. She made it out to sound like some sort of parasite feeding from your body until it took everything you had.

An entire carton of orange juice, nine pregnancy tests, two boxes of tissues, and a half pint of Ben and Jerry's Chunky Monkey ice cream later ... I was most certainly pregnant.

All the tests were positive.

Every. Single. One. Of. The. Motherfuckers.

Some had smiley faces and some had positive signs, where others just simply spelled the word out in big fat pregnant letters.

I was then curled up on my bed, with Emma, while I cried it out. I wanted to call Jameson; I wanted to scream at him and his camshaft, but then I sat there and cried.

My number one thought was, *How could I have let this happen?*

I was on birth control ... we used condoms ... well, no we didn't. We were pretty fucking careless caught up in our pornographic, dirty-talking, heathen escapades.

We were stupid, that's what we were.

Still, I was on birth control ... how could that have happened?

Ninety-nine percent effective my ass. Damn you one percent, damn you.

Mr. Jangles was curled up with us and then it dawned on me, he ate a few of my pills last cycle. "This is all your fault, Mr. Jangles!" He ignored me and snuggled closer to Emma—his newfound friend.

I wanted to tell Jameson, but decided on waiting until I saw him in person. This was *not* the kind of news you told someone over the phone that's for sure.

"It'll be okay, preggers," Emma tried to assure me, walking out into the living room with me. "Everyone loves a baby. Even my pathological asshole of a brother would."

Charlie, who was watching ESPN in his chair, immediately took notice of my appearance. I was still wearing my pajamas, my face was all red and blotchy, and God knows what my hair looked like by now.

"What's wrong with you?" he asked, and I could have sworn on a stack of Bibles he looked at my stomach. His eyes shifted to Emma. "Why are you so orange?"

"Jameson," she answered, casually strolling past toward the coffee.

"I see." Charlie looked back at me, "What's wrong?"

"Nothing," I answered quickly, avoiding direct eye contact. "Why does anything have to be wrong?"

"You just ... look like shit!"

"Thanks, Dad," I muttered, walking into the kitchen. That was the second time I'd been told I resembled feces today.

While pouring myself a glass of water, Charlie walked in.

"Sway, what's wrong? You've been crying."

"Nothing Dad, it's nothing," I lied, slurping the water. "I have the flu."

"Sway," he began looking down at my stomach, again, "the worst thing in life you can be is a liar."

I laughed. "When I was sixteen you told me the worst thing in life I could be was a slut, which is it?"

"You're right," Charlie paused for a moment contemplating, "the worst thing in life you can be *is* a slut and then a liar. Remember that, for when you have kids. Slut will be number one and then liar is a close second." Once again, he looked at my stomach and then walked away.

Well, that was strange, but surprisingly reassuring that he was still Charlie.

The next few days were spent avoiding Jameson's questions over the phone as to why I was so distant, and containing Emma from telling their whole family before I was able to see a doctor or tell Jameson.

Concerned with my lack of conversation on the phone, he was going to fly here after Pocono, so I thought I could tell him then.

By Wednesday, he was threatening to skip the race and fly home if I didn't tell him what was wrong. I couldn't justify telling him over the phone.

I made an appointment with my gynecologist and got in the same day. They didn't have much going on in Elma so you could get same-day appointments.

Emma insisted on going with me, which I was sure was a bad idea. My theory was confirmed when my feet were in the stirrups and Emma conveniently moved south knowing damn well I couldn't catch her in time. It wasn't exactly comforting since I was exposed with my bling pad on display for her *and* the doctor.

"Sway, that looks really good," Emma praised, "what did Jameson say?"

The doctor gave a look of both confusion and wonderment, mixed with fright. I'm not sure what he was more frightened from, Emma for checking out her friend's crankcase and her very bright complexion, or me, for "blinging" out my girlie pad with Jameson Riley's number and a checkered flag.

Dr. Sears gave me a smirk and continued his exam. "Judging by the size of your uterus, I'd say you are around nine weeks pregnant. Since you don't know when your last period was, I'd like to do an ultrasound to confirm this." He held up a wand, put a condom on it, and violated me.

Emma giggled, "That's fun."

"Emma!" I snapped. "Shut up."

"Hey, Sway," she exclaimed louder than I felt necessary, pointing once again to my crankcase. "They even use protection here."

Christ Almighty, they could hear her in New York.

"Get the fuck out of here Emma, right now!" I yelled abruptly, shocking Dr. Sears.

Emma, of course, did not leave; instead, she came back up toward my head and rubbed my scalp.

"Calm down, you're emotional." She kissed my forehead. "It's to be expected, my love."

"Emma," I warned.

"Yes?"

"Stop touching me."

The last thing I wanted right now was Emma touching me when there was a foot-long wand align boring my crankcase.

"Okay," Dr. Sears interrupted our silly fight, "that right there," he pointed to a flickering bubble on the screen, "that is your baby, and there's the heartbeat. You are roughly eight weeks, three days."

I was speechless. Now if only that same speechlessness would plague Emma.

"Oh my goodness." She was rubbing my head again. "When's her due date?"

"March seventh," Dr. Sears answered and pushed a button on the screen.

The baby was jumping all over the place, flailing around. The tiny flickering on the screen confirmed to me that there was in fact life inside of me. A life created by crazy-irrational-break-your-heart-logic from my dirty car-talking heathen.

Do they have support groups for crazy irrational pigizzles who get knocked up by their dirty heathen out of wedlock?

If they did, I'd be attending meetings after this. Of all the shenanigans I could get into, I get knocked up, and at one of the worst times.

The door shut behind Dr. Sears, and Emma brought me out of my self-pity trance when she snapped a picture with her phone. I ripped her phone out of her hand. "What the fuck are you doing?"

"Showing Mom, she wants to see her grandbaby."

"YOU TOLD HER?"

"Well, yeah, but I didn't tell anyone else." She looked at me as though there was absolutely nothing wrong with this.

"Fuck, Emma." I punched her shoulder after removing my legs from confinement. "Did you ever think that maybe I should tell the father first?"

"You can tell him later." She waved her arm around. "Mom isn't going to say anything. Besides, he's racing right now."

"What do you mean racing?"

It's Wednesday, why would he be racing?

"He's racing at Lernerville with Justin and Tyler. It's a charity event."

"Why didn't he tell me?" I felt sad that I didn't know, or maybe he'd said something and I wasn't paying attention, which was possible. I definitely had my mind elsewhere these days.

Emma shrugged. "It was last minute, I guess."

Later that night, after kicking Emma into the spare bedroom because she wouldn't keep her goddamn hands off my stomach, I called Jameson.

While I waited for him to answer, I laid on my stomach, staring at the black and white photo of our baby. It felt so strange to say *our baby*. I never imagined I would be pregnant with Jameson's baby. Hell, I never imagined I'd be pregnant with any baby.

"Hey, beautiful," Jameson answered after a few rings.

The anxiety hit me hard in that moment knowing I had something I wanted to tell him, but couldn't. It felt like I was lying to him, and I *did not* like that feeling.

I could hear the sound of engines in the background drowning out his voice, and the breaking in the call reception.

"Hey, handsome, where are you?" I rolled over on the bed. Lying on my stomach was starting to make me sick again; either that, or it was the five slices of pizza I consumed on my emotional eating binge.

"Oh, sorry," he apologized. "I'm at Lernerville with Tyler and Justin. It's a charity event. Mom and Emma scheduled me for an appearance, and then, of course, I decided to race." He chuckled softly. "Tyler, knowing me, already had a car ready when I got here. Ryder even showed up. He's back racing full-time."

Ryder Christensen was a USAC driver that he grew up racing with who had suffered a horrific crash at Knoxville a few years back.

Ryder, Tyler, Justin, Cody, Weldon, and Jameson were all in the same age group and had spent years battling against each other through USAC. A strong bond had formed between those boys—that's for sure.

"Oh, how's it going?" I leaned over placing the picture inside my nightstand. "Good to be back on dirt?"

"Sway," he sighed contently. "I've missed dirt track racing, so much. I wish you were here with me though; it's not the same. All the boys say hello."

It was entertaining to me that he thought he wouldn't miss dirt track racing. He grew up where dirt track racing was all he knew. Steady and determined, that love led him to what he thought he didn't want, NASCAR.

"Are you still flying home after Pocono?"

"Yeah, I have to meet with the contractor for my house on Monday, but Alley said she'd do it for me so I could be with you until I need to leave for Watkins Glen on Wednesday."

"I can come with you to that race," I suggested.

"Really?" Jameson sounded relieved.

"Yeah, I'm not really needed here for a couple weeks. We need to talk so I'd like—"

Jameson interrupted me. "That would be … great. Sway, honey, I hate to cut you off, but my heat race is up and I can't hear you very well. I'll call you in the morning."

"Okay, I love you."

He chuckled. "I love you, too."

Hanging up the phone, I slumped back against the bed.

Before long, I reached for the picture again. Every time I looked at it, my hand fell to my stomach for confirmation. I didn't look pregnant. Sure, my chest was enormous, but other than that, my stomach was still flat. The prominent ridges of my hips bones were still present, and though I was surprised I had them, the muscles in my stomach were still defined.

I didn't resemble a pregnant woman, that's for sure, emotionally yes, but not physically.

The next few days passed quickly. I spoke to Jameson twice, both times he was arguing with Kyle or Mason while we talked, so it wasn't much of a conversation.

On Saturday night, Emma helped me out at the track, and I wished she wouldn't have. She wanted to redesign our whole public relations setup.

To make my night worse, I ran into someone I never thought I'd see again.

Mike Tanner, a guy I had a one-night stand with. Let me tell you something about Mike Tanner—he was the reason women had one-night stands. You couldn't stand him longer than one night.

"Hey, Mike, what are you doing here?" I asked, and immediately felt stupid for asking when I realized he was in a racing suit, helmet in hand.

"I'm racing on the Northern Sprint Tour and The World of Outlaws on a limited schedule for Quincy." He gave a cocky shrug. "Tonight I'm going back to my roots and racing an outlaw late model. What are you doing here?" Mike asked with excited eyes.

"Oh, well my dad … actually, my boyfriend owns the track. I'm the General Manager."

"Really? Who's your boyfriend?" he asked. I could tell by the look on his face he was disappointed there wouldn't be a repeat performance of the last time we'd met.

"Jameson Riley."

Mike laughed. "Like in Jameson Riley the Winston Cup driver?"

I wanted to punch him in the face for acting as though I wasn't good enough. With all my bitchiness, he was lucky I didn't.

"Yes," I snapped rolling my eyes, "Jameson Riley, *the race car driver.*"

Mike began nodding his head in an arrogant way that really made me want to punch him. Mallory, his saving grace, appeared before I could go around assaulting the drivers.

"Hey, Sway, I need you to go control Emma," Mallory ordered breathlessly. "She's rearranging the office and something about re-painting."

Mallory, Mark's only daughter, was good people. I would hate for her to quit over Emma, or my shitty attitude these days. Mallory began working for Charlie shortly after Mark took the job seven years ago. I loved her, and even though she was ten years older than me, we got along great. I absolutely loved her husband Bryce; he was amazing. Bryce was no Jameson, but he was a pretty cool guy.

So I definitely wanted her to continue working here.

I laughed at Mallory describing what Emma was doing on our way back up to the office.

"You should have never left her in there alone," I finally told her.

It was a late night at the track, but eventually we managed to wrap everything up and head home where I once again, fell asleep as soon as I was in bed.

Sunday morning I woke up with Emma in my bed.

"How did you get in here?" I asked harshly. "I locked the door."

Emma shrugged, blowing off my rudeness. "The window."

"What are you, Spiderwoman?" I attempted to roll over, but stuck to my sheets. "Why are we all sticky?" I could see Emma's skin glistening.

"I ... spilled something," she replied softly. "I think."

"What?"

"Nothing," she avoided my penetrating glare like the plague. "I didn't say anything."

"Emma?"

"Sway?"

"What. Was. It?" I seethed.

"Uh ... I should ... go check on the twins." She bolted for the door. "I think I hear them in my room."

"Emma!" I yelled after her.

Glancing around the room, it was trashed. It looked like someone hosted New Year's Eve in Times Square in my bedroom. "Emma!" I screamed again.

Still no response.

Killing her seemed like a grand idea. And as I looked more closely around the room, the idea got grander.

When I moved, I stuck to the sheets like one of those flytraps. No matter how I moved, the sheets moved with me.

What the fuck is this shit?

It smelled like alcohol, but I couldn't be sure. It was crusty and sticky and in my hair, on my body. It strangely resembled ... *nah* ... it's not that, or was it?

It had better not be that!

I got out of bed, wrapping my bathrobe around myself in search of Emma. I found her, in the bathroom, washing her own hair.

I stood there with my hands on my hips. "What the fuck is all over us?"

"Huh?" she eluded as though she didn't hear me correctly.

"Don't huh me. Why does my room smell like a distillery and why are we all sticky?"

"It ... was an accident." Her eyes were wide with panic. "I swear."

"What do you mean it was an accident?" I scorned stepping closer to her. Trying to be intimidating, I held up a hairbrush as though I would smack her with it.

"Okay ... I climbed in your window ... I was a little drunk." I gave her a skeptical look. "All right, I was *very* drunk," she admitted. "I wanted to celebrate with you so I brought some champagne."

I sighed heavily. I knew where this was going.

"Then I realized that you couldn't drink ... so I opened the bottle and it sprayed everywhere. I tried to drink all of it so you wouldn't be mad at me, and then I don't remember after that." Emma smiled. "I mean ... I *did* drink an entire bottle of champagne, by myself. I have no idea why we're all sticky. Maybe it's from the champagne, but I can't be sure. When I woke up I was underneath your bed."

I shook my head again. "What am I going to do with you?"

This was like the time Jameson and I caught her with beer on her sixteenth birthday. She was so afraid Jameson would tell Jimi and Nancy, which he never would, that she drank a 24-pack of beer, by herself.

She puked for ten days straight.

I wasn't about to let the little twit get away with this, though, so we spent the next four hours cleaning up my room. We then realized we missed the race and our cell phones. I found mine in Logan's room, with nineteen calls to Europe.

It'd be a miracle if I allowed those little shits to see seven.

After telling him this, my threats going nowhere, I made my way into the living room to check the race knowing I missed the majority of it. I watched the highlights and read the headlines across the bottom of the TV, as nausea rolled over me.

"NASCAR Winston Cup driver of the Simplex Shocks and Springs number nine, Jameson Riley, has been air lifted to Pocono Medical Center after a post-race crash that involved him and Darrin Torres, driver of the Wyle Products number fourteen. Jameson, who won the race, was doing a burnout in the tunnel turn when Darrin crashed into him, on the driver's side. NASCAR has declined to comment on the incident, stating the crash is currently under investigation. Darrin Torres, after being treated for minor injuries, walked away from the wreck declining to comment, as well. There have been no updates as to Riley's condition."

Like a slap in the face, they then showed the crash, over and over again, as they debated how it could have happened.

There was nothing left of his car.

The video showed Jameson's car coming out of the tunnel turn after doing a burnout, and the next thing you saw was Darrin's car smashing into the side of him, at *full speed* coming out of the straight stretch.

"Oh God!" Emma choked running for her cell phone.

I could hear Charlie and then Andrea yelling for me, but I ran to the bathroom just in time to reach the toilet.

I didn't realize that Charlie was holding me until I felt him take my hand. "He's alive, Sway," he assured me, forcing me to look at him. "They air lifted him to the hospital."

I felt paralyzed, numb, and my body shaking with each sob.

Emma's voice broke through the pain; I turned in Charlie's arms.

Reflecting my own, her face was blotchy and red, tears streaming down her cheeks. Our worst fears, for the situation we tried so hard to control, came true.

"Sway," she reached for me, "Wes is coming to get us. He will be here in two hours. We need to get to Olympia."

"What did Alley say?" I asked Emma once we were on our way to Olympia.

Knowing myself, I knew I needed to be on the way to see him before she told me what happened or else I wouldn't have had enough sense to function.

Emma took a deep shaking breath; it wasn't easy for her either. "Alley said he was doing his victory lap, did a burn out coming out of the tunnel turn and then Darrin hit him. Spencer saw Darrin coming around the track and tried to warn Jameson but he'd already unhooked his radio. Apparently Spencer was one of the first ones to the car afterward." Her tears spilled over once again. "His belts were loosened, but he at least kept his helmet on."

Charlie turned up the news radio when they announced information on Jameson. Since everyone else was with him, it left us relying on them calling us to find out his condition.

We listened as the ESPN reporter spoke of the crash, "Jameson Riley, NASCAR's hot-headed rookie, was air lifted to Pocono Medical Center after his win this afternoon. While doing a victory burnout in the tunnel turn at Pocono International Raceway, Darrin Torres, driver of the Wyle Products number fourteen, hit Riley's Simplex Ford number nine on the driver side. Riley had apparently loosened his belts after he took the checkered flag. Track officials said he was unconscious when they arrived. He was immediately air lifted and is currently listed in critical, but stable condition. No comment has been made by the Wyle Products team, nor was Darrin available for comment. There were no other cars on the track so it remains a mystery as to *why* Torres was even still on the track still when he hit Riley."

"These two have had encounters in the past and without a comment from Gibson Racing, it leads us to believe that this was some sort of retaliation on the number nine. Darrin and Jameson had been battling for the lead the majority of the day, but when Jameson pulled away around lap two hundred, Darrin was unable to catch him. Twenty minutes ago NASCAR announced in a press conference that Torres has been suspended for the remainder of the season. Gordon Reynolds, Director of Competition, announced minutes ago that fines would be assessed with extreme severity. It was also announced that Gibson Racing would be allowed to replace the driver of the number fourteen."

"Jesus," Charlie mumbled, turning down the radio when Emma's phone rang.

"Hello?" she answered immediately, searching through her bag for tissues. "Okay … yeah, we are almost to Olympia …" She was quiet listening to what I assumed was Spencer and handed me a tissue. "Yes, Sway is coming, too … okay … see you in a few hours." Emma hung up and turned toward me. "He's okay, Sway." She leaned forward to capture my gaze. "Don't stress out in your condition …"

I nodded.

"Spencer said they will need to do surgery on his wrist and put in some pins, but he's going to be fine. He's got six broken ribs, a broken wrist, a fractured radius, broken collarbone, and a punctured lung."

I gasped.

"Jameson will be okay; he's still unconscious, but the doctors said there is no brain injury … just a concussion." Her eyes narrowed. "Sway." She made me look at her again. "He's fine. You need to relax and not stress out right now."

All I could do was nod.

Here, I just found out I was pregnant, and *now* the father of my baby was in the hospital.

I could be told he would be all right, or at least I prayed he would be, but that didn't stop that paralyzing numbing feeling from returning.

My mind wandered to a few months ago, knowing the change that occurred within myself. In a few short months, I went from being what I thought I'd always be to him, to being pregnant with his child.

A child I never knew I wanted until right now.

A piece of him was now inside me creating a link between us, or maybe it was strengthening the one already there. What I never understood until right then, staring off at the passing headlights, each illuminating the change within us, that the link was now a lock.

I knew, then, I couldn't settle for just a taste with him.

A taste would never be enough.

I had a thirst I never knew I had, to a substance that was vital.

About the AUTHOR

Shey Stahl is the author of the Racing on the Edge Series. She enjoys spending time with her family at the local dirt tracks. You can follow her on the links below.

Facebook: https://www.facebook.com/shey.stahl.9
Website: www.sheystahl.com

Website & Social Media:
www.sheystahl.com
Facebook: Shey Stahl

Novels by Shey Stahl:
Racing on the Edge:
Happy Hour
Black Flag
Trading Paint
The Champion
The Legend
Additional novels coming soon:
Hot Laps
The Rookie
Fast Time
Lapped Traffic
Behind the Wheel - Outtakes

Everything Changes

Waiting for You

Delayed Penalty

Made in the USA
Lexington, KY
14 May 2014